The
FIRST
STONE

To Eva —
I hope you enjoy
this — I think it may
be closer to home than it
at first appears — It was
great working with you
Thanks for everything
John

One decision can change the direction of your life in a way no amount of forethought can predict, and once taken, no God can grant you the chance to return and begin again.

Looking back—across death and betrayal . . . and sometimes pain too deep to bear—she could only marvel at how young they were that day, and, despite her nervousness, how casual it seemed.

It was on the green lawns of the UCLA campus, by the tables under the eucalyptus trees. She was carrying a coffee and Danish and an awkward load of books. He was arguing with a friend and didn't see her approach. He gestured and the coffee went sailing, streaking his pants, splashing right across her cream skirt. At first he was appalled, but then she smiled and said, "Oops . . ." At the time he thought it was the most fortunate accident of his life.

"Wow!" he said. "I'm sorry."

"It's all right." She grinned. He grabbed some napkins from one of the tables and reached to brush at the spot but glimpsed the golden thighs beneath the translucent skirt and stopped.

"Here," he muttered, his throat suddenly dry.

She blotted at the stain. He was about as described: tallish, wavy black hair, soft almond eyes, an athletic body.

"You must let me buy you a new skirt," he said anguishedly. She burst into laughter. "Well, let me pay the dry cleaning bill anyway," he insisted.

She glanced at his dripping pants. "Sure," she said. "And I'll pay yours."

And now he smiled. She was surprised by the very white teeth, but more by the unexpected spontaneity of the smile. "Okay," he replied. "We'll exchange bills. But only if I can buy you another coffee—and you promise not to splash it all over me."

Her smile was as sudden as his. It didn't occur to her that he'd have a sense of humor.

For his part he was surprised he could joke at all because just to look at her face was making his stomach react like an out-of-control camel.

They sat under the eucalyptus trees and talked for forty minutes. He had got rid of his friend when he went in for the coffee.

They did the "Where're you from?" She from Philadelphia; he would only say, "Oh, you know, the Middle East," with a nod to his darkish skin. Her name, Lisa Cooper, his name Le'ith Safadi. She was relieved that he seemed to have only a slight English accent and possessed the street vocabulary of any UCLA student. Her one fear—that he would be so in love with some other girl that he wouldn't react to her—was clearly not going to be a problem, but she had to struggle to concentrate on seeing him as just another man. When she asked and he explained that Le'ith means "young lion," he smiled bashfully. She felt he had the shoulders and the litheness for the name, but she always pictured lions as blond. He was more the panther, but the image was right for him: a young, strong, graceful animal.

Of the two, her eyes were tougher, but bright with life, a soft, speckled blue. When he got to know her, he told her they were like pieces of summer sky shining in the fields of her straw blond hair. Whenever he flattered her, his mind always framed her in these unexpected images. Later she knew it was the manner of the Arab storytellers, whose images, not adjectives, carried the imagination into someone else's world. But he had a gift for it, and the images came from him with a kind of guileless ardor she had shrunk from for years—because the innocence of it, the manifest sincerity, always melted her heart no matter how she steeled herself against it.

When at last she scooped up her books and said she had to go, he stood in sudden panic. "Have—have you seen the—*Coal Miner's Daughter*? It's—it's Sissy Spacek."

She grinned but shook her head, "No, but I have a lot of studying to do this week."

"Saturday. Could we go Saturday?"

She hesitated but then shrugged. "I guess so. We can exchange those dry cleaning bills."

He smiled, more in relief than amusement.

She would always remember their first date. He called up to the apartment so politely it was like being back in junior high. But when she walked out of the building and saw his shining new Mercedes convertible, gleaming like a symbol of arrogant wealth, an anger grew in her that almost made her turn back. She paused on the step, wondering if she could ever go through with it, but he sensed her mood instantly. He wasn't sure what it was, but he thought it might be the car. He didn't know if she was rich or poor, but he knew some of the students deeply resented "Arab money."

"One of my uncles has the Mercedes concession back home," he said apologetically. "He sort of arranged a deal. I hope you like convertibles."

She remembered that she had walked to the car without speaking. Anxious to make conversation, he later "confessed" he was from Saudi Arabia. "People always expect some kind of desert sheikh." Having disclaimed the exotic expectations, he then confirmed them by telling her that when he went home after his first year and told his family that men and women, like the two of them, actually went into darkened cinemas together—even when they weren't married—no one would believe him.

Despite herself, she found this idea irresistibly amusing. He reacted to the glimmer of interest like a Bedouin to the sight of water.

"My friend Najib told his family the same thing, but no one would believe us until my uncle who works in San Francisco told them it was true." He was grinning at the seeming absurdity.

"But why?" she said. "Don't people go to the movies in Saudi Arabia?"

He shook his head. "Not theaters. We have tapes," he said. "We certainly don't permit men and women to go into darkened halls together. All the men in my family are convinced that movie watching in America is nothing but a cover for illicit sex."

She burst into laughter. "It's true," he said. "My father said if Jineen, my sister, ever went into such a theater, he would shoot her with his own hand."

She stared at him incredulously. "Are all Saudi men so . . . randy? Maybe I should have brought some Mace or something."

"Ah—" He grinned. "It's not the *men*." She looked at him questioningly. "Saudi men don't allow their wives and daughters to have contact with other men not because we're untrustworthy but because women are by nature so uncontrollably lustful." He paused thoughtfully. "By and large, men can be trusted under temptation, but women—" Poker-faced, he shrugged at her. She tested his eyes a moment, and they twinkled just enough.

"I see. . . . Then we've been found out," she deadpanned.

"Well, at least in Saudi Arabia you have."

Deadpan too, and then the smile, and she knew that somehow she could go through with it, she *would* go through with it.

The courtship was slow and lasted through the academic year and into summer school. He was supposed to return home after completing his M.B.A. in June, but he had lied to stay on. There were two special courses he thought he really should take, he explained to his uncle. If he didn't take them, he would never get back to them. His uncle had suspected something, but Le'ith had the advantage of those who are generally truthful: On occasion he could make a good lie stick.

They went to movies, raced off to Zuma Beach in his Mercedes when they had half a day free; she watched him play soccer, discovered he could fly a plane but didn't have a license in America, was amused that for one so athletic he swam so awkwardly, hated his Saudi friends, who all treated him with a kind of deference which he seemed to take as his due, was flattered and reluctantly touched by his unconcealed devotion.

For his part Le'ith spent the year in turmoil. Every day he became more enamored of her. The mere sight of her walking in a crowd of students on Bruin Walk caught his heart as nothing in his life ever had. No girl, no woman, not even the sensuously exciting dancing girls of Egypt, who had first led him from puberty to "manhood," made him half so giddy, so helplessly "adolescent."

And as they saw more and more of each other, it went beyond the physical. The unexpectedness of her wit and intelligence, her openness with him enthralled him, sometimes tongue-tied him. And when she acted as if she were his, he was as possessive as any Saudi prince of his finest Arabian stallion.

But at night, back in his apartment with Najib, the torment began. His father's youngest brother, Sabah, was in San Francisco handling family business and acting as guardian and adviser to eight Saudis at UCLA and another four at Berkeley. No Saudi boy traveled without the guidance and protection of some elder. It was Sabah who sent them their allowances—or withheld them if he believed that was wisest. It was Sabah who monitored their grades, took reports on their habits, checked their compliance with Ramadan and other religious matters. Sabah himself had been educated at Princeton in the first wave of "oil-rich" Saudis who sought Western know-how, so he was more liberal than Le'ith's father, but on fundamentals he was as rigid as the black stone of the Kaaba.

And one fundamental was: Date all the Western girls you want, seduce as many Western girls as wish to be seduced, but never, never get deeply involved. But as the months went by, Le'ith became more and more deeply involved.

"You want to marry her?" Najib repeated incredulously. He had awakened at three in the morning to find the light on in the room of the "young lion" and knew it wasn't studies that were keeping him awake.

Najib's first guess was that Lisa had turned cold again. She did that. Le'ith could never discover what it was, what he had done or not done, that brought on these moods of distance. It was never outright rejection, just a chilling loss of intimacy. He assumed he had crossed some line of

Western culture and manners that he was unaware of. It always made him sleepless, trying to imagine what it was, fearing she might leave him. It would be years and a "life" before he would know that whatever her inner feelings, whatever hostilities or disappointments she felt, she would always have gone back to him.

But on this night his sleeplessness came from a recognition that the nearer they came to parting, the surer he was that he never wanted her out of his life. Not only did he *want* to marry her, he had to, or he'd feel his whole life would be barren of what mattered most to him.

"I've got the instant solution." Najib grinned. "Tell her you're already married."

Le'ith threw a book at him.

Najib ducked. "Why not?" he insisted. "Just say, 'Look, I've got this lovely, dark-haired, dark-eyed, olive-skinned wife, and I need a blond, blue-eyed Caucasian to set her off.' She's bound to see the reasonableness of that."

Le'ith grimaced and leaned over and poured some rum in a glass and topped it with 7Up. His uncle wouldn't approve of that, but he'd turn a blind eye to it—but never, ever to his marrying a Westerner.

"Hey, I'm not joking," Najib persisted. "You're insane when it comes to this girl. You'll never break with her. So just be honest, and she'll break with you. You'll die for a couple of months, but then you'll be back in Nayra's soft, smooth arms, and you and I can take a trip or two to Cairo"—he winked lasciviously—"and you'll have forgotten all about her."

"I'm not talking sex," Le'ith snapped.

"You haven't made her, right? I'll bet a thousand dollars once you get in her pants all this be-with-her-always crap will make you sick to your stomach. You've had a hard-on for a year. All you need to do is pop it."

Le'ith closed his eyes. "Najib, you're a fucking desert camel, and I'd be amazed if you ever even *talked* to a girl without thinking of how you might lay her."

"So would I," Najib answered proudly.

"Well, some nights I'd give half my father's estate to get inside Lisa, but I know if I was sick or she was sick and I could *never* lay her, I'd *still* want to spend my life with her."

Najib just stared at him. Then he shook his head and headed for the door. He glanced back, his face deadly serious. "*Tell* her, Le'ith. Tell her about Nayra."

Le'ith knew he should, not for Najib's reasons but because he and Lisa had built a bridge of trust beyond anything he'd ever shared with anyone, and he was betraying that. But it was an impossible dilemma. If he told her, she would leave him. It wouldn't matter that he was, by religion and law, entitled to four wives and that she would always be the first in his heart and mind. She wouldn't even listen to that. His only chance was to marry her and wait until he took her into the vast emptiness of the Saudi plain and immersed her in all the complexities of tribal and family life. There he would be able to hold her—perhaps forcibly at first—until she understood, understood and accepted that whatever else was in his life, she was its center. Perhaps by then she would be bearing his child. It was a terrible risk, but it was the only way.

Though he knew it would bring down the wrath of his uncle, to whom he owed fidelity and obedience, and of his father, to whom he owed love and respect, he was determined that he *would* marry her; he could not walk away from California without her. During their hours of lying under the sun on empty beaches, of walks, and long nights of silences, and near silences, he had come to know that she accepted all he was: his deepest fears, the weaknesses that shamed him most—from the birthmark on his cheek to his fear of loneliness. Without her he was a man in a world of strangers. With her they were a world, a sometimes prickly, unpredictable world, but a world where the worst thing that could happen was that they might lose each other. And to reveal Nayra to her was the one certain way to ensure that.

Lisa and Le'ith eloped to Reno a year to the day after that first "accidental" meeting. Le'ith wanted it that way. He was both sentimental and superstitious. It was a good omen. He even prayed that that night would produce the baby he so longed for her to have. But that first night Lisa was very careful not to have a child; she would always be careful not to have a child.

Le'ith was touchingly sincere at their wedding. His throat caught several times during their declarations, and she only kept herself from being affected by it by wondering secretly and cynically if he had been equally emotional at his *first* wedding.

They had dinner and drinks after with Najib, the inevitable best man, and his current girlfriend, a very attractive black girl from New Orleans. She was also Lisa's bridesmaid-witness, and the wedding made her almost as emotional as Le'ith.

Then Le'ith drove the new Mrs. Safadi across the California border and up into the mountains to Lake Tahoe. In the isolation of the drive, the warnings of the peril she was facing took on a reality they had always lacked till now. Her freedom to make mistakes was slipping away with each mile.

He had reserved a beautiful suite in a charming hotel overlooking the lake. His touch felt so familiar, his body so accustomed, that after the champagne and the long ride filled with anxiety but spent listening to music she loved—tapes he'd bought though she thought he'd never paid any attention—her mind wanted to relax and simply let what was to happen, happen. But she was determined to be the whore, not to let her mind or heart be engaged at all.

He undermined her resolve in a dozen ways. His touch, of course. The flowers, the necklace that was her wedding present—jade set in diamonds that made her eyes look strikingly blue. Even the moon conspired, peering through the lacy clouds, making a silver trail across the lake to their balcony.

On that balcony he put his arms around her from behind. "I've been in America many years now," he said quietly. "I know this will not be the first night you've spent with a man, but I believe you love me as I love you, and that way this will be the first night for both of us." He turned her around and looked into her eyes before he kissed her.

Lisa hung on, fighting to keep some part of herself aloof, but her poor, faithless body, which knew nothing of religions, nothing of treachery and deceit, responded to his tenderness, his passion with an excitement she had never felt before.

Against her will she held him firmly in her arms long after he had gone to sleep. She cursed her body for it—and his. Her mind kept repeating, "You cannot, must not love this man."

Chapter 2

Lisa's first real test as Mrs. Safadi came when Le'ith made it clear that a visit to his uncle in San Francisco was an absolutely obligatory part of their honeymoon.

She feared that a Princeton graduate who was described as both intelligent and sophisticated in the ways of the world might not accept her as unquestioningly as Le'ith had.

His house was an elegant white three-story building with views of the bay from every floor. There were a few Persian carpets here and there and some Eastern art on the white walls along with some very modern Western art.

After they had been admitted by some sort of subordinate manservant, it was only one of Sabah's *assistants* who came out to welcome them, and she could tell that Le'ith was shaken and suddenly far more nervous than she.

The assistant took them to a little sitting room, and a pretty servant girl immediately brought tea for Lisa. The assistant apologized that Mr. Sabah could not greet them personally, but he was on a call to Saudi Arabia. If Lisa wouldn't mind waiting for a few minutes, Mr. Sabah would like to speak to Le'ith briefly on some business matters, and then perhaps they could have lunch together.

It was clear this shook Le'ith even more. Lisa had never seen him frightened, but now the blood had drained from his face. He forced a smile at her. "I'm sure we won't be long."

The servant girl brought her some magazines and came back with a fresh pot of warm tea. Lisa roamed the room, looking at the art, and watched the boats in the bay. Lunchtime came and went. The girl brought delicate sandwiches, a fruit plate, and more tea. She said she was sure the *saids* would be finished very soon.

Then it suddenly occurred to Lisa that she had been discovered. The wise, sophisticated uncle. Her heart beat in panic, but what was the worst they could do? She had done nothing; she was in her own country. Divorce Le'ith and go? All right, she could live with that. But none of that logic stilled her heart, and the minutes stretched like hours.

It was almost three o'clock before the assistant came back, apologized for the delay, and invited her into the presence of Uncle Sabah and Le'ith.

Sabah was as Le'ith had described him: too heavy and unfit, but extremely well dressed, with big eyes, a full mouth, and a manner that sparkled with charm and civility as he held out his hand.

"It is my great pleasure to welcome you to our family home in San Francisco," he said. "When Le'ith phoned me after your marriage, he told me I would find you a woman of great beauty. I can see he was being modest."

Lisa smiled—she had come to expect that kind of compliment—but she read an inflection in his voice that suggested a purpose beyond courtesy in his flattery. And she could see that Le'ith still wore that look of impending disaster.

Sabah indicated she sit on a long couch that faced a glass table and another couch, but instead of sitting beside her or opposite her, he moved to his desk, which was on a little raised dais. Once he sat down, Le'ith took a seat in an armchair removed from them both.

"It is wonderful when two young people fall in love," Sabah said, glancing between them avuncularly. "Here in the West, where romantic love is so central to the culture, to everyday life, it is especially thrilling." Then he laughed beguilingly. "Of course it's those first moments that are the best. In fact some people spend their lives just going from one 'first moment' to another."

Lisa had to smile. It was beginning to sound as if he only intended to give her an avuncular warning about life rather than the inquisition she feared.

But suddenly the charm evaporated. He took on the look of a Middle Eastern businessman, a tough, uncompromising one.

"But in our culture—in the culture Le'ith was raised and to which he must return within the month—the *family* is the center of life. And I don't mean the American family of mother, father, and children. I mean the large family of fathers and brothers and grandfathers and uncles and half brothers and cousins. A place where a woman's life is primarily given to raising children and making the home a place of serenity in the company of the other women of the family."

He looked at her coolly, appraising her legs, her waist, her bodice. "It is unthinkable in Saudi Arabia for a woman ever to display her body to a man other than her husband in the way that you have so appropri-ately dressed for San Francisco. In fact, it is unlikely that you will ever meet any of Le'ith's closest friends, and if he were a bit more old-fashioned, not even his brothers and certainly not his half brothers."

Lisa had been warned about how hard it would be to live as a Saudi woman—but not with the harshness that tainted Sabah's words.

"The relationship you have with Le'ith now will *never* be repeated in your life within our family compound." He said it categorically and left it hanging in the air to sink in.

"It is true that Le'ith may be free to take you from time to time to Switzerland or London, and the privacy and intimacy you feel now can perhaps be recaptured for a few days, though both of you will have changed by then in ways that will be the fault of neither of you, changed simply by the vast differences in your expectations in life. Those days of anticipated 'freedom' can turn into agonies for both of you.

"You will see all around you the kind of woman you expected to be. . . . You are educated, intelligent, and you will also see the kind of life you might have had in some profession of your choice.

"The freedom to walk without a veil for a few days, to hold Le'ith's hand in public, even to dance with him will not, I believe, be sufficient to make up for the months—and *years* of living in the secluded sisterhood of a Muslim household."

"She will always be my wife," Le'ith said emphatically. It was the first sign of defiance he had shown since they entered the house.

Sabah's brows knitted slightly, but he kept his eyes on Lisa, and his attitude became more benign. "I'm sure you both love each other very much or Le'ith would never have so blatantly defied the conventions of his family and the wishes of his father.

"But both of you are adult enough to recognize that this is the crowning moment of that love. In the desert Kingdom Le'ith and I both love and owe fidelity to, the heat and dust, the submissions forced upon you will kill this flower that has bloomed so beautifully and naturally between you in this unreal land." He gestured to the shimmering bay with its spangles of boats.

"Keep it, both of you, as a *memory,* a gift whose price is a little pain. We will have the marriage annulled, and what is between you now will last forever."

Grim-jawed, watching, waiting, Le'ith just looked at Lisa.

"To go forward will destroy both your lives." Sabah went on reasonably. "And the love you feel now will grow to a bitterness that will teach you that the only thing stronger than love is hate."

If Le'ith had said nothing, Lisa believed that despite all that had driven her to this moment, she might well have given in. It wasn't just the fearsome logic of Sabah's description of her coming life; it was the underlying masculine righteousness that informed it. But Le'ith's defiant words, "She will always be my wife," had opened a tiny window in the grim prison Sabah had described. Le'ith was not Sabah, and perhaps it was enough to hang on to, to let her fulfill her promise to God and to herself.

She looked across at Le'ith. "Be fair, Le'ith," Sabah said. "You know what she faces, and there are other, even more difficult things that I have not even spoken of. Don't treat her like a prize. Love her like a human being, and give her the life a woman of her beauty and intelligence deserves. Free her."

For a moment Le'ith, clearly shaken by Sabah's words, just stared at her. "All my uncle says is true," he said in a voice she could hardly hear. "If you do not love me as I love you, then soon enough you will long for trees and hills and flirtatious laughter between men and women, and you may come to hate me." He held her eyes a moment. "But my uncle is a product of *his* past too. The idea of sharing life with a woman—her brain, her humor, her comradeship—is not something he has ever considered."

Sabah guffawed.

"But I do want to share my life with you," Le'ith continued, "all of it. If you want that, I beg you to come. But if all the truths my uncle has spoken fill you with fear and doubt, then he is right, we should stop before it is too late."

Lisa paused, and though inside she deeply wished she could push the cup from her lips, she knew exactly what to say. "All the truths your uncle has spoken of *do* fill me with fear and doubt. But I have made a pledge, and nothing will turn me from it now."

Chapter 3

They flew Saudia Airlines from New York direct to Riyadh. Fourteen hours across an ocean and a continent. From the moment they walked into the aircraft Lisa felt the full weight of her new dependence on Le'ith. The stewardesses all spoke English, of course, but Arabic was the language of the vast majority of the passengers. Even Le'ith gave their seat numbers in Arabic and chatted with the two first class attendants glibly, and somewhat self-importantly, before he turned to her and said in English, "No alcohol on a Saudia plane, of course, but would you like some orange juice?"

Lisa nodded. She had noted that the main cabin was mostly filled with men, but the few women in it were all in chadors, fully veiled.

In the first class section one woman was in a chador, but the other five or six were all dressed in the highest fashion. Too much jewelry perhaps, but apart from that, tastefully and expensively.

There were a few American businessmen in first class, but no sign of anyone who looked like a tourist.

"There's only one kind of tourism in Saudi Arabia," Le'ith explained. "Pilgrims to Mecca or Medina, and the only Western tourists you'll see are the wives of some of the businessmen who are living there, and they're very strictly confined."

When that news obviously depressed Lisa, Le'ith put his hand on hers. "We will live our own lives. Some of it may seem hard to you at first, but what if you'd married a Texas rancher?"

"Sure—or a Tibetan monk."

Le'ith grinned. "See, it's going to be easy."

A stewardess brought her orange juice, and the doors closed.

And now it began. She had been given no contact, told emphatically that no one would contact *her*. There would be a double death. First, she would be lost to her parents, mercifully just to a spot on the earth where they could not reach her. And then her parents would be lost to her. A car accident staged so efficiently Le'ith and all his family would believe she was alone in the world except for them and one distant aunt, to whom she would write every three or four months. She was to live in this isolation until her position could be of use—and then *they* would contact her.

Until that time she would make the best of life in a land she reviled with a man she was supposed to despise. If the truth were revealed, she would be stoned to death or beheaded as a traitor. That thought chilled her, of course, but what she dreaded most at this moment was the anticipated years of boredom and alienation.

The huge sealed plane, with its strange smells, its Arab music, its Arabic conversations over the Arabic newspapers, lumbered down the runway. For Lisa, the paradox was that she had initially thought it could be done only if the hatred in her heart could be focused on Le'ith. But now, in the first moments of this new, frightening life, she believed his presence was the only thing keeping her from total panic. In wooing him, she had developed a physical passion for him that she could not deny, but that, she thought, was her youth and his, and she had gotten into the secret places of his mind. Of course some of that had spilled back onto her, but she had been deliberate and calculating; only he had been riding on emotion alone.

Still, the thought of landing in Riyadh, of living years in Riyadh without him, was something she didn't even want to contemplate.

He was holding out an Arab paper for her to see. There was a rather blurred picture of hundreds of women in chadors, waving flags in front of a large gate.

"The American Embassy in Tehran," Le'ith explained. "They want the marine hostages in there so they can hang them in the streets."

"I thought the Ayatollah Khomeini was a man of religion."

"He is. He just equates the West—and the United States in particular—with the devil."

"Do you?"

He leaned over and kissed her behind the ear. "I didn't until I met
you." He glanced over guiltily at one of the stewardesses. Lisa glanced
back. The stewardess was smiling and shaking an admonitory finger at
them. "See," he whispered, "Saudi men do not kiss women in public."

"Never?"

"*Never*. When I first went to California, I used to just stop dead and
watch when I saw a couple kiss on the street, too stunned to move. Then
I took to going to the movies and sitting in the back row just to watch
people kiss. I couldn't even tell you the titles of the movies."

Lisa looked at him skeptically. He nodded: "Absolute truth."

"Is that why the Ayatollah considers us devils?"

"Not altogether." He grinned. "He's influenced a little by the fact
that the CIA overturned the Iranian government, put the Shah in power,
and built a secret police that tortured and killed his followers. He also
thinks the U.S. was the devil that created Israel."

Lisa tried to keep her voice as flip as his had been. "Is that what *you*
think?"

"Well, if there were no United States, would there be an Israel?"

"And they're *both* devils?"

Le'ith grinned. "Are you asking me or the Ayatollah?"

"I don't know the Ayatollah, so I guess I'm asking you."

Le'ith leaned very close and whispered, "Unless you know and *trust*
everyone who can hear you, this is not the sort of thing you talk about
in public."

"My," she whispered back, "there's a *lot* you don't do in public!"

Le'ith grinned. He always loved her blunt impertinence. No Saudi
woman would think like that, much less speak that way. "Okay," he
said, and whispered right in her ear. "The Saudis hated the Shah because
we knew he wanted to take over our oil and the United States was
giving him the biggest military in the Arab world. We hate the Ayatollah
because he's a rabid fundamentalist. *We* have always been considered the
fundamentalists, but compared with him, we are lurid sinners only a step

or two up from the devil Americans. As for Israel, it was a mistake, and the way the United States supports it is an even bigger mistake. . . . Now you know everything about Middle Eastern politics."

"No, I don't, because"—Le'ith gestured for her to keep her voice down—"Egypt just recognized Israel," she whispered. "You may think I'm a dumb UCLA blonde, but even *I* know that."

"Right. The devil United States poured out millions to Israel—and millions to Egypt. Money, arms, aid. So they signed an agreement. But the minute they did, the traitor Egypt was expelled from the Arab League."

"What's the Arab League?"

"The good guys, like Saudi Arabia. *Not* very effective but—" He shrugged whimsically. "And now you *truly* know everything about Middle Eastern politics."

Lisa found it a relief that he didn't seem to take any of it too seriously.

They ate in great luxury, Lisa letting Le'ith explain all the Saudi spices and condiments and, like him, shunning the Western knives and forks and eating with her fingers like a true Saudi. Very uncharacteristically he ate little and later fell asleep while they were watching a heavily censored version of Polanski's *Tess*.

Lisa tried to read for a time—they still had hours and hours to fly—but with Le'ith asleep, she coldly studied the strange Saudi faces, the Arab designs on the plane's bulkheads, the menus, the exotic Egyptian stewardesses.

Then the crew dimmed the lights again and ran another movie, *The China Syndrome*. Without her headphones on, she watched Jane Fonda and Jack Lemmon fight the forces of evil for a time, but then her eyes closed. She wanted to rest, to arrive with her senses alert, but in the drone of the jets her mind drifted back to the fateful chain that had led her step by step to this flight into the frightening unknown. . . .

She was in truth a genuine blonde, with eyes blue as the "summer sky," but, to the surpise of some, her mother's name was Bernstein, and her grandmother from Poland, whose fair hair she had inherited, carried an ineradicable purple number on her arm from a place called Bergen-Belsen.

And her father's Anglo-Saxon name was traced far back to an ancient Scottish ancestor, but all the Coopers for many generations had been Jewish on both sides. In an outpouring of ethnic pride and devotion, her uncle Noah, whose eyes were as blue as hers, had even emigrated to Israel to help found a kibbutz. Like Le'ith, he had learned to fly as a young man—and had been shot down and killed in the Six-Day War in 1987 on a mission over the Sinai Desert.

A year later his younger brother, Adam, joined the same kibbutz out of family loyalty and a vague sense of debt to Israel. So it was not strange that in college Lisa had chosen to spend her first three summers at that kibbutz. It was very near the Lebanese border, and in 1974 that had promised both adventure and purpose.

Though the volunteers all lived in a barracks they called the ghetto, each was "adopted" by a family in the kibbutz. In Lisa's case, it really *was* her family. Her uncle Adam was the youngest in her mother's family and had all the charm the baby of the family usually has. He had been her mother's darling when he was growing up and remained special long after she had her own two daughters.

When Adam and his smart, loving doctor-wife left for Israel, they had two small children, David and Ben. By the time Lisa arrived, they had added another boy, Yassi, and one adorable little daughter, Sophie. Adam, who had become rotund in fatherhood, joked that in Israel with only four children he was considered practically childless. Lisa found it was true; the families were big in the old-fashioned way and were the focus of everyone's lives.

From the first day Adam and Deborah's brood knew they owned their aunt. They pulled themselves up on her lap, usually two or three at once, led her by the hand to their sandbox, demanded she braid Sophie's hair and button the boys' pants, got her to read them stories, wipe their bottoms, fell asleep in her arms, shared her dessert in the communal dining hall.

And in the three summers she was there, Lisa, whose older sister had died of leukemia when she was twelve, came to love that part of her family as much, she felt, as her own life.

Adam and Deborah both worked off the kibbutz. The chubby fun-loving Adam, whose smile still crinkled his eyes, had somehow become a civil servant in Haifa; Deborah worked in the hospital at Zefat. Lisa and the volunteers worked in the fields from dawn till the sun boiled. Like her, most of the volunteers were young students, though there were a few very old students. There were Scandinavians, South Americans, South Africans, every kind of European, even a smattering of Asians from India and Hong Kong and Singapore. Except for the Asians, most were not Jewish, though plenty were. Sometimes in the long afternoons she and the other volunteers listened to the stories of the older members from Russia and Poland and Hungary. They all had different versions of the painful, clumsy, sometimes bloody, sometimes miraculous odyssey that had led to the building of a nation where there had been none.

She learned from those mouths of the seemingly endless history of tragedy and pursuit that gave so much meaning to those words "a land of our own"—words others spoke without thought but, to centuries of Jews, an impossible dream. Now, on that hot, arid strip of countryside beside the Mediterranean, that dream had become a reality to defend and cherish.

It was during her third summer, in the middle of a June night, that the fatal raid had happened. The first shell had exploded into the ghetto barracks. Lisa jerked awake, sitting up in panic as if from a nightmare. Her roommate, Karen, was staring at her when they heard the first screams. Another shell landed very near, the building rocked, and the glass in the window shattered. "My God!" Karen yelled.

They scrambled to grab some clothes and headed for the ghetto shelter as more shells echoed from farther up the hill.

Outside, people were running to the underground cover, some hopping along on one leg, trying to put their shoes on, others yelling at the stony ground. All the lights had gone out, but part of the barracks was on fire, and guards and some of the men were running to it. Lisa was almost at the shelter when another round of explosions thundered in. She fell to the ground as she'd been trained to do.

When she looked up, she saw for the first time that the shelling had been deadly accurate and that the housing and main buildings had been hit and were already raging with fire.

Her first thought was of the kids and, more on instinct than conscious decision, she ran up the hill to the central area. She reached it in time for another round of shells and went to the ground again. Most of this round fell short of the compound, but one exploded in the sleeping quarters, and she let out a howl of pain and ran toward it.

All around her there was absolute chaos: people running, shouting, screaming, "Check the clinic!," "Bring some sand!," and a dozen names, "Muriel!," "Zev!," "Beth!," over and over again. As she raced along in the flickering light of the raging fires, she could see people streaming from the sleeping quarters, some bleeding, some limping, all heading toward the concrete shelter of the school.

Then she saw them: Adam breaking from the building, carrying little Sophie in one arm, pulling Ben along with the other. Deborah was just behind with David and Yassi. The kids were so tiny and frightened. And then the scream of another round froze Lisa where she stood. As if in slow motion she saw round-faced Sophie explode from Adam, taking his arm with her, Adam doubled, his eyes stunned in horror, trying to grab at Ben with the arm that wasn't there as poor little Ben spilled forward spouting blood from his face and stomach. . . .

One day, after the funerals and the endless tears, Adam, whose stump of an arm had healed long before his heart, asked Lisa to drive him to Haifa. They went to a spot on the ancient bay, and he told her for the first time that he worked for an internal security branch of the Israeli Secret Service, the Mossad. Then he told her what a mole was: not a spy, who sought information and might assume a dozen different identities in a career, but someone who lived one totally false life, who became an accepted part of a world that wasn't theirs. How difficult and dangerous it was to place moles, how the Mossad's incredible record was based almost entirely on the work of such people. Men and women who had spent years toiling silently and unrewardingly in places where they did not belong, where they had no real homes. They did all this only to be called upon—perhaps—one day when Israel needed them to be called upon. Perhaps to give their lives in sacrifice like a soldier. Or perhaps one day to kill, as a soldier kills.

"No one has meant more to the preservation of Israel than some moles whose names no one knows—or ever will know," he said soberly. "And some are still placed out there in towns and villages where if they uttered a Jewish curse, they would die—gruesomely. Yet they may have to remain there until they are too old to be of use to anyone, even themselves. A daily, monthly, yearly sacrifice that may not ever be rewarded with a call to even one trivial act . . . But those who are called, and those who are not, are the real front lines of the 'home' my brother Noah gave his life to build."

Lisa's mind had raced with fear and understanding. She of course realized what he was holding out to her and could imagine her life spent in Egypt or Beirut or even some Palestinian camp someplace from Lebanon to Algeria, but despite all the rage and pain she felt—almost as deep as Adam's—she knew she couldn't do what he was asking. Work in the fields till she dropped, yes. Gladly give her life in battle, as Uncle Noah had, but live a secret life in a place she hated, and where she was hated, was not something she could truly face.

But Adam never asked. He stared silently at the sea for a time, then asked her to drive to a pretty Arab restaurant on the harbor front, where they had dinner, and he surprised her by joking in Arabic with the manager, who evidently knew him well.

Her next weeks were laced with guilt and doubt. Adam didn't change his attitude toward her at all, nor did he ever mention their trip to Haifa, but a hundred things a day haunted her. She would see the babushkas, so traditional and conservative, going to the beach with grandchildren as wild and free as only the most loved and independent of children can be. She would almost see in her head some "mole" someplace who was living in danger and dread to guarantee those babushkas' peaceful and happy old age and their grandchildren's confidence and lack of inhibition. Putting David and Yassi to bed under the pictures of Ben and Sophie and their uncle Noah brought tears to her eyes for the same reason. Their lives, their unquestioned sense that they belonged in the home their father had built, depended on some distant warrior, who never saw their smiles, their lovely brash self-assurance, would never feel their grateful hugs, could only know somewhere that these things were so because he—or she—was where he was, doing what he was.

Chapter 4

Lisa woke to Le'ith's soft touch on her shoulder. She had finally fallen asleep. As she rubbed her eyes, she looked up and saw that he was dressed in a thawb and gutra. She had never seen him in anything but Western clothes, and the change was a total shock to her. It was as if he had moved their sense of intimacy back a hundred desert miles.

He gestured to the rest of the first class cabin. The lights were still low, but all the men except the American businessmen were in thawbs, most with the gutra headdress, and all the elegantly dressed women were now in black chadors with veils.

Le'ith smiled at her. "Your turn." But there was tension in his voice. He had explained that his family would be deeply offended if she de-planed in Western clothes, and she had agreed to wear a chador, but he knew that it was a very reluctant decision and that Lisa was always capable of being the headstrong only child, and he was clearly afraid that she might balk at this last minute.

If she had seen one other woman in Western clothes, she would have, but there wasn't, and as distant as she suddenly felt toward this strangely robed Arab she had once known as Le'ith, he was now more than ever her one contact with her previous life. Conflict with him was not what she wanted. She took her bag and headed up the aisle to the toilet.

When she slipped into the chador Le'ith had bought for her and covered her face with the veil, she looked into the half mirror of the diminutive toilet. Her throat caught in a sudden paroxysm of fear. She had never tried the chador on before, and it made her feel as strange as she had found Le'ith in his thawb and gutra. Somehow during their "courtship" there had been an unreality about her mission. But now, seeing herself in this black disguise, something that covered all she really was, she grasped how fragile her dissemblance was. How could she live as this strange creature who faced her in the mirror? She was terribly unprepared, and she was filled with panic.

A stewardess knocked on the door. "We're landing. Please return to your seat." Lisa closed her eyes, clenched her jaw, and opened the door. Moving back to her seat, she caught glimpses through the windows of the land she was beginning to dread. Physically it could have been Arizona or Israel. Then she saw the vast and exotic Riyadh terminal, and her heartbeat went up again.

Once they had passed through customs and passport control and entered the massive reception hall, several men rushed up and kissed and hugged the Arab Le'ith. She was totally ignored. All around them Arab men were holding hands, laughing, kissing cheeks, hugging. The women, all looking the same—at least to Lisa—just stood quietly to one side. Occasionally one would be presented to an older man, whose hand she would kiss, and then step quickly back.

"Hi, you must be Lisa," a smoky female voice declared.

Lisa turned. A black-veiled woman in a chador stood next to her. Lisa could see enough of the eyes to guess they were smiling. "I'm Reena. From the way you're acting I would guess Le'ith hasn't told you about me."

Lisa's mind raced: Who could it be? Who could speak with this American accent? Rather than make her feel at ease, the surprise made her feel vulnerable and exposed.

"Yes . . . I mean, I *am* Lisa, but no, Le'ith didn't tell me I—I would meet a Reena who spoke English."

Reena laughed. "Well, very tactful. You'll survive. The only thing that works in Saudi Arabia is diplomacy."

Lisa didn't know what to say. If she ventured, "Are you related to Le'ith?" she might get, "Yes, I'm his second wife"—or "third concubine." Instead she muttered, "I—I expected it to be much hotter."

Reena laughed again. "Oh, very discreet, very English. No, the winters are actually pretty good."

She took Lisa by the arm and led her a little to one side. "Let me help you," she said. "Half of those around Le'ith are cousins of one degree or another; forget them. But the man holding his elbow right now—there—that is his younger brother, Youssef. Him you should watch like a hawk." Lisa glanced at her. Reena nodded firmly. "And the one just behind Youssef is Rashid. Rashid is Le'ith's half brother." She turned to Lisa. "And I am Le'ith's half sister."

Lisa breathed a sigh of relief, though she was surprised and more than a little disturbed that in all their revelations to each other, Le'ith had never mentioned having a half sister. He had talked of Jineen, his young sister, but not a word of half brothers or half sisters.

"Rashid and I are the children of your father-in-law's *second* wife. I was born two years before Le'ith, Rashid a year after. As for my English, in her youth my mother was very beautiful and very seductive—seductive enough that both Rashid and I were educated and eventually given our hearts' desire and sent to the West for degrees. It proved an advantage for Rashid, a disaster for me. It would not have taken a genius to predict that, but you must know how stubborn girls can be when they want their way. I don't imagine your parents exactly welcomed the idea of your marrying a Saudi."

Lisa forced a smile. "No. And I have been stubborn in my way too, but I hope it's not going to lead to disaster."

"Well, you may have the advantage of knowing quite soon," Reena said archly. She nodded back to the excited circle around Le'ith, which showed no sign of breaking up. "You see, Le'ith is both his father's eldest son and his favorite and, even more important, his *grandfather's* favorite, so we are witnessing a complex ceremony. Should nature take its normal course, Le'ith's power will grow each day, and then one day he will become the head of the family and all its holdings and influence. Everyone therefore wants to be in his favor, tell him how happy they are for him with his new bride.

"But since he has chosen to marry a Westerner, they all feel there is a real possibility of a family revolution. Le'ith may be reduced to cleaning up camel dung or other useful household tasks. This could produce wonderful prospects for both Youssef and Rashid, and down the line there is Abdel and Ahmad, my younger brothers, who are also expectant and hopeful. So everyone is very eager to find out just how attached Le'ith is to his new bride. Will he hold out against mother, father, and grandfather, or is this just a wild whim that a few days in the desert can convert to the magic words 'I divorce you, I divorce you, I divorce you'?''

Lisa longed to see the face behind that veil. Reena's manner was dryly cynical, as though it were all a sad, irrelevant joke. But was there spite too in that reminder that for Le'ith, divorce required only nine words and a witness?

Eventually the greeting ceremonies came to an end, and the party moved in chaotic bursts to a string of limousines. Reena and Lisa were joined by another woman, Huda, who did not speak English but was Le'ith's aunt on his father's side and, Reena assured her quietly, a woman of immense influence.

Their limousine took them only to a distant part of the huge airfield. There the three women were ushered into the back of a two-engine French jet. Le'ith finally entered and sat in the copilot's seat without so much as a glance at Lisa. She had seen that kind of arrogance in him in California, but it had never before been practiced on her. The Swiss pilot shook hands with him like an old friend. Youssef and Rashid climbed aboard. They were obviously going to accompany them to the home Lisa dreaded, the Safadi compound.

Le'ith had always spoken of it as being near Riyadh (which, she later learned, it was—in terms of *Saudi* geography), so she had expected the trip to be a short one—especially in a jet. Within minutes they had seen the last traces of the city. The landscape was not "desert," as she expected, but a shimmering palette of ochers, dun browns, huge swaths of wine red purples, hard, shimmering surfaces like ancient lava runs, then massive canyons, yellow and rust and gray. And it was endless—miles and miles in every direction.

Once, far into the journey, Reena pointed down, and Lisa could just pick out some black spots on a huge sheath of tawny, orange, and yellow rock.

"Camels," she said. "It's a caravan. Bedouin." Huda looked too and nodded. Lisa found it almost unbelievable. How could they survive, there was no sign of brush or green at all, much less water . . . and where could they be going? Where could they have come from? How in God's name in this landscape could they even know where they were?

Several minutes and several more horizons of barrenness had passed when Reena spoke again. "You can see why Saudi Arabia has never been conquered," she said. "Every country in the Middle East—Egypt, Jordan, Lebanon, Iran, Iraq—all have been ruled by the French or the English or the Turks, and sometimes all three, but no one has ever conquered the great emptiness of Saudi Arabia. Some have tried, but always the heat, the distances, the mysteries of water and survival when the sun beats on the desert shale like fiery arrows from heaven have been too much." Lisa heard the imagery, so like Le'ith's.

"Never having been slaves, never having had to bow to the foreigner has made Saudi men unlike any other Arabs you will ever meet. They're still men," she said derisively, but then her voice grew wistful. "But if you were born without a brain and longed only to bear children, it could make you happy. A lot of women in Saudi Arabia are." A little laugh. "As you've guessed, *I'm* not one of them." She sat up abruptly and turned to Lisa, her voice bearing a sudden amused but probing curiosity. "And you're not likely to be either. In fact, considering that you could not be truly stupid, there's a great puzzle here: Why did you marry Le'ith in the first place?"

Lisa was grateful at last for the chador and veil because she could feel the blood rising to her face. Please, God, don't let me fall at the very first hurdle, she pleaded silently.

"You must have read *something* about Saudi Arabia before you rushed into his arms. Why did you do it? You know if you have children and he divorces you, *he* keeps the children?"

"I—I love him" was all Lisa could mutter.

" 'Love him'! My God, you're an American. Why didn't you just take him to bed and fuck his brains out, as we used to say at Smith? Come on." Reena peered even closer. "Maybe you're not as pretty as Najib says you are." She was trying to penetrate the veil with unsubtle directness.

Huda saved the moment. She clutched at Lisa's arm and pointed below.

Lisa looked out at something so startling it almost quelled the fear that was clutching at her throat. Where all had been a moonscape of stony aridity there was a huge waving stretch of dark, vivid green. It was cut across the dun landscape in stark geometric designs and in this setting was striking and beautiful beyond belief. Like a green sea rising from the red desert. The plane suddenly banked, and for the first time Le'ith looked back at her. He had a tight, private smile on his lips. Then he turned back and took over the controls, and the plane began a series of banks and turns so that Lisa could see the whole miracle.

The straight, clean definitions made it seem as though some celestial hand had drawn a pattern on the barren floor of the continent and said, "Here will be a garden." She knew there were similar miracles in the Negev in Israel, but she'd never seen them. Then, in a small forest of date trees, she saw "the compound." She hadn't known quite what to expect, but there was a large central square with a striking white building dominating it. Several other buildings were spotted among the trees, some like miniature replicas of the master building, others very plain, all surrounded by an undulating white wall. As they swept over it, she could see men in thawbs and gutras hurrying to the cars that littered the area around the buildings.

The plane came in on a hard dirt runway that paralleled a series of warehouses. Several huge transport trucks were loading or unloading, but all work had stopped as men poured from the buildings to watch the arrival of Le'ith and his Western bride.

When the plane finally taxied to a stop, they were surrounded by cars and pickup trucks that had raced to meet them. It had a Wild West air to it that made Lisa think of Texas. Maybe Le'ith was right; it was a bit like marrying a Texas rancher.

When Le'ith stepped out at the top of the stairs—again he had not so much as glanced at Lisa—a huge shout went up, horns blasted, and he walked down into a sea of clasping hands and hugs, fervid kisses on the cheek.

When all the men had deplaned, Huda rose. Reena said, "Now it's our turn." And Lisa moved off with them, clammy with fear but expecting a greeting only a little less clamorous than Le'ith's.

Instead they were ignored. They were politely helped down the steps by the Swiss stewardess, whose arms and legs were appropriately covered, though she did not wear a veil.

At the bottom of the steps three women in chadors awaited them. One stepped forward to Lisa.

"I am Jineen," she said with the deliberation of someone who is still learning the language. "I am here to welcome you to the home of my father. Praise Allah you have had a safe journey."

"Yes, thank you," Lisa replied. "Le'ith has spoken of you often, and I feel I almost know you."

Jineen bowed. Huda accepted a hug from Jineen. Then Jineen led them toward one of the dusty Mercedes sedans. A driver promptly left the circle of men around Le'ith and carefully held the door first for Huda, then for Lisa. Reena squeezed into the middle from Huda's side, and Jineen sat on one of the jump seats.

"This is your first introduction to the hierarchy of Saudi life," Reena said sarcastically. "Muhammad said all are created equal in the eyes of God, but for practical reasons our women's world is ruled by prerogative and authority. Huda outranks us all, you outrank me, and but for her age, Jineen does too. Don't think of it as a nunnery because there will be sex. But knowing your place in the order is important to a 'happy' life."

She was really quite funny. But her quick mind had made Lisa more frightened than she'd ever been. No one had ever anticipated that her story would be exposed to the probing curiosity of a sophisticated and cynical product of Smith. Already she knew that this strange, isolated enclave with its dark and wild-looking men was not a place where she wanted to be revealed as a spy.

The car sped away from the planes. The two other women who'd greeted them had squeezed into the front seat with the driver. Huda said something to Jineen, nodding to them brusquely. "Fatima and Latifa will be your attendants," Jineen explained. At their names the two women turned to Lisa and bowed, but she could see nothing of their faces. "Fatima is trying to learn English," Jineen added. "They both want you to be pleased."

"I'm sure I will be," Lisa responded. She already felt that however dangerous Reena might be, she had nothing to fear from Jineen.

She was taken to one of the smaller buildings. It was very simple: a sitting room, a bedroom (large and well furnished), a rather derelict shower, and a standing toilet—two footpads over a ceramic hole—something she had first met in Israel but had never expected to be part of a home she lived in.

Jineen showed her around quickly, then went to the door to continue on with Huda and Reena. She started out but stopped and turned back. "You are free here to remove your veil. I would love to see your face."

Lisa smiled. She had longed to take the thing off from the first terrifying moment she had put it on. She pulled it loose and had started to slip off the chador when Fatima and Latifa came to her aid with hands that magically freed her from it all. She stood, holding her arms out, uncertain but trying to act assured. "Well, here I am, your new sister," she said.

Jineen was staring at her the way Lisa had stared at the wide, shimmering carpet of green on the desert floor. For a moment she was breathless. Then she said, almost to herself, "Now it is all clear . . . Allah be praised."

Lisa smiled, and suddenly, impetuously, Jineen removed her veil, revealing her young face, dark like Le'ith's, with large, pretty eyes and a sweet mouth, but without the bone structure that could have made her beautiful as Le'ith was handsome. She looked exactly as she sounded: a gentle, pleasing girl.

She waited for Lisa's approving smile, then placed the veil back over her face and was out the door.

Now that Lisa was "uncovered," Fatima and Latifa felt free to do the same. Lisa was amazed to see that the slender Fatima wore jeans and a loose shirt. Latifa was in a sheath dress that looked more like a servant's garment but was vividly colored in designs that seemed closer to New York than the Arabian Peninsula. Both of them had rough "country" faces but were desperately eager to please. They fixed her tea and gave her some fruit and a round soft bread full of herbs.

"You rest," Fatima said when she had finished, and pointed to the bed. "Long journey."

"Yes, I'll rest," Lisa lied, knowing her fear of Reena's curiosity would keep her awake. She moved toward the bedroom, and they followed. She turned to stop them, but bowing and smiling, they waited. "Just to lie down," Fatima said. Lisa gave up. She went to the bed, and as she started to take her dress off, she felt their silken hands disrobe her. She had to admit there was a certain hypnotic luxury to it. Latifa brought a silk robe from the closet, and with the genius of striptease artists, they uncovered her and covered her without really exposing anything, their hands never more than lightly grazing Lisa's skin.

She thanked them, but they still would not move. So she turned and stretched out on the bed. That brought smiles. They turned and left, Fatima touching a switch that activated a punkah over the bed. It moved back and forth slowly, giving just the gentlest of breezes.

She lay there for a time watching a tiny lizard in the corner of the ceiling, smelling the odd mixture of farmyard and spices that had permeated her nostrils since they'd stepped out of the car. So now here she was, in the middle of a country that allowed no Jews within its borders, that would end her life in torture and shame if anyone simply found out that she had once gone to Hebrew school.

And she was already faced with someone who doubted her story. Why, indeed, would an intelligent, fairly beautiful woman come voluntarily to live in a barren land where women had no freedom? Love was the only answer, but to a knowing woman like Reena, how credible was that kind of love in an American girl over twenty who had obviously loved once or twice before?

Lisa knew how she had made herself indispensable to Le'ith. It had come to her by accident, but it had become the key to their whole relationship. And as her mind searched for a solution, she grasped at the possibility that she could reverse it to explain why she would choose to do what she had done.

It had happened one Sunday night, when they were creeping along Pacific Coast Highway after picnicking on the beach in Malibu. There'd been a rockslide, and the traffic was backed up for miles.

Suddenly they heard a muffled explosion and screams from behind them. A car just one row back in the stalled traffic had burst into flames. Lisa twisted up and saw the passenger door of the car push open and two panicked kids scramble out, crying and screaming to their mother.

When Lisa turned back, Le'ith had already grabbed the picnic blanket from the backseat and was running toward the flaming car. People were fleeing from other cars all around them.

She got out and ran back after him. When she got to the car, Le'ith was half inside the driver's door, reaching for the latch to the hood. Flames were shooting out from under the car and all along the interstices at the top of the hood.

"Get the kids away!" he shouted.

Lisa could now see a woman kneeling on the front seat, frantically trying to free a baby from a car seat in the back. The heat from the fire was excruciating. Lisa grabbed one of the screaming boys. A man from another car had already picked up the smaller one and run to the side of the road.

When she reached the shoulder of the road, another man grabbed the kid from her, yelling, "Come on, move off, that thing is going to explode!" Lisa turned back.

Ignoring the terrible heat, Le'ith had opened the hood and a tower of flame shot up. He threw the blanket on the engine, putting his body weight right over the flame. Then he pulled off the sweater he had looped around his neck and used it to quash the flames pouring out at the sides. The fire still raged under the car, but Le'ith turned from the engine and darted around to the passenger side of the car. He jumped in, freed the baby from the car seat, and handed it to the hysterical mother.

Le'ith's courage had emboldened some of the other drivers, and two men ran to the car with fire extinguishers. The flame was finally subdued, and Le'ith became the center of a crowd of admiring spectators. He was offered balm and bandages for his burns from a dozen first-aid kits.

The mother came up to him, still holding the baby, and thanked him with tears in her eyes. Le'ith hugged her with an air of becoming modesty, but the noisy, excited praise hadn't seemed to discomfit him at all. He *was* brave, but there was a note of arrogant superiority to his awareness of it that she didn't like. It was the same in the ruthless skirmishes of the soccer he played, where Lisa'd seen him pull some miracle of speed and daring and then take the accolades as though he were Superman and this sort of thing was only to be expected, along with the praise of those less gifted.

Once they'd got by the bottleneck, they broke out of the traffic and drove up to Mulholland Drive, where they had a favorite spot to park. It looked out over the Valley—so grim in the day but like a magic carpet of light at night.

Lisa reexamined the bandages on his arm. One had pulled loose, and she took some of the balm they'd been given and smoothed it on his arm again. "You were pretty cool back there," she'd said flatteringly.

He only smiled.

"Aren't you *ever* afraid?" she asked, finishing the bandage.

"I'm afraid of you all the time," he replied. There was a touch of mockery in those words, but more than a touch of truth too.

"Well, besides me?"

He stared out broodingly over the glistening Valley, the dark hulk of the mountains beyond. The incident had been too frightening to be flippant. She slipped down into his arms. "Yes," he finally muttered introspectively, "there is something in America that frightens me . . . frightens me a lot." He paused for what seemed a long time. "When I first came here, one of the guys we met during soccer tryouts was talking about how he'd spent the year hitchhiking around the country. He said his old man threw him out on his eighteenth birthday and told him it was time he cut out on his own. The other guys laughed. They didn't see anything strange about it at all. Not one of them thought they would live at home after they finished college."

He kissed the top of her head and didn't speak for a moment. "I couldn't sleep for days," he said. "In our country you are always part of the family, you live with them, you know they are always there, and they will always have you."

He paused again, still feeling, she could tell, the fear he described. "But I've seen Americans cut off from their parents, their brothers and sisters, all their relatives, for months, even years. It always gave me nightmares when someone would tell me that about themselves.

"I can still wake up at night, thinking about it, thinking of being in the world alone, all alone . . . and I'm lost, depressed, and, to tell you the truth, frightened."

Lisa came as close that night as she felt she ever could to taking him in her arms and making love to him. They did stay in the car a long time, with her body tight against his in the erotically complex game of sexual postponement they had become adept at. They didn't speak, and by the time her passion had begun to subside she thought she knew how she was going to make him love her enough to defy all the restraints she knew he had to marrying her, how she was going to climb the very difficult mountain.

From that day on she became his family. She became father, mother, sister, cousin. . . . She could be cross with him, annoyed with him; she scolded him and was "proud" of him; she talked with an intimacy about herself as though he were *her* family, and it drew the same intimacy from him. But always she acted as if they were bound together, that no annoyance, no revelation could change the tie between them.

Except for the central basic truth about her, she told him everything: her fears, her jealousies, her embarrassments, things she would never have told a boy she wanted to capture. Ever. It was her giant risk, and it had worked. He had become as open to her, and she felt his need grow for her touch, for the look of unconditional love when he goofed or was awkward, or hurt, or stubbornly perverse. For her it was a deliberate, conscious act contrary to anything she had ever done with any boy. All the feminine restraint, the coyness, the unpredictability that she had first used as naturally as she breathed to lure him, she abandoned. She left him no doubt: Her love for him was an irrevocable part of her.

And as she lay there in her silken robe under the slowly swaying punkah, she thought that would have to be her defense against Reena's probing, cynical mind. She had come to Saudi Arabia because Le'ith had become her "family." A Saudi woman—even an intelligent, Western-educated one—might accept that.

⌇

She *was* tired from the journey, and despite her heightened sense of fear, sleep finally caught her and held her for long hours. It was a rest-less slumber; she was half awake a dozen times. Night came, and she glimpsed, through half-closed eyes, lights across the square, and she could hear voices speaking in Arabic; later the sound of a motor disturbed her again, and she realized the lights had been turned off. The next time she was aware at all, she realized someone had covered her with a soft blanket, and the punkah had been turned off. She could feel the cold night air.

As she tried to doze off again, she kept remembering the first day she had heard of Le'ith, the first day Saudi Arabia had become more than just a name on a map to her. It was only a day after she had decided she could never sleep if she turned her back on what Adam had so subtly held out to her. The day after she told him, he had her drive him back to Haifa, and she had spent the afternoon with the most ordinary-looking people: fat men with bald heads, women who needed to diet and exercise and who misplaced their glasses and jumbled up files. She might have been applying for a job at some junior college. But they knew a sur-prising amount about her, even things Adam could hardly have known: her school friends, trips she'd taken, boyfriends she'd had.

They knew quite a lot about another student at UCLA too. A boy named Le'ith Safadi. They had had his picture. He was handsome, very handsome. The eldest son in a Saudi family that was growing more and more powerful. He was married.

"In a way that can be an advantage," one of the matronly women had said. "The whole burden of marital relations won't be yours." The mere mention had knotted Lisa's stomach as though a dozen hands were clutching fiercely at her intestines. "Married?" In the nights she'd tossed and turned she had imagined she might have to engage in affairs—but marriage? She held it so sacred. She loved her parents, and she loved Adam and Deborah; that was the way she wanted it to be.

But the briefing had gone on, so routinely, so detached from any emotion they might have been discussing a concert tour. In her head she was saying, Let them send me off and call on me quickly. Let me do my duty and leave. Then I can return to Philadelphia, marry, raise kids, and die with a wonderful secret in my head, and my head alone.

"Meeting this young man will be easy," the leading fat, bald man said. "Attracting him is something I am equally sure you will manage with ease." He smiled; they all smiled at her beauty.

"The problem," another man said, "will be to draw him on far enough that he will be willing to defy convention and his family's injunctions and actually marry you."

Lisa shrugged modestly, but experience had already taught her that given the cache of physical and psychological coin God and family had presented her with, proposals were not that hard to come by. She had often felt almost guilty about these "blessings," but now she felt she might be going to pay for them. Dearly.

"Saudi men are more Victorian about their views of women than the Victorians were." The man went on. "Women are either wives to bear heirs and therefore virginal and eternally chaste or they are concubines, which they are, incidentally, allowed to have, along with four wives, and these ladies may not necessarily be virginal, but they must surely be faithful as long as they are in the employ of their master. Then there are whores. You of course must be—or appear to be—among the virginal and chaste."

Lisa had been so repelled by it all that at that moment she saw only one ray of light, and it was the certainty that her feelings and passions could never be engaged by a man who thought like that, who acted like that. Everything she did would be a job against a hated enemy.

"I'm afraid I may be the wrong girl," she had said. She'd seen a fleeting glimmer of panic in every pair of eyes except Adam's. "Not that I would not marry this man, if that is what is required," she continued.

The relief around the table was manifest. "The problem is, I'm afraid I'm not as Victorian as this Mr. Safadi. My virginity passed into history the summer after my seventeenth birthday." Adam couldn't repress his smile. Looking at him, she realized how happy she might be with a roly-poly husband like Adam rather than some Adonis like Mr. Safadi.

"That's all right, my dear," the heavyset woman with a faint mustache replied with a sigh. "We can teach you how to handle that." There were little arch smiles all round the table.

Lisa was not so relieved, but she hadn't really thought this was going to change anything.

"We know you're intelligent," the leading fat, bald man said, leaning across the table. "But the first lesson you have to learn is not to underestimate *his* intelligence—or the hold his family has on him.

"His capabilities have already suggested a special destiny for him. With that comes responsibility, and with Saudis the *first* responsibility is to family.

"To make him want you is a small hill; to make him want to marry you enough to defy his family and actually do it is a great mountain. I wouldn't begin to try to tell you how to climb that mountain, when to pull the ropes tight, when to let them fall loose, but I *can* tell you that the worst slip you can make is to underestimate the difficulty of the task."

He had brought the whole room to utter silence, and Lisa understood for the first time that looks and personality and willingness would not be enough. She remembered reading of the women who worked as spies in World War II. They had not been just sexual sirens. Spying took skill and intelligence, and the bold daring to risk all on a judgment, a conviction about someone else's innermost feelings. It was the first time the challenge had frightened her.

Later she recalled that moment often. She knew it guided her to her ultimate "victory" with Le'ith. Had she run the relationship on blind confidence or "feminine instinct," he would have slipped from her hands a dozen times. She could so easily have become just another "Western experience."

When she and Adam finally left the building, it was twilight. With his remaining arm, Adam hugged her without speaking. Then he asked her to drive down to the harbor. She thought he was going to take her to another restaurant, but at the museum *Ha'apala* he told her to turn in. The large sign said it was closed, but as they approached the gates, they opened as if on command.

The museum is only an old ship pulled up in dry dock. It had been one of many ancient craft that smuggled Jewish refugees from Europe into British-controlled Palestine after World War II. Adam, who usually had a smile in his voice that matched the crinkles around his eyes, started talking from the minute their feet touched the deck, but the words came quietly and soberly. He told Lisa how in those days the captains had to circumvent the normal sea-lanes, running mostly at night, seeking out storms to hide their movements. Everything about the journeys was a risk. The boats were barely seaworthy, the crews inexperienced or far too old; a trip that was planned for a week could take a month with food and water becoming almost nonexistent.

Belowdecks Lisa saw the rows and rows of huddled bunks, crammed with raggedly dressed mannequins as they had once been with real men and women and children. Adam told her of the days spent sitting under a scorching sun, the metal sides of the ship too hot to touch, the nights too sweltering to sleep. Of winter trips, when the seas would pound the hulls and hurl the frightened passengers in all directions, each new blow feeling as if it would tear the shuddering, fragile ship apart.

Often, when the longed-for shore had been sighted, the British would be there, and they would be *turned away,* taken to barren camps in Cyprus or returned to the refugee camps in Europe from which they'd fled.

Lisa scanned the pictures, the faces of families who had been chased and hunted across Europe, their closest relatives "eliminated" in gas chambers and concentration camps, their only possession a dream that they might make a new life in the land of David and Moses and Samuel.

It was like Adam not to have taken her there first, not to have used it to influence her, but, once she had made up her mind, to take her then . . . so that she might know her sacrifice meant something beyond their own personal grief for Sophie and Ben, something worth more than his words or anyone's could express.

She had turned to him, and he'd held her with that one arm and the stump that haunted her as she sobbed and sobbed.

Later they'd gone to the Arab restaurant he first took her to and were able to laugh and joke, but now and again her eyes filled with water and Adam would grin affectionately and touch her hair.

It still seemed dark when she heard the recorded call of the muezzin. She knew it must be dawn, but she couldn't keep her eyes open.

She was not fully awake, but it was daylight when she felt the weight of someone on the bed and turned, startled, to a smiling Le'ith, who took her in his arms and kissed her with a sexual passion that had obviously been simmering. She started to push him off, but he persisted, not brutally but forcibly enough so that she would really have to rebel if she were to stop him. For a moment she continued to resist. Seeing him in his thawb and gutra, his kissing and holding hands with brothers and cousins, his disdainful ignoring of her as though she were a piece of property to be neglected when he chose to neglect, and now to be taken when he chose to take, had disheartened her and revived in her all the images of Arab men that she detested before she actually met Le'ith.

Her instinct was to push him away, but her mind was waking, and she remembered how delicate her position was, and how dangerous. Even if she survived Reena, there would be every pressure on Le'ith to divorce her and send her back. What a glorious release that would be, but that was not an escape her pride or sense of duty would let her accept. She owed Sophie and Ben more than that, though at this moment she longed for it.

She stopped resisting and let him make love to her. For the first time it was as she always felt it would be. She hated the touch of his hands, they were invasive and crude; his murmuring her name made her wonder where he had spent the night. No, she *knew*. He had been murmuring, "Nayra," with the same husky emotion hours ago, maybe less than that. She was being the whore, acting a passion and, worse, an affection she did not feel.

She had thought it would be easy to be a whore, but she wanted to sob, just to lie there and cry and let him get on with it. Sex had never been so distasteful to her, and she had to fight consciously to keep from breaking down.

When he at last climaxed, she held her arms around his sweating head, keeping it locked in her shoulder. She could not let him see her face.

He sighed heavily and squeezed her. "I've missed you," he said playfully.

She rubbed his hair a little in response. She still couldn't speak.

"I warned you I had a big family," he said, as though explaining the night's absence. "Tomorrow you'll meet my mother, and my aunts, and my half sisters, and, well, the women of the family."

"And your father?" she asked.

She could feel his body grow taut. "My father won't be here until Friday," he said. "You'll meet him on the weekend."

"Is this my home?" she asked. He started to lift his head, but she held it down, and he relaxed, but with a sigh that revealed he was not eager to tell her what he must.

"This is your *private* home," he said diplomatically. "My father's home is home to us all, and you will probably want to spend most of your time there."

"Is this *your* private home too?"

He hesitated; it was enough for her to know that whatever he said was not going to be the full truth.

"Yes," he equivocated. "I—I still have a room in my father's house, but when we are together alone, it will be in this house."

He rolled over to look at her, and this time she did not resist. He knew her too well not to be able to read the discontent and fear in her eyes. He drew his hand along the side of her face. "I have a plan for us," he said softly. "It will take a little while, but we will have *our* house. I am home now, and it is all familiar to me and strange to you. But give it time. It won't be so strange, and I promise you, you and I will have our own life."

She was in such an emotional maelstrom, fear and anger and obligation, she didn't know what performance to give. She didn't want real attachment, yet she felt frightened and lost without it, and she needed his faith if she was challenged by Reena. She still felt repelled by the sex they'd had, yet the only thing that had cut her crushing sense of anxiety and gloom was his pledge that they would have "their house." But even if she survived Reena's cross-examination and they didn't stone her to death in the next few days, how was she ever going to live through a month of this—never mind years?

Chapter 5

Le'ith's father did not come on the weekend. Some urgent matter intervened. There were rumors of an "uprising," even revolution. Le'ith and Rashid and several of the other men were to fly off on Saturday. Lisa was to be left to face Reena's challenge on her own. Before he left, Le'ith introduced Lisa privately to his mother. Lisa, as he had instructed her, knelt and kissed her mother-in-law's hand, then rose and kissed each cheek.

Ummi ("Mother"), as she was called by all, was very overweight, but she had huge, alluring eyes and a broad, sensuous mouth. In her youth she must have been voluptuous, Junoesque, very different from Lisa's all-American shapeliness and grace. There was wit in her eyes too, and though she was supposed to be one of those most "offended" by Le'ith's choice, she reached out and touched Lisa's hair, then ran a finger across Lisa's full lips and glanced at her son with an understanding smile. She said something to him that was clearly a tease and slightly ribald.

After that meeting Le'ith hugged Lisa and told her how much it meant to him that it had gone well. She was pleased only in terms of her ultimate purpose. Le'ith in his Arab garb still seemed half stranger to her, and she resented the intimacy of his arms. He had come to visit her again the night before, and though she felt less like bursting into tears, she felt unclean from the encounter and could not wait to have him gone.

It was so disappointing, so unlike what she had expected from him. She remembered their wedding night and her fear of loving him. But now, half a world and a civilization away from Lake Tahoe, she felt that was no problem. She hated his touch, hated that he was free to make love to her whenever he chose. Hated how coming to his home had revealed this other Le'ith, this aggressive, insensitive Arab man.

As soon as he left, she had stood in the shower, touching herself as she wished to be touched. She sang in whispers and tried to find in her imagination old boyfriends who had excited her lust before, who made sex exciting and liberating, but when she finally climaxed, it was, to her distress, the irrepressible image of Le'ith at Lake Tahoe that sent her body into quivering release. She felt like crying again, but she knew she could not dwell on any of it or she would lose her mind.

Le'ith and Rashid had left immediately after her meeting with Ummi. Fatima and Latifa were vastly relieved at Le'ith's obvious cheerfulness when he returned Lisa to her "house." They fussed over her clothes with the same diligence they had earlier, because she was now to be introduced to her real home, the women's quarter. After days of sitting in her two rooms doing nothing but reading and listening to the unfamiliar sounds of life in the compound, she was almost eager for the experience, but it was here she knew she would have to face Reena again. The two servants had dressed her in a red tunic over an abu of light blue, with a red shawl over her head. It could not have been more flattering. They wanted her to put on a more vivid lipstick, and having seen the fulgent makeup Ummi used on both her mouth and her eyes, she acceded.

In order for her to cross the grounds past the scattered cars and brazen goats, all this had to be covered by a chador and veil. An old guard stood at the top of the stairs at the entrance to the quarter. He bowed to Lisa as he opened the door, seeming by the grin on his face to know who she was despite the impenetrable anonymity of the chador. Inside, Fatima and Latifa slipped the black cover from her, hung it on a knob alongside what seemed like dozens of others in the narrow gallery that led to two huge, elaborately carved doors.

Before Fatima knocked, she and Latifa fussed again over the drape of Lisa's tunic, the fall of her hair. Lisa was already about as nervous as she'd ever been about an "entrance"—Reena was certain to be beyond those doors—and their anxious fastidiousness only added to her tension.

They had told her in Haifa that if she ever felt her life was in danger, she should use the signal word "faith" in a letter to her "aunt." Now as she stood at the door to the women's quarter, she felt like screaming, "Faith!" to the sky, hoping somehow the Mossad would appear and take her away forever.

The door was opened from the inside by Jineen, whose welcoming smile almost stopped the shaking in Lisa's legs. There were gasps, and someone *laughed out loud* and said, *"Allah akbar!"* It started her legs shaking again, but Jineen came forward, kissed Lisa on both cheeks, then led her past dozens of probing eyes to three huge overstuffed chairs by a corner of the huge room. Ummi sat in one, and Jineen led Lisa to her first and with a slight pull on her arm indicated she kneel and go through the ritual kissing of hands and cheek. Ummi smiled and spoke softly, and though there must have been forty people in the room, some of them children, there was not a sound. Jineen translated, "In the name of Allah the Merciful I am fortunate to be able to welcome to our harim the beautiful wife of my son Le'ith." Lisa learned later that she would have been called beautiful if she looked like an undernourished camel, but at this moment the word embarrassed her, feeling it could not help but incite envy in a room full of women. She smiled her thanks nevertheless.

Jineen then took her to the next chair. The second wife, Harhash—Lisa knew she must be the mother of Reena and Rashid—was more delicate of feature than Ummi, but not much younger and even more overweight. Lisa knelt and kissed her hand and then her cheeks as Jineen introduced her, and then she heard a smoky voice she recognized even though it spoke Arabic. She turned to one she knew must be Reena. She knew instantly that it was she who had laughed when Lisa first entered the room.

When Lisa turned to her, Reena spoke in English. "So Najib did not lie. You *are* beautiful, more beautiful than the mountains at dawn, yet you came to live in a harim. Why? I wonder."

She was fairer than most of the women in the room, fairer than her brother Rashid, but her features were not as delicate as her mother's. She had a Semitic nose that unbalanced her face and a mouth that time or God had made as cynical and wry as her mind. What was striking about her was her eyes; they seemed to reach out at the world, seeking perpetual confirmation of iniquity or folly, the one justifying her cynicism, the other provoking her wit. As they appraised Lisa, it was clear that she hadn't quite decided which she was witnessing, iniquity or folly.

The tone of Reena's question had prompted a sharp word from Ummi. Reena bowed deferentially to her and apparently repeated the question in Arabic, adding quite a bit more.

It had an impact, for Ummi looked at Lisa with a kind of critical appraisal that had not been there before. She turned to Jineen and spoke, Jineen translating in the total silence that had once again engulfed the room.

"My mother would like to know why you chose to marry Le'ith and come to a world so different from your own, especially since your beauty and your education could have drawn many men to you from your own world."

Lisa, her legs unsteady again, thought, Why indeed? But after her restless night she felt prepared. She faced Ummi directly, "God often brings us to moments we never anticipated," she said. She paused as Jineen translated and saw that her approach through "God" had softened the doubt in Ummi's face a little.

"I met Le'ith by accident. We were both students far from home, he in a land that was as strange to him as this is to me, I thousands of miles from my mother and father, whom I'd always lived with. In our mutual loneliness we first became like brother and sister. Then we came to want each other very much as man and woman. When it came time for Le'ith to return here, I felt he was my family. I could not imagine a life without him."

Jineen was misty-eyed when she finished the translation, and Lisa was sure her sympathetic rendering of her little speech had as much impact as the words themselves. Ummi was almost as touched as Jineen;

it is not hard, after all, for a mother to believe a woman could fall in love with her son, especially a son like Le'ith. Ummi spoke again—kindly. Jineen translated: "I hope you find the happiness you seek, *Inshallah*—God willing."

The *Inshallah* was repeated around the room, but when Lisa turned to continue the introductions, Reena's look at her had grown more skeptical, not less. In the words of Smith College, the eyes were saying, "Come on, baby, cut the bullshit, what's the real story?" Lisa smiled, but she knew the effort behind it only confirmed Reena's skepticism.

The third chair was occupied by a woman not much older than Lisa. But Jineen indicated the same obeisance, and Lisa conformed. This was Toujan, Le'ith's father's latest bride, a young Jordanian, she was to learn later. Jineen introduced her with great politeness, but it was clear that in the harim at least Toujan was as uneasy as Lisa. Her power was obviously in the bedroom. Even her abu could not conceal a body at once slender and extraordinarily generous. Her face was not pretty, but there was a sultry lassitude to it that was sexually provocative even when she wasn't trying.

Jineen then took Lisa to another spot in the room by a small water fountain, where Huda was ensconced. Her wrinkled face and philosophic eyes were exactly as Lisa had imagined. She did her obeisance, and when she kissed Huda's cheeks, Huda held her head with a firm grip of affection. She spoke, and Jineen said, "She hopes you produce many blondes for Le'ith. Fill the desert with blue eyes."

Then the long ritual began. Daughters, cousins, the wives of Le'ith's brothers, of his uncles, aunts, great-aunts, some visiting friends all were brought to Lisa—to exchange God's blessing, to kiss the cheeks. She kept expecting to meet Nayra, Le'ith's "first" wife, and tried guessing which she might be, but she neither saw her nor heard her name mentioned. Had she been locked up?

When it was over, she found Reena by her side. She smiled at Lisa and said, "You need a break. Come, let me show you where you can get away from it all." Lisa expected another grilling, but she felt more up to it now.

Reena led her through one of several rooms off the main room of the quarter. Some had windows with iron grilles; some had filigreed walls. The rooms were built around the movements of the sun, so there was always shade and breeze, and there was always someplace remarkably cool, given the outside temperatures.

Reena's destination was a shaded balcony. It was filigreed in white stone so that only their forms could be seen from outside. On the first floor below was a beautiful courtyard with a pool that reflected the four archways into the different sections of the house. The details of colored marble and mosaic that trimmed the arches were complemented by groomed trees and vines with an elegance that made it seem like a fairy-tale oasis. In the middle of the pool a fountain sprinkled the air with moisture, and in one corner water flowed down an irregular mound of rocks to create the sound of a running stream. After all the miles of barren, waterless waste and the rough, unkempt barnyard nature of the compound, it seemed like a fantasy mirage.

"One of the pleasures of being a Saudi woman," Reena said with her usual wryness, "is that you are allowed to walk up here on the balcony and watch the men stroll around the courtyard in the mornings and evenings."

"Aren't women allowed downstairs?"

"Not when men are there."

"But what about parties or birthdays?"

Reena laughed. "You *aren't* very smart, are you? You really didn't read one book about Saudi Arabia, not one."

Lisa sighed. "Not really. I just listened to Le'ith."

Reena looked at her testingly and started to walk slowly around the balcony. Lisa followed, struck by how the look of the courtyard changed with almost every step, each view with its own beauty, its own symmetry.

Reena seemed reflective, touched by the serenity of the bubbling water, the emotional stillness of the courtyard, and she was apparently half convinced that Lisa was just stupid or at least stupidly improvident in not learning more about her future husband's home and life.

It was a conviction Lisa wanted to encourage. "Le'ith did tell me that this was a very religious country and old-fashioned about many things, but he said it was nothing like what one reads in the papers about Iran, for example."

"That's true. Not now it isn't, not quite," Reena replied. "But a few years ago women walked in the streets of Iran in Western dress; they attended the university in mixed classes; they could divorce; they had as much right to their children as their husbands did. Since the Ayatollah it has become more violently 'old-fashioned' than we are, but believe me, we have no 'mixed gatherings.' When the men party, *we* may party too, but we do it separately. They are at last letting women enter the university, but in totally segregated classes, and if it's a class taught by a man, his instructions come into the room by means of a television set. He never sets eyes on one of his students."

Lisa absorbed it; Sabah's description had not been exaggerated. She looked down at the sparkling pool, the peace of the courtyard. She sensed how slow the pace of everything was. No distractions, no ticking clocks. This would be where she would spend much of her time, she thought, but if she was going to be so cut off, of what possible use could she be?

"Why are *you* here if you hate it so?" she finally asked Reena.

Reena paused, as though thinking about it. "For years it was forbidden for women to be educated at all. Then we had a great king, something like your Lincoln perhaps."

Lisa laughed. "You actually believe there were *two* good men?"

Reena grinned. "I'm not sure about Lincoln, but certainly *one*." She shook her head at the idea that she could make even this concession. "Imagine what would happen in the United States," she went on, "if in one month everyone, the whole country, became ten thousand times richer than they were the month before. Can you imagine the insanity? And what would happen if the same were to befall 'civilized' England or 'cultured' France? Madness. Corrupt, uncontrolled madness. I would lay my life on it.

"But when that happened to us, when we suddenly became oil-rich beyond the wildest fantasy, fortunately that *one man* was our ruler and absolute monarch. Yes, a few million were squandered here and there, and a few young princes bought women and gambled away fortunes, but they were trickles out of the immense ocean of wealth. My grandfather was rich because he owned sixty camels and a few tents. Now sixty camels couldn't carry his wealth in gold. That man, King Faisal, took an illiterate desert people, gave them education, medical care equal to the best in the world. In one generation he turned a medieval country into a modern country and kept it sane and stable despite being in a sophisticated world that sought to grab its riches by every trick and deceit known to man. That was his good side."

"Ah, I knew something had to be wrong," Lisa jested.

"Yes. He was very religious and, like Muhammad, believed in the equality of men and women."

"Excuse me!"

"I know . . . I used to argue this at Smith all the time. Muhammad did not say women were the *same* as men, but he said they were equal in the sight of Allah and should seek education and knowledge. So, when the religious Faisal had all this wealth at his disposal, girls began going to school. *I* went to school. They were separate schools, of course, thousands of them all around the country, with building materials flown across the desert by planes, helicopters. Teachers and school lunches appearing out of nowhere—at great cost, but cost was not the object.

"For girls it was very exciting. And I decided one suffocatingly hot day when the bus came that I did not want to wear my veil. There was, of course, one bus for boys and one for girls. No one could see me but a passing Bedouin. So I thought it was quite reasonable to travel without a veil.

"My father said no. I said I was going to take it off anyway. He came into the bus and pulled me off. He took me in his car and drove off furiously into the countryside. There was little green then, just rock and shale for miles. After he had driven for what seemed hours, he stopped the car, took me by the arm, and put me out.

" 'Here,' he said, 'I am leaving you. If Allah intends you to return, you will. If not, you will not.' And he turned the car and drove off."

Lisa looked at her. Reena was staring down at the pool, but her whole body was quite stiff. Lisa hesitated, then put her hand on Reena's. It produced a little whimsical smile.

"It was two full days and a night before I found my way back. For a time I was hysterical and cried and ran in circles, covered in sweat and dust. At first I was too frightened to be hungry or thirsty, but the second day I could hardly breathe for want of saliva in my throat. My shoes were cut by the stones, and my feet bled. I prayed to Allah. I screamed to the white-hot blue sky to have my father forgive me.

"When I finally saw a bit of green, I ran on until I was sure it was a field . . . and then I just fell from exhaustion and cried and cried. It was a Yemeni laborer who found me and took me to my father's house. After they had washed me and given me water, they took me to him."

She paused again. "He looked up and said, 'So you returned. . . . Tomorrow you will wear your veil.' I ran to him, crying, and he comforted me, but he never said another word." She paused for a long time. Lisa was enormously touched by the story but could sense that it was not over.

"When I was old enough, my mother bewitched him into allowing me to go to America. My grades were better than Rashid's, and his were good. Some other mothers were also able to bewitch their husbands, and eight of us flew off from Riyadh with Salama, the aunt of one of the girls, as our guardian. She had been raised and educated in Egypt and was therefore assumed to know the ways of the Western world." She laughed.

"I loved Salama, but she was so easy to dupe. She was frightened to death herself. I had smoked hashish here, as a lot of girls had, but at Smith smoking pot became a daily routine, and I almost got hooked on coke. And for a time I got very hooked on men—boys." She grinned cynically, but there was a vulnerability in her voice and in her eyes that drew Lisa's sympathy again.

Two men appeared in the courtyard below, walking slowly around the pool. They had an air of importance, and though the sound of the running water made it impossible to hear what was being said, their manner made it evident they were discussing something very disturbing.

Reena watched for a moment. "Well, perhaps we will have some excitement," she said. "Even bad news helps break the boredom."

"So why *do* you stay?" Lisa persisted.

"I don't," Reena replied solemnly. "From time to time I go and dip myself in the desert of the West." She laughed suddenly. "Here I am probably the least religious of all, but when I am in the West, I see the competition and the incessant striving for some kind of status, the loneliness, the vanity and vulnerability, 'each man for himself' and only one ethical principle, 'Don't get caught.' It's bizarre, but after a while I actually hear phrases in my head from my school days about Muhammad's tribe and how they had become like that, and even before he heard the Messenger of God, he believed their egotism and greed would destroy them unless they found some greater purpose.

"I get caught up with it in the West. It's contagious, this striving to be special in a land of absurd conformity, and then, if I'm there long enough, I see the hole in the center of my life, and I feel the way I felt when my father abandoned me in the middle of the desert, and I desperately long to find my way back to the family."

So like Le'ith, even the cynical Reena. "Do you think of marriage and a family of your own?" Lisa asked.

Reena turned to her, those large dark eyes that had become quite soft and vulnerable suddenly cold and penetrating. "No Saudi, no Arab who did not want my money would have me. And I don't know how I could live with a man from the West, especially if I had to live in his country. And I am still perplexed that ignorant as you may have been of the whole truth, a girl like you could have been led to a place like this, even by one as becoming as Le'ith."

"I told you—"

"I know what you told me. I wait for the day when you will be as frank with me as I have been with you."

Lisa could feel herself blanch.

"Don't worry," Reena went on, "you will find that we have lots of time, and one often fills it by saying things that were never intended to be said."

Chapter 6

By the time Le'ith returned Lisa felt accepted in the quarter. Ummi approved of her; Huda approved of her; Jineen almost loved her; Reena waited but liked to scandalize her with tales about life in and out of the quarter. It was more like a girls' school than a nunnery. They sewed; they read; they played endless card games, laughing and teasing and betting everything from money to kisses on the feet. They danced and played childish games like pin the tail on the donkey.

Reena spent an hour each day teaching some of the young ones French. The younger brother, Youssef, was a wife beater, and all the women prayed he would soon take another wife so that Ulti, his sweet and pretty young bride, would suffer less. No one dreamed of protesting the beatings. Saudi men were expected to be "physical"; Youssef just carried it too far. Reena started dancing with Ulti often and writing her little love letters, and though it was clothed in a kind of secrecy, no one thought of protesting that either.

Lisa picked up some Arabic by osmosis and spent many of her free hours studying it. It was less difficult than the Hebrew she had had to learn for her bat mitzvah. She loved playing with the children. Their limited vocabularies helped her along, and they frequently corrected her when she went wrong, smiling that an adult could make such mistakes. It haunted her sometimes how like the little ones were to Sophie and David and Ben and Yassi. Men could make wars and do terrible things, but how could they become that way when they started out so much

alike, needing the same loving, having the same smiles, the same eagerness for life?

The return of the men created great tension in the quarter. Many
more returned than had left, and when it was learned that the grandfather
was among them, everyone knew important matters would be decided.
Some of the women cried; they knew the first night they would be
visited by their husbands, crudely, urgently, and if they showed an ounce
of real passion in return, they could well be slapped and beaten for
harlotry. Only the next day, when the husbands came to greet the children, would there be talk and words of affection. The second and third
wives—there were no fourth wives in this compound yet—had it easier.
Their turn would come after the "duty" to the first wife, and the young
ones like Toujan were expected to be passionate—out of singular and
undying love.

Le'ith did not visit Lisa the first night, and though she thought she
dreaded the encounter, she felt disappointed and strangely alone when
the muezzin called at dawn and she could only hear Fatima and Latifa
mumble their prayers from the little adjoining room that was their
quarter.

Later in the day she watched from the filigreed balcony and saw
Le'ith among the men around the pool. He was walking with two older
men and a man about forty with a thin gold stripe in the patterned
stitching along the edge of his thawb.

"The tall one on the left is Grandfather," Jineen said, moving to
Lisa's side. "The other one is a sheikh I've not seen before, but the one
talking to Le'ith is Prince Anwar."

Lisa turned to her, impressed. Jineen smiled. "We have more than
five thousand princes in Saudi Arabia. All are a little important, but only
a few are really important." She looked back down at them. Prince
Anwar was using his hands to explain something to Le'ith that looked
very like strangling. "Prince Anwar is one of the ones people think will
be *very* important, and he has always favored Le'ith," she added proudly.

All around the balcony the women watched the men and whispered
among themselves. But later, when they went in to eat, there was almost
silence in what was usually the noisiest part of the day. Only Huda spoke

out to them all. "It is serious," she said solemnly. "They must be comforted and supported in all things; the children must be obedient and offer small gifts." Lisa understood some of the words and certainly their import.

That night Le'ith did come to visit her, but it was very late, and she had fallen asleep. He roused her, but it was clearly not to make love to her. He held her in his arms for a time, just staring at the ceiling, and she suddenly felt very much as she had back in those days in California when there were difficult things to say to each other and they lay together, silent for many minutes, before anything was really said.

"You are to meet my grandfather and my father tomorrow," he said finally. "They do not approve of our marriage, but Ummi and Huda have spoken well of you, and that is very important." Then there was another long silence, and Lisa knew him well enough to know that his mind had gone on to other things. She had to stay his confidante, even though he had so many others around him now.

"I miss our not being together like it was," she said. Nothing for a moment. Then his arms tightened around her.

"There is so much to tell you. I don't know where to start."

"Start. I'm in a lonely place, and I have a lifetime."

He smiled and squeezed her again. "I have just seen sixty-three men beheaded," he said calmly. Lisa caught her breath. "It's much more convulsive and gory than it looks in pictures," he reflected solemnly. She didn't know if he was going to continue, but he did. "We were in Mecca, and we had fought, and our blood was hot . . . but at the beheadings I threw up, several times." She stroked his arm, trying to imagine the scene. "It was a group of fundamentalists, they attacked the guards at the Great Mosque, an organized attack on the holiest place in all the Muslim world." His voice reflected the incredible sacrilegious audacity of the act. "They occupied it for several hours before we could drive them out. At the same time there was an uprising in the eastern provinces, the source of our oil, the source of our wealth."

"Is it a revolution?"

"A backward one. Everyone knows the royal family cannot hold power forever. But everyone hopes that we can slowly, safely come to some kind of power sharing. As long as the money keeps coming and the monarchy remains reasonable, that can happen. But the fundamentalists think the modern world is the devil's world. In their eyes it creates crime and greed and the dissolution of the family. And we, in Saudi Arabia, are traitors to the Prophet because our lives and wealth should be used to promote the Sharia and to destroy the power of the United States and Israel."

"The Sharia?"

"It's a set of laws, religious laws made by mullahs and imams long after Muhammad was dead." His voice carried a thread of sarcasm.

"All religions are the same." Lisa sighed. "The Jews have a million interpretations of the Talmud. The"—she caught herself—"we Christians have ministers who read the Bible and then tell us exactly what God meant by that."

Le'ith was so absorbed in his concern about what had happened that he missed her slip.

"We have a tiny population as the world goes," he said, "and we have more oil than anyone. Two madmen want it. The Ayatollah and Saddam Hussein. And both know that they can get it without firing a shot if they can create a fundamentalist revolution and destroy the monarchy. This week taught us all how easy that might be."

"But it all seems so stable and secure, serene almost, at least out here."

"The Shah felt that way in Iran until the Ayatollah came."

"So what will happen?"

He rolled over and took her head in his hands. It was the Le'ith of UCLA, and there was genuine dejection in his eyes.

"We will go backward," he said. "We must disarm the hold of the fundamentalists on the ordinary man, and to do that, we must be as 'holy' as they are. We must reject Western ways, and you must be more Muslim wife than I ever intended you to be." He kissed her gently on the lips. "But I promise you, despite that, we will have our home." He took her in his arms again, and she knew he was sincere in the promise, but equally fearful that he could never keep it.

Chapter 7

Despite Reena's statement, Lisa *was* allowed on the first floor when men were there. She even strolled around the pool with Le'ith as they waited for their audience with his grandfather and his father. Le'ith was more nervous than Lisa, and she felt it meant that he would fight to keep her. She was grateful for the night before because though they had not made love, it was the first time since they had come into the country that she felt he still loved her, still needed her, and she was not repelled by him. She was also getting used to the look of him in a thawb and gutra.

A servant summoned them, and they were led to a tall and airy room, with lovely delicate pilasters, leading to a covered garden with another small pool.

Both men had full beards, and though he was sitting and remained so, Lisa could tell the grandfather was indeed extremely tall. Le'ith's father was big but thick-boned and looked strong as a bull, but his eyes lacked the subtlety and wisdom of his father's. Lisa could understand why Le'ith was considered next in line in terms of the family's future.

Lisa was veiled, and with the nod of the head the grandfather indicated she remove it. Very deliberately Lisa looked to Le'ith for approval. He nodded with a tight grin of pleasure.

When she took off the veil, Le'ith's father was clearly angered by what he saw and shot a severe glance of reproach at Le'ith. Grandfather, however, only seemed amused.

She was able to exchange greetings in Arabic, but then Le'ith was forced to translate.

"Since Le'ith was a small boy, learning the difference between a scorpion and a spider, a kind man and a dangerous one," the grandfather said, "he has shown exceptional wisdom, not cleverness: wisdom. We have far too few young men in Saudi Arabia to do all that must be done. If you remain here, you will see that we have to rely on Swedes, and Italians, Palestinians, the Swiss, Englishmen, even Americans, for work that should be in Saudi hands.

"Some of our young men are intelligent, but not wise. Some may be both but are not willing to work, willing to take on responsibilities.

"So one like Le'ith is especially valuable—not only to his family but to his country."

Le'ith was translating this to Lisa with a head half bowed with modesty and irrepressible pleasure. It was the first time she had ever seen him show a touch of humility. The grandfather hardly noticed—his eyes were on Lisa—but now he fixed his gaze on Le'ith.

"But in marrying you, Le'ith did something that was not wise, something that was not good for himself or his family or his country. His judgment was warped by desire—not uncommon in young men but disappointing in Le'ith."

He turned back to Lisa. "Are you Muslim?"

Lisa shook her head.

"Are you willing to become Muslim?"

Before they married Le'ith had promised she would never be forced to convert, but she could sense that what had been promised so glibly in California might be sacrificed under the pressure of these powerful family figures.

"I—I don't think I could do that," she stammered, "any more than I think Le'ith could become . . . a Christian."

When Le'ith translated, the grandfather studied her gravely, Le'ith's father just lifted his eyes to heaven as though it were all over. He said something in Arabic to Le'ith that Lisa couldn't make out. Le'ith seemed embarrassed and shook his head. His father threw up his hands.

The grandfather spoke again, and Le'ith's voice almost trembled as he translated. "Because Le'ith prevailed on his mother, and his father wasn't present when you arrived, you were deprived of the pleasure of meeting Le'ith's *first wife*."

Lisa looked across at Le'ith. He faced her with guilt, but a posture of challenging defiance too.

The grandfather spoke again. "That could be a courtesy if she knew you were coming and you knew that she existed. Did you know?"

Because she knew it would make Le'ith seem less "unwise," Lisa was tempted to say, "Yes, I knew," but she felt the probable shock on Le'ith's face would make them think she was lying to them, and that, she knew, would be the worst mistake of all.

Lisa turned back to the grandfather. "No, I did not know that Le'ith was already married. But he had explained to me that Saudi men were permitted four wives." She glanced at Le'ith as he translated. "Le'ith was a full-grown man long before I met him. When I consider the customs of his faith and family"—she turned and looked deliberately at his father—"then it does not surprise me that he married before he came to America." She turned back to Le'ith and spoke as though speaking only to him. "I confess that given *our* customs, I am a little hurt to discover it. But the only hurt that I will find unbearable is if he decides to take a third wife."

Lisa wondered whether she could have reacted so unemotionally or phrased it quite so sincerely if she had truly loved him. She could read in Le'ith's reaction the kind of devotion she had felt in California, and more than that, she had impressed the grandfather with what he saw as *her* devotion to Le'ith.

"It was still unwise," the grandfather said calmly, "but Allah has permitted it." He looked almost affectionately at Lisa as Le'ith translated. "Let us see how the golden one, who has more wisdom than some in this room, serves the husband she has chosen. If she does well, she will make Le'ith stronger and the family stronger. May Allah grant it."

She made love to Le'ith that night. He was immensely relieved and also less defiant about the revelation of his first marriage.

Lisa was, in contrast, almost exultant. A thousand times she had thought, Let them make him divorce me, let them make him send me away, but deep in her heart she wanted to do the job that Adam and fate and the death of an uncle and two little children had singled her out for, and now, except for caution with Reena, she knew she had placed herself as a mole in a family of great influence in a country that often financed Israel's enemies, that refused to accept that struggling country's existence, that one day might act to harm it, and *she* could be the instrument that could thwart that act.

She even took a little pleasure in tormenting Le'ith about Nayra. They had shared everything but this greatest of secrets he had kept from her. Was she to have one night with him and Nayra the next? She tried to look hurt but felt like laughing, so she turned away from him, and he tried to reason with her, using the whole masculine litany. It was nothing like what was between them; there was just a difference in men and women about these things, and he started telling her about all the societies where men had multiple wives, from Chinese monarchs to African tribal chiefs. There had even been Babylonian princes who had had more than three *hundred* wives! At that one Lisa turned over and glared at him.

"I want only you," he said quickly and defensively.

Again Lisa struggled to keep from laughing. "Really"—she mocked him acerbically—"and the other three hundred will be ones you *don't* want, that *won't* mean anything to you."

Le'ith smiled at *her* exaggeration; it was like of old, and she could not prevent a tiny smile back. His finger touched her chin, and his eyes grew earnest.

"I will never marry again," he said with great sincerity.

"And Nayra?" She meant it as a tease, but he took it seriously.

"I have a debt to Nayra, and I will always treat her with honor, and I beg you to do the same. But ours was a Saudi marriage; she did not expect to share my life—except to bear my children and maintain my household. I have never spent one hour talking to Nayra in the way we have talked almost from the first moment we met. Nayra went to school for six years as a child, that is all. I did not pick her, but you will see when you meet her that she is worthy of respect. I cannot with honor divorce her."

Lisa almost felt guilty. She was sorry he had interpreted her teasing as a request to divorce the woman whom she had already begun to like from his description. She held out her arms, and he came into them.

"You must remember too," he said softly, "that Nayra always expected me to have other wives. She does not have your feelings about it. You will see that she will never resent you; she will feel like your destined sister. I can only destroy that by favoring your children over hers and showing that I do."

"I can see why your grandfather calls you wise, but I take it then it is your expectation to have children by us both?"

"Please think of *this* world," he said with a touch of irritation. "A Saudi woman who does not bear children is a tragedy. Their lives are the children and the household. Our society may change so that one day women may have a life beyond that, but not in Nayra's lifetime, especially with the threat of the fundamentalists hanging over the Kingdom."

Lisa bent her head and kissed the tip of his ear. She whispered, "I shall pretend she is the wife and I am the beloved mistress."

He reached up and touched her face, grateful for her acceptance. Lisa was grateful too. Her frivolous teasing had produced a fictive world she *could* live in. To be a mistress was not to be a wife. For her to be a mistress in the service of Israel—and, from all she'd heard so far, of America—was so much more acceptable than being a wife. In her head she would make it that. And someday she would truly be the wife of a man she loved.

For now she would play the mistress to this young lion/panther whom she felt she could hold and even control to a degree. And on this night, when she felt a sense of triumph, she knew he would make love to her and her body would respond with a pleasure that would complete her sense of victory.

Chapter 8

The Palestinian said it as matter-of-factly as if he were reporting that the sun would come up tomorrow. "The Israelis have moles every-where. I'm sure if they had wanted to prevent it, they could have."

"Nonsense," Najib responded scornfully. "Jewish moles in the Egyptian Army and among the religious right! Like all Palestinians, Ghasi, you endow the Israelis with superhuman powers."

"We've seen it in our own most patriotic groups," Ghasi countered. "And we are careful. Do you think the Egyptian Army is careful about the possibility of recruiting Jews posing as fellahin?"

Lisa was picking at her food. She had lived through two long years of lonely, boring adjustment without once feeling threatened since Reena's early suspicions. Suddenly this. She tried to act as if the subject were of only minor interest to her, but she was very aware from the first mention of the word "mole" that Reena, who sat across the table from her, was watching her with a sudden, intense curiosity.

"I'm telling you," Ghasi insisted, "They have moles in *Iran* and *Iraq,* never mind Egypt and Jordan and Lebanon."

"And Saudi Arabia?" Rashid mocked.

Now Lisa knew she could not even glance at Reena or her guilt would be given away. She couldn't control it.

Ghasi laughed. "Of course in Saudi Arabia. Your money and Iran's have sustained the PLO and Hamas. You think they're not interested? I'm telling you, the Yemeni building laborer, the Swiss computer expert, the English nurse—any one of them could in truth be an Israeli mole. When Israel bombed the nuclear plant in Baghdad, how do you think their information was so exact, their targeting so accurate? When it seems there is going to be peace at last in Lebanon, why is it that some religious leader or some political giant is always blown up and the feuds start all over again? Who benefits from all that? I'll tell you: It secures the northern border of Israel, because once Lebanon is united, there aren't enough Jewish soldiers to protect it, with all the other borders they must protect."

Lisa felt the blood rise to her face. The northern border was "her" Israel, the home of David and Yassi, the home where Sophie and Ben had died. She tried to control her emotions and concentrate on the food.

"Well," Le'ith said with a note of skepticism, "if everyone is finished, let's see the tape and see if we can agree that some Israeli mole might have prevented it all."

He rose from the dining table and led them all to the big reception room. They were in their own family house in Riyadh. In the last two years Lisa had spent much of her time there. The year after the fundamentalists' attack on Mecca that had so upset Le'ith, the Iraqis attacked Iran and began a war as bloody and cruel and endless as World War I. As they watched the slaughter on their television sets, there wasn't a Saudi who didn't secretly pray that the two giants of the area would destroy each other, and when for a time it looked as though Iran might actually break the brutal deadlock and win, Saudi money went to buy American arms for Saddam Hussein, and so the war went on.

But the consequence in Lisa's life was that the fear of fundamentalist revolt in Saudi Arabia faded, and life drifted back to its conservative "normal."

They were often visited by Reena's brother, Rashid, and Le'ith's California apartment mate, Najib, whom she had never much liked but who tended to treat her more like a product of suburbia than a refugee from a harim. Occasionally there were even nights like this. Ghasi's Palestinian wife was dressed in Western dress, as were Lisa and Reena. Rashid had married a Saudi girl, Hayat, who came from a wealthy family but had never been to the West and, though dressed in a chador, was clearly embarrassed to be unveiled in front of strange men and befuddled by the unaccustomed use of the silverware.

Youssef did not bring his wife, but Najib brought that rarest of social treats, a foreign woman who was "unattached." She was an attractive, if somewhat scholarly-looking, Swedish psychologist.

They all had come to watch a smuggled tape of the killing of Anwar al-Sadat in Cairo by his own security guard in the middle of a huge public ceremony.

After dinner Le'ith poured drinks for the men—alcohol was of course illegal—but Lisa had never seen a meeting or social gathering of Saudi men where it was not at least offered and usually drunk. The one compliance to religious law that *was* scrupulously upheld was that none of the *women* were allowed to drink, though by now Lisa knew that many of them more than made up for this in their own quarters.

Reena sat next to Lisa while younger brother Youssef set up the tape. Youssef was built bluntly and solidly like his father, and Reena had been right to warn Lisa about him. He was ambitious to take Le'ith's place and, had his hypocrisy not been so obvious, might have been more damaging. He knew Lisa was Le'ith's Achilles' heel, and he never failed to inquire if she was yet with child or had decided to convert, and his sympathetic understanding of each "no" only underlined the fact that Lisa still stood on the doorstep and was not yet a true member of the household.

Despite all this, Lisa was shocked almost beyond her ability to control her reaction when he sat down across from her and said, "It's an interesting thought, isn't it, that there might be Israeli moles right here among us in Saudi Arabia?"

It took Lisa a second, but she attacked. "I think Ghasi's right," she said. "It makes a great deal of sense. I'm not sure the whole idea of Israeli moles isn't the product of Palestinian paranoia, but if it isn't, and I were an Israeli putting moles around, I'd certainly try to put a few in Riyadh."

She sensed Reena looking at her, and she knew that was a face she couldn't confront. Youssef's mind was slower, and she tried to deal with Reena through it.

"And the easiest way would be to pose as a Palestinian, like Ghasi," she said provocatively. "After all, most of them come without records or histories, refugees who have run with the barest minimum. And a great many of them obtain very influential positions."

The conversation had caught everyone's attention by now, and Ghasi was looking at her with an indignation just short of fury. "You don't know how hard it is for a Palestinian to prove himself and get employed here—or in any of the other Arab States," he stated tersely.

"I'm sure that's true," Lisa replied, "but so many *are* employed it suggests that perhaps the clever Israelis could supply sufficient background to insert a few."

"Do you resent Palestinians?" Reena asked quietly.

Lisa overreacted, she knew. "No, no, not at all. I feel very sorry for them, I am simply saying that for an Israeli—"

"Why don't you say 'Jew'?" Youssef asked bluntly.

Lisa blushed—a reaction she knew she had to defend. "Because there are 'Jews' all over the world. I assume when Ghasi's talking about moles, he's talking about Jews from Israel, therefore Israelis."

She had recovered enough to feel angry, and to think that perhaps the best course was a bit of aggression of her own. "And I must tell you, Youssef, I don't share your dislike of Jews. In fact most of the ones I've met I rather like." She looked at him defiantly.

Youssef smiled as though he'd won a little victory. "You're still too much of an American, Lisa," he said with a kind of lazy insolence. "I wonder if you'll ever become—"

"Youssef!" a stern voice barked. It was Le'ith. "When you speak to my wife, I would expect the same courtesy you would show our mother. If you can't manage that, remain silent." He glared at Youssef. To have said more would have created a humiliation beyond the rules of family conduct, especially in the presence of nonfamily members. As it was, he brought a flush to Youssef's face and a look of anger that might have frightened anyone but Le'ith.

Le'ith just held his gaze. "Now why don't you turn on the tape? It's what we've gathered for."

There was an embarrassed silence until the tape began, and through it Lisa was wondering if the clever Reena was piecing together the stupid clues she was leaving about her real purpose in marrying Le'ith.

The tape was terrifying—in its audacity, in the implications of the fanaticism and betrayal behind it. Sadat, who had won the praise of most of the world for daring to make peace with Israel, and as head of the largest Arab state having the foresight and courage (or greed and treachery, as some saw it) to accept the permanent existence of a separate Jewish state in the Arabian Peninsula, acknowledged the cheers of the crowd, walking just ahead of his alluring wife.

As he took his seat, his personal battalion of guards was parading before him in armored jeeps. Then suddenly, unbelievably, one of the jeeps stopped, and men jumped from it with their semiautomatic weapons aimed at the presidential party. They ran forward, and some in the crowd panicked, but Sadat only stood, transfixed for a moment, and then he understood and turned, but it was too late, and the bullets raked his body, making sure no life was left.

In the chaos that followed the killers might have escaped, but they didn't. They had come prepared for martyrdom and were not willing to demean it in flight like mere murderers.

The rest of the tape showed the roundup of extremists in the days following the assassination. The unrepentant fanaticism daunting and alarming. Packed jail cells with sweating, bare-chested men screaming and yelling at the cameras, defiantly flaunting clenched fists, rage and revenge in their faces. Let Sadat's fate fall on any who did the godless Americans' bidding. It made Lisa's blood run cold. This was a hatred for Israel and America that compromise and reason could never touch.

When the tape was turned off, Le'ith seemed almost as shaken as she was.

"Well, it was right to ban the tape," he said quietly. "How many fanatics we have like that in Saudi Arabia, I wouldn't like to guess, but if there were only five, I wouldn't want to give them ideas like that."

"I can assure you," Ghasi said, "I want to walk the floors of my own home in Jaffa, where some Jew now takes his breakfast and admires the view of the bay, and I condemn Sadat for ever recognizing Israel, but I would rather live out my life here in Riyadh than see the fundamentalists rule our world from Cairo to Teheran."

"I wouldn't bet my life on a stay in Riyadh if I were you, Ghasi," Reena said dryly. "We're too soft and vulnerable, especially against that kind of dedication."

"You're wrong," Youssef said confidently. "We get stronger every day."

"Do we?" Reena replied ironically. "You won't allow women to work, so yes, we now have Saudi physicists but, alas, no lab technicians, so we have to hire the French and Swiss. We have accomplished M.B.A.'s from Harvard and UCLA"—she bowed to Le'ith—"who think they know just how to use and preserve our wealth, but we have no administrators, so we hire Palestinians like Ghasi. We have doctors trained at Johns Hopkins, but of course we have to hire nurses and technicians from England and Belgium." She laughed. "If those fanatics come at this society, there are so many holes in the structure we couldn't behead them fast enough to save ourselves."

"We handled the last group that came," Le'ith said with prickly defensiveness.

Reena just smiled. "If that reassures Ghasi—" she said, and she shrugged. Lisa had seen that Reena and Le'ith had a wry, affectionate relationship based on their mutual intelligence, their sense of humor, and the perspective they had gained of their society by their experiences in the West. Le'ith could criticize her for being a cynic, and she could mock him for being so straight, but Lisa sensed that Reena would never jeopardize their bond by arguing with him in public.

And for her own part, she felt she should probably let the issue drop, but she saw an advantage in that film. "You're telling us, Ghasi," she asked challengingly, "that the Israelis had a mole in Cairo who knew this was going to happen and *let* it happen?"

Ghasi was a little discomfited but utterly convinced. "Yes, I'm sure they knew. They may have given a warning, and it was ignored. They may not have known it was the presidential guard that was going to strike, but I will wager that in those cells of screaming fanatics there are sons of David who will act for Israel when they are called upon."

"But in this case they chose to let Sadat, the only Arab leader who has recognized them, die?" Najib said skeptically.

"It's possible. It's possible he had served his purpose for them." Ghasi fumbled defensively.

"Or it's possible there were no moles," Le'ith stated bluntly.

Lisa smiled. So did Reena. Le'ith rose and poured another drink for Ghasi. "Let us ask the women to retire to their quarter, and we'll watch a film and talk seriously." It was his way of taking the sting out of his put-down of Ghasi. Since he was senior, that is of course what happened.

The "women" went upstairs, where they had their privacy, while the men stayed below, acting like the club of boys they were.

Upstairs Reena immediately found her supply of hashish, and she and Lisa broke some cigarettes and rolled joints like true veterans of American college society. "With hashish," Reena explained, "you need to mix it with tobacco, but once you've rolled them together, it smells like grass and *frees* the mind like grass."

Despite Reena's pitch, Linn—Dr. Nordheimer, the Swedish psychologist—had whiskey straight. "Our national drink." She grinned.

Rashid's new wife, Hayat, took tea. "She hasn't been married long enough to have found her sedative," Reena joked, patting the girl's head gently. "Sooner or later she will come to something."

Hayat was not exceptionally attractive, but she was young and sensual, and Lisa had come to realize over the past two years that Reena's own favorite sedative was to supply romance and love to these ripe and aimless girls who lived largely under the tyranny of their mothers-in-law and the crude neglect of their husbands, at least until the first male child was born. It filled her time, and since the punishment for adultery was still stoning to death, it was far safer than a real relationship with a man. And from the intensity of some of the interharim romances Lisa observed, perhaps more emotionally rewarding as well.

"I *am* surprised at the powerful positions so many Palestinians hold in this country," Linn commented as she looked down thoughtfully through interstices of the latticed windows at Ghasi and Le'ith talking below.

"We call them the Jews of the Arab world," Reena stated. "The educated ones are very industrious, and they have always been very clannish and entrepreneurial. We fear them, but we need them."

"But so many of them are in *government*," Linn said thoughtfully.

"That's because here all business is family business," Reena replied. "A department may be headed by a prince, even a well-educated prince, but inevitably the key people in his staff will be Palestinian. The well-educated Saudi wants to be in his family's business, not the government, but he sometimes resents Palestinian influence anyway. But they're the salt of our society. Their humor, their music, their writing have made Riyadh and Jidda more interesting places than they ever were before the exile."

Lisa was struck by how much this was like descriptions she'd heard of her own people—in America, in England, even in France.

"But if they're in such influential positions," Linn said, "there will never be peace with Israel."

"That, or there will be no Israel," Reena remarked blandly.

"Sadat made peace with them," Lisa objected before she could bite her tongue.

"And we just saw what happened to Sadat." Reena laughed. "And all the moles in the world couldn't protect Israel if it lost the support of America. And if the fundamentalists take over, I doubt if even America could save it."

Lisa felt a quiver of fear at that logic. "Why don't women rebel against fundamentalism?" she asked plaintively. "The whole thing is so awful: arranged marriages, 'honor' deaths, female circumcisions."

"And how do women rebel, Lisa?" Reena asked.

"Saudi women don't want revolution," Linn said categorically. They all looked at her curiously.

"My business is the study of women's role in society," she went on, "and I have found here exactly what I found in Iran and in Egypt: The *leaders* in the drive to fundamentalism are women."

"How did you ever get permission to come to Saudi Arabia to study *women*?" Lisa asked in surprise.

"Easy." Reena piped in. "Saudi men believe their women have the *proper* role in society. They're proud to let the world know."

"That's exactly right." Linn smiled. "And the Iranians are the same. They let me do interviews there for three years."

"You mean all these women *want* life in a harim and—and female circumcision?" Lisa posited ironically.

Linn shook her head. "The core of fundamentalism, a life that is religion-centered, family-centered, a life where women aren't seen as sex objects without relationship to motherhood—that's what they want."

"Great," Lisa said. "But all your husband has to do is say, 'I divorce you,' three times, and you're out—and he gets the children."

"Unfortunately that's true for you," Reena said with a little comradely smile, "but not for Saudi women. Saudi marriages are family-arranged. A man who says, 'I divorce you,' to a Saudi woman must answer to her father, her brothers, her uncles, a whole family army. Believe me, it's not done. Even if it were, she would have her own family harim to return to. The only ones who get 'I divorce you' spoken to them are third and fourth wives brought from Jordan or Egypt—or the United States."

Linn grinned at the somewhat stunned Lisa. "I have pursued my studies over much of the world, Lisa, and though there are always exceptions, I have found more contentment in Saudi women than I have found anywhere except among nuns."

Reena grinned. "Who were you interviewing, the husbands?"

Lisa laughed.

"No, I'm serious. Yes, some of the educated ones are among the discontented—"

"*That* I believe," Reena cut in.

Linn smiled. "When have you ever seen a Saudi woman crying on her own, lost and helpless? When have you ever seen a Saudi woman totally dependent on her husband for her sense of worth, her sense of belonging? I think never. But I can show you thousands, millions in the West who are in that position, and they are generally anxious and miserable."

"But surely the educated ones want some contact with their husbands besides an occasional bedding and a meal with the children?" Lisa argued.

"Some do," Linn replied. "But if you're *educated,* you know about the problems of a couple-oriented society, the strains of 'keeping young,' 'keeping your figure,' worrying about money and status and jobs *and* staying 'friends' with a husband whose commitment is supposed to be monogamous but whose primary focus is work and whose eyes and conduct tend toward the polygamous."

Lisa responded in heat. "I can't believe women *prefer* to live like semiprisoners, even if the jail is nice, the inmates are friendly, and they get the children to play with!"

Reena looked at her. Lisa knew she had revealed just how she really saw her life.

Reena smiled wryly. "It *is* hard to believe, isn't it?" she said quietly.

Before Lisa could react, Najib bounded up the stairs, past the protesting and startled old guard and the shrieks of embarrassment from the serving girls in the room. The ones who mattered had all been without veils downstairs, so there was only a small impropriety in his intrusion, but it was characteristic of Najib, whom Lisa found as pushy as she had at UCLA. "We have solved all the problems of the world for the next twenty years," he said as he burst into the room, "so it is safe for me to take you back to your embassy, Linn."

"I'm relieved." She smiled back at him flirtatiously. "We just seemed to be getting ourselves in deeper and deeper up here."

"Not surprising," he replied glibly. "Reena is an unredeemed feminist and cynic, Lisa is a mole for the UCLA Girls' Glee Club, and the beautiful Hayat has chosen to marry a man whose ambition is so great she will probably end up bearing him eight sons. There will be daughters too, of course, but only the sons will count."

"You must never take his word for anything about men, women, or Saudi Arabia," Lisa warned Linn, having recovered from the stopped heartbeat when he spoke that word "mole" again.

"I don't," Linn said, "but he does lead me to parts of the city where I daresay none of you have ever been. For someone interested in research, such a guide is very valuable." She smiled at him with more warmth than a guide can usually expect.

As they went off laughing down the stairs, Reena glanced at Lisa, and said, "Scandinavian women have a great weakness for dark-skinned men, wouldn't you say?" Lisa grinned. It was directed at her own Scandinavian coloring, but there wasn't malice in it.

"Well, I found a weakness for Le'ith, but I'm not sure I could have transferred it to Najib."

Reena laughed. "Well, I'll tell you something about Najib: He has a weakness for older women."

Lisa nodded and continued, "And younger women, and right-handed women, and left-handed women, and so forth . . ."

Reena laughed again and hugged her. But Lisa sensed the iota of restraint. She knew the idea of moles was new to Reena, and it had raised a specter between them again. For two years she had struggled to make their "sisterhood" a reality. It had been easy to do with Jineen. Even with Nayra. Each time they returned from Riyadh, Le'ith did not visit Lisa's "house" the first night. And she would see Nayra in the quarter the next day, her face a little flushed and wearing a touching air of triumph. But they often played backgammon together, and though Nayra was always inordinately pleased if she won—which Lisa arranged fairly often—she hugged Lisa frequently and brought her tea like a serving girl and always took her side in arguments even if she hadn't a clue to what the argument was about. She was pretty and feminine but already growing a little plump in the way of the older women. That made it easier for Lisa to feel she wasn't a real rival for Le'ith's attention, and Nayra accepted every gesture of friendship from her as a gift.

What Lisa feared now was that the talk of moles—and, worse, Youssef's clasping on to it—threatened all she had worked so hard to achieve.

Chapter 9

Time is measured by seasons in the desert, and as the languorous months slipped by, Lisa fought boredom and depression and Youssef. She was always guarded around him, but she could tell that that night in Riyadh had made up his mind. He always smiled at her as if she were going to give him the greatest prize of his life. No longer challenging her as he had initially, he feigned to embrace her as a member of the family, always asking after her health, what she was doing to pass the time. She felt like the mouse being played with by the cat. She saw him occasionally talking to Reena, and Reena would always be more watchful and wary of Lisa for days after.

It kept Lisa on edge and added to her disquiet in Riyadh. The "big city" had been a great disappointment anyway. At first there was an excitement about it. She had hoped it would become a well of significant information for her, but she learned nothing that she knew was not available in any Western newspaper. It was true the rules were much looser. When Le'ith met with a foreign banker and his wife, they dined together unveiled, like ordinary Western couples. It was at the banker's home or their home because Lisa could not of course be seen unveiled in one of the large hotels, which had the only public restaurants.

But life in Riyadh was all a man's world. In the evenings the men would often go in great caravans of cars out across the desert and by some residual Bedouin gene find a place with water and spread carpets about, roast a lamb or two, watch a movie or a soccer game on portable television, and lie around and talk under the stars until they decided to return. If the movie was blue enough or the night steamy enough, a wife or two would be abruptly awakened and crudely assaulted. From what Lisa heard in the gossip in the harims, she was fortunate that Le'ith had learned his sexual techniques as a young student in Cairo; they were no doubt polished a bit at UCLA before he met Lisa, but apparently for the Saudi man without that background, the act was blunt, brief, and one-sided.

On other nights Le'ith went to some friend's house or some business meeting. On occasion Lisa might go and join the harim in that house. The women mixed as usual, and since Lisa had become fairly fluent in Arabic by now, she was not at a loss, but seldom was the conversation worth it, and her cultural isolation often made her depressed. Her most exciting nights were those when she met some foreign woman—always the wife of a businessman or banker—who could speak English or French, and they were able to converse freely about the world outside Saudi Arabia.

Some nights the gatherings were at their own house or Grandfather's larger house. Lisa and Reena were then the hostesses for the harim, welcoming the women, knowing which group preferred cards, which backgammon. They always provided music for dancing; the "love affairs" in Riyadh among the women were much less discreet, as was the use of hashish and occasionally cocaine. Somehow, for all the Swedish Linn's confidence about the contentment of Saudi women, they, the women, were far more addicted to these little vices than were the men, at least among the wealthy.

As a woman Lisa was of course not allowed to drive. She could shop if she was accompanied by a servant. But in a society guided—at least superficially—by Muhammad's principle that no man should stand above another, all women's chadors and men's thawbs looked exactly alike. Theoretically you could not tell a rich man from a laborer, but an absolutely immaculate thawb and clean fingernails stood out like a thousand-dollar suit. And the little embroidery down the edge of them was just as revealing to the knowing eye. But such nuances were not the stuff of "shopping."

Had she been interested in gold and jewelry, it could have been paradise. Gold and jewelry traveled easily, and the Bedouins had always valued and hoarded both. The gold market was huge and noisy and always busy. When the muezzin sounded, the muta'ween would sweep through the market, flaying women and merchants with their batons, screaming imprecations at the sinners who dared trade during prayer time. It was one of Lisa's amusements to watch, but she was careful because she'd taken one of the blows once and they were not tokens; these religious police hit like prophets striking at the sin itself.

The city was supposed to be beautiful and may once have been so. It had water, and its name meant "the garden." But with the coming of money had come endless building. Le'ith told her that a *New York Times* correspondent had described the whole city as "one large building site," and the very next day the King had ordered fences to be built around every working site. Millions were made selling concrete slab fencing, but the city still looked like a building site. There were tents and old mud brick buildings next to the most modernistic glass and steel fantasies that money could buy.

Sometimes out of sheer boredom she wished she could wander among them. But though she would of course have had to take her Riyadh attendant, Bushra, with her, Saudi women did not "wander"; they moved directly and pointedly to a destination. To stand around a building site where men were working could bring the muta'ween and a dose of open chastisement, never mind what would happen at home.

One evening at a gathering hosted by a German company, she met the wife of an American banker, Anne Kregg. She was touchingly friendly and obviously very lonely. She said the bank had its own compound and swimming pool. She invited Lisa to visit.

Desperate for someone she could really talk to, Lisa took one of the drivers and Bushra and went in search of her the very next day. None of the streets in Riyadh had names, so one had to follow directions based on visible skyscrapers and marked building sites. When they at last found the compound, it was just as Anne had described. Outside, a graffitied cement wall, but inside, each of the homes was luxuriously furnished, the air conditioning was flawless, and the central area had a full-sized pool with green lawn all around.

There were a couple of American men drinking by the poolside, but there must have been twenty women, all in bathing suits, some with their feet dangling in the water, others lying on towels, or sitting under big colored umbrellas, one actually swimming. Lisa hadn't seen so much bare flesh since California.

One of the principal pastimes of the bankers was making bathtub gin and a rather potent beer derived from a German formula. So it turned out to be a rather liquid afternoon.

None of the women she met could believe Lisa had actually married a Saudi. Having lived in the country, they felt no amount of money was worth it. And if it was love, she was in for a rude awakening. Lisa only smiled knowingly, and the conversation soon turned to the daily fare: how many days or months until their tours were up, a bit of bitchiness about the women not there, rumors about the rivalries in the royal family. Each husband worked with one prince or another, and they probably had more insight into the aspirations and plans of the various cliques than Le'ith did.

One of the women who had only been there a few days asked how in God's name could a country with such a small population have so many princes.

And Lisa heard the most ribald account of the life of the great Abdul Aziz she was ever liable to hear. The teller was a good-looking, witty woman named Leone, who was by this time very well away on bathtub gin and tonics.

"Well, honey," she said, "not far from where we're sitting there was an old wooden fortress. They needed fortresses in those days because it was like the American Indians, one tribe was always attacking another. In fact the chief, or sheikh, or whatever, who was in the fort had taken it from this other sheikh. But one night our man, Abdul Aziz, who was a six-foot-four hunk of man incidentally, while the rest of these guys couldn't make five-ten standing on their toes, anyway, he sneaks into town with ten or eleven other guys and in the middle of the night puts a spear through the guard *and* the guard door. He had some arm. Well, they break in and send the whole garrison of fifty or sixty on to Mu-hammadan heaven or breaking ass across the desert.''

Everyone was smiling or laughing out loud. Leone grinned in self-approval, took another sip of her drink.

"The next day they ran up their flag and owned the town. Now this Abdul's *tribe* was very religious, which explains why we're sitting here drinking bootleg gin, and *he* was very religious. But he was also very smart. Muhammad said a man could have four wives. He also said you could divorce a wife by telling her you were doing so three times in a clear voice before at least one witness.

"So Abdul Aziz executes the chief—sheikh!—who'd taken the for-tress away from his tribe in the first place. Then he divorces one of his own wives and marries the sheikh's first, who by now of course is a widow. So he's not breaking any religious principle here. Then he hangs around until he's sure the new bride is pregnant. Given his record, this must not have taken long.''

More giggling, more laughter. Lisa, who knew the whole story, but from a Saudi point of view, was surprised at how sacrilegious she found it. She was indeed becoming a native.

"The catch is,'' Leone continued, "he had to be sure it was a son. But once that was settled, the son became an heir to Abdul Aziz, so the tribe had a stake in staying loyal.

"Now Abdul has *two* tribes. And more men. So off he goes across the desert and finds another water hole, which used to mean another tribe and another fort. But Abdul Aziz was a warrior the way Van Cli-burn is a pianist. He soon whipped the ass off this new tribe, executed the sheikh, divorced another wife, married the new widow, and got to work producing a son. And, honey, believe me, this was more heroic than it sounds because first wives were the ones with the family con-nections; that's why he had to pick them if he was to keep the new tribe loyal. Well, as you know, beauty does not always go with family con-nections, and I am told that given the looks of some of them, he was as admired by his soldiers for his work in the tent as he was for his genius in the field.

"So anyway, before long, out pops the next son of Abdul Aziz, and

Abdul's off to the next water hole and the next tribe. In an amazingly short time he has done what no one has ever done before: He has subdued all the tribes in the whole area of what we now call Saudi Arabia, which is three times the size of France!

"I suspect a critical part of his anatomy was probably three times the size of France too," she said, slapping a friend on the knee. The giggling that had been a running accompaniment to all this burst into laughter.

"Anyway, by now he had a helluva lot of sons, and having got in the habit of producing them, he couldn't stop. It's like smoking; it's just a tough one to shake." More laughter. Lisa noticed two men by the pool were listening now and were clearly not amused. "But since the prolific Abdul was good to all his sons," Leone went on, "and to all his ex-wives, the people venerated him and of course, as time went on, his sons had sons, and the happy outcome is that we have five thousand royal princes, who all have the proud title Abdul Aziz buried someplace in their names. None of them, I'm told, is six-four or a shake on the old man in bed, but for their contribution to the 'genealogical cohesion' of the nation they get a huge tax free allowance and a slice of almost every piece of business from the sale of toilets to the building of the Olympic Stadium."

"And if any one of you ever repeats one bit of this little history as seen through the eyes of an inebriated, resentful woman," an angry masculine voice cut in, "I guarantee you, you will be deported the moment you're released from jail."

"Don't be a spoilsport, Mel," Leone said chidingly. Mel was now standing across from her; his hostile posture indicated he was as inebriated as she was. "We're all bored. If we can't tell a few stories, we'll have to turn to sin, and I know you wouldn't want Doris to succumb to that!"

The implication about his wife was not the way to calm Mel's anger.

"Sin is your province, Leone," he answered vitriolically, "but jokes about the royal family are dangerous, and what is said inside this compound often finds its way outside, and you should remember that." He walked off, unsteadily, but leaving an awkward sense of guilty unease. Leone was embarrassed, but too tipsy or too perverse to give up.

"It's all factual, darling!" she shouted after him. "Well, maybe 'three times the size of France' was a bit of exaggeration, but they aren't going to put me in a dungeon hot box for that, are they?"

"You should stick to 7UP, Leone—at least till John's tour of duty is over. It'd do wonders for his career, I promise you."

He'd gone into one of the houses. "Up yours," Leone muttered as she took another sip of her drink. She turned to the newcomer who had asked the question about the princes. "Honey," she said, "the men here get to play all the games, and we're supposed to sit here in our gilded cage and dream about the dollars we'll have when we go home. Well, let me tell you, take what fun you can find 'cause there ain't a helluva lot of it around."

She paused and drank again. Then she looked at the newcomer again—her face almost somber—and in a quiet, husky, gin-roughened voice admonished earnestly, "But, honey, listen to Mama, and don't go blabbing about Abdul Aziz to *any* Saudi, no matter how friendly. Sourpuss Mel is right about their sensitivities, and if I didn't trust you all like my own sisters, I wouldn't have uttered a word that Abdul's mother herself would not have approved of." She grinned, sat up, and sighed. "You all know that for a fact." With an elaborate flourish she downed what was left of her drink and drew a halfhearted laugh that brought them at least a little ways back toward their genial bitchy camaraderie.

Lisa and Anne drifted off for a swim. "I don't really fit in here too well," Anne said.

"I can see why," Lisa replied.

Anne looked at her, sensing a possible friend. "I hope you'll come again," she said. "One friend in a place like this can make the difference between heaven and hell." It sounded as if she had experienced some of the hell, and Lisa felt she had found someone who could turn the loneliness, boredom, and uselessness she felt in Riyadh into a bearable experience.

That night Le'ith had friends and associates over for the evening, but none of them brought their wives, so once Lisa had arranged for their food with the servants, she retired to "her" room. Nayra hardly ever came to Riyadh, but there was a room for her when she did, fitted out exactly as Lisa's.

For a time she tried to read. Le'ith's business friends brought her a steady supply of books, but the most modern of them dated from about 1930. The Saudis examined every book coming in, and anything modern was suspect. Nevertheless books supplied her one release from Saudi life. But on this night her mind kept going to the afternoon at the bank compound. She wondered how many other banks or companies had compounds like that, how many American women were trapped in those gilded cages and what they did with their lives, and if there wasn't the possibility of other friends.

She turned on the television. Sometimes there was Arab singing she could stand, some of the love songs she even liked, but television was mostly dignitaries meeting the King or princes visiting local schools or factories, but on this night there was a shock. There were clear, stark images of war. Israeli tanks, American announcers patched in with the Arab commentary. She soon grasped that Israel had invaded Lebanon.

She called Bushra and sent her running down to Le'ith with the news. As she watched, she heard shouts from downstairs and curses.

Chapter 1 0

The next weeks were torture for Lisa. Le'ith was gone most of the time, and she sat for hours numbly watching the television with its Arab commentary, though when there was American or British coverage that condemned the Israelis for one act or another, that was shown again and again.

Time after time she heard Israeli officers justifying the blanket shelling and bombing of villages and whole districts of Tyre and Sidon by saying it was the only way to protect Israeli soldiers from Palestinian snipers. She knew the figures of civilian deaths that this "strategy" caused were wildly exaggerated in the Arab way, but there was enough visual evidence of shattered homes, bodies strewn in the streets, and ambulances racing off with the wounded to know that the casualties were in the hundreds, if not the thousands the Arab announcers proclaimed.

And of course the coverage dwelt on the children killed or injured, on the women, on the number of Lebanese who simply lived their lives without reference to Israel but who were paying the price the innocent always paid in war.

Worst of all for Lisa was the ever-present face of General Sharon. He seemed to her almost evil incarnate. His arrogance was so overtly offensive, and it was like granite, the verbal arrows just bounced off it, and his hatred of anything non-Jewish was so manifest it colored all his arguments, losing him points even when there was some justice to what he was saying. His was the kind of personality that people used to justify anti–Semitism, and she wished the Israelis had used some other spokesman.

She longed to talk to Adam. No one had felt more personally the problems of the security of the northern border. Sophie's and Ben's deaths proved that there was justification for what was being done, if not for the manner in which it was being done. For that she blamed Sharon and his appeal to the Israeli fanatics of the right. But as viewed from the only lens she had, the brutality of the attack, and the whole principle of invading another country, so exceeded the erratic feebleness of most Palestinian disruptions that it made Israel seem the villain and Sharon its monstrous mastermind.

Le'ith, when she saw him, railed against both. It was Israeli arrogance, possible only because of the arms and support of America. But if they seized Beirut, America would pay, the whole world would pay. She tried to draw him out, but he would only say that drastic decisions were being made.

As the Israeli Army drew nearer to the outskirts of Beirut, she wrote to her "Aunt Connie," told her she had *faith* that the war would stop soon and, with great trepidation, sent the letter express.

When Le'ith came home at night, he was always in a knot, and she tried in every way to coax him to talk, but he would only hold her and say how impotent he felt. Not only had the Americans armed the Israelis with equipment that made it madness to retaliate against the invasion, but everyone right up to the King believed the Israelis had several atom bombs—enough anyway to dare do what they were doing.

"So what will happen if they take Beirut?" Lisa asked a dozen different ways, and always his face clouded, but she sensed his feeling of impotence and dread.

"They will be sorry" was always his answer in one form or another, but she could never get from him how or why.

Every day she deliberately went out to the market with Bushra and directed her to buy things in English and then corrected herself in Arabic. Poor Bushra, who knew no English and had never before been spoken to in English by Lisa, was utterly baffled. But Lisa was hoping beyond hope that someone would contact her, and how could anyone recognize her in her chador and veil? So she set out slowly from the house each day, played her little game of English in the market, and returned slowly to the house, watching every car, every pedestrian for some sign.

When the Israeli Army actually laid siege to West Beirut, she was in as much of an emotional knot as Le'ith. They hadn't made love in days. He always came home late, and often she'd be asleep. Sometimes he put an arm around her and woke her, and they lay there in their separate agonies for what seemed hours before sleep finally took them. But no matter how late he came home, Le'ith was always up when the raucous, amplified sound of the muezzin echoed through the city at dawn. Sometimes he remembered to kiss her before he left for the mosque, and sometimes he didn't.

One day she spent the morning watching the coverage of the invasion. It included a particularly scathing account of the Israeli Army's treatment of civilians by British television. She knew how that kind of outside confirmation enraged Le'ith and Rashid and Youssef. Their own reports upset them enough, but they always knew there was bias to them, but when the Western press did it, they knew the accounts were true, perhaps even underplayed, and it united them as nothing did. They were impotent warriors watching their own kind being treated as though their lives mattered not at all, and she gleaned from their curses and muttered threats that it also united the Islamic countries as nothing else could. The same anger and impotence raged in Iran and Iraq and Syria and Jordan and Egypt.

She knew this new report would heighten tensions in the councils, where God knows that arguments were already going on, and she called Bushra and prepared to go out to the market, determined to linger there most of the day in hopes someone would finally react to her message of alarm.

As they were leaving, a car pulled up with an Arab driver, and Lisa's heart took a leap, but when the driver opened the door, it was only the Swedish psychologist Linn.

"Hi," she said blithely, "is Najib here? I've been looking for him all over the place."

Lisa signaled Bushra to close the door behind them. "No," she said, "I haven't seen Najib in days. In fact I seldom see *Le'ith*."

"He wouldn't be in now, would he? I'd like a word with him too. Our embassy is a little—"

"No, no," Lisa answered, walking right toward her. "I probably won't see him till midnight, if then."

"Well, too bad for the embassy, but at least it gives us a chance for some chat, eh?"

"I'm off to the market," Lisa explained weakly. It was not a likely excuse to avoid a chance to talk to a Westerner, and Lisa knew it.

Linn grinned and took her arm. "The market's open all day. It's so hot, treat me to a tall glass of iced tea, I'll trade you some invaluable gossip and be out of your hair in half an hour, eh? Less."

Lisa couldn't refuse, but she couldn't force a genuine smile either, and she glanced up and down the street looking for a parked car, a lingering man, anything before she reentered the house, but there was nothing.

Linn was infuriatingly domineering once she was in the house. She ordered the tea meticulously from Bushra—a large pitcher—and when Lisa led her to the air-conditioned sitting room, she said, "Oh, no, let's sit out by the fountain, I love the sound of the water." So Lisa ordered one of the men to put a table and two shade umbrellas on the patio. When he was gone, she closed the door from the house and removed her chador and veil. It was still hot on the patio, despite the shade and the fountain. Linn sat and smiled, running her hand through the water blissfully *and* appearing blissfully unaware of Lisa's sense of urgency, though Lisa was sure she was aware of it.

Bushra brought the tea. Linn thanked her; Lisa thanked her; Bushra left. Linn assumed command and poured them each a glass. Then she lifted her glass and looked at Lisa. "Faith," she said quietly, as though offering a toast.

Lisa stared at her, almost dropping her glass. Linn's eyes crinkled in a little smile, but they developed a new seriousness too.

"Are—are you—" Lisa stuttered.

"When we met, I didn't realize that your aunt Connie and I had some mutual friends."

For a tiny second Lisa expected a trap, but it was too impossible. The Saudis might have read her letter—probably did—but who would know "faith"? And it was so logical, a Swedish psychologist traveling the world studying the life of women, three years in Iraq, who knew how long in Egypt, and now Saudi Arabia. Think of a better cover for an agent for the Mossad.

Linn kept smiling, and her gestures suggested some light gossip, but her words were severe. "Unfortunately you now know what I am and I know what you are. This is bad for us both because should either of us be caught and tortured, the other will almost certainly be destroyed as well. So I'm praying that what you have to say is very, very important."

Lisa sipped her tea. She was shaken now by the seriousness of what she'd done and uncertain suddenly that it was justified.

"Stay calm." Linn smiled. "Think of a joke and laugh. Your attendant at least will be watching us. Relax and make it look like you're settling in for a morning of delightfully useless female conversation."

Lisa suddenly felt so incompetent, such an amateur and fool. She searched for a thought or story that amused her. Then she remembered Le'ith's frantically embarrassed shyness at being seen naked and his gymnastic efforts to cover himself. It didn't produce a laugh, but it did evoke a genuine smile. She sipped some more tea and sat back in her chair. She twisted it, putting her feet on the pool surround, so her voice was facing the fountain.

"It's about the invasion, of course."

Linn gave a social laugh. "Of course."

"When the army headed toward Beirut, Le'ith, who's been at government council meetings with his grandfather every day, said that if they dared take Beirut, America would regret it, the whole world would regret it."

Linn spread her arms as though taking the coolness from the fountain. She smiled at the pleasure of it.

"Have you been able to find out what that meant?"

"I've tried and tried, but no. My feeling is that it's real because whatever it is, he seems as much haunted by the damage it will do to Saudi Arabia as to America."

"Not Israel?"

"He says 'they,' and it usually means the United States and Israel, but the phrase he's used two or three times is 'America and the whole world.' They feel so impotent and so angry. I think they really would do something rash and incalculable."

"Let us talk a little, and then you go on to the market."

"I was just going to the market to—"

Linn cut her off with a lift of her hand. "Whatever you planned to do, do. Don't let them think our little tête-à-tête has changed your plans in any way."

Again Lisa felt like a foolish amateur.

"You must remember that there are agents in the field, as well as your kind. At times like this it's very dangerous because we're pushing to get as much information as we can. I must tell you that what you have told me today is very valuable, but it is not something we did not know."

She turned to Lisa, a beaming smile on her face. "And if taking some of the risks I've taken in the past three weeks has made someone in their security decide to follow me around for a while, the fact that I visited you for a long morning's chat will not go unnoticed."

Lisa felt like looking guilty, but she had the sense to smile back.

"It was, as the Americans say, a tough call, and don't condemn yourself for it"—now she smiled genuinely—"but in the future don't assume you are Israel's sole intelligence source."

Lisa smiled sheepishly. It only remained for them to gossip for a time, and the tale Lisa wanted most was Linn's own story. Was she Swedish? Definitely, born and raised there. That was the legality; the truth was she was Danish. Her parents had been smuggled out of Denmark to Sweden near the end of World War II, when the German SS, which had left Denmark pretty much alone, decided to round up all the country's Jews and send them off to the gas chambers before the war ended.

Her father, like most Danish Jews, was not at all religious. At the time the SS cracked down there was only one Jewish synagogue in the whole country, and it was attended mostly by the very elderly.

But when the Danes put up a tremendous fight and saved almost every one of the eight thousand Jews in Denmark, smuggling the bulk of them to Sweden, her father began to take an interest in what it meant to be a Jew: why they were pursued, why they were worth fighting for. Then came liberation and the pictures of the camps, the stacks of bodies, and her father became, if not religious, very actively Jewish. They went to Israel several times, the whole family spent a couple of summers at a kibbutz, and it was there that she was recruited. She went back to her university in Stockholm, taught for several years, and was called into service only four years ago.

"I might not have done it," she said reflectively, "but my father died the month before the call came. It seemed like a sign, and I'm not sorry— yet." And she contrived a falsely frivolous smile and sipped the last of her tea.

When Le'ith came home that night, he was more agitated but less ex- hausted than he usually was. He wanted his meal served in the room he called his study, and when all the servants were gone, he turned on the shortwave radio. It was early morning in America, and as he ate, he had Lisa pick around the endless ads to find a newscast. She finally got one that was about more than the traffic and weather. The Israeli Army remained in West Beirut but had stopped its advance. Le'ith leaned toward the radio expectantly. Yasser Arafat had signed a document ac- cepting a UN resolution that recognized Israel's right to exist as a separate state.

Le'ith smiled tensely. Lisa thought, God, if the PLO accepts Israel, the rest of the Arab countries will *have* to go along!

But, the newscaster continued, neither Israel nor the United States would accept the PLO as the voice of the Palestinian people.

Le'ith stood up, glaring at space for a moment, then threw his cup against the wall and pushed the table from him, spilling half the dishes on the floor.

"God damn them!" he said. "They don't want victory; they want humiliation!"

"They think the PLO are terrorists," Lisa said appeasingly.

Le'ith turned and looked at her incredulously. "Lisa, where do you live? The British called George Washington a terrorist! And Jomo Kenyatta! Israel's prime minister Mr. Begin *was* a terrorist! The Palestinians are fighting for their homes and their country, and if one Israeli is killed, you've seen on television what happens: They bomb what they call terrorist targets, and you've seen the women and children carried from the rubble their airplanes leave." The radio was still crackling, more ads, baseball scores. Le'ith reached over and slapped it off.

"The PLO *does* represent the Palestinian people. Only they want to humiliate them and reduce them to nothing so they can put up some puppet group that they can control with money or power or fear."

His voice had calmed a little, but he was still pacing like a caged panther. "Well, it will never happen. No such group will come into being, whatever they do to the PLO; they've created too much hate."

Lisa wished they could talk, just talk, let him tell his side, let her tell Adam's and Noah's side. There *was* too much hate, but it was on both sides.

Le'ith took a bite of a mango. His anger was subsiding, but it was still there. He stared out the window for a moment, his posture stiff and belligerent. Then he sighed angrily and came back toward the table. "One thing more, Lisa. We said we would create our own life here, and before all this, I felt we were beginning to. And if it ever ends with the world intact, we will yet. But I've been told that you spent a day in the compound of the Chemical Bank of New York."

Lisa grinned. "Yes, I met a woman at a party, and she invited me. It was sort of fun to spend a day with a bunch of Americans."

"Never do it again," he said sharply.

She looked at him in disbelief. He'd never talked to her like that. Was this the beginning of the Saudi man?

"I liked it," she snapped. "And I intend to go back often."

For a moment she thought he might strike her. "Those women are whores," he said with quiet venom. "No one who does business with that bank, or any of the banks, has not had an affair with at least one of them."

"Maybe some of them are bored and restless, but I'm sure *all* of them do not have affairs. Are all Saudi women so saintly—Reena, for example?"

She again thought he was going to hit her, and she was sorry she had said it, but she was so angry, and she felt it was a critical struggle for the tiny bit of freedom she might have.

"You will not go," he said, his eyes so fired with anger, his body so tense she dared not answer because he seemed ready not only to hit her but to spring on her and beat her.

"I will instruct the drivers and Bushra that you are not to go near one of those compounds." It came with a fierceness she had never seen in him. "If you ever defy me about this, I will see that you are confined to the house whenever we are in Riyadh."

Had his fury been less impassioned Lisa would have shouted back some defiance, but his rage frightened her. It was as though he were begging her to say something so he *could* hit her. She stared back at him with as much hauteur and courage as she could muster, but her hands were shaking.

He finally turned from her and turned the radio back on. "I want you to go to your room now," he said flatly. The crackling static returned, some male voice was pitching the virtues of new Toyotas.

Lisa turned and went to her room without looking at him.

Chapter 11

Le'ith drove the two of them to the airport. Reena was the only one who spoke. It was late afternoon, almost sunset, and as usual on the broad boulevard out to the airport, luxury cars—Rolls-Royce, BMW, Mercedes—were parked every hundred yards or so on the spacious grass divider and along the grass borders. Whole families were spread around each car, sitting and lying on carpets, watching portable televisions, smoking, talking, eating. Later they might return to their homes, or they might spend the night under the stars.

"You see, we're still Bedouin," Reena commented as they drove past the first few of them. "They have million-dollar homes with air-conditioning and electric lights, but they prefer to live under the sky as they have always done. All our newfound wealth has only made us prisoners of Western chattels."

Le'ith grunted derisively but said nothing.

Lisa had unexpectedly—and much sooner than planned—been called to the American Embassy, where she received the news that her parents had been killed in an automobile accident. Lisa was so genuinely surprised at the timing that her reaction was more appropriate than she might otherwise have been able to stage.

Le'ith had accompanied her and for the first time since their argument had actually touched her. He quietly put his hand on hers. She was in a chador but once inside the embassy had removed her veil. When the consul gave the details of the funeral, which was being delayed until she could return, she turned her head into Le'ith's shoulder. He put his other arm around her, not firmly, but for a Saudi man in public it was more than just a gesture. The loss of mother *and* father is tragic in any society. In Saudi life it is a blow almost beyond bearing, and she could feel his compassion even through the ice of his anger.

That night, as she and Bushra were packing her things, he came into her room, again something he had not done since their argument. She only glanced at him and continued packing. After a few minutes he left—so quietly she didn't know he'd gone.

Later that night he came again. She was not yet asleep. She lay absolutely still, her eyes closed, and she heard him move toward the bed. He stayed there for a long time. He used to tell her that with her bare shoulders and long hair she looked like the wife of a monarch who could choose from all the women from the snow-capped mountains to the farthest reaches of the desert. She knew all men were jealous, and the Saudis fanatically so. Now, when she was, in his mind, looking her most desirable, was he feeling compassion or only worrying about her going to America without him?

She was still angry with him, but the chance to leave Riyadh had lessened her feeling of captivity. She even had to admit that the women in the bank compound reminded her of Somerset Maugham's novels about Englishwomen in the social prisons of the colonial Far East. How their lives revolved around illicit affairs and forbidden loves. Perhaps he had a right to be worried. But she was still shaken by the ferocity of his anger and the raw use of his power against her.

She expected a touch, something. But she finally heard the rustle of his thawb and the door closing softly.

The next morning he went off as usual at dawn, but he had told Bushra that he would return to take Lisa to the airport.

Reena took breakfast with her and asked about the kind of clothes that would be appropriate for a Christian funeral. Lisa had never been to a Christian funeral either, but she just said, "Black. Black is always appropriate." It was the opposite in Saudi Arabia—mourners always dressed in white—and Reena shrugged.

"I thought that's what I remembered," she said. Then she looked at Lisa with unaccustomed gravity. "I don't know how much Le'ith has told you about basic things, but he may have explained that the word *Islam* means 'surrender,' surrender to the will of Allah, the will of God. It's a comforting belief because when things happen, even the worst things, you know they're not real accidents, they're destined. They are, in that way, the 'will' of Allah."

Lisa looked at her, surprised by her solemnity and the talk of religion. "I'm a cynic"—Reena smiled—"and, *I* feel, a woman of intelligence who has more than normal ambition, but I'm married to a society that doesn't want my intelligence or my ambition. But I do believe in that 'surrender' to destiny. You do all that you can, but in the end the best and deepest wisdom is to accept whatever God delivers to you." She had of course read Lisa's surprise, and her tone reflected it, but there was a dark sincerity to her mood and her words.

"I don't know how much prayer," she went on, "or how much alcohol it would take me to accept what has happened to you. But if you 'surrender,' I know it will help take away the pain." She smiled. "I'm not asking you to become a Muslim. I'm just saying that if you can believe it was God's plan for them, and for you, their destiny, and yours, the next few days and weeks might be easier for you. . . ." She bowed her head for a moment, then looked out into nothingness. "I was once almost lost to cocaine in America. I had been betrayed and was destroyed. It was only someone telling me what I am telling you now that saved me—such as I am."

She touched Lisa's hand and smiled. "I know you would probably have preferred to have Jineen accompany you home, but I promise, I go not as your guardian but I hope as your friend, and I will help all I can."

Tears came to Lisa's eyes. The death of her parents was a sham, but Reena had surprised and touched her so that the sham meant nothing. She reached across and put her arms around her and cried. Reena touched her head and said, "Surrender . . . surrender. . . ."

Later, in her room, all packed and waiting, she watched television. The Israelis were pulling out of West Beirut, but before they left, they stood by and watched as their allies, the Christian Falangist Militia, went through two Palestinian camps, slaughtering men, women, and children. The scenes almost made her sick to her stomach. There was so much coverage of it by Western news that there was hardly any Arab commentary as the cameras moved past the bodies, the gasping, sobbing faces of the few survivors, the long-shot glimpses of Israeli soldiers in the distance.

She turned it off and cried again. She knew only too well that through the ages there had been pogroms where Russian soldiers, and Polish soldiers, and Hungarian soldiers, and even English Crusaders had carried out the same kind of merciless slaughter against not two but hundreds of Jewish settlements, but for her this didn't justify what had been done that day. It hurt to think that those she truly loved, that she would willingly give her life to sustain, those who above all should understand could allow this to happen. There was even something malign and cowardly about the fact that they didn't do the deed themselves but used someone else to do it.

When Le'ith returned, her eyes were red from crying, and her mood was so depressed it was easy to believe she was mourning the death of her parents.

Except to ask if she was ready, Le'ith said nothing to her, but he was unusually curt in ordering the packing of the luggage into the car that was to follow them to the airport. His aide Khalid was to check the luggage through and attend to the details, and Le'ith's mood made poor Khalid so edgy he almost jumped at every word.

When they arrived at the airport, there was someone from the airline to greet them and take them to the VIP lounge. As in most public places men stood around talking to each other, holding hands, laughing. The women sat or stood quietly by themselves. But after a hostess had given them soft drinks, Le'ith turned to Lisa, looking into her face directly for the first time since the argument.

"Lisa, could we talk for a moment?" It was almost like the uncertain student Le'ith she'd met a hundred years ago back under the eucalyptus trees at UCLA.

"Of course," she replied. He looked around and saw a spot by the corner of the huge windows overlooking the runways. "Perhaps over there," he said. Awkwardly, as though it embarrassed him, he walked ahead of her, and she followed in her chador and veil, like the Saudi wife she was.

They sat in two chairs across from each other, and he threw a newspaper and some magazines on the chairs beside them to ensure their privacy.

He glanced out the window for a moment, and Lisa could see how nervous he was. "I intended to accompany you to your parents' funeral," he said quietly. "I know I belong there, but with all that's going on with the Israelis, my grandfather refused to give me permission to go." For a moment he didn't move. Finally he faced her.

"I know these last weeks have been very lonely and trying for you." He looked out the window again. "I never expected it to be this way, but in *my* head this time, when I must establish myself in the way my grandfather has in the councils of the royal family and those who matter, is just a phase of our life. And then there was the invasion—"

"I understood all that, Le'ith," Lisa replied. "And I have tried to accept most of your traditions that were not mine, including your first wife."

"I—I thought that was settled."

"It's been accepted," she replied coldly. "But what is not acceptable is that I am your prisoner and may have no life of my own unless you approve. You promised me *our* life. *My* wishes are part of *our* life."

There was a little lightning flash of anger in his eyes, but then he leaned toward her, trying to reason with her. "My honor, my family's honor are affected by all you do. You've shown you understand that, and I've been proud of the way you've made yourself acceptable to all my family. My grandfather thinks you are a prize. So do I."

He put his hand on her arm, and smiled tentatively. "I know that no matter how hot it was, you would not go to the market in shorts and a halter."

She smiled. "I'd be beaten to death by the muta'ween."

He grinned. "Probably. But you know what I'm saying. You have made sacrifices to our customs and understand the importance of them to us. I know you must miss America, and the American business compounds are like little pieces of America."

He was interrupted by the announcement that Lisa's flight was now boarding.

Determined to finish, he gripped her arm firmly. "The women in those compounds are bored. They have no religion, they drink, and they have affairs."

Lisa just looked at him.

"This is not my jealousy talking," he insisted. "But I tell you openly it *is* my pride. That my wife would go to those places implies that the golden one is not Allah's special prize to Le'ith; she is an 'available' American woman like the others. That I would let you go is a reproach to me in the eyes of all; that you would go without my permission emasculates me in the eyes of my family and my colleagues. 'I have married a jewel from the West, but she is not a Saudi wife; she is a banker's wife or a merchant's wife,' and her very beauty becomes my humiliation."

The announcement came again: "Last call."

Lisa stood. Le'ith released her arm, but when he stood, he turned her to face him. "When you come back, I promise there will be a surprise for you that you will like. I have already spoken to Huda about it."

Lisa nodded noncommittally. She didn't know what Huda had to do with them, but she did understand why she would never visit a bank compound again, and though it made her less angry at Le'ith, it saddened her that the little window of light that had opened in her cloistered life had closed as fast as it had been opened.

Reena was approaching them, and Le'ith took Lisa's arms and turned her so that Reena could not see his face. "Lisa . . ." he stammered. He tried to find her eyes behind the veil, but she could see his eyes clearly, and there was water in them. "I love you, Lisa." It was a young man's plaintive sincerity. "Please, please come back."

His unconcealed heartache moved Lisa, and now she understood. She had never doubted that she would come back—she had to—but Le'ith didn't know that, and he knew that he was sending her to America and all that meant to her, and from a Saudi Arabia where there had been few pleasures and many disappointments and constraints. He feared this was good-bye forever.

She squeezed his arm lightly. It was not a commitment; it could even be interpreted as a kindly good-bye.

"We'd better board," Reena said, coming beside them.

Lisa turned to her. "Yes, we'd better. It's not a plane I want to miss."

Le'ith didn't move, but when they had cleared passport control, Lisa looked back, and he was there. She lifted her hand and waved. He only stared at her stoically.

Chapter 12

Once aboard the plane, they were served a meal that Lisa and Reena only nibbled at. When the dishes were taken away, Reena offered Lisa a couple of sleeping pills. She said it would make the journey easier, and Lisa wouldn't be just sitting and thinking about what had happened. But Lisa shook her head. "I *want* to think about what has happened—things that went before and things that will follow."

Reena smiled understandingly. "Well, I'm going to get out of this male concept of propriety and take a couple myself. I prefer sleep to the censored movies." She got up and went to one of the toilets. Getting out of her chador and veil sounded good to Lisa too, so she went to a toilet on the other side and came out looking blond and Californian and, if not quite as porcelain, far more interesting than she was when she took her first ride on a Saudia plane. Several of the men in the first class section could not hide their amazement—or interest—in this blonde who had emerged from under the black chador. The Saudi men gaped; the American businessmen tried to look smoldering. Lisa couldn't keep from smiling; she had once been used to this, even gloried in it, but it had been a long time.

Reena was already curled up in a blanket when Lisa returned to her seat. She twisted over and put her hand on Lisa's shoulder.

"Now if you want to talk or cry or curse the world, God, and fate, you wake me. I'm very good at all those things. I'm also your sister, and you have rights over me." She moved her hand to Lisa's neck and squeezed playfully. "And remember, there's no pleasure for an old cynic like the pleasure of actually being wanted." Another smile, and she turned back to her huddled position on the stretched-out chair. "Remember," she finished.

Lisa tilted her own chair back and raised the footrest. The cabin lights had been turned out, and she lay there aware of the flickering light of the movie and "remembered."

For all this time her mother and father had believed she was in the tiny town of Popondetta in the rain forests of Papua, New Guinea. Lisa didn't know who had devised all this, but it was Adam who had told her. Her parents knew that above all, she wanted to do something useful with her life, something where money wasn't the object and physical beauty was irrelevant. Adam knew it too, from the time she was sixteen and already a little tired of boys chasing her because of her looks.

So the day Le'ith proposed and they decided to elope, she sent off the letter she had composed in the boardroom of the Mossad in Haifa months before. It sounded excited and upbeat. She was sorry she couldn't return home at the end of the school year as planned, but a very special opportunity had come from two women who had visited the campus from Australia. She was going to teach English and elementary math (!) in a village in New Guinea! It seemed the Australians and twentieth-century commerce had forced this tribe from their normal hunting and gathering life. They needed to learn the mixed blessings of money and paid-for work. There was plenty of available work, but most of it required English and at least some math. The women said they were a happy people and, though not very organized, were willing students.

Unfortunately she had learned about all this only three days before the group had to leave. It was perfectly safe, four of them were going, and they were sponsored by the Australian government. They were not to worry; she'd write the moment she arrived.

When Lisa sent the letter, she felt a little ache at the deception and an immense longing to see her parents just one more time. But her mind was set then on what she considered a more worthy purpose, and the fact that Adam, her mother's brother, was a co-conspirator somehow made it easier.

From then on her letters were mailed somehow by someone in Popondetta, Papua, New Guinea. The first one had been the toughest to compose. She made it sound buoyant, but she knew how much it would hurt. She told them she was already working. She had two classes of adorable children and one of very funny elderly adults. The food and housing were like summer camp. The good and the bad! She wished they could visit and see it, but with Dad's heart problem it would be suicide. The temperature was staggering, and the humidity killing. It was a place only for the young and healthy.

One thing she had to confess was that she'd signed on for three years. She knew it would upset them, but it was the only way the Australians could do it, with the cost of flights and everything. She knew she'd miss them, but it was not a lot different from being off to Chicago for a job, and here she felt so useful. No one judged her on her looks, and she knew they would be proud of her. She signed it, "I love you both so much—and always will."

She had to sit and not look up at anybody when she finished. There were two others there besides Adam. After a minute or two they each got up and touched her shoulder and left the room.

"You can still call it off, Lisa, and no one will condemn you, no one," Adam said quietly.

She just shook her head.

Later that week she sat with Adam and Deborah and did stacks of birthday cards, Hanukkah cards, Rosh Hashanah cards, and tons of post-cards saying: "Terribly busy, love you, thanks for writing." Then ones adding: "I'm sure everything will work out," "Sorry to hear about Dad." "What a vacation, wish I could have been there." "Don't complain to *me* about the heat!" "Thanks for all the news."

They did them endlessly over three days. Adam kept the stack from her, but she figured that in all they covered some *fifteen* years.

That last night she was doubled up in grief. She cried and cried and couldn't stop crying. She tried to think about the truth of it, that if she had gone to work in Chicago, except for Thanksgiving and the Jewish holidays, her absence would have been the same. It helped a little, but not much.

She remembered that in the predawn she had walked through the orange groves, and when she turned back toward the kibbutz, Adam was leaning against a tree, watching her. He was smiling as usual, but there was melancholy in it. She moved to him, the tears flowing more freely with each step. He held her tightly in his one and a half arms.

"It's all right," she said. "I'm going to make it."

And she did make it. Now she was going back to complete the story of her isolation. When she went back to Saudi Arabia, Le'ith would believe he was her only intimate family. He would certainly trust her more, trust her commitment to him, but would that make him more "Saudi" in his treatment of her? She cared "professionally" because she knew if it did, she would have less access to what she felt she was there for. But as she stretched out next to the sleeping Reena, she knew she cared personally too. Much as she liked Reena, she knew Reena still doubted her. Jineen, her only true friend, would soon be lost to marriage and another family's harim. The only times she felt "normal" and not walking through someone else's dark and perilous life were when she received letters from home and when she was with Le'ith. Now that she would no longer receive the long pages from her mother and the hasty notes from her father—which had gone from Philadelphia to New Guinea, were edited and rewritten there to change any references to New Guinea into ones about Saudi Arabia, and then by some Mossad chain sent back to Philadelphia to be mailed again—she would be more dependent on Le'ith than ever. She did not love him, but she needed his presence because paradoxically he was still her only connection to what she thought she really was.

Chapter 13

When Lisa flew back to America from the kibbutz, she was always ill tempered at the raw commercialism of everything and the selfishness it seemed to engender. The kibbutz was like a family, not in the Saudi way, exclusive and self-protective, but in an open, accepting, sharing way. Israel seemed relatively poor and backward, but America had chosen a way to wealth and progress that was so spiritually flawed she wanted to shout, "Fools!" and longed to be back on the kibbutz with all its "inconveniences."

But when she returned this time, she could think only one thing: Let freedom ring! From the moment they entered the terminal she felt an enormous elation. It was like discovering a new land. It was not just that there were women everywhere, laughing, talking, working, pushing in front of men in lines, complaining(!), shrieking in delight at greeting someone, but the men too were a spectrum of colors in a range of attire that went from the elegant to the absurd. It was like a wonderful circus.

They entered at Kennedy and had to transfer to American Airlines for the short trip to Philadelphia. Just walking in the terminal, feeling free to stop and gape, take a drink at the drinking fountain, scoop up a runaway two-year-old and hand him, laughing, to his father, being bumped by a young guy in a Michigan sweater and having him turn and apologize in an outrageously flirtatious manner, seeing people kissing(!): It was all enough to make Lisa feel she had awakened from some terrible nightmare and found that life was really technicolored, exciting and fun. She could imagine now how it had first struck Le'ith.

It was too powerful a feeling to hide from Reena, but it was obvious what it was too, and Reena just smiled at her a couple of times and said, "It seems good to be back, does it?"

Lisa nodded. "Does it at all for you?"

"I have very mixed feelings about America," Reena replied mordantly. "But the first two or three days I'm always fascinated watching it all, and I enjoy being able to sit in a restaurant by myself, and going to the movies, and dressing in a skintight dress and watching the men leer, but after a time all that wears off."

When the plane took off for Philadelphia, Lisa didn't need to pretend. The thought of being so close to home, of seeing buildings and streets she knew so well made her truly melancholy. Reena touched her hand a couple of times and seemed tense for the first time on the trip.

They were greeted by a man from the funeral home. Lisa had no idea how much he knew. Was he Mossad, or was he just a poor undertaker who had been given a lot of false information? She was never to find out, as she was never to find out who the people were who were buried and how they had come to be identified as Howard and Ruth Cooper.

The man, who identified himself only as Frederick, said he assumed Lisa did not want to stay in the family home, and Lisa quickly agreed. Reena looked a little surprised, but Frederick said he had arranged a suite for them at a hotel, and he suggested he take them there so they could check in and refresh themselves before they went to the funeral home.

Once he was in the car, he avoided looking at Lisa but said he hoped she would understand that the wait had been so long they were forced to close the caskets. Lisa simply said, "I understand."

At the funeral home they signed in and were led to a room where two caskets were placed side by side. There were flowers all over the room and some on the caskets. Lisa moved forward to the little kneeling stool in front, and in doing so, she could see over the flowers. There was a picture of her mother on one casket and one of her father on the other. She burst into tears. It was so real, they were the kinds of photos put on caskets, and it just got to her. She knelt, crying, and then it occurred to her that all this had happened earlier than planned because it *was* real, her mother and father *had* been killed in an accident, and she let out a piercing sob she could not control. She felt Reena's arm around her shoulder, and she wanted to shove her off, shove off the whole false life she'd taken on.

Through her tears she could see the faces of her mother and father, so like them, yet so posed and unlike them. She could see her mother in the kitchen, frowning and pursing her lips, and her father with the shuffling walk he'd developed after his stroke. God, she never should have left them; she was their whole life.

As she was crying, she suddenly felt another hand touching her shoulder. She wiped at her tears and looked up. An elderly but still-attractive blond woman was bending to caress her shoulder; her hand lightly touched Lisa's cheek. "You won't remember me, dear, because you were only eight the last time we saw each other, but I am your aunt Connie Baylor."

Lisa lurched up and put her arms around her and clutched her as she sobbed in relief.

"There, there," "Aunt Connie" kept saying, but Lisa felt she had been to hell and back in sixty seconds. If she had an Aunt Connie, her mother and father were still alive, and she was just Lisa doing a job and had a life to come back to. She could only gradually stop the sobbing, and she began to feel so good she knew she had to act as if she were being brave, not euphoric.

"I know it's a terrible blow, dear," Aunt Connie said, "but they were so proud of you and you gave them so much joy. Be thankful for all that has been."

Somehow Lisa got through the funeral. It was held in a small Episcopal chapel. The minister made a touching oration. Quite a few people were there, and they all greeted and commiserated with Lisa, but she didn't know one face.

At the cemetery Reena held her hand, and Lisa found it all solemn enough to perform like one desolated by the loss of loved ones.

And she actually felt the emotional release that normally comes after a funeral. Aunt Connie and four "close family friends" had prepared a little wake with wine and snacks and conversation about Lisa's new life.

She and Reena were scheduled to go back in three days, and Aunt Connie suggested that Lisa might like to spend a couple of days in the family summer house on the coast. Lisa looked surprised because the family summer house was in the mountains, but she knew enough to say yes, that would be very nice.

When they went back to the hotel and got ready for bed, Reena offered her a couple of sleeping tablets again. This time Lisa took them. "I think I would like to sleep tonight," she said. "I feel exhausted, but I'd hate to wake up with jet lag and spend the night thinking." It was only too true.

After she'd taken them and settled in, Reena came in from her room and sat in the chair near the bed.

"Do you need me these next couple of days," she asked sympathetically, "or will you be all right with your aunt?"

"I think I'm all right," Lisa replied. "Somehow the funeral—" She shrugged.

Reena nodded. "I know the worst moment was seeing the caskets, but if you feel something is liable to hit you like that again, I want to be with you."

Lisa shook her head. "No. I won't say that I won't cry again"—she smiled—"but I've accepted it now."

"If you're sure, I'd like to go to Boston for a day or two."

"Of course. Aunt Connie's here. I'll be fine. Old friends from Smith—or just old friends?" she asked with a smile.

"A little of both," Reena replied with a hint of deviltry.

She got up and sat beside Lisa on the bed. "You know," she said, "Youssef and I had more or less convinced ourselves that you were Jewish and probably married Le'ith at the behest of somebody in Israel. It seemed the only logical explanation." She ran her hand along Lisa's arm. "But you really did need a family, didn't you?"

Lisa managed a catch in her throat. Reena had scared her enough so that it wasn't faked. "I do now," she said.

Reena shook her head. "No. One thing we're good at in Saudi Arabia is family. You have one, imperfect as it is . . . and you will never be alone."

She leaned forward and kissed Lisa on the cheek. "Sleep and sur-render," she said. Then she turned out the light. "Anyway, you're much too Nordic to be Jewish. It was the one thing that didn't really fit." And she was gone. Lisa sighed. She knew so many blond Jews, but providentially, the world didn't seem to notice.

Before sleep took her, she thought of how inept she'd been. Both Reena and Youssef had seen through her, and but for an "accident" at the funeral home, Reena might have remained suspicious enough to question the Episcopal service and Lisa hesitantly making the sign of the cross, something that would have been enough to give her father another stroke! She grinned at that thought and promised herself to be more convincing as the pills gently did their work.

She learned Aunt Connie's real name was Sandra during their drive to an old beach house some twenty miles south of Atlantic City, where they both watched the angry sea and talked.

Lisa felt compelled to tell her about the conversation with Reena. Sandra listened and asked a dozen questions about what Lisa could have done to have made them so accurately suspect her. Lisa recounted it all as self-flagellatingly as she could. Even so, she was uncertain how Youssef had guessed. Reena could have talked to him first, but that seemed very unlikely.

Sandra was unusually disturbed by that and asked questions Lisa couldn't answer about Youssef's friends, where he spent his evenings in Riyadh, whether he traveled beyond the city and the family compound.

"Be careful of him," she said at last.

Lisa smiled, and Sandra quickly asked why. "Because those are the very first words Reena said to me about him."

"All the more reason then," Sandra said. She had grown more and more displeased with Lisa through all this. A storm had blown up, and it was like her mood. Rain pelted against the window, and the old wooden building trembled in the wind. Lisa felt Sandra's displeasure, but she loved the sounds of the storm; it made the desert seem a million miles away.

Sandra paced and lit a cigarette like a veteran of the habit, though Lisa had not seen her smoke in the last two days.

"Do you have any idea how difficult and expensive the last two days have been for us?" she asked severely.

Lisa had thought quite a bit about the difficulty, of who the bodies in the caskets were, if there were bodies, and if not, how did they get a Christian funeral home to go along with the hoax? Where had the people come from at the funeral? Who was the minister and what did he know? All these had occurred to her, but the expense hadn't, but just the mention made her realize how staggering it must have been.

"We have invested an enormous amount in you. And not just in money. Dr. Nordheimer has been an invaluable asset to us, but after her meeting with you, we felt you both would be compromised if she remained in Saudi Arabia. She has had to 'abandon' her research for 'lack of funds' and has returned temporarily to her university."

Lisa stammered, "I—I thought it was so important."

"Didn't it dawn on you that we had other sources of information about something so monumental?"

Lisa nodded. "Linn told me that was the case, but to be honest, I hadn't really thought about it."

Sandra gasped in incredulity. "Lisa, you *must think,*" she said pleadingly. "We didn't know anyone suspected you, and we decided in the long run you could be more valuable where you were placed than Linn was likely to be in the next few months. We brought you out early to make it clear to you that your service is more likely to come when your husband is more important than he is now. In all probability it will be because we know something you *don't* know, and *we* will contact you to take some action."

Lisa felt chastised and knew the reprimand was just. It wasn't a game she'd undertaken, and however well intentioned she was, she hadn't acted intelligently. But what truly disturbed her was that Sandra was implying that they expected it to be years before she would be called on for her "service." When she returned to Saudi Arabia, it was going to be for a long, long sentence.

She and Sandra drove back to Philadelphia through rain. As the windshield wipers swished back and forth, a sight that itself gave Lisa a sense of melancholy homesickness, Sandra told Lisa what the great crisis over Beirut had been about.

"Once before when the Arabs felt fury about American support for Israel, they arbitrarily raised the price of oil four times. At first no one thought they could stick to it, that one Arab state or another would need to sell at any price and then the others would follow. But they did stick, and it changed the world's economy forever.

"Now things are a little different. There is North Sea oil, and the United States has oil reserves, and there is more nuclear power, and the Arabs have grown to need their oil revenues.

"But the threat was that if Israel took Beirut, they would stop all oil sales to Japan and the West. For a short time the West would be all right, Japan would suffer, and so would the Arab states for the loss of income. But if they stood firm—and there was every sign they would—it would have led to economic catastrophe for everyone. While you were worrying in your house in Riyadh, the Saudis made all this clear to the United States. And the United States was using every pressure it could to have the army stop short of Beirut.

"In Israel there were those who were against the invasion altogether, and more who were against taking Beirut, but there were some who said, 'To hell with it, take Beirut, and damn the consequences.' You can guess who those were.

"It was a fight, but in my mind anyway, the forces of reason prevailed."

It all made Lisa realize how insignificant she was, how insignificant Le'ith was in all this. No wonder Linn had been angry, Sandra reproachful. It was a lesson in humility she realized she needed. For her it was her whole life, but in the wide scheme of things she and Le'ith were only tiny cogs in a big, big wheel.

Sandra never lost her chill or sense of doubt about how secure Lisa was in her appointed role, but when they reached Philadelphia, she was sincere in offering Lisa a chance to see her parents.

"We can do it," she said. "But think about it a moment. Believe me, sometimes it's better to cut yourself off sharply." She looked at her watch. "But if you want to, they go to the market in the mall every night about this time. He buys *The New York Times,* and she usually buys frozen yogurt and two Mrs. Fields cookies." She shrugged wryly at it.

If she'd left out the inconsequential *New York Times* and Mrs. Fields cookies, Lisa might have said no, but just the image brought water to her eyes, and she said, "Please, I'd like to see them."

The last time she'd gone home was just before she and Le'ith had eloped. She told Le'ith she wanted to make one last visit to her parents, and though he was nervous about it, he had of course understood. Unlike him, she knew it might be years before she would ever see them again. They were surprised by the number of spontaneous kisses and hugs they received, but they suspected nothing. They had even encouraged her to go out on dates and not "waste" all her time on them. It seemed so long ago. She had been a girl then; she was a woman now.

She and Sandra sat in the tree-lined parking lot for about fifteen minutes before Lisa saw them pull in. They had a new Volvo, and her mother was driving. They got out without speaking and just walked to the market, her dad moving slowly, but they came together at the side-walk, and her dad held the door for her mother. They were so familiar it was as if Lisa had seen them yesterday. The thought of all the lost years—for them and for her—made her heart ache, and she could not check the tears that coursed down her cheeks.

They were in the store for only a few minutes, and through the trees Lisa could see their heads moving around and her father talking to Sid at the cash register. When they came out, they were grinning, and her dad said something that made her mother laugh, and she hit at him with the package she was carrying, and he put up his arm in defense, laughing and saying something else outrageous. It was like a gift to Lisa that they seemed so happy, yet when they pulled away, still smiling, she was racked with a sense of loneliness whose pain seemed to fill her whole being.

On the flight back with Reena her mind was not only filled with anguish about the years yet to come but haunted by Sandra's warnings about the danger from Youssef and the need to be wary of Reena's quick mind. If she thought her cover had been penetrated beyond repair, she was to notify Sandra immediately ("my faith in God is stronger than ever"), and they would try to get her out. Until then she had to prepare herself for exposure by either of them, and she had to convince Le'ith that there was only one truth about her: She loved him more than anything in the world.

Chapter 14

She and Le'ith drove across the flat shale of the desert surface in a British Land Rover equipped with a double radiator to deal with the heat. Two trucks followed them, whipping up a little cloud of dust that traced their progress into what seemed like endless nothingness.

It was almost 140 degrees outside, but the Land Rover was air-conditioned, and though Lisa knew the men often drove across the desert, she'd never done it and was amazed at how firm and relatively even the surface was. And it was empty to the horizon. A few hills—and nothing. She felt as if she were exploring the moon. Each mile took her farther from Riyadh, farther from the compound, farther from Youssef. By now she knew the real danger was Youssef, not Reena.

Just before they had started out on this trip into the barren nothingness, 241 marines had been killed in Beirut by a fundamentalist suicide bomber. It was the *second* bombing since Lisa had returned that targeted the United States for its role in sustaining Israel, and like fundamentalist activity anywhere, it sent a shiver through the tents and palaces of the Saudi royal family. Their fear of fundamentalism was far greater than their fear of democracy. Patronage, the Army, and the National Guard could control the few who sought political power or civil rights, but government is religion in Saudi Arabia, and religion is government. And the fundamentalists claimed *they,* not the "corrupt" royal family, were the true followers of Islam.

Le'ith explained all this to Lisa when she was astounded that the first bombing had hardly been referred to in the press or on television. The

ability of fundamentalists to use terror as an instrument to gain influence
was not something those who controlled the news agencies wished to
publicize, Le'ith told her. When the second, more devastating bomb had
been exploded, there was the same slighting of the event by the censored
press, but Youssef used it as a means of putting more pressure on Lisa,
something he clearly believed would eventually produce the crack in
her mask that he was seeking.

They were in Riyadh, and Le'ith was going to a meeting with
Grandfather. Youssef asked if he could give his personal condolences to
Lisa for the tragedy that had happened to so many American young men.
Le'ith had reluctantly agreed, provided Bushra was present and he met
Lisa in Le'ith's study.

Lisa had only been informed of the meeting, not what it was about,
and she chose to go downstairs in a chador and veil. Since coming back,
she had already had one unnerving challenge from Youssef; she didn't
doubt that this was going to be another.

When she went into the study, Youssef was sitting in Le'ith's chair,
and he did not rise.

"You can safely remove your veil in front of me, Lisa," he said
insinuatingly.

"I don't think Le'ith would approve of my being unveiled when he
was not present," she answered stiffly, and sat on the couch opposite
him, signaling Bushra to sit beside her.

"I wanted to tell you how sorry I am about the death of all those
young American marines in Beirut."

Lisa almost smiled. She could believe him sorry that any survived
but hardly that he sympathized with her or the families of the marines.
She simply nodded.

"In these moments when it must be very difficult to be separated
from your own country and your own countrymen," he went on, "it
occurred to me that it might be very helpful for you if you had your
aunt come over to visit. She would certainly be welcome, and I'm sure
Grandfather could arrange to have her admitted."

Now Lisa knew where he was going, and she was grateful she had
left her veil on. "That's very thoughtful of you, Youssef," she replied,

keeping the sarcasm from her voice; there was no sense making him more of an enemy than he already was. "But as I've explained to Le'ith, my aunt is very sensitive to heat. Her legs swell, and she finds movement very difficult. It's why she chose to live in Oregon." It was a story they had concocted on the beach.

"Oh—" Youssef responded slowly. "Like your father's heart condition when you first came. How well thought out. Your aunt must be a very intelligent woman." And he stared at her as though they both knew how they stood. She excused herself, and it was over—for then.

"How do you ever know where you're going?" Lisa asked as they continued to race across the desert floor.

Le'ith was in a buoyant mood. "We're Saudis!" he shouted. Then he glanced at her. "We have the sun, and shadows, we have the colors of the rock, and if we go a little wrong, we have the stars at night, and we can put ourselves right."

Lisa was still amazed. "I think it was a matter of survival of the fittest," Le'ith asserted. "You can't live in the desert without water, and many of the wells aren't marked by more than a few stones, you can't see them until you're almost on them, yet men go out across the desert knowing only that the next well is so many hundred or thousand stone throws in a very particular direction. They go confidently, and they find the wells. I believe it's a gift, like music or dexterity, and those who didn't have it died out. It's why Saudi men are so independent. All they need is directions to the nearest well, and they'll survive."

They were heading for a valley, almost 250 miles northeast of the family compound. It was land owned by Huda. To Lisa's surprise, despite all the other restrictions on their lives, women were allowed to inherit—both land and goods. And favored daughters, and even favored wives, could accumulate great wealth. Huda had been a favorite daughter *and* a favorite wife of the elder brother of Le'ith's father. He had died of smallpox before Huda had given him any children, but he willed her land and money that made her a powerful figure in the family and a fairy godmother to those who did not win the favor of their own fathers.

Le'ith was not one of those, but he was a favorite of Huda's anyway.

She was going to lease Le'ith her valley—more than five thousand acres—for which she would receive 40 percent of the profits. He then presented a proposal to the government to build a farm that would initially require hydroponic cultivation, a small but expensive desalinization plant, and thousands of dollars in investment in machinery, plastic, hybrid seeds, and ultimately hybrid cattle from Morocco. For the first years his primary field crop would be buffalo gourd. It could grow on almost barren land and produces seeds with more protein than soybeans. And the pulp that is the residue from crushing the seeds is excellent cattle feed. He would plant date trees and palms and forage sorghum, and as the microclimate of the valley changed, he would add hard durum wheats and corn. Eventually the farm would produce hydroponic vegetables, tons of buffalo gourd oil, cattle, wheat, and corn, and in time Le'ith intended to add orange and lemon groves.

The plan had been developed with expert help, part of it financed by the Ford Foundation. Le'ith had spent hours on it when they were in Riyadh without even telling her. When the government accepted the plan, Le'ith received the right to claim 50 percent of the cost from it. He then went to a bank where Grandfather had contacts and borrowed another 25 percent. Huda donated the last 25 percent, which would have to be repaid, but without interest. Islamic law forbids the taking of interest, though of course many ingenious alternate ways of making profit from lending have been developed through the ages. Huda spurned them. She gave the money, and all she wanted was the money back.

This was the surprise Le'ith had for Lisa when she returned from the States. Unlike everything else he did, this was to be for them alone, not for the extended family, and it was critical that he could arrange it all without drawing on family funds. He had received final approval when she was in America.

It was some months before it all was put together, but except for her two confrontations with Youssef, they were surprisingly easy, even pleasant months for Lisa. In part this was because Le'ith had been inordinately pleased at her return. She almost thought he was going to hug her at the airport, chador, veil, and all. But he restrained himself until they reached the house and her luggage had been taken to her room and she had shed the black and gray garb.

He took her in his arms and squeezed her again and again, saying, "I love you, Lisa. I love you." She found his body comforting as always, and through all the upheaval in the States she had longed to hold some-one, and to be held. She didn't think it had to be Le'ith, but there was no question by now that Le'ith would certainly do.

Somehow coming back had seemed natural. All the things she had recalled with dread in the States—the mandatory dress, the implicit as-sumption of the superiority of men, the lack of any life outside the home, the need to defer to Ummi and live in the harim, the separate rooms and houses for her and Nayra—none seemed so grim to her now because none of them was a surprise. This was her life in Saudi Arabia, and without noticing it, she had become accustomed to it.

For the first few weeks they had stayed in Riyadh, and it was clear Reena had made a most favorable report. Everyone, even Grandfather, assured Lisa that they were her family, to be so always, and that anything she needed they would provide if they possibly could. Jineen was like Le'ith. She just could not stop hugging Lisa, and it made Lisa aware that Le'ith was not the only one who had thought she would not return.

While she was gone, Jineen had been introduced to the harim of the family of her future husband. Ummi had made the arrangements, but her father of course had the final say. They all liked the boy, whose picture Jineen had seen. "He's so handsome," she told Lisa, "and he's the third son, so he's going to the university in Riyadh and we can be married almost immediately.

"I've decided," she said earnestly, "that I want to be like you and Le'ith. I want us to really love each other. And his mother is so nice; she is going to let me visit home whenever my husband agrees."

Fresh from America, Lisa was appalled and pleased at the same time. She held Jineen's head in her hands and kissed her cheek and said, "I know you're going to be very happy."

It was almost a life, Lisa thought. She had resigned herself to a long stay. She knew the rules now. As for Le'ith, he seemed to be making

up for all those days in California when they did not make love. He was
in her room every night. He always left at the muezzin's call at dawn,
but he was back in bed with her before the sun had bleached her window
shutters with its dry white light.

Sometimes he returned during the day, and they made love again
under the fan, its breeze cooling their bodies and rippling the silk cur-
tains. She could hear the sounds of the street, and they made her feel
she was doing it in some exotic setting with this lion of a man who was
besotted with her. He had learned the secrets of her body, the places to
begin, the times to be soft and caressing, the times to use every muscle
of his body. If she was going to have to survive for years, she thought
this was a "price" that could make the passage of time more tolerable.

Often when they were finished, she would be embarrassed that
Bushra would find the sheets so wet, but then Bushra was probably
listening somewhere, her own hand wet at the sounds of their lust. For
so Lisa wanted to think of it. She was playing mistress to a lustful man
who touched her own desire for lust, but she still held to herself that
piece of her heart that would provide the alchemy to turn that lust into
love.

At long last the time came when Le'ith had to return to the family
compound to get Huda's signature on the final documents. Lisa was
almost relieved they were making the trip. She needed a little vacation
from continuous sex, and the confinement in Riyadh seemed much
more severe than it did in the compound, where she was at least free to
wander in the palm forest and could be taken on expeditions around the
farm by the children.

Youssef had been there to greet them. It was their first meeting since
her return. Four of them—Le'ith, Lisa, Reena, and Jineen—had flown
together with Le'ith's aide, Khalid, who handled the briefcase full of
documents. Reena preferred Riyadh, but Lisa guessed that she had come
down to "run interference" for her, especially with Youssef. They were
still wiggling into their chadors when Khalid opened the door of the
plane, and Youssef burst in past him.

"Well, the golden one has returned!" he exclaimed.

"You knew she'd returned weeks ago," Reena said acidly.

"Ah, but it's so hard to believe all the stories from Riyadh. I had to see her with my own eyes."

Lisa had her veil on by now, and he missed her irrepressible look of anxiety and doubt.

Le'ith had taken off his earphones and finished his log. He stood and glowered at Youssef. "When you want to see my wife, you will do me the courtesy of asking my permission first," he said. "Now please get out of the doorway and let us deplane."

"I thought I might help carry gifts," Youssef protested. He seemed almost pleased that he'd made Le'ith angry.

"They're all in the hatch," Le'ith replied, "and the servants can bring them in. Now, please—out!"

Youssef glanced at him defiantly for a second, then turned and ran down the steps. "Let me help the ladies deplane!" he blustered, and stood at the foot of the little stairs and ceremoniously guided them all to the ground. Jineen hit him on the head. That made him laugh and softened everyone's mood.

He had turned to Lisa with a look of sincerity and said, "I'm sorry about your parents. I know it must be very painful. I hope after you've made your greetings to Father, Mother, and Huda, Le'ith will allow you to join us and tell us a bit about them. They're a part of the family we all regret not meeting."

Lisa found the request sinister and frightening. "Lisa's much too tired for that," Le'ith said. "She'll be quizzed enough by Father."

Youssef nodded acknowledgment, but Lisa could tell even then that he was waiting, that he believed even less in the Lisa she was presenting.

That night when Le'ith didn't come to her house, she was surprised. He had been so loving she couldn't believe he'd just turned it off to go to Nayra, even though she understood there was an implicit obligation that he do so. She was hurt, and she reproached herself for it, but her mind kept saying, but he was so much in love, so much. She also felt vulnerable in Youssef's presence, and she realized she needed Le'ith's love for her for more than tactical reasons.

The next day she and Reena went to the harim together, with Fatima and Latifa carrying bags of gifts. Reena had warned her what was expected, and they'd spent two hours and several thousand dollars in the duty-free shop at Kennedy. Jewelry was the desired gift, but Reena assured her that giving the right gift was far more important than the cost.

Reena proved right as usual. Each new bit of jewelry was greeted with exclamations and cries of delight. Lisa had picked toys for the children, and they mimicked their elders with cries and signs of fainting with shock.

Nayra was there with her little smile of triumph, but she greeted Lisa with a weighty sense of sympathy. Before the gifts Lisa had to go through the ordeal of receiving condolences from everyone, and of them all she felt Nayra's was the most genuine. The night before Huda had made her cry with grandmotherly affection and sympathy. She thought now that if Adam could see how much they'd wrapped her in the family for protection, he'd believe he deserved a medal for the wisdom of his plan to "terminate" her parents. She prayed she had not inadvertently destroyed all his brilliant planning.

While all the arrangements for the farm were being worked out, she and Le'ith flew back and forth to Riyadh frequently. Sometimes Reena accompanied them, and sometimes Youssef. Lisa tried to joke with Youssef about being a bachelor in Riyadh, never bringing his wife. Whom was he seeing all those nights he was out on his own? She could tell the teasing made him uncomfortable even though he pretended to enjoy it, but through it all she learned very little; even Le'ith didn't know who some of his friends were.

But one night he surprised them both by saying he would like to bring one of those friends for dinner, and he hoped Lisa would join them. Le'ith was as astounded—and almost as wary—as Lisa. He was far more liberal than the vast majority of Saudi men, but the idea of his wife's dining with someone who was not a selected guest of his own was more than an irritant to him.

"He's a man who's been to the West often," Youssef said in extenuation. "He won't be shocked, and I guarantee his good behavior with my own life." His exaggerated posturing about it annoyed Le'ith even more, but he gave his approval.

On that night Lisa was unveiled, but she wore a traditional abu covered by a dun tunic. The guest proved to be Colonel Ansari of the Army. Le'ith knew him, and though he treated him distantly, he listened to him intently. Two days before, the paper had reported the *first* Beirut bomb. An Islamic fundamentalist suicide bomber had wrecked the U.S. Embassy, killing sixty-three people including sixteen Americans. The news was buried on one of the inside pages among news of import deliveries and religious festivals. Colonel Ansari's invitation had gone out long before the incident, but the chance to quiz the colonel about it was something Le'ith obviously welcomed.

"It was retaliation for the invasion, surely," Le'ith posited.

"Of course," Ansari answered.

"Do you think it was the Islamic Jihad?" Le'ith asked.

"I don't think they have the organization for it," the colonel replied. "Apparently the quantity of explosives was huge. It was probably Hamas; they have the support of the Iranians."

"But they're all linked in their opposition to America and Israel, aren't they?" Youssef asked with affected innocence. Lisa looked at him. He was staring fixedly at the colonel though she was certain the question was put for her benefit.

"Of course," the colonel answered, " 'the Great Satan and her hated daughter.' They all agree on that. But I don't think anyone has been able to organize them. Iran tries to mastermind them, but Gaddafi wants his say too, and Assad, and the extreme wing of the PLO. Put five of them in a room together, and you will have six different views on how to destroy Israel *and* the United States."

He smiled, and Le'ith grinned back dryly. The colonel was not a likable man, even when joking. There was something sinister and with-drawn about him.

Youssef turned to Lisa with his own unpleasant smile. "Colonel Ansari is head of the Army Secret Service, Lisa. He has the difficult job of tracking any illegal activity by fundamentalists or those countries—like Israel, for example—that are enemies of the Kingdom."

Lisa knew she blanched. So that's why the colonel had been asked to meet them. She was as stunned by Youssef's audacity as she was by his clumsy and blunt reference to Israel. She could have no doubt that he had her in his sights, but what did he *know*?

"Well, I hope that means the colonel does not himself regard America as the Great Satan," she said, turning to the colonel and trying to deflect the conversation from the source of her unease.

"No, indeed," the colonel responded. "Most of these fundamentalists see Israel as only one piece of a monstrous American plot to destroy Islam. And they believe it. That's a joke. But Israel and America *are* two faces of the same coin. The fundamentalists hate Israel not only because they think it's America's instrument, but because it brings the corruption of materialism to the heart of Arabia."

"Youssef tells us you visited America. Did you find it so terribly corrupt?"

Now the colonel looked awkward and embarrassed. Lisa suddenly suspected he had partaken of some of America's "corruption" with more pleasure than he'd care to admit.

"No. No, much of it I like," he stammered.

"I told the colonel about Ghasi's theory about moles, and you know, he agrees," Youssef said with feigned wonder. "He believes Israel has moles in *all* Arab countries—even ours."

Now he was looking directly at Lisa, and again his audacity astounded her. Did he actually know something? Was the evening going to end in some terrible revelation that would make it impossible for Le'ith to protect her even if he wanted to? After all, he could not defy the Army Secret Service.

"Well, we'll have to keep an eye on Ghasi." Le'ith laughed. "A good way to cover your guilt is to point to someone else." His tone revealed his cynicism about the whole idea, and he certainly missed any allusion to her.

Lisa waited on tenterhooks through the rest of the evening for some startling new disclosure from Youssef, but nothing came, and she decided in the end he had nothing concrete; he was only probing in his crude and unsubtle way, doing it in the presence of the head of the Secret Service, thinking she might give herself away under the pressure.

Five months later there was the second bombing that killed all the marines, and he had tried again. Just the two of them and Bushra in Le'ith's study when she felt all the pretense had been dropped. He believed she was an Israeli mole, and he was after her.

A week or so after that meeting she and Le'ith had returned to the compound again. Le'ith, as usual, spent the first night with Nayra, but a few nights later he was in Lisa's house, and she lay, curled up, with her back against his chest, his arms encircling her. He had just turned out the lights. The punkah was swishing back and forth above them, and the bright desert moon lit the whole room in a soft glow. It was beautiful, but her mind was full of Youssef.

"I'm going to fly to Riyadh alone tomorrow," Le'ith said. She turned to him, a little surprised. He smiled. "I'm bringing six men back with me tomorrow night, and there won't be room for you."

He held her closer. "I always told you we'd have our own life. Well, two days from now we're going to leave for Huda's valley and the farm. I'm bringing back the foreman and five workers. It'll take two days of travel to reach the valley, so five nights from now I'll be making love to you in 'our world.' " He grinned. "For now you'll just have to be satisfied with my making love to you in *my* world." He was still smiling when he kissed her. She fought for a time, chasing Youssef from her mind as Le'ith slowly brought her body to want his, but in the end he proved right: She was satisfied.

About an hour before sunset on their first day of driving north, Le'ith honked the horn and waved his arm in signal, and the two trucks split, one going wide on the left, the other wide on the right, and they all slowed down. Le'ith leaned forward over the wheel and kept scanning the desert in front of them.

"What are we looking for, a pile of rocks?" Lisa asked.

Le'ith smiled, "Well, you *are* becoming a Saudi wife. That's right, we're looking for water."

From the look of the desert the chances of finding it seemed about equal to the chance of finding a palm tree in the middle of Antarctica, but after about ten minutes the truck on the right honked its horn over and over again, and Le'ith smiled and turned the Land Rover as the second truck swung over toward them.

Lisa had been in her chador and veil when they started out from the compound, but once on the way she took them off. She was wearing jeans and a light blouse. Le'ith glanced over at her. "I brought something for you," he said, and leaned back behind his seat and tossed her a long-sleeved UCLA sweatshirt. "You don't have to get in your medieval rags," he said, "but bare arms and the fit of that blouse would have the muta'ween coming cross-country on camels to get you."

Lisa grimaced wryly. She was amused by the UCLA sweatshirt, but she'd worn blouses more revealing at dinner parties and thought maybe in the wilds of the desert she could be a little more flexible.

"And I do want you to wear a hijab and veil," Le'ith said more firmly, having seen the exasperation in Lisa's eyes. "These are strange men to you, and from the beginning they must know your status as my wife. They will not speak to you until I give them permission, and I ask you not to speak to them." Lisa was putting the sweatshirt on, and she grunted her annoyance. "Tomorrow, when we reach the valley, if all is well, I will introduce you to them, and you may treat them as you would the male servants at home."

He had stopped the Land Rover. There in front of them was a circular pile of rocks not more than two feet high. The men in the trucks were getting out, but they avoided looking at the Land Rover, and Le'ith just waited calmly until Lisa covered her hair and slipped on her veil.

Le'ith looked at her with an amused tolerance. "Have you ever slept in a tent?" he asked.

"No," Lisa said tersely. "And as your number two wife I'm not sure I wouldn't rather spend the night in the Land Rover."

Le'ith just laughed and jumped down into the heat.

The men were exultant that they'd found the well before the sun set. There was no twilight in the desert. The sun was there, low in the sky, and then it was gone, and with it, the light. Within an hour the worst of the heat would be gone too. Le'ith and all the men but one (who was apparently not a Muslim) faced Mecca, knelt, prostrated themselves, and prayed. Lisa stayed in the Land Rover with the motor idling and the air conditioner on.

They erected two large tents. It was cooler by the time they finished, and Lisa got out and stretched. Le'ith sent one of the men to her with a cup of water from the well. The well was deep, it had seemed to take forever for them to haul a bucket up, but the water from it was cold and clear. "*Zain* [it's good]," Lisa said. The man smiled sheepishly without looking at her. Like the others, he was covered in a sweat-streaked patina of sand and dust from the ride across the desert.

In the darkness a fire was started to roast a lamb, and Le'ith finally came to her. He smiled at the pique he saw in her stance. "As a Saudi wife would you mind following me into our tent?" he asked. His smile broadened as he saw her stiffen.

Nevertheless he turned immediately and walked to the tent. She hesitated a moment, but she knew, however annoyed she was, however arrogant he was being, she could not in any way humiliate him in front of others. Aside from adultery, it was the one unforgivable sin. She followed him dutifully, head lowered, to the tent, but once inside she gave him a shove in the back. He staggered and turned to her. She drew her finger across the "UCLA" on her sweatshirt and said, "*Our* world, huh?"

He laughed and pulled her to him. He slipped off her scarf and veil. "You are more beautiful than the curtain of stars that walk the desert night," he said softly, "and men not used to you could lose their direction altogether."

She huffed, but when he kissed her, she responded in a way that let him know all was forgiven.

Their tent, lit by two vapor lamps, was huge and luxurious. It had three layers; the inner layer was silk, through which she could see, here and there, geometric designs that created the optical illusion that they were close and other parts of the tent were distant as the horizon. Their meal was brought to them, and as soon as they were finished, Le'ith said they should sleep because they had to be up before dawn.

As they lay on an air mattress disguised with silken sheets, she could hear the men outside feeding the two goats they had brought as part of the cargo. Goats, Lisa had learned, were the garbage collectors of the desert. They would eat almost anything, and they provided milk. Lisa didn't much like the animals, but she'd already nicknamed these two Jekyll and Hyde. She had considered calling them Le'ith and Youssef, for her the same image, but she thought better of it. But hearing them munching away at the remains of dinner brought Youssef's menacing figure into her mind.

"When I told Reena of our visit from Colonel Ansari, she told me that Youssef has friends in the Army and you have friends in the National Guard. Is that a family strategy?" she asked without looking at him.

"In some families, yes," Le'ith replied lazily. "The Army is headed by one branch of the royal family, and the National Guard by another. If you suspect one or the other is going to get dominance, it might be wise for a family to cover themselves in that way. But it just happened with us. I've spent more time around Grandfather, and his ties are to the National Guard side."

"How come two branches of the royal family?"

"Their mothers. One mother bore the last three kings. They were full brothers, and it is the function of the National Guard to protect the King. Prince Sultan, who is the head of the Army, was also a son of Abdul Aziz, but he had another mother. It is natural to suspect some rivalry, and rebels tend toward the Army—and Youssef tends to be a rebel, as you've noticed."

"Jealousy of you?"

"I suppose. If I were in his place and he in mine, I'd be jealous."

"And Rashid?"

Le'ith grinned. "The jealousy in that part of the family seems to rest in Reena. But I'm sure Rashid has his moments of envy."

"And so with the royal family."

Le'ith chuckled. "They're royal, not supernatural," he said. "Our greatest king, Faisal, was *assassinated* by a royal prince, another heir of Abdul Aziz."

"Then Reena is right: You aren't as stable as you seem."

"Don't become as cynical as my half sister. The Army and the National Guard cancel each other out. The National Guard even has its own air force just like the Army. It's all been arranged that way. What she says about the fundamentalists is more true, because the King is not the law, the Koran is, and the fundamentalists always appeal through the Koran—very selectively, but the average Bedouin is not a refined philosopher. But don't worry about our stability, as long as Iran and Iraq keep fighting each other, we can all sleep at night worrying about next year's crop, not about what Youssef conspires with his drinking friends in Riyadh."

So Youssef *was* more than a little irritant, even to Le'ith. What would happen if he should succeed in finding out why she was really there before she had even done anything? Would Le'ith simply divorce her and let her go back, or would his Saudi pride be so hurt that he would have to do what Saudi fathers did to adulterous daughters, throw the first stone of however many it took to kill her or, almost worse, turn her over to Youssef to dream up an even more painful way to die?

"Speaking of Youssef's friends," Le'ith said sleepily, "Colonel Ansari called me to ask if I'd ever met your parents. Did you talk with him about them that night?"

Lisa's heart jumped. "I—I don't remember. Maybe I mentioned their . . . accident."

"He's a peculiar man. He probably wondered if they were rooting for the Iranians or the Iraqis to win the war."

"It would have been an amusing question to have put to my father," Lisa responded.

Le'ith chuckled and yawned an end to the conversation, but Lisa was well and truly awake.

Chapter 15

Huda's valley had at its head a tiny oasis with three palm trees and some rough desert grass. There was a brackish pond that spilled over into a little stream that traced down into the valley for a couple of hundred yards and then died out, its winding, broken trail of green a thing of beauty in the desert and a promise of what might be.

Lisa first saw it when the desert was at its most awe-inspiring. The sun was low, and the searing heat of the day was passing. The valley was long and wide, and every little rise along it had its purple shadow, like dark brushstrokes on the golden landscape. The light wind that came with the change of day was sending runnels of copper sand chasing across the hillsides. From the oasis to the sandstone horizon that echoed the dying colors of the sky it was about as beautiful as the desert could be.

On that first sight Lisa knew that if she survived, this *was* her valley, and if there were anything in Saudi Arabia that she would love, it would be this.

The men pitched their tent down the valley floor near the end of the stream. Le'ith and Lisa's tent was placed so it opened onto the oasis and the valley beyond. The two of them ate outside by a fire the men had made. They looked out over the valley, seeing the men moving about their fire and their tent, Jekyll and Hyde tethered near the stream. The clear night with its thousands of stars peered down at them.

When they finished, Le'ith took Lisa's hand and pulled her up from the carpet they'd put down for their meal. He had her face the valley and stood behind her with his arms around her.

"This is our home. Tomorrow I will introduce you to the men, and after that you may dress as you please, though I beg you to be moderate. Soon some of the men will bring their families, and though none of them are Saudis, we don't want our valley to get a reputation for scandal."

"I promise, no bikinis," Lisa said, already shocked by his concession.

Le'ith smiled. "And someday," he said, "we will stand here and look out and see a valley that could be California, so it will be *yours,* and mine." He hugged her, and she was so taken with the thought that it was not hard for her to lean back into him.

"And now, wife number two, I'm going to take you home." And he picked her up like a Western bride and carried her into the tent.

It was not quite the *Arabian Nights* for Lisa. She had done part of her job, she had made him love her, and she had kept him loving her, but somehow the very act of making her a home, and so romantically, reminded her of how much she wanted a real home, wanted to be the bride of a man *she* loved. For Le'ith the night was obviously special, but for the first time since the awful nights he had first made love to her in the compound, she had to pretend.

The next day Le'ith very ceremoniously introduced her to the men. Lisa knew that no Saudi would ever be a farmer, or carpenter, or laborer. No Saudi woman would marry a farmer. A cabdriver, yes, that was acceptable; it was like being a camel driver. That is why the workingmen of Saudi Arabia are Yemenis, or Pakistanis, or Egyptians, in numbers so great the government hides the figures from all but the most trusted.

So Lisa was not surprised, when Le'ith brought the foreman into the tent to greet her, that he was Italian. She was in jeans and a black long-sleeved blouse that fitted very loosely. The foreman, Paolo Mirenda, could not repress a flicker of response to the unexpected blue-eyed blonde, but once over the shock, he acted toward Lisa as he might toward any other employer.

"Lisa, I would like to present Paolo. He is the engineer and foreman who will supervise the initial stages of our building."

Paolo, a stocky, balding man in his mid-fifties, bowed with a matching formality, then looked up with a smile, responding to Le'ith's use of

English with an accented English of his own. "I am much honored to meet the *said*'s wife, and please forgive my saying, but especially because she is very beautiful." He smiled again. "Please may I question, are you English or American?"

"American," Lisa answered.

"And you are choosing to live in Saudi Arabia!" he asked with amused wonder.

She glanced at Le'ith instinctively—and guiltily, she felt—and quickly tried to recover. "I chose my *husband*," she replied lightly. "Saudi Arabia came with him."

Paolo laughed. And Le'ith smiled. Lisa relaxed again. Though his English was less than perfect, Paolo was a well-educated and talented engineer, and his three-year contract would cost a fortune. But he had already done major work in both Jidda and Riyadh—that was why he knew that meeting the *said*'s wife was a singular honor—and he spoke Arabic, especially technical Arabic, fluently. Beyond that he knew how to get work out of Yemenis and Egyptians. He was a priceless asset, and Le'ith treated him as such.

They exchanged some pleasantries about the heat and Lisa's reaction to the valley. Then Le'ith instructed him to gather the men to meet Lisa. For this, Le'ith expected Lisa to wear a hijab, a covering scarf. His one demand, besides asking her to dress "moderately," was that she never appear outside the tent without her hair being covered. A woman's long hair was such a provocative sexual symbol in the Arab world its "privacy" was sacrosanct. The fact that Lisa's hair was blond only made the symbol more potent. The men who worked the farm, though all skilled at their trade, were, like most workers in the world, basically conservative. And Le'ith demanded she respect this.

It was a minor annoyance but, given the Saudi sun, a burden she could easily live with. So when Paolo called, "*Said*, ready!" Lisa, her face exposed but her hair covered, followed Le'ith from the tent, and they stood on one side of the little pond while the five men stood sheepishly on the other. As Le'ith introduced them, each glanced briefly into Lisa's face and then looked down. There were three Yemenis and two Egyptians. Le'ith thought it best not to have his workers too clannish, and if rivalry grew up between the groups, he knew Paolo could handle it.

The men seemed relieved when the meeting was all over. Lisa too suddenly felt a sense of freedom she had never felt in Saudi Arabia. They had seen her face, openly and with the *said*'s permission, so she could roam the valley freely and acknowledge the workers or not as she felt fit. It added to the feeling that this was indeed her valley.

Later she and Le'ith took the Land Rover and slowly explored it all in air-conditioned comfort. When they drove up one of the hills that framed the valley, Lisa could see that they were on the edge of a range of small mountains; arid, barren, and forbidding, they stretched from horizon to horizon like a turbulent sea of frozen stone. Le'ith said, "Those are our guardians to the north." She knew he was thinking in the instinctive Saudi tribal way, and in her thoughts she responded in *her* tribal way, He's right, we don't have to worry about the neighbors.

The valley was much bigger than it seemed at night; there were half a dozen smaller valleys off it, and some of these were several hundred yards long. In one of the larger ones there was another tiny oasis with but one palm tree, some rough desert scrub, and sagebrush around it. Pitiful as it was in an absolute sense, it gave that whole branch valley a feeling of life.

She and Le'ith drove to it. When Lisa eagerly jumped out to inspect it, the heat hit her as though she had been shoved into a blast furnace. It took her breath away. "God," she gasped, "how many months is it like this?"

Le'ith only answered, "We can spend the summers in Riyadh if you like." He was in a gutra and white thawb, and though he too was affected by the change from the coolness of the Land Rover to the oven of midday, he walked slowly to the pond and bent to taste its water. Lisa was already covered with sweat and struggling to breathe, but she followed him. He was sweating too as he turned and smiled up at her. "Taste the water," he said. He cupped his hands and scooped some up for her. It was terribly brackish, and she spit it out, licking the salt from her lips.

Le'ith laughed and swirled his hands in the water. "This is our gold," he said. "The land is soft and basically rich in minerals, but the water is so salty it kills anything but the toughest scrub. But there is plenty of it down deep. Paolo's first job is to pick the best site for the desalinization plant. We have to dig for water as you would for oil, then pump it up and through the desalinization plant." He stood and looked around. "I want it in one of these branch valleys as far from the head of the valley as possible, so we won't hear the pumping and generators. But this stuff"—he bent and swished his hand through the water—"is going to make 'California' possible."

He turned and looked at her. She was panting from the heat. It was really insufferable. She had been through three summers now, but she had spent the days in air-conditioned rooms or rooms cunningly designed to give air and block out the heat. She had never stood on the hot desert floor, taking the scorching sun at its fiercest, and she could not even respond to the lighthearted reference to his dream. In her own heart all that he said made her think only of years of exile. Better here than the compound, better here than Riyadh, but the thought was as suffocating as the heat.

He smiled at her sweat-soaked breathlessness. "Come on," he said, "I'll show you how the Bedouin survive days like this."

They drove back to the tent. Its sides had been raised about two feet to allow what air there was to circulate. Since it was midday, the whole tent was open that way. As the sun shifted, the sides on the part of the tent exposed to the sun were lowered, so direct sunlight never penetrated the tent. Adjustable flaps created vents around the top, so the warm air went up and out, creating a flow of air even in the worst heat. To say it was cool would be an exaggeration, but it was an enormous change from the blast furnace outside.

The men had no such comfort. They had erected canvas shades over the two centers of their work. The oil generator was pumping water from the pond to a spot on the valley floor where they were making mud bricks, the building blocks of Arab homes before the coming of oil money. The second shade was to the side of Le'ith and Lisa's tent, where string and marker sticks already outlined the base of a small building.

For three days, aside from rides with Le'ith and Paolo in the Land Rover to look for sites for the main pumping station, the greenhouses for the hydroponic production, the first planting area for the buffalo gourd, Lisa sat in the tent, reading her Penguin editions of nineteenth-century novels—Hardy, Flaubert, Jane Austen, de Maupassant—about other women in bondage of one kind or another and watching with mild fascination as the men made the bricks, set them on planks to dry in the blistering sun, then aligned them in the walls of the little house they were building. As each new line was completed, they were rewarded with a bucket of water over their heads.

Like most mud brick houses, it would have only one room and a roof with a crenellated surround about two and a half feet high. This house was different in that it would have the usual little ventilated openings for the circulation of air, but it would also have a large window that overlooked the oasis and the valley. And it would have an air-conditioning unit in the wall, run off the generator.

Le'ith would have preferred to live in the tent, but he knew the midday heat would be a daily torture for Lisa, and he wanted her to love this valley. So he'd set the construction of her daytime shelter as the first task for the men. Much as she dreaded the years ahead, she sometimes thanked God that Adam and his confreres had sent her to Le'ith.

In this case there was only one tiny reservation in her gratitude. The cement of the bricks was camel dung. One of the trucks had carried a large crate of it, and once wet, it gave off a horrific smell. Le'ith assured her it would soon pass, along with the flies it attracted.

"Why couldn't you use straw?" she pleaded as the smell grew in proportion to the height of the walls, and the buzz of the flies began to sound like a small aircraft.

"We could"—Le'ith grinned—"but straw wouldn't keep out the insects, like scorpions."

He knew that was all he had to say. One time at the compound Lisa had gone to shower and a scorpion scooted down the wall and across the floor toward her! She'd run out—nude—in front of Le'ith, Fatima, and Latifa.

"My God, it's a scorpion!" she screamed as she covered her mouth with one hand and her pudenda with the other. Le'ith had laughed and gone calmly into the shower with a broom. When he came back, he gave the broom to Fatima and asked her to take some paper and dispose of the dead scorpion.

"Now you can have your shower." He grinned.

Lisa, covered by now with a robe, shook her head. "I'm *not* showering."

The next day, and ever after, she examined the shower floor and walls carefully before she entered. Having seen the size and speed of one, she dreaded scorpions even more than when they had been just a word to her.

Apparently camel dung, attractive as it was to desert flies when it was wet, dried into an effective insect repellent, and it was why one of the modern buildings in Riyadh could be infested with cockroaches and the little mud house next to it be immune to them.

Fortunately the sun, which was then as hot as most ovens, dried the bricks relatively quickly.

Within the week the house was finished, and Lisa moved in. No smell of camel dung. No flies. At first she felt confined because the tent always had an air of freedom and access about it, but when she opened the door and felt the blow of suffocating heat, she gladly accepted the window's wonderful view across the valley and her cache of paperbacks and tapes. She ventured outside only in the first hours after dawn, walking, watching the men work, feeding Jekyll and Hyde.

Sometimes when the men had no need for it, Le'ith let her take the Land Rover to explore on her own. Those were the moments she truly loved. It took her a time to master the gears, even after Le'ith's meticulous lesson. But no woman is allowed to drive in Saudi Arabia, and even on the first day when she cursed the gears and her ineptitude, she felt she'd burst one of the worst bonds of her "Muhammadan exile." When she was out of sight of the men, she pulled off her scarf and let her hair blow freely. She raced across a long ledge on the western hillside that gave her a whole new view of the valley. The sense of liberation was almost like her first day away from home at college. She felt if she could escape Youssef's and Colonel Ansari's probing and spend enough time in this valley, she would survive until she was needed.

That night there was a three-quarter moon. It created shadows in the valley and gave a bright silvery sheen to the hills. She and Le'ith had their dinner on the roof of her house. A carpet had been laid, and they ate, as Saudis do, without a table. Zia, one of the Egyptians, was the cook, and he was very good. Among the goods Le'ith had brought some sidacki, the mildly alcoholic drink that was legal in Saudi Arabia, like the 3.2 beer that had been permitted in the American Prohibition era— or at least that was how Le'ith justified it.

It was just potent enough to give Lisa a little buzz. When that mixed with her elation about the day, the moonlight, and her muted hope about the future, she suddenly found Le'ith's mouth extraordinarily attractive. They were listening to a tape of Egyptian love songs, as sensuous as her thoughts. He was wearing slacks and a shirt open at the neck that revealed the bit of hair on his lion's chest. She could see the bulge in his trousers as he pulled the gutra from his head and ran his fingers through his dark wavy hair. He stared at her with those luminous dark eyes, and she slipped a handful of pomegranate seeds into her mouth and leaned over to him, half-facetiously, kissing him with open mouth, sharing the tart taste on their tongues. He groaned a little in surprise and pleasure when she stroked him and her hand slowly unbuttoned his pants, touching him. He gently lifted her blouse and caressed her breasts, then moved his head down, brushing her nipples with his lips, finally taking them in his mouth until she was wet with passion. It was a wetness he soon found with his tongue, and she curled to take him in her pomegranate red mouth. How often she climaxed that night she could not remember, but she had let herself yield to the taste of lust she felt for him and was more hungry for his body than she had ever been.

After, they lay nude on the carpet, both breathless and covered in a tiny layer of sweat and sex.

"We'll catch our death," Lisa panted, and got up, crouching, and went to the stairs. She brought back a cotton blanket and spread it over them as she lay down next to him. He held her tightly in his arms. The night chill had set in, but their blanket and their bodies were the exact match for it, the chill making them cozy, the moon and stars dazzling them with a clarity only the desert sky can give.

"When we were children," Le'ith said, "we would often sleep on the roof: Mother, Father, Youssef, Jineen, all of us."

"Did your father make love to your mother?" Lisa asked, pulling close to him.

"Not while I was awake." He smiled.

"And Youssef, was he jealous of you back then?"

"When I took a psychology course, I read about the difficulties of second sons. I think our society probably makes those worse, and Youssef seemed to be born with a desire to bully. He would taunt Jineen when he could get away with it, and he would have bullied Rashid and Reena, but Harhash had seduced the will of my father, and she watched Youssef like a falcon, and if he dared touch them, he knew he would feel the whip."

Thinking of Harhash, Lisa twisted away from him and glanced up at the night. "Do you really think it's right for a man to have four wives," she asked, "not to mention unlimited concubines?"

Le'ith spoke thoughtfully. "I know it sounds strange to you, but remember, in the desert there was no radio, no television, almost no one knew how to read, there was nothing to fill the days—or nights. Sometimes they would light a run of torches and race horses and camels in the cool of the evening." He grinned again. "And some nights there were concubines."

Lisa thumped him—not too hard. Le'ith smiled, and his eyes became very nostalgic. "Grandfather had an orchestra of girls," he continued. "Young girls. They seemed beautiful; the music seemed beautiful. And the men of the family came to his great tent and drank tea, and listened to the music, and had sex with the girls."

It was obviously a fond memory of his youth. He glanced at her. "The girls were well taken care of in terms of life at that time; they were part of the household, fed, tended to, cared for, and still are, though the orchestra has long since passed."

From his tone it was clear he found it all very reasonable, and Lisa couldn't truly fault it in the world he had grown up in. She sneered nonetheless. "*Four* wives too?" she chided. "I suppose they also fill the nights."

Le'ith smirked. "Sometimes." He prevented her from thumping him again by turning quite serious. "Before Muhammad, the custom was to have *many* wives, however you could take care of them. Muhammad said *only* four, and you *must* treat each equally."

"And the educated, sophisticated Le'ith believes in the word of Muhammad."

Her tone implied he would take his allotted four. "He didn't say you *had* to have four wives," he said dryly, pulling her back to him. "And the educated, sophisticated Le'ith believes in the words of Muhammad the same way the educated, sophisticated Lisa believes in the words of Christ."

Lisa would skip that one. But she accepted the point. There were plenty of things in Judaism that demanded a lot of credulity—or simple faith.

"In fact," Le'ith said, "we believe in all the prophets you do, Abraham, Noah, Moses, Christ. We, more 'rationally,' I would say, believe there is just *one* God, that it is sacrilegious to call Christ God. He was only a prophet, but the same angel Gabriel who appeared to Mary, the mother of Christ, may she be blessed, also appeared to Muhammad and made him the messenger of God. Muhammad was just the *last* prophet—which you do not accept, but the educated, sophisticated Le'ith does. And he believes that as prophets go, he was the True Prophet."

Lisa sighed. "I guess I like your being religious. I just don't think I'm ever going to like your religion much."

Le'ith laughed. "Well, you don't know much about it, but since you don't like it much, I'm glad *you're* not very religious."

His tone carried the insufferable confidence and superiority Saudi men used on women, and she wanted to throttle him. She leaned up and glared at him. "How can you say that? I'm *very* religious."

Le'ith was still grinning. "I've never seen you pray. I've never even seen you make the sign of the cross." Lisa started to mumble a protest, but Le'ith went on. "And you never ask to go to church, or—"

"Where would I go to church in Saudi Arabia!?"

"At the American Embassy," he responded calmly.

"Well . . . I—" Lisa stammered. "Why didn't you *tell* me they held services at the embassy?"

"You never asked, and you never seemed concerned."

"Well, I don't think you have to go to church to pray," she blustered. Her aggression had become defensive, and inside she was kicking herself for being so stupid. Of course she should have asked if there was somewhere she could go to church. Another way she had made Youssef suspicious of her. Dumb, but if that was the kind of clue he had, she knew she could handle him.

Le'ith was just looking at her. He smiled. "Well, I'm glad you feel you don't need a minister or priest to get to God. That's very Muhammadan." It was that supercilious tone again, but mocking and facetious. "We believe you read the Koran and speak directly to God. The imam is not necessary. Only justice and charity bring you blessings, not the mosque or the imam."

Lisa saw an escape from the conversation. She snuggled up to him and whispered, "Well, I guess in that way I *am* Muhammadan, but don't ever tell anybody. I'll deny it to your face."

Le'ith grinned and kissed her. Lisa could feel him rise against her body. They made love and dozed, made love and dozed again. She was too tired to think beyond that night and found it all as delicious as the pomegranate seeds.

And when dawn came, Le'ith slipped his shirt on, knelt, prostrated himself, and prayed to Mecca.

Chapter 16

Months, years, can go by in the heart of the Saudi plain without much happening beyond the change of seasons and the inevitable growth of children. So when there is occasion for some legitimate celebration it is made into a festival of enormous proportions. So it was with Jineen's wedding. For Lisa it began as a wonderful break from routine; it ended in heartbreak.

The core of the ceremony really lasted only two days, but the celebrations began ten days before the wedding itself, and the excited and joyful preparations started months earlier. No relative, however distant, no friend, however casual, would miss the wedding of Sheikh Safadi's granddaughter. Dozens of tents were set up all around the family compound to house and feed the prospective guests. Commercial refrigerators were hauled in to store all the food and drink that would be consumed. Musicians and dancers were contracted for, airplanes and crews were leased to carry people back and forth from Riyadh and Jiddah and Dharan. Lisa thought it was a little like organizing the Olympics!

Because much of it concerned women and the harims, Lisa and Reena became the executive directors of the distaff arrangements under Ummi and Huda. Their Western educations—in the eyes of the others—gave them an incredible mastery of logistics, and they handled hundreds of details, from places to store clothes to toilet facilities, with a thoroughness and calm that brought constant exclamations of wonder.

The first formal step in the ceremony is for the bridegroom to visit the home of his prospective bride and sign a marriage contract with the bride's father. That meant that the initial partying began at the Safadi compound. The bridegroom and his family arrived days before the contract signing itself.

Le'ith had flown back and forth from Riyadh several times during the preparations, but had been too distracted by his own obligations to pay much attention to Lisa. But the night before the first great party he had come to her quarters and flopped into bed playfully. For the next ten days only the wedding mattered and he was prepared to enjoy it.

"You see what you missed by not having a Muslim wedding," he said, dragging her into his arms and biting at her ear.

"Oh, yes, I get all sentimental at the thought," she replied. "Just think of the joys I missed. Tomorrow, if she's lucky, Jineen will get the first look at her husband. Now if that had been the way it'd been between us I might have raced off the UCLA campus on a camel never to be seen again."

He bit her again. "Listen, women have their advantages in Saudi Arabia."

She laughed. "Of course. They can bear children, get beaten by their husbands, and share his bed with three other lucky girls."

"You're being unfair. A bride gets a dowry—a mahr—and it's hers always. If her husband divorces her, she keeps it, and she can will it to whomever she chooses. Lots of American women don't have that financial security."

"Ah, perhaps I should've asked for a dowry. Why are you only telling me this now?"

He grinned at her teasing, and held her closer. "A Saudi woman is obliged to give her husband obedience—"

"Now we're getting near the truth."

"*But,* in return, she has the right to suitable clothes, maintenance, and—most important—the right to sexual intercourse with her husband. A right I want you to feel free to exercise at this very moment." He started to nuzzle her neck and his hand slipped below her waist to pull her close.

"And if I don't choose to?" Lisa said softly.

"Then you are being disobedient," he responded as softly.

Lisa laughed. "Ah, heads you win, tails I lose—a perfect Saudi compromise."

"Exactly," he said, and his lips found hers and the talking stopped.

The next day, the bridegroom's plane landed in midafternoon. Lisa, Jineen, and Reena watched from a latticed window as the car bringing him and his father and his two brothers entered the compound. Grandfather, Le'ith's father, Le'ith, and Youssef were there to greet them. When they stepped out of the car, Jineen was uncertain for a moment which man was hers. In their gutras the three brothers looked very much alike, but she had studied her picture of her groom endlessly and at last she was certain.

"It's the one talking to Le'ith now," she said.

"He's the tallest," Reena observed cheerfully.

He was indeed long and angular, almost as tall as Grandfather, but extremely thin. Lisa looked at Jineen. The prospective bride was watching the men enter the house and she was trying very hard to looked pleased, but Lisa could read the doubt and uncertainty.

Later, when Lisa was alone with Reena, she said that she had at first thought it almost a joke that someone would have to steal a look at her husband to see him at all before she became his bride. But having seen that look on Jineen's face, she thought it wasn't a joke. It was a tragedy.

"Arranged marriages can be the happiest," Reena replied. "Good families will try to pick mates that are suited to each other. It's better than making your choice in some bar or dance hall when you're half lit."

"Well, I don't recommend that either," Lisa said.

Reena touched her head affectionately. "Don't worry about it. Jineen is not expecting a 'Western' marriage. Let her produce a few sons and she'll be happier than most of your girlfriends back home. Remember what that Swede said."

Lisa did, and the mere mention of Linn brought to the surface her fear of Youssef and Colonel Ansari. She had only seen Youssef face-to-face once since the wedding preparations began, and he had smiled at her as if she were the vessel bearing all his dreams.

She met Robert the third night of the celebrations. All the partying for the women had been in the harim of course, but Le'ith had told her that two former members of the soccer team at UCLA were in Europe and he had invited them to the wedding. Once when she and Reena were looking down at the men from the obscurity of their filigreed balcony they had glimpsed two men in Western dress, but they hadn't been able to see their faces.

Then, on the third night, Le'ith had asked her to stay in her house. She thought he wanted to make love; they hadn't been together since that night before the festivities began. She knew that Egyptian belly dancers were part of the entertainment the men were enjoying each night and she felt he was probably getting a bit randy.

But it was Reena who came to her door. Le'ith and some of the men were on a picnic out in the desert, and she and Reena were going to join them. Le'ith's factotum, Khalid, was going to drive them because he was the only one who could be counted on to keep it secret.

They drove for about an hour into the desert and then they saw the fire. Three cars were parked around it, and when they got there they found Le'ith, Rashid, another UCLA graduate Lisa had met in Los Angeles, Jamal Massari—and two Americans. Rashid had brought a beautiful Egyptian dancer and Jamal had a girl almost as pretty who, Lisa learned later, was from Lebanon.

They were already in high spirits when Lisa and Reena arrived. It was like a slightly illicit fraternity party, and all the more fun because it was outside the law.

Le'ith was eager to show off Lisa, and helped her out of her chador before he introduced her to the two Americans. She was wearing a party gown, because that's what everyone was wearing under their chadors. She looked radiant, she knew. Donald Dillard was a broad-faced, amiable man, gone to fat since his soccer days, but looking like he was having the time of his life. And then there was Robert.

"Lisa, this is Robert Peters," Le'ith announced jovially. "I kept him from you at UCLA because he was so sainted a man, so monastic in his practices, I thought he might turn you from me altogether." The mocking irony drew a slow, devastatingly wise smile from the very handsome Mr. Peters. Lisa vaguely remembered his face. But in a soccer uniform it didn't have the impact it had on her now. He shook her hand and it was like some kind of electric shock. An indescribable emotional spark went from his intensely focused eyes through his body to hers and she quivered from it.

For the rest of the night she didn't dare look at him when Le'ith was liable to be watching. But she stole a hundred glances at him, and whenever their eyes met he seemed to understand exactly what was going on inside her.

They drank quite a bit, the Egyptian girl danced, they talked of the West and particularly Paris, where Robert was living. He was an executive at J. Walter Thompson, the ad agency, and he made it sound more exciting than everything that had ever happened in the desert since God first created it.

Later, they all danced, and when Robert came to take her as partner, he held her discreetly, but his hands clutched at her repeatedly in an almost invisible message of desire. She felt like fainting, and could feel the warm moisture between her legs.

When they drove back to the compound, Robert piled into the front seat with her and Le'ith. Reena and Donald were in the back. And as Le'ith drove, intensely studying the terrain ahead under the headlights, Robert's hand stroked her leg . . . along it, under it. Again, she could hardly breathe. She slipped her hand down next to his and their hands clutched in embraces as passionate and exciting as any embrace she'd ever felt.

When they neared the compound, Le'ith stopped, and Lisa and Reena transferred to the car Khalid was driving. Robert embraced her "sociably," but again his hands clutched at her fiercely. "I hope I'll get to see you again before I have to go back," he said. "It'll be your turn to tell me about all the excitement of life in the desert."

She wished she could make some witty remark, like "It won't take long," but she was numb from passion and only muttered, "Hmm," and reached up to touch his face in farewell.

She hoped against hope that Le'ith wouldn't come to her that night, but of course he did. She tried to feign exhaustion, but when he persisted she took him with an aggression he was not used to. She let herself go completely, only controlling her body enough to keep from crying out, "Robert, Robert," instead of "Le'ith."

She didn't see him for the rest of the wedding, though she stood on the balcony staring down at the men as long as she dared every night.

On her last day at home, Jineen was dressed like a princess, and the harim was decorated with flowers. The centerpiece was a huge floral throne, where she sat in her moment of glory. Downstairs, Le'ith's father and her groom, Ossama, were holding hands under a woven cloth held by an Imam. Her father was saying, "I give you my daughter, Jineen, the adult virgin, in marriage according to the law of Allah and his prophet. Do you accept her?"

And Ossama was saying, "I have accepted her."

"Allah bless you with her," her father intoned.

"I hope in Allah she may prove a blessing," Ossama responded. Then all the gathered men said in unison the first chapter of the Koran.

When they finished, the bride's father and the groom signed the *Aqd,* the wedding contract, specifying Jineen's dowry and how much more must be given if Ossama were ever to divorce her.

Upstairs, the women heard the cymbals and the drums and the lutes and the trumpets signifying that the wedding ceremony was complete. As one they began their excited ululating cry of celebration. And the sound swelled as the doors to the harim were opened. Lisa could not imitate the women's cry, but smiling beneath her veil, she stood next to Reena, who was ululating as loud as any, as Ossama and Le'ith's father entered the harim.

Jineen's face was covered too, but Ossama walked to her throne, looking at her almost totally covered body as though he were looking at the most beautiful woman in the world. Lisa's throat caught. That is how she would want Robert to look at her. Oh, God, how she would love to be his bride.

The next day the celebrations moved to the Mahamedi compound, Ossama's home. Planeload after planeload took off, starting in the early morning. Lisa did not go till late afternoon, but she and Reena were organizing the women passengers from before dawn. They went on the plane with Jineen, Ummi, and Huda. It was Jineen's farewell to her beloved home, and nothing could stop her tears. Huda tried to comfort her, telling her how lucky she was. When she, Huda, was a girl, women went out of their house only three times in their lives. To go to the home of their bridegroom, to go to the funeral of their parents, and to go to their own grave. But Jineen was going to be able to return home to visit, to go to Riyadh on special occasions, and probably to visit the homes of her new sisters-in-law. Her freedom was immense compared to the old days.

Jineen tried to sniffle her gratitude, but her joy through the last five days had all but dissolved in the agony of leaving those she loved most.

The Mahamedi compound was not as grand as the Safadi compound, but it had spawned a similar appendage of tents and outbuildings for the wedding party. Tables sagged under the weight of food, bands played, beautifully dressed children ran in excitement from one adult gathering to another.

On this night, Jineen would once more be put upon a throne, and this time her bridegroom would come to her and only the intimate families would be present. He would remove her shoes and wash her feet, and he would say, "O, Allah, bless me with her affection, her love, and her acceptance of me. Make me pleased with her, and bring us together in harmony." He would then raise her veil and have his first look at her; then he would kiss her forehead saying, "O, Allah, guard any child of our union from the grasp of Satan."

Lisa and Reena remained in one of the women's tents while all this proceeded in the Mahamedi harim. Nothing had stilled the excitement that coursed through Lisa's blood. She performed all she was supposed to do, but she could feel a flush come to her face whenever she let her thoughts dwell on Robert. She longed for another picnic, but she knew it would never happen at the home of another family.

Reena sensed something was wrong, but never suspected its cause. She thought Lisa was feeling sorry for Jineen—which indeed she was, though not to the degree Reena assumed.

"You know, it may not work out, and she can come back home with us tomorrow," Reena told her with a touch of deviltry.

"How do you mean?" Lisa replied.

"Well, to show you there is some justice for women even in Saudi Arabia, if the dear boy Ossama fails to get an erection between now and dawn, she can divorce him." Lisa stared at her. "Absolutely true," Reena declared puckishly.

"Does that happen?"

"I'm told it has," Reena replied. "No one I know. On the other hand, it can turn out that Jineen doesn't bleed. She comes home then too—only in disgrace. In fact, if someone sterner than Grandfather ruled our household, she'd probably be stoned to death for bringing dishonor to the family."

"My God, what if she doesn't bleed?"

"I think she will. I'm a cynic, but it would be too much even for me if *Jineen* were not a virgin."

"But what happens if a girl loses it on a bike, or a horse or—God forbid—on a young lover?"

"Oh, believe me, no one raised in a decent harim reaches the age of sixteen without learning how to insert blood-soaked sponges in her vagina, or splinters of glass. Saudi women know how to stick together."

"Splinters of glass?!" Lisa grimaced.

"I'm told it's not too painful, and it convinces the man how very tight you are."

"God—it's almost worth remaining a virgin to avoid it," Lisa said and they both burst into laughter. It was the first genuine laugh she'd had since she met Robert.

Later that night in the midst of the party in their tent a huge cry went up from the main house, and there was a clamor of music and shouting that was quickly taken up all around the compound. Reena too had let out a shout, and she leaned over to Lisa in the sudden exuberant chaos and shouted, "Ossama has just displayed the bloody sheet! All is well!"

And then the partying really started. Many of the women cried, either out of relief for Jineen, or remembering their own wedding nights.

Alcohol slipped secretly from hand to hand among the younger women, and Lisa was sure more of it was pouring freely among the men.

Two nights later they returned to the Safadi compound. Lisa had not seen Le'ith the whole time. The next day, Huda told her he had gone to Riyadh on business and he wanted her to go on to the valley. In a few days he was bringing his American friends down to see it.

Lisa's knees were shaking from the time she saw the plane come in to land until Le'ith actually brought Donald and Robert into the tent. She was dressed informally and had let her hair fall down over her shoulders. She knew she looked more appealing than she had that night in her formal gown. And he did too. He wore a light shirt, open at the neck, and she could see the hair on his chest and the muscles of his shoulders.

His greeting was as casual as the others, but when he stepped close to her, his hand clutched her arm with a firmness that told her he had been thinking of her as much as she had of him.

They had a meal in the tent, then took the Land Rover out to view the farm. They had harvested several crops of buffalo gourd and hydroponic vegetables, and though it all looked arid and as though the desert might claim it back at any moment, the greenery was sufficient to make a striking contrast to the land around and the parts of the valley that had not been planted at all.

Robert sat in the front with Le'ith. Lisa longed for his touch, but she knew it was probably safer than if he were next to her. He was so witty. There was constant irony in his compliments to Le'ith on all he had accomplished in introducing a little green to the desert, and yet it was without malice and made Le'ith laugh as genuinely as the rest of them.

They stayed one night. They ate outside by the oasis, and she sat across the fire from him. The light flickering on his face made her so lovesick she could only pick at her food. Toward the end of the evening, he turned from Le'ith directly to her and started asking her about herself.

"Aside from Le'ith's soccer-playing ability, whatever drove you to a life in Saudi Arabia?"

"Oh, the excitement of the nightlife really," she answered. "That, and the shopping. Where else can you get lamb's wool at the price you can get it here?"

He simply smiled and nodded his head. "What did you study at UCLA—geography? Or animal husbandry?"

Le'ith laughed. Robert didn't take his eyes from her.

"Comparative literature. I always wanted to be a writer. I was a junior before I realized almost everybody else did too, and a great many of them were better than I was."

"So you chose the desert because there wasn't so much competition?"

She smiled, but the look in his eyes was making her stomach turn. "No, I had decided I would make a career in one of the institutional charities—Oxfam or Save the Children; it may not please an advertising man, but at heart I'm a do-gooder."

"Some advertising men do good once in a while," he grinned. "But Le'ith was able to take you away from all that?"

And suddenly Lisa felt very vulnerable. She was saying more than she should say, revealing more than she should reveal. "I also wanted a marriage to someone I loved," she said, though it killed her to do so. She wanted him to know that in her heart she was free, except for being madly in love with him.

Robert looked at Le'ith. "Well, I would say both of you are lucky."

They went on to talk about horses, but whenever Le'ith was not looking, he glanced at her across the fire. She knew he still wanted her, and she died to have him.

In the morning Le'ith went off to talk to Paolo. Lisa tried to escape Donald and the servants, but someone was always at her heels whenever she was near Robert. Then she was in her little house and Bushra went out to get water. The door closed, then opened again, and closed. She turned and he was standing in it. He held out an arm to her and she hesitated only a second, then went to him and he kissed her with all the heat and violence she felt toward him. His hand pulled her bottom into him and she felt him huge against her stomach. Then he held her away.

"He can't find us," he said. "But someday, someday, I will have you." And he pulled her to him again and kissed her as violently as before.

Then in one move he was out the door, and she was left quivering and breathless.

For months after they'd flown off, her head pounded from it. She knew he was the man she really wanted in life. And for a long time the image of him was like a sickness in her blood.

But what they say about time is true. She got so she couldn't call up the image of him. She couldn't remember really what he looked like, and the sensations of those brief meetings were only memories incapable of inciting emotion. Her mind dwelt for a time on all she was missing, all she was giving up, but the fantasies of the life she could have in Paris with him gradually gave way to thoughts of the new crops, the fear of Youssef and the way he continued to treat her like the messenger who was going to deliver the golden egg. She even found that Le'ith's arms brought her comfort and pleasure on the days when they shared their pride in the growth of the farm.

Most of the valley had been planted and her little house had grown to four rooms when Le'ith returned one day from Riyadh with the letter from Aunt Connie that she had always prayed for—and feared.

In the past months she had remained at the valley when Le'ith made short trips to Riyadh or the family compound. Even when the memories of Robert had faded to the point where they seemed to be from someone else's life, she chose to remain away from Youssef, to make a life in this spot that she felt belonged to her.

After Le'ith changed clothes from the flight, he left her to go inspect the new planting of wheat. She held the letter he had delivered limply in her hand. She knew it was *the* letter because it was still weeks before the routine correspondence was due. Standing at the front of the tent, she looked out over the changed landscape and remembered an afternoon of their very first summer. There had been a thunderstorm out of Wagner. Huge, towering thunderheads, reaching thousands of feet into the sky, marched slowly toward them across the desert, flashes of lightning darting along the immense front of cloud.

Le'ith, Paolo, and the men scrambled to cover machinery and reinforce the stakes on the tents. Lisa got the tethers of Jekyll and Hyde, already skittish, and, with the help of Zia, who pushed while she pulled, dragged them into a mud brick toolshed that had been built near the men's tent. There were three families on the farm then, and she could see the women and children pounding down the stakes of their tents.

As the sky began to darken and the cool wind of the storm whipped up the dirt and sand along the valley, Lisa ran back to her house and went up to the roof to watch. The first light rain had begun. Le'ith ran up the stairs. He watched the battlements of clouds close on them. "I'd feel a lot safer in the tent," he said.

"But then we couldn't see anything," Lisa protested.

"It's coming from the southwest," Le'ith replied. "We could probably open the front flap a little."

Lisa shook her head. "I want to watch it from the window."

"If this house gets wet enough, you're liable to start smelling camel dung again."

They both were wet already. "It's worth it," she said. "How often are we going to get the chance to see a thunderstorm?"

She pulled him to the stairs.

"I'll take you to England and you can watch it rain all day," he said protestingly as she dragged him along and the first crash of lightning with its thunderous aftermath lit the sky.

They darted into the house and watched as the rain poured down on the valley. There were lightning bolts that shuddered the windowpane and hailstones so big they seemed to lay a carpet of snow across the desert floor.

Lisa loved it. She lay on the cushions in Le'ith's arms as the lightning and thunder raged. The teeming rain, the hail: they all transported her back to their summer home in the mountains when she and her mother and father and her dear dead sister used to sit on the screen porch and watch the storms roll over the pine-covered hills. She was usually in her father's arms, as she was now in Le'ith's, feeling secure and frightened.

As the storm passed, the lightning only distant flashes in the gray clouds, followed seconds later by thunder that was only a mild echo of the booming tumult that had surrounded them, Le'ith's iron grip on her finally relaxed.

She turned to him, grinning. "You were afraid."

He tilted his head ambiguously. "We don't see many thunderstorms. I was worried about us"—he glanced toward the ceiling to indicate he didn't think the house as safe as a tent—"and I was worried about out there." He nodded toward the farm.

There was another roll of distant thunder. Lisa grinned at the vulnerability she saw in him. "You're laughing at me," he said. And she did laugh. He took her by the arms. "I think I need to show you I am still master," he growled. She smiled, and he pulled her to him, and they made love among the litter of her books and in the faint odor of camel dung.

They had slept in the tent that night as they usually did. When Le'ith got up at dawn to pray, Lisa rose, slipped on a robe and a scarf, and stood in the opening of the tent. In the soft light of the morning the valley looked like an endless sea of flowers. It was covered with color, a bed of green and tiny blooms everywhere. She could see yellow and pink, scarlet, lavender, crimson—a capricious, unbelievable garden.

She changed quickly and walked out into it. Up close the flowers and bits of grass were sprinkled here and there on the valley floor. They didn't cover it as it appeared from the tent, but everyplace she turned it was the same illusion, an iridescent blanket of color. Seeds that had been lying dormant for decades through the burning heat of the days and the frigid cold of the nights had bloomed with the touch of water. It was a miracle.

Now, almost three years later, standing before the tent as she had that day, she could see that their own miracle had changed the look of the valley almost as dramatically. Distant rows of buffalo gourd gave a rich sheen of green and yellow to the eastern hillside. Across from it, young date trees swayed in the wind, and near the tent there was a large orchard of young palms, already four and five feet high. Near one of the valley branches a huge plastic greenhouse shimmered in the sun, and from it hydroponic vegetables poured in regular harvests. The desalinization plant was working, the pumps brought them freshwater every day, and the quantity kept growing.

There was a single-lane track from the valley to the compound for trucks; there was a mechanic and a garage and a dirt landing strip for Le'ith's plane. Paolo had returned to Italy, and a Moroccan was foreman to a work force of more than twenty men.

Without noticing it, Lisa had become attached to it all; she had come to look forward to each day. She participated in the planning of the crop rotation, the location of buildings—she even engaged in some of the physical work. It was so vastly different from life in the harim. Only occasionally would thoughts of her mother and father, of Robert, of Adam and Deborah and David and Yassi, of her "lost" years, send her into a funk of melancholy. It was almost as if Le'ith had given her the baby he so much longed for from her.

And now the call from "Aunt Connie" had come. She felt it odd that she would feel even a tinge of remorse at receiving that for which she had so often prayed. There had been so many things along the way, the fear of Youssef's secret knowledge, even furious arguments with Le'ith, the uncontrollable passion for Robert, to make her wish to return to her own life. But life on the farm had become essential to her. Only in my Saudi life, she told herself. In her real life it meant nothing at all. But would she survive what they wanted of her? And if she did, what would it be like to go back now and live as a twenty-nine-, almost thirty-year-old single woman in America? Would Robert be married? Would he even remember her?

Chapter 17

The note from Aunt Connie read that she was on a rare visit to Europe and "she had faith" that Lisa would be allowed to come visit her for a few days in Switzerland; she'd be there February 4, 5, and 6.

Le'ith said that of course she could go, but Grandfather had been ill off and on this last month; he was not sure Grandfather would let *him* go. Reena was in Paris; they could wire her, and she'd fly down to Geneva. Perhaps Rashid could accompany Lisa there.

"Can't I just fly on my own?" Lisa asked wearily. "Reena does."

"Reena is not married. I don't want you sitting next to strange men in planes."

Lisa wanted to explode, but she knew it would only make matters worse.

"Rashid may be able to get free—or Youssef."

"I don't want to go with Youssef!"

"Don't worry, if I send him with you, he'll have enough warning that he wouldn't dare offend you."

"Youssef offends me by *being*," Lisa replied.

Le'ith smiled. "Well, perhaps Rashid can make the trip, so don't worry about it until we find out."

She did worry about it. She spent one night in the compound and received the blessings of Ummi and Huda, who complained that they saw far too little of her now that she had her valley. They saw more of Jineen, and Jineen had married *out* of the family.

Huda pinched her cheek and said she was thinking of revoking the lease if she and Le'ith didn't come home more often. Lisa hugged her and said she should come see what they had made of her valley. "I'm an old lady who likes her comforts," Huda replied. "But one day when you've made it truly civilized."

Nayra had grown still more plump since Lisa's last visit, but even the extra weight could not disguise that she was pregnant. It was a shock, though when Lisa caught her breath, she didn't know why it should be. Le'ith slept with Lisa that night. He said he'd spoken with Grandfather by phone, and he wouldn't let him go. Le'ith and his father had called Rashid in Riyadh. He thought he could but wouldn't know until morning, so Youssef was going to fly with them tomorrow just in case.

Lisa didn't know whether it was because she was upset by that or whether she was truly jealous, but her response to that news was "I see that Nayra is pregnant."

Le'ith was not the least bit defensive. Instead he smiled and put his arms around her. "I hoped for a long time that my first son would be yours. I even tried to plan it that way. But then I began to feel we would not have children at all."

The thinking was pure Saudi, but more understandable to her than before. "What if it's a girl?" she replied.

Le'ith hugged her again. "Then there will still be the chance that my first son will be yours."

Lisa shook her head; there was something charmingly naive about a Saudi man's self-centeredness when it came to sons.

He kissed the top of her head. "You know," he said, "all my life I have felt this compound was my home. Now for the first time I feel like a guest here. I feel my home is in the valley with you."

He meant it even though Nayra was bearing his child, and just as surprisingly Lisa felt it too, even though she was probably about to betray him and his country.

The plane no sooner reached its flight altitude and the seat belt sign had been turned off than Youssef said, "Why don't you take off your chador? You'll be more comfortable."

As usual there was something sexually insinuating in it. He was always very discreet about the way he looked at her when Le'ith was watching, but she'd seen him appraise her like a fetching product in the slave market more than once.

"I'm quite comfortable," she replied. "I think I'll doze for a while." She knew it was going to be difficult enough to get free time with Sandra, and she wanted to establish from the beginning that she was doing things her own way on this trip. She knew there was probably no chance of going to Paris, but she might make a phone call or two. Even the thought of that sent her daydreaming.

She didn't eat when Youssef ate and ordered only after he had left his seat to talk with some men in the back of the first class cabin.

She'd removed her veil and thought she'd escaped him, but just as she was taking a last sip of coffee, he slipped into his seat with a broad smile.

"We were just talking about Israel," he said. He had that look of assurance that he was getting to her.

Lisa paused. "Really? I'm afraid I'm not much into politics these days. I'm more worried about our first crop of sorghum."

"Have you ever been there? To Israel?" he asked. The same smile, the same unsubtle look of piercing interrogation. The question made her blush; she could feel her color rise but couldn't stop it. She turned away to signal the steward for more coffee. It was enough time to create an answer.

"After my senior year in high school some of us took a cruise around the Mediterranean," she lied. "We stopped in Tel Aviv, I think, and went up and saw the ruins at Caesarea."

"Did you like it?"

"Oh, it all became a blur, Athens, Delphi, Cairo and the Pyramids. It was very hot, we giggled a lot, and I became lovesick for a dark-haired French boy named Jeannot."

Now she looked *him* in the eye. He was not the kind of Saudi man who thought it appropriate for girls to flirt at any age—unless it was with him. She could see in his instant reaction that he would have liked to have given her a knock or two as he did Ulti and his new wife, Ayesha. The reaction pleased her no end.

"I think what bothers me," he said, unable to keep the anger from his voice, "is that Israel considers itself above the law. The United Nations orders them out of Lebanon, and they ignore it; they bomb Tunis, a sovereign country, just as they earlier bombed Iraq. They really need to be put under some control."

She knew she should keep her mouth shut, but it wasn't altogether her nature. "Yes, I suppose you're right," she said as casually as she could. "And didn't the United States mine a port in El Salvador, sinking ships and causing several deaths? And the CIA overthrew Allende in Chile, I remember. And French commandos just sank the ship *Greenpeace* in New Zealand and ignored the UN order not to explode atomic weapons in the South Pacific. And the Russians—well, we won't go into that." She faced him. "I think it's a worthy ambition to try to bring the rule of law to the world, Youssef, but it seems to me you've taken on a very difficult task."

He was piqued to fury that she had put him down so chillingly and personally, something he could not hide. But he gradually absorbed the fact that though she didn't mention its name, she had defended Israel's actions by analogy, and his look of anger gradually turned to triumph.

"Well, for someone not interested in politics, you seem very well informed," he said smugly.

"Oh, Le'ith and I watch the news sometimes. Now, if you'll excuse me, I think I'll get out of my chador. We should be landing soon."

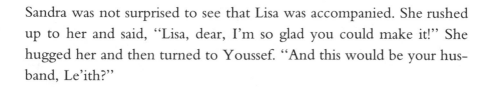

Sandra was not surprised to see that Lisa was accompanied. She rushed up to her and said, "Lisa, dear, I'm so glad you could make it!" She hugged her and then turned to Youssef. "And this would be your husband, Le'ith?"

"No. Aunt Connie, I'd like you to meet my brother-in-law Youssef. Le'ith couldn't make it, and Youssef was kind enough to be my escort."

"I'm so glad to meet you," Aunt Connie said. "But, oh, dear, it presents a little problem. You wrote that Le'ith might come and I've booked you a lovely room at my hotel, but they're absolutely packed." She smiled encouragingly at Youssef. "There are several hotels along the lake, and I'm sure we can find a splendid place for you in one of them."

Youssef was clearly not pleased. "What hotel are you in?" he asked.

"The Beau Rivage," Sandra answered, "but don't worry, let's get your luggage into a taxi, and we'll go to the hotel and make a few phone calls." She put her arm around Lisa as she guided them out to the taxi stand. "I'm so glad to see you looking so well. Is it a thrill to see snow again?"

Youssef, unused to being preceded by women, followed sulkily with the luggage and the porter they'd picked up in the customs area.

Sandra had not shown any reaction at all to the name Youssef, but it had set off alarms in her head. Fortunately the Beau Rivage *was* full. She got the concierge to find him a room in a small hotel three blocks away, and the moment they put him in a taxi, she took Lisa to her room, quizzing her all the way.

"Did he ask to come with you? Is that why he's here?"

"No," Lisa answered. "He was the last resort. They couldn't let me come alone, and no one else could get free. It wasn't *his* idea."

Sandra didn't look reassured. "Do you think he still suspects you?"

Lisa nodded dismally. "I almost feel he 'knows,' but for some reason he just keeps hinting to me. I know he hasn't said anything to Le'ith or his grandfather."

"How could he *know*? Is there anything you haven't told me?"

"No . . . They noticed that I never asked to go to church, but that's hardly proof of anything. Most of the Christians I knew never went to church, unless they were Catholic."

They had reached their floor. Sandra guided her to the left. "My room is right next to yours," she said. "You wait in your room until they bring the luggage up. I want to make a couple of phone calls. Do you need any Swiss money?"

Lisa smiled. "You forget, the Saudis have been money changers for centuries."

"And that fur coat? Did that come from China on the Silk Road too?"

Lisa was at her door now. It was the first frivolous thing Sandra had ever said to her. Lisa grinned and shook her head. "No. So many Saudis travel now you can buy fur coats in Riyadh. They aren't considered provocative."

Sandra had the key in her own door. She smiled but then became Sandra again. "Please don't answer the phone. Let the desk take messages, and then you can return calls after we've talked about them."

"Can you tell me why I'm here?"

Sandra hesitated. "Not yet."

Lisa nodded and went into her room. She was sure of only two things: Youssef thought she was a mole, and Sandra thought she was incompetent. In a short time she knew those two elements would come together somehow.

She went to the window and looked out at the half-frozen lake, its waterspout, the snow-covered roofs and the distant white-capped Matterhorn dominating the black and white landscape. It was only three-thirty, but it was twilight already, and the car lights, white and red, made winding patterns through the wet streets.

It was beautiful and so busy and full of life. It made her melancholy in a strange way. It was too "foreign" to make her homesick, but she could imagine the people shopping and talking in coffeehouses and bars. In the lighted offices she knew people were working, talking on the phone, flirting, or hating their bosses, or waiting for closing time. It was a whole active world, the twentieth-century world, in which she no longer had a part to play, an entire life she was missing, yet the strangeness, the "busyness" made her think fondly of the calm, purposeful days in the valley. She'd truly been away too long. She didn't belong in either world.

The bellboy came, and she tipped him and unpacked. She'd need to buy a suit and a couple of sweaters even if she was only going to be here three days. And shoes and boots. She'd just about finished when there was a knock on the door.

She opened it, and Sandra stood facing her. "Never open the door until you've asked who it is," she said. Then she stepped aside, and *Adam* moved into the doorway.

Lisa was so stunned she didn't move for a moment. Then she ran into his arms and held him, tears spouting from her eyes.

Adam squeezed her firmly, then said, "Come on, let's get out of the hallway. The Swiss are so proper we might get arrested."

He put his arm around her waist, and she leaned into his shoulder, hardly believing what was happening. She knew she missed him, but she never knew how much until she saw him. He was the only part of her real life she could still touch, still be truthful with, and those smiling eyes brought back memories from her entire life, from all that was Lisa before she gave herself to a Saudi kingdom half a globe away from her own world.

She sat on the couch, holding his hand, touching the flecks of gray hair, not letting him go while she asked him about Deborah and David and Yassi. David had had his bar mitzvah. Lisa could hardly believe it, and tears came to her eyes again. Little David saying his haftorah. Her dad couldn't risk the trip, but her mother had come with the other relatives from the States, and that news made her ache with homesickness.

He said he would have brought a picture, but when they traveled "on business," they never carried pictures of their families, well, their real families. Anyway, David was as tall as Deborah now, constantly washed his face because he had a tendency to pimples, and believed he was in love with a sixteen-year-old volunteer from Venezuela. Yassi was due for his bar mitzvah next year and had already invited half the thirteen-year-olds in Israel. Lisa grinned sadly and shook her head. In all these years she had held the mental image of the two boys as those little ones who had sat on her lap and played on the beach. But kids grow like palm trees. Each year the farm had become more green David and Yassi had been changing too, and soon only an old photograph would be true to her memories.

"Do they consider themselves American or Israelis?" she asked with a smile.

"That's one of the shocks of being a parent," Adam replied. "Deborah and I have always been Americans doing our bit for Israel and the memory of brother Noah, and if you're American, you feel your kids are American. But these kids have grown up in Israel, and they are very belligerently Israeli. When they tease us, they call us Yanks. When they're really mad at us, they call us stupid Americans."

Lisa laughed, touching his head again. "I love the gray," she said.

"From worrying about you," he replied wryly.

"And this," Lisa said, touching the artificial arm that ended in a gloved hand.

"It's quite useful," he said lightheartedly. "It reminds me of Sophie and Ben, and I can do almost everything with it."

The mention of the two lost children brought Lisa's mind back to her reason for being there. She glanced at Sandra. "Well," she said soberly, "perhaps you'd better tell me why I'm here."

Adam released her hand, stood, and walked to the window. It was something he didn't want to tell her, that was certain. Did they want her to kill some diplomat or, worse, Grandfather? They'd given her those lessons in firearms for something. Could she really do it? The words had been so easy then, and the hate so strong, but she knew the act would be a world apart now.

Adam spoke without looking at her. "Lisa, Howard died three weeks ago." Howard was Lisa's father. She gasped, slamming her fist to her mouth. "He had another stroke," Adam went on, "and according to your mother's letter to you, it happened in his sleep, and he suffered not at all. She wrote the same to me, so I'm sure it's true."

He had turned to her, and his face reflected her grief. Once again she was too stunned to move. She felt an enormous sadness, a sense of disbelief, but there were no tears.

"We sent a cable in your name from New Guinea," Sandra said, and handed her a copy. It read: "Dear Mom, I have been up-country and only received your cable and letters today. I am so crushed I cannot find words to tell you how sorry I am and how hard it is for me to be away from you at this moment. It is too late for me to come home for the funeral, and for a million reasons I can't explain I should not leave here at this time. I will write soon. I love you, Mom, and you are always in my prayers. Love, Lisa."

As Lisa read it, water did come to her eyes and her heart felt like breaking.

"Adam wrote it," Sandra said needlessly.

Lisa was about to say something when there was a knock on the door. Adam and Sandra glanced at each other. Sandra stood and said, "Yes, who is it please?"

"It's me, Youssef," came the cheerful response.

"Just a moment," Sandra said casually. Adam took the copy of the cable from Lisa's hand, glanced around the room for evidence of his presence, then went quickly and quietly into the bathroom. Lisa heard him slip behind the shower curtain as she wiped at her eyes.

"You needn't cover up for me," Youssef declared facetiously through the door. "I'm one of the family."

Sandra opened the door with a gracious smile. "Lisa was just putting away her things, some of which are not appropriate even for some of the family to see."

Youssef came striding buoyantly in. "I'm a married man. There's nothing that can shock me." He was so full of himself he didn't notice Lisa's red eyes. "With the use of a little oil," he said, slipping his thumb across his fingers in the universal gesture for a bribe, "I've found a room in your hotel. In fact I am only down the hall. So I thought it proper that I take you both to dinner."

For once Lisa saw Sandra buffaloed. "We—we were just going to talk family." She was flustered. "I'm afraid you'd be very bored."

"Not at all," Youssef declared eagerly. "I would *love* to hear about Lisa's family."

Sandra had recovered. "Oh, in that case we shall be very discreet," she said. "Lisa has told me how gossip travels in Saudi Arabia."

"Ah, but I think Lisa knows how very discreet *I* can be," Youssef said, glancing at Lisa with that sinister cat-and-mouse look of his. Then he turned social again. "She's been trying to wheedle the truth about my nocturnal habits out of me for years, and she knows no more today than when she first came to Riyadh."

"Well, we shall see if we're clever enough to follow your example," Sandra said blithely. "I'm sure you're both a bit tired, so why don't we have an early dinner?" She was unceremoniously leading him to the door by his elbow. He was not used to being physically induced to anything, much less by a woman, and he was incapable of disguising his fury. "We'll meet you in the dining room at six," Sandra went on, ignoring his glare altogether and smiling warmly at him as she ushered him out the door.

The minute it was shut, she leaned her back against it and closed her eyes. She just stood there for a moment frozen in anger and foreboding. Then she turned and checked through the peephole in the door to be sure he was gone. "Clear," she muttered.

Adam came out the bathroom. "He knows," he said desolately.

"Of course he knows," Sandra hissed. "I've felt that since Philadelphia."

"But why hasn't he turned her in?" Adam groaned.

"He must have told someone," Sandra said.

"I feel if he had proof he would have done something," Lisa said. "He invited a Colonel Ansari, who's head of the Army Secret Service, to a dinner. There was much of his 'hinting' as usual, but nothing came of it."

Adam slouched to the couch. "Holy God, Ansari."

Lisa felt guilty, certain something she had done or said had given her away.

"Perhaps we need to arrange something more serious for young Youssef," Sandra said weightedly.

"No," Adam answered. "If that happens, they're sure to turn on her. I think we should go ahead as planned."

He faced Lisa, speaking more like her uncle than a control. "We have no set assignment for you, Lisa. We may never have need of you. And if you go back now, they may seize you at any time. If they don't and if we need you, you will have to act knowing that Ansari and Youssef will be watching, and you must be smarter and faster—and perhaps more ruthless—than they are. I'm not sure you can do that, and if you want to give it all up now, which would be a very sane decision, we will fly you to New York tomorrow. Your mother, for one, will be deeply pleased."

Lisa was truly confused. She'd given years of her life to be exactly where she was. But was Adam right? Did she lack the guts and ruthlessness to do something truly brave, truly lethal? And it was true her mother needed her, this moment. Of course that meant something to Adam, but she knew she could not live her life for her mother, nor would her mother want her to.

"But why hasn't he turned me in? Why hasn't he at least told Le'ith?"

"Well, he's clearly known—or had a deep suspicion—for some time. Maybe he's waiting for proof. Maybe Ansari thinks you'll tip them to something bigger."

"Or perhaps Youssef wants to hold it over Le'ith . . . to use when Le'ith is about to become the head of the family," Lisa added thoughtfully, believing she had found the real reason.

"That too is possible," Adam said.

"Look," Sandra said decisively, "if we have something she must do, we know the situation and can probably get her help. We've lifted people from more dangerous situations. The question is, What is liable to happen to her if Youssef gives her away before she's done anything?" They both looked at Lisa.

Lisa paused. "I think Le'ith would probably send me back. Certain things have grown between us, and I don't think he would want to kill me. . . . On the other hand, he can be arrogant in unpredictable Saudi ways, and with his pride and his position so deeply hurt it would not totally surprise me if he had me stoned to death to redeem his honor."

Adam turned away. Sandra sputtered and slapped her forehead. "God"—she sighed—"if we only had Linn in there. She had a dozen contacts in the Army; we'd know just how much they know and what they're waiting for."

"I know you've spent a lot of time and money and effort placing me with Le'ith," Lisa said quietly. "In a few months I'll be thirty. I knew my whole life might be spent in futility, that was part of the bargain, but now, maybe through my own fault, the stakes have changed. To be honest, before I go back, I want to know if you really think there'll be any use for me or am I likely just to spend my life in the desert, waiting?" Now that she had met Robert, the question was more critical to her than it had ever been.

Sandra gestured to Adam and flopped in a chair with a heavy sigh.

Adam hesitated. "We know—or at least we have strong reason to believe—that Le'ith's grandfather sits on the committee that hears appeals for money from Hamas, the PLO, and probably the Islamic Jihad. We also have reason to believe that Le'ith has sat in with his grandfather on several sessions of the committee. They know not only how much money is disbursed but by what channels it goes, and when.

"Saudi Arabia is trying to play a neutral game. The Saudis truly need the West, so they give enough to keep those groups alive but not enough so they can ever really win. But none of us has forgotten that when Ibn Saud was king, he said his one wish in life was to die at the head of his troops as they retook Jerusalem. We believe that soon Le'ith will be in a position to know, and even influence, critical decisions. We're not worried about the present Saudi leadership, but the key people are no longer young, nor are they secure, especially against the fundamentalists.

"If that leadership changes—an upheaval in the royal family, pressure from the fundamentalists—it is always within their capacity to finance and support the Palestinians in a real civil war in Israel and, when that is being fought street to street, *then* to join Syria or Iraq and seriously march on Jerusalem. Should that happen, a soldier we could count on in Riyadh might be priceless."

From all she'd heard in Saudi Arabia, all she'd seen, Lisa was shaken by how plausible that scenario might be. As he spoke the words, she no longer questioned that her service was worth what it was costing her, worth even the imagined loss of Robert. And she didn't need to express it to Adam; he could read it in her face.

"Nobody in the National Guard trusts the Army, and nobody in the

Army trusts the National Guard," Adam told her. "Even if Youssef tells Le'ith—unless he has some concrete proof that we don't know about—Le'ith may still not believe him."

"It's true," Lisa said. "Everyone in the family knows his ambition to take over from Le'ith. Unless he has something that simply cannot be denied, then I will win over him. I know."

Suddenly the three of them were feeling a bit better.

"Why were you so certain Youssef was suspicious of me in Philadelphia?" Lisa asked Sandra.

Adam answered. "Someone had sent a registered letter to 'Mrs. Connie Baylor' at the address only you have. We have the mail forwarded, and a very close friend runs the receiving post office. We read the letter, though they wouldn't have known, and it was stamped 'Return/Registered Letters Not Accepted in General Delivery.' "

"What did the letter say?" Lisa asked tensely.

" 'Dear Aunt Connie, Did you go to the synagogue today?' " Sandra answered.

It stopped Lisa's heart for a moment. "Was it sent from Saudi Arabia?"

"New York," Adam answered, "but that doesn't mean anything. *You* are the only one who has that address."

"Well, now that he's seen 'Aunt Connie,' " Sandra said, "we must cover my departure very carefully."

"And your arrival." Adam nodded thoughtfully. "He's certain to check that."

At dinner Sandra proved a master at deflecting Youssef's questions about them and showed so much fascination about his life that Lisa learned things she'd never known. Like Le'ith, he'd gone to a school in Cairo, where the teachers were English and used willow sticks to enforce discipline. He proudly asserted that he felt the stick far more often than Le'ith had. He claimed he hadn't wanted to go to a university in America, so instead he had spent two years in college in Alexandria and then gone to the University of Madrid.

There, he said, Arab power had ruled for over eight hundred years, four times as long as America had been a nation, and while the English and French were trying to keep warm over wood fires in wattle huts, the Arabs had built a civilization that still stood, a wonder of science, architecture, and beauty.

There were two women, each sitting alone at tables near them, and as he expanded on the virtues of Moorish culture, both half listened and seemed impressed and amused. One had reddish blond hair; the other looked Persian. Neither was a stunning beauty, but they were attractive and dressed in that expensive European way always evident in Switzerland.

Youssef's roving eye was not unaware of them, of course. He pitched his voice a little higher and smiled frequently.

"Medicine, mathematics, astronomy were all created and advanced not in factories or ugly cities but in gardens with water and flowers and a recognition that beauty is as important to men as what they eat." He glanced at the reddish blonde.

Lisa was caught between amusement and amazement. Though the words were coming from Youssef's mouth, she well knew he was about as interested in gardens and flowers as he was in camel dung. The facts of the Great Sultanate were a common and repeated source of conversation—and boasting—in Saudi Arabia, and though Lisa was a little amazed that Youssef could repeat them so glibly, she knew the only beauty that actually interested him enough to be moved to action was not the product of men but what nature invested in women.

"The Spanish appreciate all this." Youssef went on expansively. "The Alhambra is their greatest tourist attraction, so they expect the Arab mind to be interested in many subjects, but most of all in the true philosophy of living."

Where he got that phrase Lisa could not guess, but even with the tension of the night, it almost reduced her to laughter, and she had to cover her mouth with her napkin.

The two ladies seemed impressed. So did Sandra.

"So, besides Arabic, you speak English and Spanish," she said in flattering amazement.

"Fluently," Youssef responded.

He had ordered a brandy with his coffee, and he sniffed it expertly and sipped.

"Well, it's been fascinating," Sandra said as she gathered up her purse. "I look forward to tomorrow, and perhaps we can talk again."

She had already stood, and Lisa followed her lead.

"But it's early," Youssef protested.

"For you." Sandra smiled. "But I know Lisa is tired, and so am I. Why don't we plan on lunch tomorrow? Give us a ring when you get up. If we're out shopping, just leave a message, and we'll be there."

Youssef was half standing, trying to protest, but Sandra had never let him get his mouth open, and she and Lisa were already halfway to the maître d's stand. Sandra turned from Youssef, smiled at the maître d', tipped him, and they were gone.

When they got back to Sandra's room, Adam asked how it went. "Perfect," Sandra replied. Lisa was amazed at her élan.

"You still betting he'll take Talia?" Adam grinned.

"Absolutely. Now you two have work to do, and I want to muddy the record of my arrival here, and I'll need some time, so why don't you go to Lisa's room?"

Adam nodded and picked up a bulging briefcase. When they went into her room, he tossed the briefcase into a chair and went to the minibar and mixed himself a vodka and tonic. "Do you want something?" he asked.

"No," Lisa replied, "I had wine with dinner. I'm not used to it. It's quite enough."

Adam took a hefty drink and then faced her, a smile half real, half forced. "Unfortunately we only have three days," he said, "and we can't be sure how clear of trouble they're going to be. I'd like to leave you and let you crawl in bed and sleep off the wine, but as you must have guessed by now, you have some letter writing to do."

Lisa nodded. Youssef had almost driven the thoughts of her father into the darker recesses of her brain, but the thoughts were still there.

Adam reached into his briefcase and took out some very thin airmail stationary that had "From Papua, New Guinea" printed in one corner.

The first letter was the hardest. And took the longest. After she had finished it, Adam gave her a letter from her mother written two weeks after the funeral.

She was going to sell the house—too many memories of them both—and buy a place in Tampa Bay. Nancy Stein had lost Art about eight months ago, and she had been down there and loved it. They were buying adjoining condos in a lovely gated complex with swimming pools and tennis courts and saunas and all sorts of things for keeping old ladies from getting too old. She hadn't totally given up on Lisa's returning from New Guinea someday with her aborigine husband; at least that was what she'd assumed had happened. And she wanted to be fit enough to throw spears with any aborigine grandchildren she might have. Then she became serious and wrote how much she loved Lisa, and though she missed her beyond measure, more than anything she wanted her to live her life as she wished to live it.

That finally brought the tears that Lisa had been storing, and it was several minutes before she could write again, but when she did, the words flowed easily and swiftly.

She had written four letters and about fifteen postcards when the phone rang.

Youssef was torn. If this were Egypt, he would have made his move on both of them and had them both, but if he tried that here, he might lose them both. Western women could be very peculiar.

The dark one had the bigger tits, and it looked as if she had great legs. But the blonde had a great mouth, and he could think of some good uses to put that to.

A waiter decided it. He dropped a spoon on the carpet near the dark-haired one, and when he stooped to pick it up, she moved her legs, and Youssef caught a glimpse of the top of her silk stockings and the white flesh above it.

After they'd shared a drink, the ever-subtle Youssef invited her to his room. Her dark eyes were very sensuous when she turned it on, and she did.

"I know a little club only two blocks from here," she purred. "We can have a little walk in the crisp night, have a drink or two and a dance, and you can tell me how it happened that I had the good fortune to find a man like you all on his own."

Youssef hesitated. Maybe he should have taken the other one. "Then tomorrow when we're having breakfast in bed," she went on, "you can tell me whether you felt you were fortunate to find me all on *my* own."

She was leaning close to him, and while she took another sip of her drink, her free hand slowly slid along his crotch. She could understand instantly why he was in such a hurry to get upstairs, but that was not the plan, and that little bit of encouragement was enough to get him out the door.

The combination of Youssef's weakness for telling extravagant stories about himself, his love of alcohol, and the arousing delight of flesh-to-flesh dancing kept them in the club for more than three hours.

When they came out, the air was so crisp it stung their throats. They laughed and watched their breaths turn to frosty clouds. Youssef slipped on the ice and called a cab, but Menijah, the dark-haired one, waved it away, telling Youssef they needed the fresh air to be wide-awake enough to enjoy the rest of the evening. She kissed him flush on the mouth, plunging her tongue into his, and he joined her in waving the cab on.

A block later near the corner Menijah appeared to slip, and she bumped Youssef toward the curb. He laughed and reached out for her, but he suddenly felt the whack of a car that had slid across the little mound of snow on the curb and caught his legs, bouncing him off the hood and dumping him on the ground.

Menijah ran after the car, cursing and shouting at it. The car had no lights. At the next corner it slowed; Menijah hopped in; the car turned on its lights and sped off.

The telephone call was from the Hôpital de la Tour. Lisa had answered, but Adam held the phone so he could hear. The operator identified the caller. It was a nun. She put her through.

"This is Sister Claudel at the Hôpital de la Tour," she said in a voice so soft it was almost a whisper. "I'm sorry to tell you that your brother-in-law Mr. Safadi has been in an accident. It is not serious, he is fully conscious, but he has broken two bones on his lower right leg, and we will have to keep him in the hospital tonight and operate tomorrow morning. He would like you to bring some of his personal things if you would."

"Tonight?" Lisa asked, not able to keep the surprise out of her voice.

"If you would," the sister answered. "He would like his shaving equipment, some underwear, and, most important, his copy of the Koran. He is of course in a mild state of shock, and he was insistent that you bring this to him tonight. I have spoken to the concierge at the hotel, and there will be no difficulty in getting into his room."

Adam could not be seen with either of them in public, so Sandra accompanied Lisa to the hospital. Adam had revealed to Lisa that the incident was no accident. The minute Sandra knew it was Youssef who had accompanied her, they felt they had to make sure he kept out of their hair. The job had been done just about perfectly. He would have to stay in the hospital at least the three days and then, as a bonus for the trouble he was giving them, have the inconvenience of a cast for several weeks. Their one surprise was that he had taken the dark-haired Menijah over the blond Talia.

"But do you think he suspects it *wasn't* an accident?" Lisa had asked nervously.

"I don't know," Adam answered. "But given what he thinks he knows about you, I don't think it makes much difference."

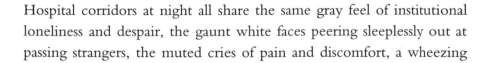

Hospital corridors at night all share the same gray feel of institutional loneliness and despair, the gaunt white faces peering sleeplessly out at passing strangers, the muted cries of pain and discomfort, a wheezing voice calling, "Sister, Sister!" It made Lisa more anxious each step along the way.

When they reached Youssef's room, the door was closed. They knocked and heard his gruff voice respond, "Yes?" They opened the door. He was in a temporary cast and a hospital gown. The only light was the bed light over his head.

Lisa had hastily wrapped his things in a plastic laundry bag. Sandra had taken the flowers from their two rooms and put them in another. Youssef hunched up when they came in, his eyes narrowed in anger.

"So it is the two of you," he said malevolently. Then he saw the flowers and laughed. "Oh, that was thoughtful of you."

Lisa hadn't moved from the door. Sandra calmly walked to the cabinet beside his bed. She found a flower vase and placed the flowers on the cabinet. His eyes watched her the whole time.

"There," she said. "That makes the room a little brighter. Are you in much pain?"

He smiled with amused bitterness. "Not much," he said. "They've doped me up, but I was determined to stay awake until you arrived." The sheer resolve was so fierce it made the statement a threat. There was no doubt he knew what had happened.

"We brought your things," Lisa said, holding up her sack. She still hadn't moved. There was so much malice in his mocking play with them she half expected him to lash out and hit them. She'd seen him do it in sudden, violent outbursts to animals and workers, and she'd seen the bruises on Ulti and Ayesha.

He just looked at her. There was a smiling confidence in his eyes, but there was also burning hatred. "Would you please bring them to me?" he said slowly. She was aware of his eyes on her, but she didn't look at him as she brought the laundry bag to the side of the bed.

He took it from her, reached in, and hurled the shaving equipment across the room. Lisa started. He pulled out the Koran. "Look at me!" he commanded.

She glanced up, and he placed his hand solemnly on the Koran, his eyes burning into hers. "I swear to you on the Holy Koran," he said venomously, "that you will pay a hundred times for tonight and for all that has passed." He held her fixed in his pledge of vengeance. Then he turned to Sandra. "And this oath I make to you *too*," he said bitterly. "On the word of Allah."

Then he put the Koran on the bedside cabinet, knocking over the flowers. "Now get out." He sneered. "I'm going to sleep."

Chapter 18

The next day and a half Lisa spent hour after hour writing postcards and letters, to "Mom" only. Most of them she did in a numb stupor, only Adam's encouragement and suggestions keeping her going. Every once in a while the reality of her father's death sank in, and with it came the sense of her mother's loneliness, and she became so depressed that she felt nothing in her life had worked. She was a failure in everything, even the simplest things, like being a good daughter. Leaving her parents for years seemed so easy as a young college graduate, but as she herself had grown older, she realized how punishing it must have been for them. Now her poor father was never to see her again, and she knew how much he had doted on her.

Here she was, almost thirty, locked in a passionate, deceptive relationship with a man she had come to believe was too basically decent to pour out his love to someone who was only using him physically, mentally, and politically, someone whose job was to betray him.

And she had even bumbled that so she might not ever be able to do what she was assigned to do, but failure or not, she would still betray him and reduce the life he had built to ashes.

Even Adam couldn't drag her out of these moods. Even the memories of the tiny graves of Sophie and Ben. The best Adam could do was to press her to keep writing, and slowly the numbness returned. Again he kept the size of the stack discreetly from her, but she knew Yassi would be a college graduate before they had used the last of them.

They had visited Youssef on the first day, in the afternoon, after he had come out of the operation. More flowers, and Swiss chocolates. Lisa told him that she'd called Le'ith and told him about the accident and that Youssef was not to worry. They expected Reena to come down from Paris sometime that day or the next.

In his semidrugged state there was less fire in Youssef's anger, but he still watched her as though he might pounce on her and beat her to a bloody pulp at any moment.

"And I suppose you told my loving elder brother that I had been out drinking with a woman and been hit by a car," he said as though adding up the score against her. And Lisa blushed because that was exactly what she had said. Youssef simply nodded.

Sandra asked how his operation had gone, and he turned to Lisa with his answer. "He said he had to put clamps in my bones, but if I'm careful and let them heal properly, within *a year or so* my leg could be as strong as ever." He had lingered punishingly over the words, another addition to the tally of retribution.

The visit was as short as they all wanted. Lisa and Sandra left with courteous platitudes about hoping he would feel better soon. Youssef didn't respond.

Lisa went on her own to meet Reena at the airport. They would of course have to go to the hospital, and neither Lisa nor Adam thought it would be wise to expose Sandra to some kind of accusation before Reena. Given Youssef's temper, he might do that even if it was not his plan. If he did intend to tell Reena what he believed, it was still better that Sandra not be included. Reena had memories of the Sandra at the "funeral" lodged in her mind that would be a better defense than a false denial in the flesh no matter how skillful. Rather than take a chance, Adam had Sandra write a note of regret to Reena that she'd had to leave before she could see her again. Sandra departed Geneva only a few moments before Reena was due to arrive.

Though she knew how precarious her position was, Lisa was almost eager to see Reena. Since Jineen's wedding their relationship had developed so they could admit almost the worst about themselves and still remain friends. Reena had twice come to the valley to visit. She enjoyed the physical freedom of the place, but she shook her head in wonder at

Lisa's attachment to it. "What do you do with yourself except fuck Le'ith when he isn't too tired?"

Lisa responded that Reena didn't appreciate how much was going on because she hadn't seen it in the beginning. Lisa's mud brick day shelter had only one room at the time of that visit, the desalinization plant was being constructed, and only a few acres of the buffalo gourd had been set down with water hauled all the way from the compound.

"Holy God"—Reena had laughed—"if it was worse than this in the beginning, you must be a closet Bedouin!"

The second time she came, Lisa had driven her out to the hydroponic greenhouse and shown her all the growth now that they had some water. She made her get out of the Land Rover and walk among the dates and the palms. They had five goats now, but Jekyll and Hyde always followed Lisa whenever she was near and trotted after them into the palm orchard. Reena kept trying to shoo them off, but they would only raise their lips and bawl at her—and then follow on.

"Praise Allah," she cursed. "You must even be feeding the goddamn goats." Lisa laughed, tossed the goats some scraps from the Land Rover, and then drove Reena out to the desalinization plant, where they watched the Yemeni laborers working the pipes as they dug deeper for more water. "Our gold," Lisa repeated proudly. That branch of the valley was the ugliest part of the farm, not only because of the machinery but because it was spotted with pools of oil from the tankers that made regular visits to supply the two generators; oil in Saudi Arabia was cheaper than water so it was treated more carelessly. It smelled like an ill-kept garage, but Lisa was proud of it all.

As she had the first time, Reena had brought along some hashish, and when they returned to Lisa's air-conditioned quarters, which now had three connected rooms, including a shower, Reena took out a cigarette case of already rolled joints, and they started laughing even before they'd lit up. "I never could understand why you married Le'ith"—Reena grinned—"but now I find out that underneath that glamour girl exterior you're a fucking farmer." They both burst into laughter.

"It's *true*," Reena insisted. "Here I picture you as this patrician bitch from Philadelphia, only interested in country club dances, trips to Europe, wearing the deepest décolletage Bergdorf's offers, and cuckolding your husband with the tennis pro, and lo and behold, it turns out you're not only bedazzled by camel shit as fertilizer, but you go orgasmic over an ugly goddamn buffalo gourd, you carry scraps for a couple of mangy goats, and you expect me to pass out with envy when you show me a factory yard that looks like an industrial dump!''

Lisa's face ached with laughter.

"You're living in a mud hut, girl! And you tell me breathlessly that it's got *three* rooms! And even *then* Le'ith makes you sleep in the tent! In all my time in America I never met a hillbilly. I have to bounce ass three hundred miles across the desert to discover one, and all the time it's been disguised as this blond bombshell direct from a California beach party."

Lisa had doubled up and was coughing from laughing and smoking at the same time. "Talk about sophistication," Reena mocked after a deep draw and a convulsion of her own husky laughter, "Le'ith'll bring in the cattle next, and you'll be squatting outside the tent getting your kicks from feeding a flea-ridden calf from a bottle!"

"I'm—I'm looking forward to it!" Lisa stuttered, and they both rolled over laughing.

They had talked about everything that night. Reena had even spoken openly about her little affairs with some of the young wives. She said she'd lost her certainty about what she was. She had loved men and liked women, but now, when she went West and took up with some man, she found herself thinking of some young bride's soft flesh and their uncomplicated passion. Everything was so difficult with men. By the time you truly got intimate with them and could actually relax, either you were tired of them, or they were tired of you, or the whole thing became stupidly routine and very dependent on some guy's ability to keep an erection, a problem one never had with a dildo.

Lisa had laughed off and on through the night until her stomach actually ached. Those two trips to the valley farm had made them companions, and when Lisa went to Riyadh, they always functioned together like old friends or even, Lisa admitted to herself, like sisters.

Lisa was certain that if Youssef ever exposed some proof of the truth about her—and she had still done nothing—Reena would fight for her release without some fatal punishment.

When she'd cleared customs and come through the gate, Reena grinned at Lisa, and they hugged each other. "So my brilliant half brother has managed to do something stupid again," she said.

"Well, it was an accident," Lisa said. "Do you want to go to the hospital first, or would you rather go to the hotel?"

"Oh, let's go to the hospital and get it over with," Reena replied. She sounded tired, and looked it too.

In the cab she sighed and told Lisa, "You don't know how much trouble this buffoon has caused. I was in Paris shopping with Ulti, his lovely first wife, whom he now largely neglects—except for a beating or two—for the fresher charms of Ayesha. So Rashid has had to fly to Paris to accompany her home. I had to wait for his plane, which is why I'm so late—Well, that isn't true. I'd never have come at all if I had my way, but we did have to wait for Rashid's plane." She turned to Lisa. "And your jealous husband does not want you to remain in Geneva after your aunt leaves even if *I* am here. I think he correctly believes I will try to lead you astray." She nodded to Lisa. "I'm sure I'd pick up a better quality of man with you as my partner."

Lisa laughed. Reena was trying to be lighthearted, but something was obviously wrong in her life.

"Anyway," she went on, "the young lion is flying up here tomorrow morning to take you back to your goats and buffalo gourd."

Lisa's heart flipped. Youssef might vent his spleen on Reena, and there was every chance Reena would not say anything to Le'ith. But if Le'ith went to the hospital and the broken leg was hurting badly, there was no predicting what Youssef would do. He so envied Le'ith, and he was so fiercely angry with her.

Youssef affected to be pleased to see them both and even thanked Reena for agreeing to stay in Switzerland until he was well enough to go home. When he told her how Lisa and her lovely aunt had brought him flowers and candy, he wasn't subtle enough to make his gratitude sound genuine, but gratitude wasn't much in his character, and Reena noticed nothing at all.

Lisa had been able to get Reena a room at the hotel, and when they got there, Reena wanted Lisa to join her for dinner in her room. She was too tired to face the dining room. They ordered and chatted about Sandra's having to leave and unfortunately missing her and Le'ith as Reena unpacked.

After the service waiter had opened the wine and left the room, Reena lifted her glass to Lisa. "Here's to us," she said wistfully.

They touched glasses and drank. "Can you tell me what's the matter?" Lisa asked sympathetically.

"Sure," Reena responded. "I'm in love. And as usual, it isn't working out."

"Is it a Western man?"

Reena looked at her over her wineglass. "It isn't a man, Lisa. . . . You might have guessed that after all my trifling with others' emotions, Allah would contrive to punish me in a suitable way."

Her dejection was so profound that Lisa was as touched by the vulnerability under that hard-shell exterior as she had been when Reena had told her the story of her father's leaving her in the desert. There was also a little twinge in her own consciousness about "trifling" with others' emotions and the punishment God—or life—might contrive for it.

"Is it someone at home—or here?" she asked.

Reena laughed. "Oh, it's someone at home—*really* at home."

"In Ummi's harim?" Lisa asked in apprehension.

Reena looked at her, then grinned and shook her head hopelessly. "It's Ulti," she said.

"*Youssef's* Ulti . . . ?" Lisa stammered.

"To me, the most beautiful woman in the world, even including you."

"Have—have you—"

Reena smiled. "Yes, we have. We've made love at the compound, in Riyadh, in Paris, but she wants it to stop."

She was lost in her despair again. "She loves Youssef." She huffed cynically. "Can you believe that? Above all she wants to give him a son, and she believes that will bring him back to her bed. . . . That callous, brutal pig who couldn't say a nice word to her unless it was prompted by lechery, he is what she wants, and she's afraid that if he ever finds out about us, he will turn from her forever." She sighed glumly. "I wonder if God will punish me for wishing that car had done something a bit more 'fatal' to my charming half brother. . . . Probably. Perhaps I should just wish it had hit him a little higher." She forced a smile.

She looked up at Lisa, who was staring at her in confusion and sympathy. "Don't worry," Reena said, her husky voice slipping into its usual ironic cast. "I'll get over it—or I'll die, that's all."

Chapter 19

Youssef did not tell Le'ith anything about Lisa in Geneva. But it was not long before she learned the reason for his restraint, and it was as she had guessed.

Three weeks after she had returned to the valley, Grandfather died. Le'ith had been with him in Riyadh. The custom in Saudi Arabia is to bury the dead quickly, but they flew Grandfather and his two surviving wives to the compound and set the funeral back a day so that Le'ith's uncle Sabah could fly from San Francisco.

They hadn't yet strung a telephone line to the valley farm, but the foreman and several others had CB radios, and it was Zia, who had been with them from the beginning, who brought Lisa the news. She and Bushra were to be driven back to the compound, and Zia was to be her driver. He had never driven the Land Rover before, and there was an irony in her sitting in the chador and veil showing him how to work the gears.

He made a shaky start, but once they were on the single-track road, he drove swiftly and confidently. Lisa was a jumble of nerves. She told herself that unless he had proof positive, she could win out over any accusations Youssef could make. But now that she thought the moment was near, her certainty waned.

The harim was crowded with relatives, all wailing and crying. She made her obeisance to Ummi and Huda, who both hugged her, crying anew.

Jineen, happy with her husband now and heavily pregnant, could not keep her smile of joy from Lisa. Only when she actually spoke of Grandfather and remembered his chasing her around the palm trees when she was a little girl did she cry.

Reena was in genuine mourning, smiling wanly at Lisa and holding her hand. "He was an older Le'ith," she said. "I loved him very much, and I would have been far less free without him. He was always so vigorous and so much in command. . . . Time goes too fast . . . I wish it would stop." Her eyes had gone to Ulti, but she turned away and walked on with Lisa.

The mosque at the compound was the size of a small chapel. The men washed their hands and feet at a wooden trough that was fed with a spigot faucet. Inside, the body of Grandfather—Sheikh Ibrahim ibn Muhammad Safadi—lay in a white linen shroud on the floor of the mosque, its head facing Mecca.

The imam, flown from Riyadh, stood behind it, and just behind him stood Le'ith, his father, Uncle Sabah, Youssef, Prince Anwar, Rashid and Harhash's younger children, Abdel and Ahmad. Behind them the mosque was crowded with cousins and workers and some elderly sheikhs who had flown from Riyadh and Jidda and Dammam. The imam began with the opening prayer. "All praise is due to Allah, the Master of the Day of Requital. Thee do we serve and thee do we beseech for help. Guide us on the Right Path, the Path of those upon whom thou hast bestowed favor."

And all knelt, their heads to the floor.

After the ceremony the body was carried by Le'ith, his father, Uncle Sabah, and Rashid to the plain, unadorned graveyard. Lisa was with the women who followed, wailing their laments. Youssef, who limped angrily on a crutch in the chaotic maelstrom of mourners, had another score to settle with her. He should have been one of those bearing Grandfather's body, but his leg had not healed enough to take even his own weight yet.

There was no casket. Just a white linen shroud, and Grandfather's face was exposed. Showing their respect and grief, all the men repeatedly surged in to touch the shroud, making the pallbearers weave and stagger. It was frenzied and melodramatic in the way Saudis can sometimes be in the face of grief, but Lisa could see that however ritualized, there was genuine mourning on the faces of many inside the family and out.

As she was jostled along with the other women, anonymous in her chador and veil, she realized that she too had been touched by whatever quality it was that made Grandfather so powerful, yet loved by so many. To her he was always kind and seemed amusingly pleased that she was there. She knew he had a reputation as a great warrior in his youth, fighting at the side of Abdul Aziz when the great conqueror was past his prime and Grandfather was a strong and muscular youth. How many heads he had chopped off, she could not imagine. She knew too that he was an enemy of Israel, not out of some passion, just on principle.

All in all she had felt secure with him at the head of the family, and she was glad that it was Le'ith and not his father or Uncle Sabah who was destined to take his place.

At the graveyard there were no markers or monuments. The procession moved to a newly dug grave with a large pile of stones next to it. Grandfather's body was placed on the ground. The imam bent and freed the shroud entirely from his face. It was to be the last look, and all the relatives sang out a piercing wail of lament.

Then the imam spoke. He said the words flatly, unemotionally. "He was a man who honored Allah, who was fierce in warfare but generous to the poor and just to all. From the time he was a boy he could recite the Koran by heart. He was a true son of Abraham and a follower of the Prophet."

There was a moment's pause. Then Le'ith turned and started to walk back to the compound. The others followed. Only the imam remained.

When everyone was gone, he covered Grandfather's face. The two workers lowered the body into the grave and stood stiffly as the imam spoke.

"You are Sheikh Ibrahim Safadi, son of Ali al Muhammad. You are a Muslim, one who submits to the will of God. You believe in one God and that his Prophet was Muhammad. . . . God save you." He paused for a moment, then left the graveyard. The two workmen climbed out of the grave and began to fill it with stones.

The harim was, but for a few whispers, almost silent when they all returned. Huda hobbled around, quietly telling each guest what the sleeping arrangements were. She had been close to Grandfather and of them all was probably the most affected by his loss and the nearness of death. She was the one Lisa had come truly to love, reminding her so much of her Bubbie, her father's mother, and when she came to her to tell her that Jineen would be sharing her house that night, Lisa squeezed her, and both their eyes were wet when she moved on.

After they had eaten, Lisa and Jineen went to the house and lay on the bed. Fatima and Latifa kept coming in to see if they were ready to get out of their clothes, but Lisa just shooed them away. Jineen chatted aimlessly about Grandfather, about how she prayed she would have a boy, how generous Ossama was in letting her come back to the compound, for as happy as she was, she still missed it. And missed Lisa and Le'ith.

Lisa half heard her. Her mind was on Youssef and what might be going on among the men. Jineen finally wound down in exhaustion, and they let Fatima and Latifa put them in their nightgowns and were ready to go to sleep when a huge ruckus arose across the compound. There was shouting and the crash of glass and someone's voice shouting, "In the name of Allah, remember Grandfather!"

The cursing and shouting continued only slightly subdued. Lisa had an insane urge just to run. To run across the desert or perhaps take the Land Rover and drive to the valley, where she felt, equally madly, that somehow she would be safe.

Jineen was already half asleep. She rolled over and said, "What's the matter?"

"I don't know," Lisa whispered. "It sounds like an argument. Maybe they're splitting Grandfather's estate. Go to sleep. We'll know all about it in the morning."

Jineen touched her face affectionately, patted her own swollen belly, and was mildly snoring in seconds.

Lisa could not sleep, even after the shouting had stopped. She tried to control her fear. It was no good trying to think it was something else. If it was Youssef telling Le'ith what he believed, she had to be prepared to speak to Le'ith without blushing, without nervousness, without giving herself away by any sign of fear or hesitancy. She had felt she would be so good at it. She had "acted" loving him almost flawlessly and with no sense of panic.

Now the stakes were higher, much higher, and she didn't know if Youssef had some big surprise up his sleeve.

She tried deep breathing and repeating a mantra over and over, but she was still tense and full of dread when she heard a soft knock on her door.

She got up and slipped on a robe, moved to the sitting room, turned on the light, and threw her shoulders back, taking a deep breath. She forced herself to walked calmly and slowly to the door. When she opened it, it was a woman in chador and veil. She had started to come in when Fatima came around the corner.

"It's all right, Fatima. We don't need anything," Lisa said, letting the woman enter and closing the door. When she stepped forward, Lisa had recognized Reena.

Reena stripped off her veil and shrugged off the chador. Lisa was surprised to see that she was in her nightgown.

"Who's in there?" she said softly, nodding to the bedroom.

"Jineen."

Reena went to the curtain and peeked in. Jineen was sound asleep. She turned back and looked at Lisa almost as though for the first time. "I don't suppose you'd have any hashish?" she asked without much hope.

Lisa shook her head. Reena sat resignedly in a chair and signaled Lisa into the other. "You heard the eruption?" she asked.

Lisa nodded. Reena studied her again, like an unknown candidate for a trusted position.

"About an hour ago I was summoned downstairs. By that time only my father, Le'ith, Sabah, Youssef, and Najib were there. I have never seen Le'ith so out of control. His face was red, and his knuckles were bleeding. There was a smashed vase still on the floor, and the stand with the Koran had a broken leg."

Lisa was saying the mantra to herself over and over and trying to look concerned and puzzled.

"It seems Youssef accused you of being an Israeli mole," Reena said. Lisa frowned. "Again?"

Reena nodded coldly. "He said you had duped Le'ith from the beginning. That was in front of everybody. Apparently Le'ith leaped across at him and grabbed him by the throat. When they pulled him off, Youssef claimed you and your aunt had arranged to have him hit by a car in Geneva."

Lisa raised her eyebrows at that preposterous claim and shook her head. She kept repeating the mantra.

"Apparently that was the general reaction, nonsense, but Le'ith shouted, 'You're a liar and a *fool!*' That prompted Youssef to charge at him. He actually hit Le'ith with his crutch. When Father finally got them under control, Youssef said he had proof."

Now Lisa's heart was beating so fast her chest was thumping. She hoped she was only looking stunned and flabbergasted.

"And he pulled out a letter addressed to your aunt. It was registered, and it was *returned.*" Lisa shook her head and shrugged as if she didn't get it. Now Reena was looking at her testingly. "He said he had discussed you and the letter with Colonel Ansari of the Army Secret Service, and the colonel had said that was a regular method used by the Mossad. There would be no forwarding address, so your aunt couldn't be traced."

Lisa said, "But you've met my aunt, and so has Youssef. She doesn't have to be *traced*."

Reena nodded without conviction. "Apparently Le'ith said something along those lines, but Youssef went to the Koran and swore on his life that what he was saying was true. It shook everybody, especially Father.

"Le'ith shouted, 'You swear on a *letter*? You accuse my wife,' and, I guess, other such things, and attacked Youssef again, calling him a 'blasphemer and coward.' That really set them off. Even Father couldn't stop it, but finally Sabah and the others got control. Sabah said that he'd met you and doubted very much that you could be Jewish." Lisa thanked God for her blue eyes and blond hair. "Then he asked Najib what he thought, and Najib said he thought it was a joke."

Lisa cursed herself for never liking Najib. From now on they were friends.

"That's when they called me," Reena continued. "Youssef barked, '*You* think she's a mole, I know!' the minute I came into the room. I didn't even know they were talking about you. And as you know, I have no great reason to be very accommodating to Youssef right now. Father was just staring at the floor, so I asked Sabah what the madman was on about. And he told me roughly what had happened."

She looked at Lisa with some question in her eyes again. "You know that except for Huda and Le'ith you've become my favorite person in life. . . . I would accept anything from you—except that you could hurt Le'ith in this way. If you are a mole, I don't expect you to tell me, but I have always wondered why you married him and agreed to come here."

Lisa shrugged wearily. She had said so many times, but her heart was pounding again. What had Reena told them? She started to speak, but Reena shook her head and cut her off.

"I know, I know, you love him. That may be true, I'm in love enough right now, I'm so miserable when I'm not with her that I could see myself running off to Alaska and living in an igloo with her if she would only have me. But somehow I can't see you being in love that way."

"Maybe not that way," Lisa said as calmly as she could. "But the same underlying feeling that life with someone you love is better anyplace than a life with the wrong person. Now that I'm damn near thirty I can imagine that if Le'ith had returned here without me, I might have fallen in love with someone else in time. But at twenty-two I didn't feel that way." She knew how intelligent Reena was and hoped this was the kind of comment that would at least satisfy her.

Reena sighed; she still had doubts. Youssef had done his poison. "Well," Reena said, "I've seen you on that damned farm looking as happy as if you were at the president's ball, so maybe underneath you're as screwed up as all of us."

She stopped, and Lisa waited. But nothing came. Reena just stared at the floor, thinking and looking as drawn and desolate as she had when she came to Geneva. Finally Lisa had to find out.

"So how did it end?" she said.

Reena looked up as from a dream. "Oh," she said, "I told him he was crazy. In the beginning you looked so beautiful I couldn't understand your wanting to live in a harim, and the idea that you were a mole was as plausible as anything. But that was for about five minutes. It was clear that you were not only in love with Le'ith, but you even loved his damned goats."

"Youssef yelled, 'You're blind, you're all blind!' Then Sabah asked him when he had sent this letter. And Youssef started to sputter and finally admitted that it was over a year ago. 'And you bring it up *now*—at Grandfather's *death*!' Le'ith shouted. And that effectively was the end of it."

She looked at Lisa with that tiny trace of doubt and grinned despairingly. "I hope."

"I hope so too," Lisa responded. She was beginning to breathe almost normally again. "You know you warned me to watch out for Youssef the first day we met. I hadn't even seen your face."

They both smirked at that. Lisa got up and went over to Reena's chair. She sat on the arm and put her arm around her. "Thanks for telling me all this," she said. "I've felt very secure and welcome here, but even life on the farm has its up and downs, and when I'm down—and believe me it happens—the fact that we've become friends is more important to me than I can tell you. I do miss the West, and you are my West, among other things." She hugged her, and Reena clutched her arm.

Lisa knew that everything she said was true, and she prayed that whatever she might ultimately have to do, she could somehow do it without hurting the people she had come to love in this, her false life, too much.

They flew the next day to Riyadh. Le'ith piloted the plane, Najib sat in the copilot's seat, and Sabah, Rashid, and Reena sat with Lisa in the back. Najib and Sabah made some light conversation about California and San Francisco as they drove to the plane, but everyone was strained. Le'ith avoided looking at Lisa the whole trip.

His personal assistant, Khalid, was at the airport in Riyadh to greet them, along with several other assistants and lackeys. They all made ceremonial farewells to Sabah. Then Le'ith and Rashid went off immediately with Khalid. Najib said he would have accompanied the two ladies to the house, but a poor woman from Lebanon had been languishing three days at the Intercontinental Hotel, and he feared for her life if he made her wait another hour.

So a driver and one of the lackeys took Reena and Lisa to the family house. Reena didn't speak until they were in the privacy of the women's quarter. "Well, we're in a funny fix, aren't we?" She sighed as she shed her Muhammadan outer garments. "You don't want Youssef here, and I don't want him at the compound. Somehow that stupid ass has taken charge of both our lives."

Lisa was too much on edge to say anything about Youssef. "I suppose I'll be seeing much less of Le'ith and the valley now." She sounded—and felt—as depressed as Reena. Just wearing her chador and veil on the plane and being treated like a nonexistent entity at the airport reminded her how important the valley had become to her sanity, and seeing Khalid and the phalanx of subordinates waiting to do Le'ith's bidding as they had Grandfather's made her realize that her life was going to be circumscribed again by the rigid customs of this city she had long ago become bored with.

"Oh, yes, your little sojourn with buffalo gourds and mud huts is over, my dear," Reena said without much sympathy. "You'll be moving to Grandfather's house; it's more impressive for meeting all those bankers and ministers, not to mention royalty." She looked at Lisa with that tiny grain of suspicion she still carried. "You of course will be spending most of your time with the wives or the concubines, and you know from the times we've been at Grandfather's most of that company will be elderly and 'traditional.' "

"It sounds like fun," Lisa said ironically. "You *will* come and stay with us?"

"Not as often as you'd like." She was fixing a drink from the shelf hidden behind a panel of arid mountain scenery. She raised a glass to offer one to Lisa, and Lisa nodded. She disliked the taste of whiskey, but the thought of some kind of oblivion was too tempting to resist.

"I prefer younger groups, as you know," Reena reminded her ironically. "And when the chance comes, I've decided to make one more serious, funny, romantic effort to seduce Ulti from her misery . . . and if I fail, I think perhaps I need a long trip abroad."

It saddened Lisa more than she could say. They all would be suspicious of her now. It meant that her own life would be Le'ith, when she saw him, and trying to keep an eye on Youssef without a family ally.

Reena could read the dejection in her face and laughed. "Don't worry," she said, "when you move, I'll come along for a week or two and teach you how to whip those tyrant servants over there into submissive puppy dogs. Once you make yourself the real mistress of the household, you can at least be miserable in your own way. But you can't give an inch; they've got to fear your moods more than you do."

Le'ith came home very late that night. Lisa was sleeping, but very lightly because the moment she heard him greeted at the front door, she awoke. She wasn't sure he would come to her room, and she lay there waiting, her heart beating faster every moment. When he finally came in, he was in his robe and simply stood at the door looking at her. She wasn't sure that he could tell if her eyes were open.

"I'm awake, Le'ith, if you want to come in."

He came to the bed and took off his robe. She had to make him love her; she had to convince him that she loved him. When he got into bed, she put her arms around him. "I know how close you were to Grandfather," she said. "And I know from when I lost my father—and mother"—she had almost slipped but went on without a break—"that nothing much helps. But I love you, Le'ith, and your family loves you, and your grandfather thought you were everything he wanted you to be."

She felt some of the resistance in his body slip away. She held him tighter. "I know your life is going to change, and mine, but we have done so much together we can make this change too. I love 'our world' in the valley, but it would not be 'our world' without you. I want you in my world." Until that phrase she had spoken without a sense of duplicity, but she could feel the guilt rising in her as she went on. "And I hope you will always want me in your world."

Le'ith responded to her words, not her sudden feeling of deceit and hypocrisy. And the words were what he needed. He turned and kissed her. It was possessive and ardent and redemptive. He held her so fiercely she almost cried out in pain, but she clung to him, trying to reciprocate his ardor.

They made love, and she moved and whimpered and murmured his name and cried out in feigned ecstasy. They knew each other's bodies so well now that the pretending was mechanically easier, but mentally she was tortured by the act of doing what she had come to do.

When it was over and she was resting against his shoulder, he squeezed her and spoke his first words. "Lisa," he said softly, "your aunt Connie, is she your father's sister or your mother's?"

Lisa's pulse raced, but she tried to answer casually. "My father's." It's what they had agreed on long ago in Haifa.

"You know Reena has spoken so highly of her, Sabah would like to meet her."

Lisa's heart was racing. "That would be nice; they might enjoy each other," she said. "Though her idea of a woman's role in society might shock him."

"And vice versa." Le'ith grinned.

That little bit of humor lowered Lisa's heart rate twenty points. She was able to laugh. "Did he want her to come to San Francisco?" she asked, hoping against hope that was what they wanted.

"No, no," Le'ith replied thoughtfully, "he thought he would go up to Oregon and see her. That *is* where she lives, isn't it?"

And Lisa's heartbeat was up again. That was the address, Portland, Oregon, but Lisa knew the mail ended up in Haifa and was generated from Haifa. Where Sandra might actually live she had no idea.

"Yes," she said. "I've never visited her, and the last time she came East I was only a kid. Somehow at the funeral, and in Geneva, we always talked about *my* life. I don't really know much about hers, except that she's widowed." That too had been programmed in Haifa.

"Do you know her phone number?"

"Ah, no. Isn't that silly, but I've never thought of calling her." She hoped it sounded as genuine as she tried to make it.

"Well, she'll be in the book," he said.

And that terrified her. "Why don't I drop her a line"—she improvised desperately—"and tell her she has this admirer, and if he doesn't get through to her, perhaps she'll ring him?"

"All right, we can try that way too," Le'ith said sleepily. "I can't tell you what I have to do tomorrow." He yawned. "But I always sleep better after we've made love, so I guess you were worth the time." He nuzzled her neck, and she slapped at him.

His immediate doubts had been laid to rest, but now absolutely everything depended on Sandra. Lisa knew any letter she wrote was likely to be read before it left the house. One of the manservants always mailed the letters, and if she tried to take it to a mailbox, Bushra would have to be with her, and Lisa knew that however much Bushra might like her, her primary loyalties were to the family. And the postal service, like everything else in Saudi Arabia, was vulnerable to influence. Le'ith would see whatever she wrote, so she was going to have to tell Sandra exactly what she had told Le'ith: that she had an admirer in San Francisco, and if she didn't hear from him by phone, Lisa had *faith* Sandra would call *him*. He wanted to come up and visit her.

How Adam and Sandra would deal with that she had no idea, but she knew she had to send the letter tomorrow so that they had some time because Sabah would probably call Portland information the moment his plane touched down.

Chapter 20

Fortunately the next few days were extremely busy. The family business was really a large distribution conglomerate. It handled industrial and medical gases, automobiles and motorcycles, fertilizer, cement, electric water pumps, agricultural tractors and machinery, diesel pumps and electric generators; it even distributed household soaps, toilet paper, and soft drinks.

But since ultimately everything—licenses, import permits, land rights, even the right to incorporate—came from the Crown, the most important role of the head of the company was to maintain a good relationship with the members of the royal family controlling the various ministries.

It helped to be successful and produce wealth, but if you were close enough to the right people, it was not absolutely essential. Grandfather's genius was that his relationship with the relevant members of the royal family was almost avuncular. And with the King, the Crown Prince, and Prince Sultan, he was a man who had earned his privileges by fighting at the side of their father, and they treated him with respect. Beyond all that, he had made the business enormously successful.

It was all this that had led the Mossad to target Le'ith. And its judgment had been right because from the beginning Grandfather had made Le'ith more partner than apprentice. There was no person of importance, even the King, to whom Le'ith hadn't been exposed in working sessions. His restraint and his wisdom had made their mark. His one failing—his marriage to a Christian Westerner—had become the source of amiable teasing and thus paradoxically had become an asset. It explained in part Le'ith's rage at Youssef. If what Youssef said were true, not only would Le'ith's Saudi manhood be destroyed, but it would destroy his role in the business and probably the business itself.

In those first days after Grandfather's death it was essential that he receive condolences from all the right people in the right order. Like Grandfather, he was not a worrier and felt confident that he would make the right moves. But he knew his presence was necessary, and he had to establish his authority among the subordinates in the firm who would never have dared bamboozle Grandfather but were certain to test Le'ith.

Despite her overriding fear about Aunt Connie, Lisa had to deal with her own immediate problems. The move to Grandfather's house was complicated and urgent, and Reena had been right again: The servants intended to run the house their way and to put the young new mistress in her place quickly. But Reena had primed Lisa brilliantly.

It started right at the beginning. A truckload of personal things had been sent to the house, and Lisa and Reena followed to organize it and determine how to dispose of Grandfather's things. A manservant accompanied them and rang, as they told him to, at the *front door.* A woman servant opened it and stood openmouthed as they calmly entered past her. The head of household, a tall Pakistani, strode toward them with a look of shock at a faux pas he was going to be quick to rectify. The manservant who accompanied them was terrified. "*Said* Safadi's wife and sister," he muttered fearfully.

"Let me identify myself," the imperious head of household said, though he knew they both knew him well. "I am Moustafa, the head of household, and, praise Allah, always here to serve you." He bowed but then stiffened like a disciplining schoolmaster. "But it is the custom of the sheikh to have his wives enter at the women's entrance. I will have Simona"—he nodded to the stunned woman who had opened the door—"take you to that entrance and to the women's quarter."

He started to usher them out, but Lisa stood firm. She removed her veil coolly. It was shockingly bold, but no sin, Moustafa had seen her face before at dinners with Prince Anwar when they had dressed in

Western clothes. "Let me identify *myself*," she said in her now almost perfect Arabic. "I am Said Safadi's second wife, and the harim will be under my care. I thank you most sincerely for informing me of the sheikh's customs, but please inform the servants that I will enter the house by this entrance unless I choose to do otherwise. Now would you please see that refreshments are sent to the harim. I want to talk to my two grandmothers." She turned to the woman servant. "You will please accompany us, Simona." As she reached the stairs, she turned back to Moustafa. "I shall meet with you later, Moustafa, to tell you how I want our personal things arranged." And she led a veiled but chuckling Reena toward the interior stairs to the women's quarters.

And so it went with many challenges and return engagements for a little over two weeks. By then Lisa felt in charge in a way that she had never felt in charge of anything.

But it didn't still her fears. Reena stayed for almost three weeks, and Lisa dreaded her going, but Youssef had come to Riyadh. He stayed in the old family house and almost licked his lips as each day passed with no word from Sabah about Aunt Connie. Reena was unaware of Lisa's apprehension, and she longed to get back to the compound and Ulti. Lisa and Bushra accompanied her to the airport, and Lisa hugged her desperately before she got on the Swiss charter. Reena couldn't guess how much, but they both were in dire need of a friend; only Reena was going back to hope, and Lisa to fear.

Le'ith had been loving to her for four days after that first night when they returned to Riyadh, but he chilled suddenly, and the few times they were together spoke to her only formally and, when others weren't looking, studied her as though he were trying to analyze her very soul.

She guessed that Sabah had called Portland and there was no Constance Baylor listed in the directory. He might have followed that up by hiring a private detective to search her out, which would explain her brief little sojourn of acceptance. But now that there was apparently no "Aunt Connie" Youssef became buoyant, and Lisa could see a creeping malaise of spirit take over Le'ith's personality.

She knew he was managing the business well. Rashid had always worked at the family offices. Unlike his sister, he accepted his second-tier position without envy. He had been blessed with fewer brains but a good deal of common sense, and he made an ideal number two. Le'ith could have the ideas; Rashid was happy to see that they were executed.

One night, after the usual entertainments, he came up to the women's quarter to get his wife, Hayat, and to see Reena and Lisa. In admiration and amusement he told them that Le'ith ran the business the way he played soccer. He was always going ahead, and he could be as ruthless as a Mongol warrior when the need was there. He was more like Grandfather than any of them had realized. It frightened Lisa. She knew how dire his position would be if Youssef were proved right, and now that her life hung in the balance she feared that ruthlessness.

He never came to her room. They were waiting for some final proof. Late one night she went to him when he was in Grandfather's study. He was sprawled on the carpet, leaning on a large cushion, with a drink in his hand, staring into nothingness. He looked up at her emotionlessly as she entered. She took off her veil. She knew he still loved the look of her.

"Le'ith," she said supplicatingly, "these last weeks have been very tiring. I wonder if you would allow me to go to the valley for a few days? Everything is in order now, and I'm sure Hayat could manage the harim for a time."

Without taking his eyes from her, he seemed to weigh it a long time. Finally he said, "Of course. Speak to Khalid tomorrow, and he'll arrange a plane."

"Thank you," she replied. He looked so lonely and dispirited she was tempted to go to him and put her arms around him, as she had in the past. It was how she had won him, getting him to reveal and share the things that were hurting him. It was when he first allowed her to see the loneliness he felt in Los Angeles that she knew she was winning him in a way that went beyond sex or looks.

But she dared not ask what was causing his despondency now.

"I'll stop at the compound and pay my respects to Ummi and Huda," she added in propitiation.

He still hadn't taken his eyes from her. He simply nodded.

The flight to the farm was not totally irrational. A phrase of Sandra's stuck in her head when it became clear that Sabah had not made contact with Aunt Connie. She had said, "We've lifted people from more dangerous situations." Lisa knew it was not likely they could "lift" her out of Riyadh, but perhaps they could lift her from the valley. She had told them about it in Geneva, even saying it was a couple of hundred miles north of the compound.

When she left Riyadh, she was accompanied by Bushra and Le'ith's chauffeur. She told Bushra to tell the chauffeur to stop by the main terminal because she wanted to buy something before they took off.

The driver pulled the long Mercedes right up to one of the main entrances and parked with the arrogance Lisa expected. When he pulled open the door for her, she said they would only be two minutes and went in quickly with Bushra. They hurried to the area of shops, and Lisa gave Bushra two hundred riyals, and said, "I need suntan lotion up there because I'm outside so much. You go that way, I'll take this aisle. Buy whatever you find—the highest number, Bushra."

Before Bushra could summon a protest, Lisa had gone down the aisle they faced. She hurried along, then checked back to see that Bushra had taken the other aisle. There was no sign of her, and Lisa moved to one of the clerks and asked if there was a mailbox near. The clerk pointed back to a wall in the main area. It meant she could be seen from any of the shops. She had to take the chance that if Bushra looked, the back of her chador looked like everyone else's. She walked as briskly as she dared to the box and deposited another letter to Aunt Connie. Even with these precautions, she only dared write that she hoped Aunt Connie had liked Sabah and that she was taking a short holiday at the farm in the valley.

She followed two tall men back to the area of the shops and knew she had been unseen because Bushra was still at a chemist's shop, nervously trying to decide which of a dozen lotions to buy. Lisa made the purchase, and they hurried back to the car. If there was any chance of rescue, it was now in the mail.

It was late November, and she was able to take long walks through the valley. She would take the Land Rover and drive to places where no one was working, then walk through the fields. Sorghum was now growing where they had first planted the buffalo gourd. There were almost three hundred acres of it, and most of it had survived. In the little branch where she and Le'ith had first seen the oasis with the single palm tree, an orchard of growing palms and ten acres of a hybrid durum wheat had been planted. The wheat was only about knee-high, but most of it was surviving too. And the tentacles of the tough old buffalo gourd now lined the hillsides as well as the farther reaches of the valley.

She climbed one of the giant wheels of the automatic sprinkler to get a better view of it all. When she cupped the corner of her eyes and looked across the waving green stalks toward the valley proper, she could almost believe she was in California. There was even the hum of insects, and swooping over the fields, birds that had appeared from nowhere.

At night she slept in her four-room mud hut rather than the tent because she felt it was safer. She kept Bushra with her; she didn't want to be surprised all on her own. Sometimes she would listen to the BBC Arabic Service on the shortwave and think of the other life she might have had. Prince Andrew married Sarah somebody, who evidently was not a virgin. Three cheers for him. Pope John Paul had made a visit to a synagogue—the first time in recorded history, though it all began in a synagogue. Three cheers for him too. Donna Reed died, which was almost like her mother's dying, and it made her dismally aware of the passing years. *The Phantom of the Opera* was a huge success in London. The radio played some of the music, and she longed to see it.

But she found that of all the news, the item that affected her most was that of Reagan's admitting he had approved the sale of arms to Iran. She had become so afraid of fundamentalism that even in seeking some contact with the West, she realized her orientation was still locked in the Arabian Peninsula. Arming Iran threatened Israel, and it threatened

Saudi Arabia, and as more than two hundred dead marines testified, it threatened the United States as well. It was, she thought, stupid and frightening beyond belief.

For a time the arrival of every vehicle, especially at night, made her think her time had come. But one day slipped into the next, and though her anxiety never left her, she roamed the farm, sometimes helping planting seed or sorting the dates for packing or stapling down the tendrils of the buffalo gourd so they would sprout new roots, all with a paradoxical sense of melancholy at the thought of leaving it.

Except at three o'clock in the morning, when her fears often overwhelmed her, she truly believed that the worst Le'ith would do would be to send her back in some humiliating way. And she hoped, against hope, that a blue and white helicopter would appear and lift her out of all of it.

Then one day, just before sunset, she was walking in the shade of the palm orchard, Jekyll and Hyde at her heels, when she heard the sound of a plane. Again her first urge was to run and hide. She wanted to know what they'd discovered before she faced Le'ith. Suddenly she feared that maybe he'd sent Youssef. It would be, after all, Youssef's victory. And that *did* make her want to hide.

But as the sound came closer and she could catch glimpses of the plane through the palms, she decided to face it with dignity. She was unashamed of her purpose, and unfortunately her method was dictated by the state of war with Israel, which only Egypt of all the Arab states had ended.

She walked back slowly toward the tent. She saw the plane come in to land. She stood in the tent for a moment, looking at the carpets, the bed, the beauty of the silken surround, and she decided no, no, she would meet whoever came in the place she thought of as her own. She left the tent and entered her mud hut.

She told Bushra to stay in the front room, and she went to the second room that she had made into a bed-sitting room–cum–library. She took off her scarf and brushed her hair. She put on a long-sleeved black blouse and white slacks. She feared thirty like most women, but when she looked in the mirror, she felt only some of the naiveté had been lost from her face. The punishing marks of time were still ahead of her.

She heard Le'ith's voice shouting, "Where is she?" and one of the men responding more quietly, "There, *Said*."

She heard his footsteps, and he opened the door. "Where is she, Bushra?" he asked.

Lisa came out of the second room and closed the door behind her. "I'm here, Le'ith," she said stoically.

He looked at her almost as he had when he first met her. "You— you said you were only going for a few days," he said.

Lisa shrugged. "It's hard to leave this place."

Le'ith's eyes moved slowly from her newly brushed hair to her black sandals. "It's hard to live without you," he said with melting sincerity. He half grinned, almost guiltily, and Lisa, in her relief, ran into his arms.

In the intensity with which he hugged her and kissed the side of her head, she could feel his relief too. Sandra had done it. She couldn't imagine how, or with what ingenuity or cost, but she had done it. She had made Aunt Connie exist for Sabah.

When they went back to Riyadh, she found it difficult to believe that it had been only weeks since Grandfather had died. It seemed like years. Unexpectedly she found it easy to avoid Youssef. Le'ith was even more furious with him now that Lisa had been exonerated, and though Youssef sometimes came to the house, Le'ith never invited him to dinner and Lisa was never forced to leave the harim to meet with him. But however disappointed he was that she had escaped this time, Youssef knew and Lisa knew it was only a tactical defeat. He was the one person in the family who now *knew* the truth about her, knew she only had to make one slip and he had her.

Knowing his personality, she was convinced that his humiliation in front of Sabah and his father had deepened his hatred of her. So when Le'ith suddenly decided to make the hajj—the pilgrimage to Mecca that all Muslims hope to make before they die—she packed up and returned to the valley. It would be far too easy for Youssef to arrange dinners for Colonel Ansari and his wife and others and their wives. While Le'ith was gone, Lisa would have to manage the harim and put up with any cross-examination the husbands instructed their wives to give.

Le'ith had chosen this moment for the religious experience of his life because Nayra was almost due, and *Inshallah,* he was going to have his first son. The night before he left he had held Lisa for a long time in his arms, saying again how much he had prayed that she would bear his firstborn, how he had often neglected Nayra simply to give them more time.

She had been in the harim long enough to know he was actually being kind—not callous—in saying this. But being a Saudi man, in giving one wife a child, he felt duty bound to give his other wife a gift as comparable as he could. He told Lisa that he was going to build a home for her at the valley, one that would overlook their whole domain, and he had already ordered the workmen to begin.

It was a gift that delighted her, and she let him know it warmly. She was feeling an isolation again that only Le'ith seemed to ease. Reena, who could sometimes make her feel she had some life beyond pretense, had come back from the compound—and Ulti—filled with unhappiness and tears. She had failed, and she poured out her despair to Lisa one night—without seeking relief in alcohol or hashish—and the next day left for Rio and God knows where, telling Lisa she didn't know when, if ever, she would return.

When Lisa got to the valley, she discovered the workers had already moved the tent out of the work site to a place below the oasis, and she and Bushra made it their home because her own little palace, which had grown by another room for Bushra, had already been knocked down. Lisa was amazed at how desolated she was by its disappearance. Some of the mud bricks had been tossed carelessly down the hillside, and she retrieved one to keep as long as she was in Saudi Arabia—and even longer if she could arrange it.

Le'ith had ordered a television disk too. It was not permitted, and it was a sign of his growing power that he was trusted to receive programs that hadn't passed through the censorship of the government channel.

Lisa thought she might catch up on the world or even find some comedy show from England or an American basketball game on the Armed Forces Network, but to her surprise, what entranced her, and held her before the set, came from the Saudi government channel itself.

It was showing the annual pilgrimage to Mecca. It began with the planeloads of pilgrims from India and Malaysia and Indonesia, of course, but also from Africa and South America and the Balkans and Russia and even some from China and the United States.

It was frightening—if you were Jewish—to think of all the Muslims there were in the world, at least as the world's animosities stood now.

But her fascination was not with that; it was the thought of Le'ith going through these acts. They were not as obsessively ritualistic as those of the Hasidim at the Wall in Jerusalem, but as a whole, the ceremony suggested a depth of belief that she only came remotely close to at Rosh Hashanah and Yom Kippur.

The TV showed a great throng, of which Le'ith was part, she knew, on the Plain of Arafat, praying to Mecca, the city where no non-Muslim can set foot. It was a sea of white, with here and there a car or a bus or truck or a row of tents rising above the landscape of kneeling pilgrims, each one, from Caucasian to darkest African, wearing the ihram, the white garment of Abraham. Each was praying individually, you could tell as the camera panned along the endless rows, but an imam in the studio was explaining what the prayers were: "Here is your book . . . read it. Enough for you this day that your own soul call you to account."

Later the pilgrims moved to what the imam identified as "the pillars of Mina, the white pillars of Satan." As the pilgrims passed them, they each slowly threw pebbles at them, the imam recited the two prayers they were saying—"Begone, Satan, you are accursed. We shall destroy the wrongdoers"—and, the imam proclaimed, the most important, "I cast stones on my weaknesses, O Lord."

Lisa cringed at the next step. The pilgrims were still outside the city near Mina, and were kneeling all up and down the little valley and the surrounding plain, most holding tiny lambs, but a few with baby camels and goats. One by one, at their own pace, they slit the throats of the infant animals, then raised their faces to the sky. The imam intoned their prayer: "Like Abraham, Lord, I offer the lamb to God to obey His Commandments and to give Him thanks."

It was nearly sunset before they finally moved into the Great Mosque. The courtyard was immense, and already the balconies and minarets shimmered with lights.

The camera gave shots of the throng, which looked like a great wheel of humanity moving around the black-draped monolithic Kaaba in the center. The Kaaba in Muslim belief was the stone on which Abraham prepared to slaughter his son, Isaac, as God had ordered. When the camera moved closer, it picked out the aged and crippled being carried, the blind being led. "Before the sacred stone," the imam narrated, "all are equal before Allah, rich and poor, strong and weak. And each mouths the same prayer as the circle turns, 'I am a part of the flow of life . . . it goes endlessly on. . . . How far I've come. . . . How far there is to go—' "

Suddenly there were shouts and gunshots, and the camera froze, and the circling mass of pilgrims, so seamless in their shuffling ring around the Kaaba, began to come apart, fighting broke out, and some fled in panic to the walls of the courtyard. Then the camera cut abruptly outside, where the huge mosque was a single mass of white light against the purple sky. But there was shouting and more gunfire among the seething crowd outside the mosque. The screen went black for a moment, a test pattern came on, and sacred Arab music.

Lisa watched for an agonizingly long time, but there was no announcement, no explanation. Bushra was already in tears, saying, "The *said* . . . the *said*," over and over again. Lisa left the television on but shouted to Bushra to bring her the radio. She turned on the shortwave band for the BBC Arabic Service.

". . . before our direct coverage from the Great Mosque was cut off, the riot seemed to have spread to the courtyard of the Kaaba itself. All direct communication from Mecca has ceased, but prior to the cutoff our reporter outside the mosque said there was fighting in the streets and police fire had evidently killed two or three. We will broadcast any further information as soon as it becomes available. In the meantime we have a report from our own correspondent in the Lebanon on Munir Makdah and the Fatah splinter group of the PLO, which advocates—" Lisa switched it off. She knew all she wanted to know about the Fatah.

Lisa sent Bushra for the foreman and used his CB radio to contact the compound. She spoke to Le'ith's father, who had heard the news. She asked him to call Khalid and send a plane for her; she wanted to be in Riyadh.

As she sat in the plane with Bushra, she thought of her first flight to that city and how she had felt that her only contact with her "real" life was Le'ith and how the thought of being in Saudi Arabia without him had been intolerable.

She felt exactly the same now, despite Reena and Huda, despite her valley. She loved Robert, but that was a different life. Le'ith had been so central to her Saudi life, she knew she would rather hurt him in the end, as she would inevitably have to do, than have him die in a religious riot.

Riyadh was full of rumors and anxiety. When Lisa arrived, Rashid told her that scores had died. There was no word from Le'ith yet, but that was because there was no official news about anything.

Lisa called Najib. His family was rich and influential too. It dealt in the real gold, oil products, but Najib enjoyed the wealth and cared little for the power, so a cousin was destined for Le'ith's place in his family, but Najib still had access to royalty and often to inside news earlier than Le'ith.

He was very amused that Lisa would call him directly. "Before you say anything sexually endearing," he said cheerily, "you should know that phones can be monitored here." Lisa paused for a second; she was after all seeking forbidden information.

"Aha!" Najib exclaimed.

"Najib, I did not call you about *sex*!"

"Ah, too bad. But I am relieved for Le'ith's sake."

"Najib! What have you heard about Mecca?"

"It's not a very good place to be right now, but otherwise it's a very beautiful city."

"Has anyone heard from Le'ith?"

"No, but we will soon. The news has leaked out that more than a hundred died, and there is enormous pressure from all the Muslim countries—and the Western press—to get a detailed report of what happened and a list of the casualties, of whom, I am sure, Le'ith is not one." He was sounding like the normally intelligent man he could be when his mind was on something other than women.

"Does anyone know what happened?"

"I can only say one word—the Iranians."

Lisa paused. "You *will* tell me the minute you know anything about Le'ith?"

The sincerity of her concern got to him. He hesitated, then: "Le'ith is organizing the cleanup with Prince Hakim. Now that *is* all I'm going to tell you unless your real desire is to rendezvous with me at the Intercontinental, in which case—"

"Thank you very much, Najib." That came with relief and sincerity too. "Next time I call we'll talk about a rendezvous in the valley—you, me . . . Le'ith, and the goats."

"Oh, Lisa"—Najib sighed—"I warned Le'ith when he first met you that you were one of those all-or-nothing girls. Say, those goats, what do they look like?"

"You ought to be arrested." Lisa laughed and hung up.

She was surprised at how relieved she felt, and the three days before Le'ith's return to Riyadh seemed to stretch endlessly. Aside from Le'ith's well-being, the big news for the family was that Nayra had given birth to a son. Rashid and Hayat already had a son and daughter. Ayesha, Youssef's second wife, was apparently pregnant, but for Le'ith's father, for Ummi and Huda, not to mention all the cousins and aunts and uncles, it was Le'ith's son they had been waiting for.

When Le'ith finally came back to Riyadh, he returned to the house only to change his clothes and spend an hour on business in the study with Rashid and Khalid. It was already late in the afternoon, and he rushed up to see Lisa at the last moment. He looked drawn but elated.

Lisa was furious he hadn't come to see her immediately. As usual, she told herself it was only because it showed that she hadn't made him love her as much as she thought.

But when he walked into the room, she was more pleased to see him than she was piqued. "I'm relieved to see you alive," she said. She had dressed to make him glad to come home.

He smiled at the look of her and took her in his arms. "I must go," he said. "I want to make the compound before dark. We'll talk when I get back." He squeezed her and turned to go.

"Congratulations on your son," she said.

He stopped and looked back at her. He signaled her to his arms and held her again. "Don't worry, you are my life. Nayra will make a fine mother, and you will come to love my son too." He kissed her head and left. She heard him rushing down the stairs, calling out, "Rashid, Khalid, let's go!"

She convinced herself it was all to the better. When she left, he would have Nayra and his son.

The child was named Ibrahim ibn Le'ith Safadi in honor of Grandfather. Le'ith came back from the compound after only two days, but he was full of himself and the child and told Lisa casually that he would have stayed a week but that the crisis about the bloodshed in Mecca meant he had to be in Riyadh.

It had been the Islamic fundamentalists from Iran again. After they had seized the Great Mosque years ago—in the first year of their marriage, he reminded her—elaborate security precautions had been set up, but they proved just barely sufficient.

"There were Iranians making the hajj, of course, even though they are at war," he said reflectively. "And Iraqis too. I could see that there was some effort to separate the two, but the truth is, no one expected trouble."

"How could you tell which was which when you all wore the same garment?"

Le'ith shrugged. "You can make mistakes, but the Iranians are not Arabs. They're a different race, they're Persian; they're more Caucasian than Arab. We can usually tell the difference."

He smiled wanly. "They were converted by conquest, and now they're the most fanatically religious Muhammadans of all. They wanted to control the hajj, to take it from the soiled hands of Saudis who are hypocritical allies of the 'Great Devil' America. . . . And they were like those men we saw when they assassinated Sadat. They kept coming, wildly, in a fury so unrelenting that death meant nothing. Two hundred and seventy-five of them were killed. And they killed over a hundred. It was a slaughter. Worse than before, except that they did not take over the Great Mosque."

"Well, I can see that the loss of life was terrible, but it was just an incident. Given the expectations about Iran, why is there so much panic?"

Le'ith snorted. " 'Incident'? Believe me, if Iran were not at war with Iraq right now, they would be at war with us, and Iraq would probably attack too, rather than let Iran take all the spoils."

"Because some fanatics tried to take over the Great Mosque?" Lisa asked incredulously.

"Because the primary duty of the Saudi Kingdom is the maintenance of the holy shrines at Mecca and Medina. If they fail in that, then the Kingdom will not survive. And the Iranian 'fanatics' who died trying to keep the Great Mosque 'pure' even now will become martyrs—not only to the Iranians but to fundamentalists here and in Egypt and Algeria and a dozen other places.

"We have a tiny population and a great responsibility, and how it's executed is the difference between survival and extinction—at least for this government. The biggest task now is how to handle the growing influence of the fundamentalists. What happened at Mecca was a disaster. There should have been no deaths, no martyrs."

"But if you used a gun, you added to it."

He nodded grimly. "Yes, because it would have been a worse disaster if they'd taken the Great Mosque again. Then the Muslim world would say this Kingdom could not be left with the responsibility of the most sacred places on earth. And believe me, the Kingdom would have fallen, and so would we."

When Le'ith came back to Riyadh, he was apparently the only royal adviser who was sure what to do and how to do it. The Iranians were a lost cause, but nevertheless he advocated assuaging them, having the King himself speak to the Ayatollah, saying he knew the Ayatollah would never approve of any attack on the sacred grounds, but however misguided the attacks were, the Saudi Kingdom deeply regretted the loss of life.

After that there was a continuous succession of meetings with ambassadors and heads of state from all the Muslim countries, all in the presence of the King, the Crown Prince, and Prince Sultan. It was Le'ith who outlined the new security arrangements, the issuing of rubber bullets and stun guns so that, Allah forbid, if such an outbreak ever happened again, there would be less loss of life. It was left to the royals to pledge that nothing was more important to them than the preservation of the sanctity and approachability of the sacred shrines.

Lisa could tell by the way he was treated that Le'ith's stature and influence had grown immensely. Even Prince Anwar, the royal who was closest to the family because his father had been trained and protected by Grandfather in the border skirmishes at the end of World War II, deferred to Le'ith in conversation. And many nights Le'ith would be invited to dine with other royals. Sometimes Lisa would accompany him, but only to the harims, of course, which she found much stricter—no alcohol, no hashish—though they were physically lavish and the games they played slightly more intellectual.

The age and power of the first and second wives, with their control over their royal children, and the freedom with which they discussed the politics of the Kingdom, made Lisa believe she was at last nearing the position Adam and the Mossad wanted her in. They seldom saw Youssef, but he too clearly believed she was getting near her goal. He spread rumors about her, and he knew no secrets could be kept in the harim. She could tell she was watched by everyone with a note of distrust, but Le'ith's growing power kept it all beneath the table.

She and Le'ith made only occasional trips to the valley, and it was always punishing for Lisa to leave. Now that change there had started, it had come rapidly. They had planted the first orange and lemon trees. It was Le'ith's idea to plant them along the line of the old riverbed instead of in symmetrical orchards. It made the fruit more difficult to harvest, but the weaving line of green along the valley floor added to the beauty of everything around it.

Her one lament was that since they were away for such long periods, Le'ith had put his younger half brother Abdel, who had not proved the brightest of students, in charge of the farm. In Lisa's eyes it made the valley a family affair and one subject to the shadow of Youssef's stories, rather than something that belonged only to Le'ith and her. But Le'ith argued that they needed someone they could trust absolutely to oversee things. If she had been in America, Lisa would have said Abdel didn't have the brains to oversee a high school picnic, but she had learned to be silent about an encyclopedia of things her tongue would have abused on the other side of the Atlantic.

Le'ith always stopped on the way to see his little Ibrahim at the compound. It was six months before Lisa was invited to do so. She had been warned by Le'ith not to praise the baby. That was an invitation for the demons to take him away.

Lisa had learned long ago that the Saudis were as superstitious as the Italians or the Irish. The women in the harims were constantly having their fortunes told. She first saw the object of Le'ith's superstitious concern in the harim. She had made her usual obeisance to Ummi and Huda when Ummi, smiling as if she had some great secret, clapped her hands, and everyone turned to the door of the quarter. A servant girl opened it, and Nayra came in holding the baby. He already had thick black hair and, of course, huge dark brown eyes. Nayra held him as if he were sacred.

Lisa went to them and hugged Nayra and kissed her cheek. Nayra was so proud and pleased it was impossible not to share in her happiness. Lisa was tongue-tied for a moment because she knew she could not praise the baby. Finally she said, "May I hold him?" Nayra could not have been more flattered.

The baby was obviously used to being handled and loved by many besides his mother. He willingly accepted Lisa's arms around him and gurgled back at her smiling face. Lisa had come to the age when not having a child was no longer just a casual decision, when it seemed more important than all the deadly hide-and-seek of her daily life. Now, feeling the warmth of the little body against hers created a longing far beyond the "little ache" she had felt across the years when she had played with or caressed the other children of the harim.

She squeezed him and said, "Oh, Ibrahim, Ibrahim," and kissed his forehead and cheeks. She looked at Nayra, her eyes saying all the things she was forbidden to vocalize. She knew that in that warm, lovely, soft bundle with the huge eyes she had a genuine rival for Le'ith's love now, but somehow it didn't matter. All that mattered was the ache she felt when she handed him back to his enraptured mother.

Chapter 22

"The source of all our troubles is America. And Israel belongs to America. Unless people see with their own eyes that the *agents* of Israel are shedding Muslim blood, we shall not be able to perform the duty set for us by Allah.' Ayatollah Khomeini." Le'ith looked up at her. They were having breakfast in the garden in Riyadh and he was going through some correspondence. Lisa was taken totally by surprise by the quotation, and she knew her face reflected her shock.

Le'ith shook his head gravely. "My brother Youssef believes you are an 'agent of Israel.' " Lisa tried desperately to change the shock of fear on her face to the shock of disbelief.

"As far as I know," Le'ith continued, "he's kept his suspicions in the family—except for Colonel Ansari. I've tried to keep it from you, but he's already caused a certain amount of mischief." He smiled wanly. "I confess I've lost more than a few nights' sleep over it myself."

Lisa reached out and took his hand. "Le'ith, you—"

He cut her off. "No, no, I don't. But he's taken some circumstantial things and woven a whole plot around them. I've always thought he was crazy, and I still think he's crazy." He grinned. "But marrying a Westerner—especially being in love with a Westerner—carries certain risks in this society." He shook his head wryly. He held out the letter. "He has asked that we invite him and Colonel Ansari to dinner again, and to make sure I'd agree he dug up that quotation of the Ayatollah." He looked at the letter again and could not keep the concern from his face.

"He underlined the word 'agents.' I don't know if the Ayatollah did or not."

Lisa's heart was beating too fast to do more than try to keep her hands from shaking. What would give Youssef the courage to call for another showdown after the debacle of his last attempt? The fear that he had found some new evidence kept her in turmoil for an entire week, but when the evening finally came, it ended in laughter that took her back to her early days in college.

On the night, she had asked Le'ith if he wished her to wear a veil, hoping to God he would say yes, but he shrugged the suggestion off. "No, you don't have to do that. Ansari has seen you before, and I'd rather both of them could see your face and perhaps grasp what fools they're making of themselves."

Lisa had then done what she knew she shouldn't. She went to her room, rolled two joints and smoked them slowly. More, she felt, would make her foolish. Less could not touch her panic. She knew that Le'ith was her only hope, and she could not look guilty or suspect, no matter what they brought to the table. As frightened as she was, she knew she would give herself away the first moment without the help of some sedative.

Even with the hashish, the sight of Youssef and Ansari together filled her with dread. They both were so sinister in their different ways: Youssef blunt and aggressive, Ansari malign and perversely secretive.

It began very sociably, with chat about this prince, that scandal, but then Le'ith showed his impatience. "You asked to come here tonight to discuss something," he said brusquely to Youssef. "Could we please get to that?"

Youssef was only too eager. "I suppose you both read last week about the murder of Abu Jihad by Israeli agents in Tunis?" This was the sort of news the papers and television did carry, anything that implied that Israel was lawless or menacing. She had seen a comment on it and was certain Le'ith had too.

"Yes, I saw what was printed about that," Le'ith answered.

"Abu Jihad was number two in the PLO behind Yasser Arafat,"

Youssef went on. "Number *two,* head of the PLO's military and intelligence operations. A minister of state, even if they don't recognize the state. And he was killed in his own bedroom in Tunis."

"Are you trying to tell me that Israel's Mossad is an effective organization, Youssef?" Le'ith said ironically.

"Effective and *ruthless,*" Youssef replied.

"All right, I think we can agree on that," Le'ith said coldly.

"Colonel Ansari has discovered exactly what happened. I would like you to hear it."

Lisa had her first flash of regret at taking the hashish. She couldn't see what the hell she had to do with Abu Jihad or Tunis and thought she might have missed something.

"Well, we've discovered that three Mossad agents with false Lebanese passports flew into Tunis and rented two vans and a car. They drove to a point about ten miles north of Abu Jihad's villa where a motorboat from a cutter offshore unloaded twenty more agents dressed in Tunisian uniforms."

"You're positive about all these details?" Le'ith asked skeptically.

"Absolutely certain. It's taken some work to reconstruct it all, but the combination of some witnesses, the van rental, footprints on the beach . . . They even had the audacity to cook a meal on the shoreline before they left for his villa, and they left the remains there. I think they wanted us to know exactly how 'efficient' they were," he said contemptuously.

Le'ith nodded, and the colonel continued. "They obviously had discovered that Abu had just returned from Cairo. Once the larger unit was onshore, an Israeli Boeing 707 flying a short distance out at sea jammed all communications. The agents went to the villa just after Abu Jihad arrived. They killed his chauffeur, a guard in the car, another guard in the house. Then four of them went upstairs.

"Abu Jihad was with his wife and two-year-old child. He had heard scuffling and gone for a pistol. When he turned, he was cut down by automatic weapons. The autopsy revealed he had been hit by over sixty bullets."

He stared at Le'ith. "As I said, efficient and ruthless."

"They did not kill his wife and child," Ansari said with a smirk, "although his wife begged that they shoot her too."

Youssef leaned toward Le'ith. "The interesting thing about this murder, Le'ith, is that it appeared to be led by a *blond* girl who photographed it all with a video camera. She appeared to be the leading agent."

Le'ith stared at him grimly, waiting. Youssef just stared back. He had apparently finished. When Lisa realized it, she started to laugh. And now the hashish really took over. She could not stop her giggling. Trying very hard to be straight-faced, she looked at Youssef, but the more glowering he looked, the worse her convulsions. She turned to Ansari, and he wore an expression of reproof that would have given a subordinate a heart attack but that only reduced Lisa to more laughter.

Le'ith began to smile. "I should explain that I told my wife of your suspicions, Youssef. I suspect she finds it 'amusing' that having discovered one blond Mossad agent, you should assume *all* blondes are Mossad agents."

And Lisa burst into another paroxysm of laughter.

Youssef was too incensed to remain sociable. He tried, but his anger ignited every word. "Maybe not *all* blondes! But Sabah and Najib and Reena all exonerated *this* blonde"—and he stood, pointing at Lisa—"on the grounds that her hair was fair and her eyes blue!"

Le'ith jumped to his feet. "Don't ever point at my wife or speak to her in that tone again! Now get out of the house! Colonel Ansari, I apologize for my brother and for my abruptness, but I ask you to leave with him." He glared at Ansari with all the fury that was missing from his words. Youssef started to speak, and Le'ith slammed his fist on the table. "Get out! And get out now!"

Youssef glared at him, but Ansari pulled at his arm, and Youssef stormed from the room, his face red with anger.

Lisa had stopped laughing. She looked at Le'ith. He heaved a sigh and then smiled at her, and she started to giggle again. Then he laughed. Then they both laughed . . . and laughed.

Lisa made love to him that night with such happiness she thought they ought to legalize hashish.

She and Le'ith were having one of their more serious arguments when it happened. Abdel had accused Zia, the Egyptian who had come to the valley with the first group of men, who had been their cook for the first six months as well as laborer extraordinaire, of false counting on several shipments of dates and, in collusion with one of the truck drivers, making money on sales of product that belonged to the farm.

Lisa could think of a thousand reasons why the miscount might have happened, one of them being Abdel's inability to count straight. But Le'ith had had Zia and the truck driver arrested and brought to Riyadh.

Saudis do not steal. You can leave a suitcase full of money on the hood of your car, walk across the street to talk to someone, and the suitcase will be there when you return. Money changers go off and have coffee, leaving their tables heaped with money, and never even bother to count it when they come back.

Lisa knew the reason. When you are found guilty of theft, the authorities cut off your right hand. That punishment would seem enough, but it is only the beginning. In Arab cultures, where there are very few inside toilets and toilet paper is largely a Western mystery, one uses the left hand for washing one's self after defecating. The concomitant of that is that one eats *only* with the right hand. To use the left hand is, in Saudi eyes, a disgusting act that would drive others from the meal.

So the punished thief becomes a social pariah, condemned forever to eat alone, even in his own family, and shunned on sight by every other self-respecting person.

The severity of the punishment makes theft among Saudis as unusual as a snowstorm in the desert. But the thousands of immigrant workers have to be taught the lesson by official warnings, by word of mouth—and by example.

Lisa knew that the courts almost always accepted the word of the accuser and, if presented with "evidence" as concrete as an invoice, would condemn Zia and the driver, Farid, with hardly a hearing.

"You can't do this to Zia," Lisa began plaintively when Le'ith first told her.

"I can do it to Zia, as I would Abdel or—or *Jineen,* if I thought they were guilty of stealing!"

They were having lunch by the fountain at Grandfather's house and, as usual, eating with their right hands.

"But you're *assuming* he's guilty. A miscount isn't proof."

"One trip maybe, two trips perhaps. *Three* trips, that's proof."

"I've seen them load those trucks, three or four cases—"

"Stick out like a sore thumb! They stole, and if we let them get away with it, it only becomes an invitation for others."

"They could've been stacked wrong! Why not give him a *warning?* My God, he's been with us from the beginning. You'd give more tolerance to Jekyll and Hyde."

"You come and see. It's very humane. They—"

" 'Humane'! To cut somebody's hand off!"

"Would you rather it was like America, where people break into your home and shoot you for ten dollars' drug money?"

"I don't think Zia did it, and you're going to ruin his life, and I don't think Saudi society will fall apart over a few cases of dates even if that idiot Abdel has the facts straight!"

"That's Western thinking, and it's *wrong!* The reason people don't steal in—"

Moustafa, the head of household, hurried out to the patio with unaccustomed abruptness. "*Said,*" he said, "you are wanted urgently on the phone."

When Le'ith came back, he slouched in his chair with a heaviness that signaled some disaster. From his expression she knew it was not about her. She reached across and touched his hand. "What is it?"

For a moment he didn't answer. Then he shrugged bitterly. "The madman Hussein has invaded Kuwait."

He got up and started for his room. Lisa followed right after him. She knew the threat had been in the air for weeks, almost since the time the UN had finally negotiated an end to the Iran-Iraqi War, but there was the assumption in Riyadh that Washington had warned Hussein off. "Are they just openly defying the United States?"

Le'ith shook his head. "Our people don't know. Some think their last emissary gave him the silent go-ahead."

"But why would America ever condone invading Kuwait?"

"They want to pacify the monster in Baghdad because they think he's better than the Iranians. They've been selling him arms; they figure, let him take a slice of Kuwait and he'll stop when they say 'enough.' "

"Kuwait's tiny. How do you take a *slice*?"

"The Kuwaitis are using angled drills to draw oil from a field that lies just across the border of Iraq. To be fair to the madman, he's tried to get them to stop by threats and appeals, but the Kuwaitis are greedy, and they've gambled that he wouldn't dare invade."

He dressed in an immaculate thawb and gutra with a mustard-colored silk cloak draped over one shoulder. Lisa could tell one cloak from another now, and she knew he had been summoned by royalty.

"Are they expecting you to go up and stand between the two sides and make them listen to reason?"

Le'ith laughed. "No, someone has reminded the Royal Council that it's only a hundred miles of flat desert between the Kuwaiti border and our oil fields, and if he decides to let his tanks keep coming, they need advice on which way to run."

Lisa grinned and blew him a kiss as he hurried out, shouting for Khalid.

Lisa missed all the excitement of the war. When Hussein had taken not his slice but the whole of Kuwait, there was a period of genuine fear in Riyadh. America threatened all sorts of things if Hussein's armor crossed the border into Saudi Arabia, but there was nothing to stop him, and if he took the oil fields and threatened to set them on fire if they attacked him, Le'ith and all those around him thought America would almost certainly be forced to make an accommodation with him, buying the oil he would then have to sell and telling the

Saudis they would kindly help them economically with what was left of their country.

In those tense weeks Le'ith wanted Lisa to go to the valley, but it was the very time she felt she might be called upon. Saudi Arabia was no friend of Israel, but Hussein was a dedicated enemy. Lisa dreamed that she might even be asked to do something positive. In war the enemy of my enemy is my friend. Could she assist in making the Saudis accept Israel as an ally? The thought that she might do something that did not involve betraying Le'ith and the family in some devastatingly destructive way was enough to lift her spirits for a month. Youssef came to the house from the compound and set up watch on her, and Le'ith tolerated it. But for once his younger brother didn't terrify her. He had overplayed his hand so much, and in this cause she was certain she could outsmart him if her call came. She waited in eagerness.

But Hussein hesitated, and gradually the alliance was formed, and ships started steaming up the Persian Gulf to Dammam. One night at an "American" dinner they laid on for Prince Anwar, an American general, and an attaché of the U.S. Embassy whom they all assumed was CIA, she heard Prince Anwar say, very casually, "Of course, if the Israelis were asked to participate in any overt way, all the Arab states would leave the alliance."

"Oh, we're well aware of that." The attaché laughed.

The conversation went on to other things.

So she sat out the war, even bearing some snide remarks when Hussein sent his rockets into Israel. "Well, the demon can't be all bad," one elderly royal wife joked as the women watched the televised views of the damaged houses.

The very best result of the danger was that Reena had flown back to Riyadh. If the country was going to be attacked by the damned Iraqis or anyone else, she was going to be there to poison someone's soup or give him a case of venereal disease at the very least! She had arrived unannounced, and Lisa heard her voice even as Bushra was rushing excitedly up the stairs to tell her.

Lisa ran down from the quarter sans chador, sans veil, and with her short-sleeved blouse unbuttoned at the top. Moustafa turned his back and ushered the other male servants out of the hallway as the two of them hugged each other like a pair of schoolgirls. The man carrying Reena's bags simply stood and stared at Lisa—luxurious blond hair, bare white arms, and svelte body—as though frozen by an image of the hereafter. Moustafa took him by the collar with one hand and the seat of his pants with the other and escorted him on flapping feet out the door.

Reena had slipped the knot of her depression. She hadn't found a "new" love, but she had intermingled religious experiences in the Andes and the High Sierras with romantic ones from Rio to San Francisco, where she was when the war broke out. She had met with Uncle Sabah and was going to go to Oregon to see Lisa's aunt Connie when Kuwait fell and everyone was saying there was no real way to stop Hussein if he decided to march on Saudi Arabia.

Lisa had never believed she would be grateful to Hussein for anything, but at that moment her spirit nodded politely in his direction.

Reena had an itch to run to the compound and see Ulti and hoped that she'd find her just a pretty, empty-headed nothing. But she was terrified of it too. "She's like a drug," Reena said. "I still see her image in the shadows, I can taste the softness of her mouth, I can feel my head under the urgent pressure of her legs. . . . I hope it's all in my imagination, dreams, and the reality will be terribly mundane and disappointing, but if it isn't—" She shook her head, and Lisa knew she was still haunted by that love that she had so casually and recklessly sought and that now possessed her beyond her will to resist.

But it didn't spoil their reunion. Reena had already heard from Sabah that Youssef, having tired of personally keeping watch on Lisa when all around him others were experiencing the tense intoxication of war, had pulled some strings with friends in the Army and gone to the United States as liaison with the two brigades being trained there. Before he left he had pointedly let her see him, Colonel Ansari, and another young Army officer talking intensely to Bushra. Lisa knew that anything Bushra discovered they would know too. Reena grinned ironically at the thought of Youssef in America as they puffed at the first recreational joint Lisa had touched since Reena left. "They teach them how to torture people to get information. Can you imagine, for once Youssef will be head of his class."

Lisa laughed, but the thought of Youssef's learning fancier ways to extract information chilled her. She didn't think she could stand even *un*sophisticated torture, never mind something exotic that Youssef might learn from the Special Forces veterans of Guatemala and El Salvador.

Lisa was grateful that while Reena was in San Francisco, Sabah had also told her that Ulti was pregnant. Lisa assumed the news would hurt Reena, but she was wrong. "If I go back and find her a bore," Reena said flippantly, "fine. She'll have what she wants, and I don't have to feel sorry for her. If she still knocks me dead, I've got two options. One, I just turn and run. Or two"—she leered—"pregnant women are always horny, and with Youssef gone for a month already, I can sensually try to reawaken her to someone who really cares for her."

"You think you *could* run?" Lisa grinned.

Even under the benign glow of hashish, the pain seeped into her eyes. "Oh, I can run," she said in that husky voice of hers. "If I sense that even now, when she's pregnant and can have her child, she still wants three nights a month with that brute more than she wants the life I can give her, I will seal my eyes like a young hawk and fly away to parts unknown."

Chapter 23

When the war ended, Le'ith was permitted a long holiday. He had spent most of the war in the allied headquarters outside Dammam, and his occasional visits to Riyadh were always filled with meetings and royal audiences. He had become one of the few the royal family trusted for an honest view of the realities, both of its enemies and its allies.

Lisa was always so concentrated on extracting information from him when he spent a night with her that she found their time together a strain, even though most of it was spent in relieving his (and her own) pent-up sexual longings and watching him sleep the sleep of the exhausted soldier.

When she looked at him closely, she could see a gray hair or two at his temples and a few at the very back of his head. They bothered him, but like the birthmark he so hated, they gave character to his face, and when there were more of them, he would be even more handsome, she thought. But she knew they were a measure of his concerned involvement, as were the dark stains under his eyes. When the end came, he needed a rest.

He spoke of going to Europe, and her heart leaped, but first he wanted to visit the family compound. Impatient as the thought of Europe made her, Lisa was delighted to see Huda and Ummi and Nayra and baby Ibrahim. He was walking now and a charming bundle of mischief. Reena had taken the risk and gone back. She looked smug and happy, and Ulti quite blissfully pregnant. Youssef was still in the United States, and Reena's only fear was that he might tire of Las Vegas and

L.A. What happened when that moment came, she didn't even want to consider.

Le'ith was now the established sheikh, and it gave a gravity to all he did, even in his role as a father. Young Ibrahim had to learn to kiss his hand before he got his hugs, and even he was silenced by the stillness and air of tension that arose when his father entered the women's and children's quarter.

The young sheikh's first duty was to hold the majlis, as Grandfather had done. He sat in the great hall of the house, making judgments on all the disputes and complaints of the workers and the families bound to the tribe. Lisa learned by word of mouth that he was almost Solomonic in his judgments on these occasions. He was not yet loved and deferred to as Grandfather had been, and for all his decisiveness, Lisa wondered if he ever would be. She only had to think of Zia.

Zia had of course been found guilty. Punishments were inflicted in the square outside the Great Mosque, and Le'ith had demanded she accompany him to Zia's. The scene reminded her of public executions she'd seen in movies about eighteenth-century England. There was a huge noisy mob, all freshly come from midday prayer on the Sabbath. The imams led the "guilty" out into the square, where the plinth for their punishment stood. There were three that Friday, each held by two guards. Zia was the first. He was pulling back but seemed dazed and confused.

"They've been drugged," Le'ith whispered to her in English. "You see, it's not quite as barbaric as you'd like to believe."

Lisa felt fortunate that she couldn't see over all the pushing, crowding heads to witness it all. But she saw the great ax of the executioner rise and heard the terrible scream that indicated the pain had penetrated far more deeply than the drugs. A huge cry went up from the crowd. Then there was a wild swirling of the heads and bodies, and Le'ith grabbed her arm, turning her and pulling her forward at the same time. "There! Look! Look!" he shouted over the yelling horde, and in patches of vision between shoulders and heads she saw four men in hospital garb hurrying the giddy, blood-soaked Zia to a long Cadillac ambulance, its lights flashing.

She jumped so she could see as Zia was put on a stretcher in the ambulance and immediately given a shot by a medic. Two of the men in hospital garb had piled in the back and began bandaging Zia's bleeding arm. Then the doors closed, the siren sounded, and the ambulance sped away through the crowd. Lisa saw two more just like it, waiting for the next victims. Le'ith had relaxed. He turned to her calmly. "He'll be taken to King Faisal Hospital," he said, "and he'll be released only when they're sure he has no infection and he's strong enough to carry on by himself."

Lisa was dumbfounded not only by his calm sense of self-righteousness but by the combination of medieval barbarity and high tech compassion.

From what she'd read of the brutality of life in American prisons, and what she knew of the fear of crime that haunted American streets, a fear that was nonexistent in Saudi Arabia, she could not fault the paradoxes of the Saudi system, but knowing Zia, knowing what would now become of him, she believed that Grandfather would not have acted with the rigidity that Le'ith had.

She believed that as time went on, and Le'ith became more sure of his strength, he too might be capable of rising above the book and become as confidently humane as Grandfather was. Ironically, "the book"—which was wrong, she thought, about Zia—was right about her. She should never have been accepted into the family. But she still admired the wisdom and magnanimity of Grandfather, even if in her case he had been tragically wrong.

They had only been at the compound for a week when Le'ith told her he didn't want to go on to the valley, he wanted to go to Europe immediately so both of them could get the family, and the desert, and the war, and the politics of the court out of their systems. Her heart pounded. She had thought Robert had become no more than a distant memory, but the possibility that she might see him again revived her emotion the way water brings dormant seeds to flower on the desert floor. She did not dare to ask that they go to Paris; she knew there was no way her voice could keep from betraying her.

But Paris was where Le'ith wanted to go. On the flight out, they both changed to Western clothes immediately and she was aware of how dignified he looked with his firm face and the temples of gray. He still looked a bit tired, and he held her hand for long periods of the flight. When this all began she never would have believed that she could have felt guilty about betraying him in any way, much less in the secret recesses of her heart, but watching him doze, his hand still in hers, she did feel guilty that all that was in her mind was the hope of seeing Robert once more, of touching him and being touched by him.

They stayed at the George V. The first night they strolled down the Champs-Elysees hand in hand and had a lovely touristy dinner at La Tour d'Argent, looking down the Seine through the long glass windows at the lights of the city and the Eiffel Tower. They danced, and as she watched the other couples she remembered what Uncle Sabah had said, how trips to the West would only incite in her longings for all she was missing.

It was true. She thought of being Robert's wife. She could be working for UNICEF, filling her days with what she believed was useful and beneficial, spending her nights in his arms, going to the Opera, dining with friends, showing him and the city off to her mother. How much she was missing—how painfully much.

The next night Le'ith took her to dinner on a bateau and while she was sipping her champagne, looking off at the city as it glided by, she became aware that someone was staring at her. She looked at him. It was a dark-skinned young man leaning against the rail down the deck from them. He was watching her so intently that she thought he was coming on to her, and then he turned away nervously and moved on. And she felt flattered. Even with all the beautiful women in Paris, she could still rivet some men.

But when she looked back at Le'ith she realized the young man's skin color was exactly the same as Le'ith's, and it slowly penetrated that it was a face she knew. She tried all through dinner to remember where she had seen it before, but she couldn't. Then, as they were leaving the bateau, she caught a glimpse of him on the upper deck. He was staring at her again, but the moment she saw him he turned away. But that brief glance was enough. She remembered instantly. The young man was the young army officer she had seen with Youssef and Colonel Ansari talking with Bushra before Youssef had left for the States. They had followed her. They would follow her everywhere.

She went shopping on her own the next afternoon and glanced in every store window to see if she could see his reflected image. She felt sure he was there, but she never saw him.

When she got back to the hotel, Le'ith announced that they were having dinner with Robert—did she remember him, one of the ex-soccer players who'd visited them during Jineen's wedding?

"Oh—oh, yes, I do remember him," Lisa said with feigned effort. "He was in advertising or something, wasn't he?"

"That's the one," Le'ith replied. "He's going to take us to this special restaurant in the sixteenth arrondissement. One of those places only the French know," he added sardonically.

Lisa primped for an hour before they left. She still wasn't satisfied with herself. She wanted to wear the jade necklace Le'ith had bought her for their wedding night—it was still the piece of jewelry that flattered her most—but she couldn't bring herself to do it. She wore an emerald lavaliere that hung down to the beginning of her cleavage. She thought Le'ith might object to the low-cut dress and the position of the lavaliere, but he only told her how appealing she looked. "In the desert you're like an exile from a more wondrous world; here you're a jewel among jewels, no man with eyes can fail to envy me." He kissed her softly on the cheek so as not to spoil her makeup, and she wished he'd snarled, "Change your dress," or "Put a chador over that," or "You look like an Egyptian whore."

Robert was not yet at the restaurant when they arrived. They were sitting at the table sipping kir royales and discussing the clientele when she saw the young army officer enter and scan the room. She looked away so their eyes wouldn't meet. Later, she glimpsed him at the end of the bar, trying to look inconspicuous. She realized that if she was ever going to see Robert alone, she would not only have to create an excuse to free herself of Le'ith, she would also have to find a way to elude this unwanted watchman. And what would he make of that: that she was meeting with the Mossad? But she was so eager for that moment to come she knew she would manage it whatever the consequences.

When she saw Robert through the window, her heart started to race. He made a great show at the door with the maître d' and she was grateful for it because it gave her time to calm herself a little. When he came to the table he shook hands with Le'ith and clapped him on the back; then he turned to her and stopped. "More beautiful than I remember," he exclaimed too loudly and clasped her in his arms. There was no hidden squeeze, but he kissed her firmly on the cheek.

The next two hours were like the gradual thaw of a giant iceberg. Robert was this dazzling obstacle in the path of her life's work—impressive, majestic, but something capable of sinking her and all she had given so much to achieve. And as he sat there opposite her, disillusion peeled sheaths of glamour from that brilliant white image.

He began by making so much of this intimate little café he had discovered, not seeming to realize that everyone who has ever been in Paris for three days finds an "intimate little café" none of the tourists know. And he was the same with the menu, ordering for them all in huge paragraphs of dialogue, questioning the waiter on every detail of the choices, then unnecessarily explaining it all to them in English.

He selected the wines with the same mannered punctiliousness. Lisa looked at him closely for the first time. Not a hair was out of place. His fingernails were manicured and gleamed with some kind of polish; his clothes looked like they had come from the cleaners five minutes ago. He looked more like a model than a man.

When he started to talk, it was just as it had been in the desert. He could not stop talking about his own life. He told Le'ith with a leer that he was closing a deal with one client for the use of Emmanuelle Béart as their spokesperson. If it went through as planned he'd have to spend *days* escorting her around Paris. Le'ith didn't know who Emmanuelle Béart was; neither did Lisa. Robert spent the next five minutes assuring them she was the young movie star most desired by men the world over.

And as he went on in a half-joking manner about the famous clients he was handling, and how his success was envied by his colleagues in

London, Rome, and Madrid, Lisa realized how hugely insecure he was. Looking at Le'ith—so calm, so self-contained—she could see how he made someone like Robert even more uncertain of himself. If Robert had had any idea at all of what Le'ith had been doing, even he might have realized how insignificant all his little triumphs in the advertising world were.

By dessert, he was ready to turn his attentions to Lisa. By now the iceberg was nothing more than a few scattered pieces of melting snow. He was incredibly handsome, and his eyes promised more depth than the man could deliver, but she could face his most ardent gaze with nary a quiver. He wanted the chance to show her Paris—his Paris. She realized, looking into those falsely romantic eyes, that he must attack every vulnerable woman as he had her. Each little conquest giving a tiny boost to the insatiable need to reassure his battered ego that he was half the man he projected to the world.

"Le'ith and I have so little time together," she answered, "I want to spend these days with him, even if he forces me to attend some awful soccer match."

She could see the blow it delivered, like an icicle in the throat.

Le'ith didn't take her to a soccer match, but he did take her to the races. Like all Saudis, he loved to see horses race. And for her the atmosphere at Longchamps, with its stunning, flirtatious women in their extravagant hats and dresses, parading about not as chattel but as empresses of the world, was like a bath in champagne. She loved every moment of it. Twice she caught the young army officer watching her, but it only made her smile. She hated the idea of being followed everywhere, but now that she had nothing illicit planned, she felt a report to Colonel Ansari that she had been nothing but an innocent tourist in Paris might do her a lot of good.

On their last night, Le'ith confessed that he had had enough of the West. He wanted to go back to the valley and take a real rest. Lisa could have stayed a year—or maybe ten, but she had to admit to herself that she too missed the valley. As they lay arm in arm in bed she thought of her hopes on coming to this city. How could she have been so intoxicated with the man? She recalled the night in the desert. He was so intense, so perfect. Half dozing it came to her that he was *one* Western man in the desert, singular, the personal embodiment of her chance to escape to the possibilities of that other life she might have had. And he came in such a glamorous package. In Paris, he was only one man of many—and a surprisingly shallow and inadequate one at that. Even the package was artificial.

She had been so besotted with him she might have risked her mission—even her life—for him. When she put that thought next to the image of him in the restaurant—an immaculate, burnished fop—she sniggered out loud.

"What's so funny?" Le'ith muttered sleepily.

"Oh, nothing," she answered. "Just Paris . . ."

He grunted, pulled her closer, and went to sleep with his head on hers. She was going back to Saudi Arabia without even a dream of escape.

Their house at the valley had been completed. It was not a palace, but it was beautifully designed, with Moorish arches, elegant pillars, the sound of water in every room. Cascades of it trickled down the sides of a rock wall in the main room; there was an exquisite fountain in the atrium at the center of the house and little fountains outside the windows of the bedrooms.

Every room that Lisa inhabited looked out over the oasis and the valley, silken drapes gave her privacy when the long glass doors were opened, and at night the roof of their bedroom could be opened to the stars. And it was "their" bedroom. It was not "her" bedroom, which Le'ith visited. It was a Western bedroom that had a dressing room for him off one side of it and one for her on the other.

It was a home only a millionaire could build, of course, but with the mature palm trees that had been planted around it and the long strands of bougainvillaea on the walls, it belonged to what was now the landscape, a fantasy Arabian home on a fantasy Arabian oasis, and though Lisa thought at first that it was too lavish, too ideal, and yearned a little for her mud hut, she told herself with a smile that she would grow used to it.

During Le'ith's vacation, she came to love the long rides they took through the valley in the early light of day or at sunset. He had bought two beautiful Arabian horses. Lisa hadn't ridden a dozen times in her life, and the horses were skittish and temperamental, but desert life gives Saudis wonderful patience, and Le'ith helped her and Jamalle, "Beauty," her swift, surefooted stallion, learn to move almost like one. Not only did the thrill of riding him take her by surprise, but because he became the vehicle for her truly experiencing the valley in a "natural" way, she came to love him more than any animal she ever had.

When they raced through the wheat fields, or wove in and out of the orchards, or just paused to look out over it all, Jamalle seemed to love it just as she did. He was handsome, graceful, a delight to look at, but Le'ith's horse took her breath away. Strong and majestic, like a Black Prince with a long mane and a glistening coat. Le'ith had picked him for himself and named him Saladin . . . so right for the look of the horse, so right for Le'ith. Riding beside them, she thought they looked like a sculpture in motion.

For days they both enjoyed it all, and then Le'ith was called urgently to Riyadh. On the day he was to leave, Huda at long last decided to fly down to see her investment. Now that they had a house with all the amenities she would at last make her visit. Le'ith stayed an extra day.

For all their enthusiasm Huda could not disguise that to her, their valley was not greatly different from the compound. The same miracles existed; the only real difference was the hilly terrain, and that was uncomfortable for her. She did like the view from their house, but she was clearly shocked that Le'ith and Lisa shared a bedroom and there was no "quarter" in the house. She told Le'ith she was making him a loan to add one to the structure immediately. And she scolded Lisa harshly for not keeping proper purdah when there were so many men around. When Le'ith left, the general impact of her visit was one of disapproval. They were youngsters who had been given their head and not used it properly.

Le'ith was disappointed, and so was Lisa. When they went to see Le'ith off, he whispered to Lisa as he hugged her, "Keep her here as long as she'll stay. It may grow on her."

"I never dreamed she was so conservative," Lisa replied.

Le'ith grinned. "We've become too Californian out here. For the sake of Allah, *don't* let her see you working with the men or riding in jeans!"

She shook her head. He kissed her, waved to Huda, and entered the plane.

When they returned to the house, Huda made the servants erect a large screen before the entrance to the two guest rooms, making the area into a miniquarter. Then Huda's servant, Om, cleared the kitchen of men and said that until a quarter was built, no men were to serve in the house at all.

Lisa bristled, but she recalled Reena's explanation to her when she first met Huda about rank and the role of authority in Saudi life. Huda was only doing what she had been raised to think was her prerogative.

To deal with her irritation, Lisa took Jamalle for a ride. She wore a chador. Le'ith had bought a sidesaddle when he bought the horses, but she'd never used it. She found it awkward and the chador uncomfortable, but the ride and the valley soothed her temper.

When she returned, she shed her chador and went behind the new screen and called out to Huda, "Sittau." It was as close as Arabic came to "Bubbie"; it meant "grandmother," and it was what Lisa had come to call her.

"Come, come," Huda responded quietly, "I need you." When Lisa went into her bedroom, Huda was sitting propped on two large cushions, looking out at the fountain in the atrium. She didn't turn but held out one arm, and Lisa sat beside her and Huda pulled her close.

"We heard all the stories about you being an Israeli," she said softly, not looking at Lisa, but stroking her arm affectionately, "but though Youssef swears they're true, I have never believed them. I know you love Le'ith, and I felt your need of family when your parents died. Your heart, my Lisa, I know, and there I feel secure for you and for Le'ith."

Now she glanced at her and stroked her blond hair. "But this golden head of yours is a wandering camel that has not found a home or a master yet. And that worries me very much."

"I feel this is home," Lisa responded solemnly, and snuggled down into her arms, where indeed she did feel as much at home as she had in the arms of anyone since her own Bubbie had died.

"Ha." Huda mocked her pleasurably. "But this valley, this place is your 'other' home. This is the West. I may not have been there, but I recognize it when I see it."

Lisa laughed. "Only a little West, Sittau."

"No. You have no harim; you share Le'ith's bedroom. Your face and body are seen by your own workers *and* workers who only come for a day or a week. What is your life when Le'ith is gone?"

"Well, I—I go to the fields and inspect the crops. I—I feed the goats." She smiled. "And I read and—"

"You inspect the crops with Abdel?"

"No. Abdel and I don't get along very well."

"You go only with Bushra?"

Lisa hesitated. "Yes, often."

Huda looked at her gravely. "And often you go alone."

Lisa nodded slowly. "Except for some of the drivers who are never here for long, none of the men are Saudis."

"They are *men*." Huda snorted emphatically. "Surely you don't ride in anything but a chador?"

"No," Lisa lied. "In fact I hardly ride at all." She hoped Huda wouldn't cross-examine Abdel on that. And if Bushra ever told her that she and Le'ith often swam nude in the pool of the oasis at night and that Le'ith was still the shy one about it, Huda would decide that the landslide was rolling fast and would probably move in to save the family.

She pushed her head against Huda's warm body. "We have tried to make a compromise between Le'ith's world and my world," she said. "Both of us feel it is fair."

"Nothing in life is fair. 'Fair' is for simpletons and those who have not lived. You will find as life goes on that you need the harim—need it for love and strength and for something to live for beyond your husband, who already has far too much to think about than your 'fairness.'

And it will only get worse with time, and if you have no children, you will wither here like an unwatered vine."

Those were thoughts Lisa had long wrestled with, so her spontaneous response would have been a grim "Tell me about it," but for Huda's sake she tried reason.

"All the West is not bad, Sittau. Many women and men have close relationships, are husbands and wives—*and* friends."

"They tell me of such 'friends.' More than half divorce, women are left with children, and husbands run off, leaving their wives to beg or work as prostitutes."

Lisa smiled. "Some women work as lawyers and doctors and even engineers. Not all divorced women in America have to turn to prostitution."

Huda could sense the teasing. "Ha!" she said again. "What about people living in the streets? What about young girls going to movie houses to see shocking films in the dark, and some even going with men who are not their husbands? And people stealing and killing everyone with guns? And drugs? Is all that 'not bad'?"

"None of that will be here in our valley," Lisa promised, turning to her seriously.

Huda touched her cheek. She paused for a long time. "In the desert we know that one stone starts the landslide," she said with true concern. "The best safety is in the words of Allah. I will pray every day for your conversion."

Lisa was touched by her sincerity and hugged her.

Later they dined together. Huda would eat only in her "quarter," refusing to go to the lovely dining area overlooking the oasis even if there wasn't a man in the house. "One stone starts the landslide."

Huda did not get the chance to let the valley grow on her. The next day Le'ith called to say he was sending the plane back for them. He wouldn't tell Lisa what the trouble was over the phone, but he did say that one day in the city had convinced him they had much more to worry about than Huda's approval or disapproval.

Chapter 24

L e'ith spread them on the table of his study. There were faxes to their number at the house and to Le'ith's office. Each showed a severed head falling from a body and a sword dripping with blood. They were drawn crudely, but with graphic force. They were designed to terrorize some- one, but whom? Lisa's reading ability was far behind her verbal com- prehension. She could make out "death" in the coarse scrawl at the bottom, and "men," but she had to ask Le'ith to read it for her.

"Death to all secularists, death to the men without beards."

"What does it mean?" she asked in alarm. "You?"

Le'ith nodded. "Since the war ended, there's apparently been an enormous struggle between"—he hesitated—"our own fundamentalists and the 'men without beards.' Western-trained 'secularists.' Rashid kept it from me because he thought in the end the monarchy was never going to let anything happen to all the 'beardless' products of Western edu- cation who were keeping the Kingdom running. Initially he was right, but then these sheets began circulating in the streets, at first a few, then hundreds. Then they were faxed to our houses and offices. Last week they were posted on the Grand Mosque—which means they have the support of the imams."

The personal intrusion of the faxes to the house sent a chill through Lisa, and the image of that executioner's sword striking at Zia's arm and rising bloody from the plinth was fixed in her mind. But what chilled her more was the audacity of the fundamentalists behind it all. Their power had seemed to have waned during the war. They protested the presence of American soldiers, especially American women soldiers, on the holy soil of Islam, they forced restrictions on allied religious ceremonies, but the general feeling was that the presence of so many outsiders and the daily view of them on television had created a loosening of the fundamentalist hold on society. But that perception was clearly wishful thinking.

"I asked you to come back because I'm going to have some gatherings here at the house," Le'ith told her. "And I need you to supervise the harim. This situation is much too delicate for Hayat."

"Is there any *real* danger from these?" Lisa asked.

Le'ith laughed cynically. "The one certain way the monarchy can secure itself is to behead a few beardless sheikhs. The Army and the National Guard are Bedouin. Loyal—but archconservatives when it comes to religion. If the imams convince them that the 'beardless ones' are pawns of the West, the King will be forced to act against us or face a revolution like the Shah did—with much less chance of surviving."

"What are you going to do?" she said anxiously.

Le'ith looked at the faxes reflectively. "I'm going to have some dinners . . . and you must be very careful; many of the wives of some of my most 'Westernized' friends are very conservative. Keep them talking children, or cards; plan games for them. Don't let discussions of this even begin. You know how rumors fly in this town. No one must suspect a thing until we are ready." He turned to her with a tiny smile. "And, I beg you, please be the model Muslim wife."

"But you're not a secularist; you're Muslim to the core," Lisa argued. "So is Rashid. Even Reena is truly a Muslim."

"There are two kinds of fundamentalists," he said solemnly. Then he grinned. "We had one kind visit us just yesterday. They believe in the Koran; they fear materialism; they fear 'sin'; they do an untold amount of quiet good. Then there are others who *call* themselves fundamentalists. Narrow, unforgiving—revengeful. All the things that true religion is not. And worst of all, driven by a fanatic need for control." He stared at the fax and then looked up at her wryly. "Back at UCLA they taught me it had something to do with bowel training. Absolute control and absolute conformity. Unfortunately, their numbers are growing, and their power too."

The thing Lisa knew about the "retentive" fundamentalists was that they hated Israel with a fervor and pledged its destruction. She knew Iran wanted to destroy Israel, and so did Iraq, and Syria, and now, if Saudi Arabia, with all its wealth, turned from Le'ith's kind of mild disapproval of a Jewish state in "Arabia" to the obsessive hatred of the Ayatollah and Hussein, Israel would be surrounded by a sea of fanatic hatred. David and Yassi would be grandparents before they could draw a free breath—if indeed they survived to be grandparents.

Le'ith took the concern that lodged in her eyes as a sign of her anxiety about him. He took her in his arms. "Don't worry," he said. "The royal family is more afraid of them than I am. And I think I know how to win—at least for now."

Lisa knew that any meeting of more than three persons for political purposes was banned in Saudi Arabia, so she grasped the danger of what Le'ith was attempting with his "nonpolitical" dinners. And she was a little awed by the fact that by the time he finished he had obtained the signatures of almost fifty of the most powerful "beardless" businessmen of the regime on the royal petition he had framed. Le'ith's name came at the top, of course, or none would have dared sign. But the boldness of them all was propped up by an almost panicked fear in each that, as the fly sheets and faxes continued to multiply, each more violent and threatening than the last, the country would fall to the hard-core imams if the royal family did not act.

Lisa had never seen Le'ith as apprehensive as he was the morning he was to present the petition to the King. Le'ith had often described him to her: kindly but short-tempered with age and, like most old men, convinced he knew what was right. Unlike most old men, however, he held the power to enforce his beliefs. Treason was the unforgivable sin. When he thought he saw it, there was no appeal. One gesture meant torture and beheading. And as Youssef had once chillingly told her, that fate fell to more than a hundred Saudis every year.

Lisa stayed clear of his bedroom while Le'ith dressed. He had been pale and silent at breakfast, but he wanted her there. They had received three more faxes during the night, mutilated "beardless" bodies, eyes gouged, ears and tongues cut off. Each bore a message: "Islam speaks of the *equality* of men, yet see how the beardless, godless men live." "Islam speaks of the common good, yet who brings us alcohol and filthy American films!" "Islam speaks of the religious life, but the beardless ones bow at the altar of the West, they fornicate in the cities of the West, they gamble in the casinos of the West!" It was damning but it would be a rare royal prince who could read those words without a blush.

Le'ith's petition proposed that the King stamp down hard on the imams behind this underground campaign. That was dangerous in itself because the monarchy's primary function was the protection of the faith. A blow at the imams could provoke the kind of religious revolution the royal family most feared.

But the genius of his idea was the most dangerous element for him. At the very moment government police were to arrest the rebellious imams, Le'ith proposed the King publicly announce the formation of a Consultative Council to recommend "reforms" to the Royal Council of Ministers, which was what the dominant members of the royal family called themselves.

It was, by implication and historical precedent, the crack in the door that questioned the absolute sovereignty of the monarch, the sort of concession that had led to the downfall of monarchies throughout history. Le'ith knew the King would see that danger instantly, and so would his aging and powerful brothers, the Crown Prince and Prince Sultan. He, one of their most trusted counselors, had schemed behind their backs to lead some of the greatest benefactors of the crown's wealth to call for a move they all knew would one day lead to the end of the monarchy. A Consultative Council soon became a parliament, and a parliament soon led to independent courts and laws that determined what a king could or could not do. If that was not treason, what was?

Le'ith's hope was that with the rising tide of violent fundamentalism at home and abroad, he could convince them that that crack in the door was a way of alleviating the pressure before the door was sundered by an explosion beyond hope of controlling.

Lisa grasped quickly that he had to succeed—for his reasons and hers.

If the King did nothing, the flood of pamphlets would become a flood of avenging mobs. The National Guard would never attack them. The "beardless ones" would be executed in the streets, and the country would be in the hands of extremists. Helping Le'ith prevent that might save her life, but beyond that, if she did nothing more for Israel than ward off a fundamentalist takeover of the Kingdom, she would have done enough to justify all her years in this false life she had undertaken.

He came to see her in the quarter just before he left, and he wore a look of nervous fear that she had never seen on him.

As he stood there, with the pallor of death, she smiled with a warmth that came without pretense. She went to him, put her arms around him, and pressed her head into his shoulder. "I am on your side, and I will be here for you as long as you want me, and whatever the cost."

He clung to her tightly and didn't speak, pressing his head against hers. At last he turned and went out the door. She glimpsed moisture in his eyes, but his shoulders and his gait were a bit more like that of the young lion/panther she knew so well.

The roundup of the extremist imams was swift and thorough. It was reported widely in newspapers in the West, but of course no word of it appeared in the Saudi press. Nevertheless there wasn't a household in Riyadh, Jidda, or Dammam that didn't know about it. Rumors ranged from one hundred militant clerics to a thousand. Only a few insiders knew the true numbers, and this time Le'ith was not among them.

What the Saudi press *did* report that day was that "in his concern for furthering the religious solidarity of the Kingdom, the King was establishing a Supreme Council of 'Islamic Affairs.' At the same time a Consultative Council of technocrats was to be formed to recommend social and governmental reforms to the Royal Council of Ministers. These steps were taken to deepen Saudi Arabia's service to Islam."

Le'ith came home on the day he presented the petition almost as shaken as when the day had begun. It had not been easy. Unpredictably the thing that had kept his head on his shoulders had come from the militant clerics themselves. Unknown to Le'ith until after four hours of only slightly veiled hostility was the fact that the clerics had submitted their *own* petition the day before. It was far bolder than Le'ith's. It violently denounced the government for straying from the true course of Islam and demanded that all concourse with foreign banks be ended immediately and all relations with Egypt, Algeria, and Morocco, which were persecuting religious fundamentalists, be severed.

Part of the King's anger at the daunting boldness and arrogance of those demands spilled over onto Le'ith. He had the sense to bear it, and when some of it had spent itself, he quietly told the King that the imams' bellicose petition showed how far things had gone, why some action was necessary. He himself had demonstrated his loyalty to the monarchy several times over, but if the King doubted it, he should surely recognize that if there were a religious revolution, he, Le'ith, would suffer more than any of the royal family, who would certainly be given asylum as the Shah had been. . . . The reference to the Shah was not accidental but not absolutely necessary. He knew the King's anger was a measure of his own fears.

Slowly the King had thawed. In the end he thanked Le'ith with his customary ceremonial politeness, but he pointedly stated that Le'ith would not be a member of either council.

Lisa was shocked. "You should have been on them both," she exclaimed.

Le'ith shook his head. "Well, I won't be. And until they told me about the clerics' petition, they hadn't even planned a Supreme Council of *Islamic Affairs*."

"*You* thought of it?" Le'ith only looked at her silently. "You mean they used both your ideas and won't let you on either council!"

"It may work in my favor. When his temper cools, he may make amends with generosity. That's his way. And to be honest, I don't want to give time to them. I think I can be just as effective with a few dinners."

Whoever got the credit, the strategy worked, at least for the time. The faxes and fly sheets stopped abruptly. There were some violent mutterings in some of the mosques, a remaining undercurrent of unrest, but the frenzied momentum of a fundamentalist "revolution" against the "beardless ones" was stymied. Everyone knew the danger remained, that the followers of the militants only became more determined, and even the more moderate imams continued to preach against the growing Westernization of Saudi life and brashly denounced the lavish living of the rich, whose numbers included most of the royal family.

Youssef came home in the midst of all this. Le'ith spoke to him only in chill monosyllables, but Youssef was, if anything, more determinedly provocative than ever. He grasped immediately how precarious everything was and sensed that it gave him greater power, not less. The least religious, and in his "corruption" the most Western, of all the family, he began spouting the slogans of the religious right almost from the day he arrived.

"Present parties excluded, of course," he said, smiling at Lisa with a false air of solicitousness, "but we all know where the discontent in the Arab world comes from. America is right at our doorstep, trying to colonize our minds and souls, corrupt us with their godless philosophy of greed and envy and unrepentant selfishness."

Had he not been so obnoxious, Lisa would have laughed. It was hard to think of anyone more greedy or envious or "unrepentantly selfish" than Youssef. But she was amazed again at his ability to parrot phrases from someone else's creed. They were dining at Najib's. Najib was not unaware of the dangers ahead, but he was one of those who could not summon the will or self-discipline to alter their lifestyles no matter what.

"Well, I can avouch that it was California that corrupted me," he said in mock penitence. "Before that I was as steadfast a Muslim as Youssef. But all that lechery and greed just warped me beyond repair, I fear."

Everyone smiled at the reference to Youssef's putative religiosity—except Youssef, and he was getting bold enough to let the dangerous side of his nature show.

"I know some imams who would not find that funny, Najib," he said with a menacing bluntness.

But Najib was not to be intimidated. "By Allah, you *have* reformed,

Youssef. Keeping the company of imams. I'm proud of you, and if it ever comes down to revolution, I know you'll put in a good word for me."

Again there were smiles all around, but though he could indeed parrot the phrases of the day, Youssef was not quick-witted enough to joust with Najib's casual drollery.

"When it comes to revolution," he said, "you can all be sure I'll have a *lot* to say." It was bluster, but not empty bluster. Youssef was just the one to ride the wave of bigotry, and Najib knew it as well as Le'ith.

"I'll tell you what, Youssef," Najib rejoined, "you take care of *me* in the revolution, and I'll keep *you* in lovely Egyptian and Lebanese ladies until the scimitar falls. Now that's a reasonable deal, isn't it? Look at Nagwa here." He nodded to the absolutely gorgeous girl who was with him for the night. "Her charms took me particularly, but I assure you, I can supply you with a dozen equally charming ladies within the week." Youssef had been eyeing Nagwa brazenly from the time they had sat down, so Najib's words were not without a trace of vitriol. Youssef enveloped her in his eyes again and started to speak, but Najib raised his hand and cut him off. "No, no," he said, "the sin will be mine. You need not worry. As a faithful Muslim you are allowed a concubine or two, and it will be my profligacy that purchases them. There is no imam so zealous as to find you at fault for that." They all were grinning and looking at Youssef with some of Najib's mockery.

Youssef stared at Najib, then looked up and down the table. Rashid was there with Hayat and four of the beardless "California Mafia," as the Saudis called the close-knit graduates of the California universities. All were old friends of Le'ith's and Najib's. And all were dressed in Western clothes. Only Youssef was in a thawb.

"You remind me of the court of Louis the Fourteenth," Youssef said. "So superior—and so *blind*." He turned forcefully to Lisa. "And America's other fifth column, Israel, is soon to be surrounded—not by peasant shepherds—but by disciples of Allah, who, like their ancestors of the Grand Sultanate, are masters of science and technology. America, its bastard daughter, Israel, and those who have swallowed its shallow philosophy are doomed in Islam. The clock is ticking!"

Lisa had blushed red at his sudden, blunt linking of her to Israel. That he would do it hadn't surprised her, but that he would do it so blatantly in public took her completely off guard. But Youssef's venom was so unmasked, and so universally directed to the whole table, that her particular reaction went unnoticed—except for Le'ith.

After a moment's silence Najib spoke again, as lightheartedly as before. "So good of you—and so *learned*—Youssef, to associate us with Louis the Fourteenth. He had such a full and luxurious life. For a dreadful moment I thought you were going to allude to poor Louis the *Sixteenth,* who of course was guillotined with the beauteous Marie Antoinette. But, Allah be praised, sinners that we are, you don't think of us in terms of *that* court."

Now it was Youssef's turn to blush. He stared at Najib, stammering wordlessly. Then he rose, still crimson with anger and embarrassment. He swept his arm along the table, knocking his wine flying. "All this Western crap—the knives and forks, the fancy wines, the Armani suits, the shameless women—it's all going! And sooner than you think!" And he pulled the tablecloth, making a litter of everything, then strode out of the room past the alarmed stares of the servants.

"By Allah, we are getting bold, aren't we?" Najib said after a moment of startled silence. "Perhaps I had just better check my bank account in Switzerland."

"He was with the units in America, wasn't he?" Saleh el Sayed stated more than asked. They all were trying to reset the table with the flustered help of the servants.

Saleh was a graduate of Berkeley and one of those monitored by Uncle Sabah. He was a brilliant engineer, according to Le'ith—and a good Muslim—but very Westernized.

"Yes," Le'ith responded soberly. "I apologize for him. He has always had connections with the Army, and as you might imagine, he gets on with soldiers very well."

"I didn't realize the Army was so much in the hands of the imams," Najib said. "Have I not been paying attention?"

"I don't know," Saleh replied. "Maybe none of us have been paying attention."

"The Army's volatile right now, and so is the National Guard," Le'ith said with informed confidence. "But they won't *start* the revolution. Whether they would fire on a crowd led by imams is a different question."

"You fill me with confidence," Najib groaned.

"Well, if you happen to be lounging around in a UCLA sweatshirt drinking booze with a lady out of purdah, I would recommend you have a secret exit and a pilot standing by at the airport."

"Where did the world go wrong?" Najib sighed.

"With Adam," Lisa said. "The first Middle Easterner." They all smiled. But nothing could redeem the night. The "beardless secularists" sitting at that table, sipping their expensive French wine, all knew in their hearts that Youssef was right: The clock was ticking.

Chapter 25

Shortly after the crackdown on the imams Lisa had gone to the compound for a rash of births. Ulti gave birth to a boy. Jineen returned with her second child, another girl. Le'ith was given another young half brother by Toujan, his father's young Jordanian bride. And another son by Nayra.

The experience was a confirmation of all Huda and Linn had said about the value of the harim to the lives of women.

Ulti was redeemed in the eyes of Youssef because she had given him a son. For the first seven years of the boy's life she would be in charge of him and treated with respect, even by Youssef. Lisa had waited for her visit until Youssef had returned to Riyadh, but all the harim were pleased that Ulti no longer faced regular beatings or scornful neglect. Even Ayesha, Youssef's second and favored wife, was elated by it.

Jineen, who wanted so much to be in love with her husband that she brainwashed herself into that state, was brokenhearted because after producing two daughters, her loving husband, Ossama, was in eager pursuit of a new bride who could give him sons. Though the pride of every woman who had produced a son was worn on her face like an indelible beauty mark, all of them smothered Jineen in understanding and compassion.

Toujan, who had always been an outsider in the harim from the time Le'ith's father first brought her from Jordan, had by the painful but relatively simple act of giving birth been inducted into the sisterhood of the household as though it had always been waiting for her to apply. Lisa had seldom seen her smile, and she had almost always been on her own. But now the smiles flowed from her face, and there were eager arms to put around her and hands to take and hold her baby on high. To Lisa's surprise, Ummi minded not at all. Her husband's plaything had produced a lovely baby that belonged to them all. And how often he visited Toujan's chambers had long since ceased to bother her. She, Ummi, was the mistress of the harim, and he needed her as she wished to be needed.

And Nayra had borne another black-eyed son for Le'ith, not as pretty a baby as Ibrahim, but thick-boned and formidable-looking even as an infant. Lisa thought fleetingly, Another Youssef, but tried to shut the image from her mind. Everyone else thought he was splendid, and most important, he insured Le'ith's heritage. All the harim knew about their valley, gossiped endlessly about Le'ith's "Western" love of Lisa, even under the attack of Youssef's rumors; that much Reena had told Lisa many times. No woman they knew had a relationship like hers with Le'ith. Men lived their own lives; brothers, cousins, and friends were for companionship; concubines were for sex; wives were for children and managing the household. "Sharing" a life was to them as wondrous as flying to the moon.

But in producing sons Nayra had done what was important, and she had gained a stature that was exceeded only by Ummi's and Huda's. That shift reflected Le'ith's new status, of course, but it did not come automatically. Nayra's simple and loving nature had made her place, and she was happy in it. Her girth seemed about to rival Ummi's, but that bothered no one either. And secretly Lisa had to admit she was relieved by it. She liked Nayra and loved the devilish and witty Ibrahim, but it was comfortable to feel that Nayra didn't want, or seem to care about, a "physical" competition for Le'ith. Where Nayra was in the private household of Le'ith's heart Lisa didn't know, or believe she could understand, but it seemed to satisfy Nayra in a deep and fundamental way.

Reena came to Riyadh three days before Youssef went to the compound to greet his new son. She regaled Lisa with stories of the harim, as usual, but of her own romance was less irreverent. It seems that as Ulti had progressed into the last weeks of pregnancy, her sensuous attachment to Reena had paled. She became concerned about the baby; she wished Youssef were there; she felt awkward and ugly and wanted to spend time only with her servants or Huda. But Reena was not disturbed.

"I've gotten into the secret places of her mind," she told Lisa confidently as they lay on Lisa's bed, puffing their joints. "I've brought her alive in ways she never dreamed of," she purred.

"You're sure you aren't just making her feel guilty? It sounds a little perverse to me." Lisa grinned.

"No, you're too straight. It's all that Christian upbringing. She may want to get laid now and then by Youssef, and beaten up by him, but I know she'll always come back to me."

Lisa was tempted to say, "Famous last words," but she didn't want to throw seeds of doubt on Reena's unaccustomed mood of contentment.

"What does Ummi feel about all this, and your mother?" she asked instead.

"I think Ummi is worried that Youssef will find out and beat Ulti to a pulp. My mother only looks at me as she has for years, a bewildered, hauntingly disappointed search for the bright-eyed little girl who was going to marry some sheikh and produce offspring like a she camel." Her voice had dropped to a husky mordancy, as though she too somehow had lost touch with that promising little girl. Then she puffed and grinned. "The truth is, we're the harim's scandal, and every good harim needs its scandal." And she laughed.

"And when you tire of all this physical stuff?"

"Oh, it's not *all* that. We have moments of unbelievable tenderness that aren't sexual at all. My worry is not tiring of her; it's that with a baby she will be stuck in that harim for years. I need to travel. I need to get away from here, and I love to travel with her. . . . That does bother me." And she had lost some of her contentment again.

After her own visit to the compound Lisa continued on for a short trip to the valley, and Reena flew down from Riyadh to be with her again. Reena loved the new house. "Now this is the way I pictured you," she shouted as she ran with outstretched arms from one room to another. "God, you've got to let me bring Ulti down here."

They rode brazenly in jeans and blouses with their hair streaming in the wind. Lisa felt pangs of guilt at breaking her promise to Le'ith, but Reena led her to things she would never do on her own.

Lisa took her to the "ranch." They now had twenty head of cattle and a small barn. It was fenced with steel piping that Le'ith had laid like a wooden plank fence and painted white. From a distance you could think you were in Kentucky. She told Reena that she had indeed held the first sticky, blood-soaked little calf in her arms and fed her from a bottle.

Reena laughed but then nailed Lisa with one of her looks of world-weary desolation. "It's probably as close as you and I are ever going to get to feeding a baby."

For all their frankness, they had never spoken about Lisa's "inability" to have a baby. And that look was the first hint Lisa had that Reena felt the lack of motherhood as deeply as she herself felt it.

Later, back in the house, they talked about it briefly. Reena was amazed that Lisa could live in a harim and not understand that anyone so raised would long to have children, long for it more than for a husband or a lover or a life of luxury.

"But Hafez, Ulti's baby, won't you be close to him?" Lisa asked.

Reena guffawed bitterly. "Hafez is Youssef's. And much as Ummi and Huda might tolerate my little affair with Ulti, if I ever showed the *least* partiality to him or an ounce of possessiveness, I would be given the option of leaving the harim voluntarily or being stoned to death."

"Ummi could never do that."

"You're still a 'foreigner,' aren't you, Lisa?" Reena sighed. "Ummi and Huda would have tears in their eyes, but if they had the right, they would themselves throw the first stones. A man's sons are more important than all the oil under the desert. And the one child I must never love is Ulti's."

Lisa stared at her and gradually accepted the unbelievable truth of it.

They were aimlessly watching television, a CNN broadcast from Europe—the idea that Le'ith was allowed a disk and could actually see anything that was on satellite entranced Reena; it was like a delicious open window on that part of the world she so often missed—when suddenly the announcer cut into the program and said, "We are now taking you to the South Lawn of the White House in Washington, where President Clinton will introduce Israeli Prime Minister Yitzak Rabin and the Palestinian leader Yasser Arafat after their signing of the historic Peace Accord between Israel and the PLO."

Reena glanced incredulously at Lisa. Lisa was too stunned to do more than open her mouth. They both watched, riveted, through the whole ceremony, the speeches, the faces of former American presidents, of Kissinger, of Arafat's delegation, and finally the incredible, soon-to-be-famous handshake.

The comings and goings in the outside world were always irrelevant to life in the compound or the valley, curiosities at most, but even so, Lisa and Reena felt slightly less benighted when the announcer stated that until August 29 even the *President* of the United States had not known the scope of the secret meetings that were held in Norway and Egypt between representatives of Israel and the PLO. The Accord had taken the whole world by surprise. Peace had been talked of for years, but no one had anticipated that the "insoluble" problems of that long, bitter struggle could be settled without decades of haggling. The Accord was as "earth-shattering" as the breaking up of the Soviet Empire and the fall of the Berlin Wall.

When the ceremony finally broke off, Lisa switched off the set, and they sat for a long time in silence. It was past midnight, they both were tired from a day of riding and talking and had had too much wine with dinner, but neither could bring herself to think of going to bed.

Reena finally turned to Lisa. "Well, this rather changes things for Israel, doesn't it?"

Lisa was not so sleepy that she didn't recognize this as Reena's desire to deal with that residual doubt she carried about Lisa. This would certainly be a justifiable time for Lisa to confess. After all, if the Palestine issue was settled, what reason was there for the war with Israel?

As the momentous consequences of that Peace Accord worked their way through Lisa's mind, she was very tempted just to throw her hands in the air in relief and say, "Yes, I am an agent of Israel. I have done no harm, except perhaps to Le'ith, and now I am going home."

What stopped her were sudden thoughts of how easily that miraculous Accord might fall apart. She knew all about Hamas, the Islamic Jihad, and the other "fundamentalist" groups that declared there would never be peace as long as there was an Israeli state. She knew too about the settler fanatics in Israel—most of them, it seemed, from the United States—who were also of the religious right and were prepared to die and kill to maintain their Jewish "right" to all Judea and Samaria, the West Bank to the rest of the world. That peace was now possible she accepted with eagerness and wonder; that it was certain she knew was not true.

"I would say it changes everything for the Middle East, not just for Israel," she replied at last. "Wouldn't it be nice if everyone started trading oranges and fashions instead of bullets and insults?"

Reena studied her with undiminished skepticism. It wasn't a conviction like Youssef's, it was just a "doubt," but nothing Lisa had ever been able to do had really succeeded in stilling it.

"Well, I'll be amazed," Reena said, "if it alters Hussein's view of Israel or the Iranians'. And I really wouldn't want to be Mr. Arafat right now. I should think it might be a little difficult to get life insurance."

Lisa laughed. It was true, he'd made himself a target for almost everyone. Then the smile dropped from her face because she realized that if he *was* assassinated—by anyone—it would almost certainly be the end of any "peace." "We live in a precarious world," she said grimly, thinking too of the fundamentalist imams in Riyadh and their savage faxes and fly sheets.

"Is it true," Reena asked, "that Le'ith is in trouble with the King?"

Lisa shook her head. "Not trouble. Perhaps a little disfavor right now. The one who is in trouble I think is the King."

"And Le'ith told him so?"

"Something like that."

Reena groaned. "I love my brother, and I admire his courage, but you can't imagine the disaster he would bring down upon himself and the family if they ever thought him disloyal."

"I think he weighed that," Lisa replied defensively. "He also considered what would happen to the family if the Kingdom fell to a party of zealots."

Slowly a huge smile spread across Reena's face. It contained her cynicism but also an unusual degree of warmth. "You really do love Le'ith, don't you?"

Lisa blushed uncontrollably. She had to face that she did somehow "feel" he was her husband and she was defending him. Had she played this role too long?

"It's all right," Reena said, leaning across and squeezing her arm. "Once in a while life dishes out a tiny bit of justice. Le'ith deserves to be loved, and nobody on this side of the Jordan River will ever blame you for it."

And Lisa blushed again.

Chapter 26

Lisa waited with some hope and some tension as the months went by, watching television and the outside world as she had not since the day she first arrived in Riyadh. A Dr. Baruch Goldstein, an American immigrant settler, massacred scores of Palestinians in morning prayer at the Ibrahim Mosque in Hebron; a Hamas "martyr" took out himself and a busful of Jewish women and children in Jerusalem; a follower of the Islamic Jihad did the same for a group of Israeli soldiers; Israeli police and Palestinian police exchanged gunfire; Israeli settlements continued to be built in the West Bank despite the agreements in the Accord that they would not; Arafat called for a separate Palestinian state with Jerusalem as its capital despite the pledge in the Accord that he would not.

Yet the peace held. Jordan even joined the PLO and made its separate peace with Israel.

Then, when things seemed most promising, the greatest cataclysm struck. Ironically, it was not, as she and Reena had grimly anticipated, Arafat who fell to his multitude of enemies; it was his unlikely partner in peace, Yitzak Rabin, who was struck down by a bullet delivered by a right-wing Israeli law student. Despite all the hate she had seen—and felt—both in Israel and in Saudi Arabia, Lisa could not accept that this could happen to a leader who was so loved, who had done so much for the very existence of Israel. From her time in the kibbutz she knew this man's whole life had been dedicated to the survival of a Jewish state. It was in his every act, every drop of his blood. Yet he was gunned down by a religious fanatic who called him a "traitor."

Sadat, who had also believed the nations of the Middle East could live in peace, had been killed by the murderous right of his country, Rabin by the maniac zealots of his. To her surprise, when the news came, Lisa did not have to bury her shock and grief; Le'ith seemed as stunned as she was—and as repelled by the sight of Muslim fanatics in Syria and Jewish fanatics in Israel celebrating in glee the assassination of this extraordinary man. Later they watched together in fascinated silence as Yasser Arafat emotionally spoke of Rabin's bravery, called him "partner" and "friend"; and as King Hussein of Jordan, almost in tears, praised his role in bringing the peoples of the Middle East together, and at the funeral embraced his family, and was embraced by them; and as President Hosni Mubarak, Sadat's successor as the leader of Egypt's government, called him one of many brave and principled men who had fallen on the path to peace.

The next day, when they watched the funeral with its collection of world leaders, with Arabs and Jews present, Lisa had a sense of the "nationhood" of Israel stronger than she had ever felt. It was as if now it really existed, a nation accepted like America, or Ireland—or Saudi Arabia. It seemed confirmed when the Israeli leader of the opposition, Benjamin Netanyahu, said that governments in Israel were changed by ballots, not by bullets, and though he remained opposed to the peace process, he would support Rabin's government coalition and not use this tragedy to challenge its right to office.

So, once again, against all the odds, the "peace" held.

It was winter and the weather was glorious when Le'ith suddenly told Lisa they were going to the valley. He had slowly worked his way back into the King's favor, and he had been right: The King had rewarded him with a stunning jeweled sword for his "services to Islam," and once more the Royal Council seldom met without his presence.

So the sudden decision to go to the valley took Lisa by surprise. They left the airport at Riyadh at sunset. Bushra accompanied them, but Le'ith chose not to take Khalid or his personal servant, Musa. He flew the plane alone.

Lisa sat in the copilot's seat, and flying over the great central plain at night, with the minutes droning away in the sound of the jets and seeing not one tiny beam of light from horizon to horizon for miles and miles and miles, reminded her of the vastness of the land she had become so accustomed to—and its emptiness.

As they approached the runway at the oasis, lit on both sides by kerosene pots, the few lights of her valley seemed a fragile, tiny outpost in a forbidding world of darkness.

Her sleep was restless, and so was Le'ith's. At dawn he rose and knelt to Mecca. When he finished his prayers, she thought he might come back to bed, but his mind was as withdrawn as it had been on the flight to the valley.

"I want to ride," he said. "Will you come with me?"

They rode for more than three hours, and though they stopped to let the horses drink and to view the fields several times, Le'ith never spoke a word. He looked so physically commanding on Saladin, yet his face was a knot of indecision. Lisa sensed that he wanted her with him but did not want her to speak.

Near sunset they rode again. And it was the same.

It went on for three days. On the night of their third day he had a fire built at the side of the oasis and a lamb roasted by the servants. They sensed his mood as much as Lisa and presented the food and cleared quietly and quickly. When they had gone and all was silent at their end of the valley, Le'ith stretched out on the carpet and stared at the stars for a time.

"I want you to tell me I am crazy," he said soberly.

"I can do that." Lisa smiled. "Is there any particular reason?"

"Yes," he answered. But he didn't speak for a time. Then he said, "Iran is buying arms from what was the Soviet military—submarines, sophisticated aircraft; our informers even think the list includes atomic missiles. They have certainly been trying to obtain weapons-grade plutonium. And despite everything, Saddam Hussein is stronger than he was when he invaded Kuwait. The fundamentalists have taken over in the Sudan, and they are so strong in Egypt that whole areas are in their control."

He paused again. "Our Kingdom has gradually been surrounded by those who want to destroy the monarchy. And there are far too many inside the country who are willing to help."

"I'm afraid that all sounds very sane to me," she said, picking up some of his solemnity.

He nodded, but there was clearly more. "There is one other country in the Middle East that is alone and surrounded by enemies. . . ."

She looked at him penetratingly. He only stared at her. "Israel?" she dared say at last.

"Yes, Israel," he uttered. "We think of it as Western, a pawn of America. But America isn't up to protecting Israel any more. Even if it had the will, which it doesn't—look how long it took the Americans to mobilize for Kuwait, and they had a country at their disposal to put their forces in and prepare them. There would be no such haven in a war over Israel. Their nearest friends would be in Europe, and the Europeans would be more intent on securing their oil than securing Israel.

"So like it or not, Israel can't afford to be a pawn of the United States anymore. It is part of the Middle East."

Lisa held her breath. "And if the Palestinians and Jordan and Egypt can accept Israel, why can't we?" He rolled on his back and looked at the sky again. The words came slowly, phrase by deeply considered phrase.

"And if we do, and Israel is just another country in the Middle East, then *we* are its natural ally. Our dangers are its dangers: Iran, Hussein, the fundamentalists. . . . It has atomic missiles, we know. But where can it place them that can save it? The country is too small. It is the perfect target for those who will soon have atomic missiles of their own. But if atomic missiles were placed around Saudi Arabia, even the most insane aggressor would have to hesitate. Where are they? And how do you take them out in a land of desert shale?

"The Israelis have an infrastructure of scientists and technicians; they have a highly disciplined modern army, all things we need to survive. For their part, they need our money, our oil, the vastness of our land."

He paused and looked at her. For a fleeting second she wondered if it was a trap. Had something prompted him to doubt her again? But this was not how he treated her when he doubted her. And he had been seething with some thought for weeks, ever since Rabin's assassination and funeral; she had seen it grow in him, and she knew him too well to think he could "act" this.

"I'm going to disappoint you," she said at last. "I don't think you're crazy at all." She paused. "But I thought you hated Israel."

"I hate some of the things she's done, but I intend to see that this monarchy does not fall to the imams."

He sat up, wrapping his arms around his legs, staring out across the valley. "But the King is deeply religious; he rages against Israel's control of Jerusalem and the Dome of the Rock and the Al Aqsa Mosque. I think he would rather die in a revolution than conspire to leave it all in Israel's hands."

Lisa was cautious. "I thought the control of Jerusalem was one of the issues in the Palestinian agreement."

He smirked. "It is the 'last' issue on the agenda, and the Israelis say over and over again the sovereignty of Jerusalem is nonnegotiable."

"Isn't that what negotiators always say?"

"Hmm . . ."

"If you suggested it to the Royal Council, maybe their interest could get it moved up on the agenda."

Le'ith was smiling. "The Royal Council? Lisa, if one word of this idea leaked to the streets—that a certain 'beardless' sheikh was urging the King to make an alliance with the godless American puppet Israel—it would not only be the militant imams who would tear the palace apart but the Bedouin Army, the Bedouin National Guard, and most of the citizens of Riyadh." He looked at her. "And you and I would be strung up on a lamppost and hacked to pieces."

"So—so what can you do?"

"I can ask for an audience with the King alone. That will put me in enough danger . . . but if he grants it even over the protests of the Crown Prince and Prince Sultan and I fail to convince him, well, the worst, I suppose, would be torture and a beheading; the best would be a lifetime in exile here in the valley."

"He wouldn't call you a traitor just for the idea," Lisa protested.

Le'ith shrugged dubiously. "I would hope not."

"A life here wouldn't be so bad, Le'ith," she said winsomely.

His answer was quick and short. "I was not meant to be a farmer. . . ." He stared out over the valley in silence again. "But I wasn't meant to be a coward either. . . . And I think this is the only way this Kingdom will survive until Ibrahim is a man."

She was caught off-balance again that he was thinking of his son and not of them. "Would it really be so drastically opposed?"

Le'ith grinned. "How many imams can you imagine supporting an alliance with the devil Israel? Remember, this is a Kingdom based on the Koran. No, if a deal can be struck, the King would have to get the agreement of the Crown Prince and, most important, Prince Sultan."

"The Army?"

"Yes. And if they harbor a desire to challenge the role of the King, you couldn't present an issue more likely to carry the mobs and most of the military."

"Is he that way, Prince Sultan?"

"He's an enigma, but he's human. I think he would like to be king, but he well knows that a fundamentalist revolution is brewing here, and Iraq and Iran are just waiting to exploit it. My guess is that if he can be convinced that this is a way to neutralize the danger from the north, he will settle for being a great prince of a thriving country rather than the king of a seething cauldron that would soon be in the hands of the imams and then only Allah knows who."

"Then why seek an audience with the King alone? Why not deal with the three of them from the beginning?"

"They each have their own counselors; the opportunity for mischief would be enormous. Any single counselor who opposed it for religious reasons or personal ambition or jealousy could ruin it all with one phone call to a leading imam. It would never have a chance." He had obviously gone over the possibilities a hundred times himself in those days of indecision.

"There is only one way," he continued. "I must convince the King, I must convince the Israelis, and if it ever comes to pass, it must be set before each country as an accomplished fact, but with the advantages to both sides so clear only the worst bigots could oppose it.''

She could see that he was right. No other way would work. But it was such a long shot. Yet in its vision it was like Alexander's cutting of the Gordian knot, the Gordian knot that tied together all the strands of discord in that whole quarter of the world.

"And until that time," he went on, "everything must somehow be done with more secrecy than even the Peace Accord between Israel and the PLO. That taught me a lot."

The fire was nearly gone. The stars were bright above them, and the desert chill was closing in on their little space before the dying embers. "Why have you come to me with this, Le'ith?" Lisa asked, studying the lines of his face and the little patch of gray at his temples.

He turned to look into her eyes. "You're the only one I can trust with something so dangerous . . . the only one . . . and I had to talk with someone." He said it with such profound sincerity that it brought a rush of water to Lisa's eyes—not because he trusted her but because he did so with such faith when in fact she was the last he should trust.

He saw her tears in the red glow of the coals and pulled her to him. "It's almost like California," he said softly. "There are the two of us— and everyone else."

Lisa closed her eyes and accepted his arms around her. In this cause he was right. Perhaps God had answered her prayers.

Chapter 27

As Le'ith expected, a private audience with the King was not that easy to achieve—even for him. But when it came, it was exceptional. Le'ith was called in the early morning. He did not return home until after nine P.M.

Lisa was already a wreck by two o'clock in the afternoon. She wanted desperately to get the advice of Adam, but she could think of no way to contact him that wouldn't throw suspicion on her, and she couldn't risk that now that she had Le'ith's total confidence. By six o'clock she had stopped worrying about getting advice and had begun to worry that Le'ith was under arrest. She knew the King was in the habit of napping in the afternoon, and it was long past the time for that.

She couldn't eat; she couldn't read or watch television; she just paced and paced.

When he finally came home, she wanted to rush down to him, but when she came into the hallway, she could see that he was hurrying with Moustafa to the kitchen. Then she heard footsteps running up the back stairs. She decided she should return to her room in the quarter.

One of Grandfather's wives had died, and the other had gone back to her own family, so the quarter was empty except for Lisa and Bushra and three servant girls who didn't know what to do with themselves. It was not only empty but silent, and Lisa could hear Le'ith speaking again, but she couldn't make out what he was saying.

He came to her room about half an hour later. It was one of the longest half hours she'd ever spent. When he came in, he didn't even greet her. He simply closed the door and asked where Bushra was. Lisa assumed she was in her sitting room.

"Go find her," Le'ith said. "Then tell her to go to the kitchen with the servant girls and stay there until our meal is prepared and then bring it up here."

Lisa looked at him questioningly, but he snapped abruptly, "Go, do it now!"

Even as concerned for him as she was, she hated to be ordered about that way, hated being treated as if she were only an instrument of his will, and for a second her temper flared, but he only met her glare at him with another gesture of impatience, so she grunted angrily and did as she was bidden.

When she came back, Le'ith had turned out the lights and was standing at the door seeing that Bushra and the servants had actually left the quarter. Again he just gestured her into the room as though she were another maid. When she finally closed the door, she turned on a table lamp and stared daggers at him. "I have been waiting and worrying all day and half the night. You could at least—"

"Go pull the drapes on the window," he interrupted.

She closed her eyes, then walked stiffly across the room and pulled the drapes. When she turned, he was lying on the bed. He signaled her to him.

"I must speak quickly," he said in a hushed voice. "I have been with the King the whole time. All I can tell you now is that he has agreed— with a number of qualifications. But once he accepted it in principle, he grew very excited and had as many positive ideas as he did qualifications. Most important, he agrees that there are only two things that can kill it: the Israelis—or if the idea is in any way exposed before there is agreement."

"That's wonderful, but why are you—"

He put his fingers to her lips. "You do not spend eleven hours with the King without its being noticed. I was followed home, and I am sure it was the Army Secret Service." He nodded to the drapes. "The listening devices they have these days mean we have to be scrupulously careful where we talk and what we say."

Lisa nodded. All his abruptness made sense now. She wondered anxiously if Colonel Ansari would connect Le'ith's activities with what he considered hers to be.

"I have spoken to Moustafa and the servants," Le'ith went on, "telling them that we are going away and that I know their loyalty and know that the privacy of our household will be safeguarded by them." He grimaced sardonically. "But we have to be realistic. They will certainly corrupt one of the servants at least, and they will certainly plant bugs in the house by the time we return and perhaps before we leave. Say nothing to Bushra or any of the servant girls from tonight on, and say nothing to me. They all sense that something is up, and they'll eavesdrop or they're not Saudis."

"Do you think the Army *suspects* what's going on?"

Le'ith shook his head. "No. They only know that the King doesn't give eleven-hour audiences, and they know I asked for a *private* audience. They are just immensely curious and immensely paranoid about Prince Sultan's position."

Lisa was a little relieved. "Then while we are alone, may I ask *where* we are going and when?"

Le'ith smiled for the first time in weeks. "I'm taking ten days to establish what 'happened' in my meeting with the King," he said. "In that time Rashid and I will, with royal help, set up the financing for a major, ultramodern chemical plant, which His Majesty suggested be our cover." He lifted his eyebrows, "What do you think of that?" Lisa was properly impressed by the royal cunning. "Then," he continued, "you and I are going to Casablanca to arrange for the import of potash and uranium for the plant."

"Casablanca?"

"Yes." Le'ith grinned. "I learned some extraordinary things today. Morocco's kingdom is having trouble with the fundamentalists too, and is more than a little concerned about the fundamentalist upheaval next door in Algeria. Morocco's borders are like ours—miles of porous emptiness, terribly vulnerable to the import of everything from hashish to revolution. All that I knew, but what I didn't know was that King Hassan has been quietly encouraging contacts with Israel, that he has even allowed an outpost of the Mossad to operate in Casablanca."

Lisa stared at him in amazement.

He nodded. "It's true. And it's there we stand the best chance of making a high-level contact that can keep the possibilities of this absolutely secret."

It was a lot for Lisa to absorb, and the most dizzying fact of all was that after all these years she was now truly on Le'ith's side, that they were what he always thought they were, a partnership. "And why are you taking me?" she asked.

He rolled over and put his arms around her. "Because I need sex," he answered playfully. She grinned at him. He was obviously feeling better; they hadn't made love in weeks.

"I see," she said, "and you think I'm better than those voluptuous dark-haired dancers you'd find in the casbah?"

"Listen, don't talk me out of it," he replied.

She punched him, and he pulled her closer, nuzzling her neck. "I do want sex with you right now," he murmured. "Go lock the door."

"Oh, God, Saudi men," she groaned. "*I* have to lock the door."

He sighed, kissed her neck again, and got up and locked the door. He shed his thawb before he got back on the bed. She started to undo her blouse, but he stopped her. "No, I will do that."

"What if the Army Secret Service is listening?" she whispered as he undid one button and kissed her breast, then another button.

"Good," he said. "It's time they learned of these things."

The sex was marvelous. She wrapped her legs around him with a force that even took him by surprise. When it was over and Le'ith had shouted to Bushra to bring their dinner back in ten minutes, he held her close to his sweating body.

"I'm taking you," he said solemnly, "because this is all so precarious . . . and so important. I need to be sure I'm not making mistakes. I need somebody I trust completely to question every move I make. . . ." And he squeezed her and kissed the top of her head.

Chapter 28

If Lisa had to live in an Arabian city, she decided Casablanca was it. Its graceful boulevards, the sidewalk cafés, the lush restaurants, and the luxurious hotels were only part of it. The touch of French culture was everywhere: films, theater, fashion. And the city sat on the sea, its landward approaches protected by, of all things, beautiful green golf courses. On top of that there was just enough Arab exotica to give a pinch of spice. Women in chadors walked along the street next to girls in the highest and most risqué French fashion. A few men in thawbs and beards mixed with the casually dressed businessmen of the city, and the young men sported everything from T-shirts to garish polo shirts over baggy trousers.

Le'ith's contact, Mourad Nusseibeh, was a very influential Moroccan businessman, who was also a close confidant of his King. His assistant, Bassam, met them at the airport with a long Mercedes limousine and two servants to handle their luggage. Because the city was new to them, he had the driver whisk them along the seafront and through the city's palm-lined central section. Then they sped past trucks and donkey carts and wandering families of Arab workers to a large estate outside town.

On the way Bassam chattered amiably about the city, the country, the excitement of this year's English football season, which was received on television. Perhaps to show the importance of his boss, he explained that he himself had been editor of the leading business magazine in the country when Mr. Nusseibeh tapped him to be his assistant.

As they approached the gates of the walled estate, the doors opened, controlled by two servants, who bowed deeply as the car passed.

"Were they waiting for us?" Lisa asked.

"Yes and no," Bassam answered. "They wait all the time. Their chief is in the tower"—he pointed—"and he warns them when a car is approaching." Even after her life in Saudi Arabia Lisa was impressed.

Mr. Nusseibeh was a short, stout, swarthy man with close-cropped white hair and a white mustache. He was exceedingly polite, but the response of his servants to his slightest glance gave a sense of his power. His home was imposing and filled with extraordinary art; in the central room there were two Picasso sculptures, a Pollock that almost covered one white wall, a Matisse, a Braque, two Murillos, a stunning Klee, and, in a special alcove of golden light, a Holbein Lisa had seen in a dozen art books. It was like a very special gallery. The eye was focused on the art, but when you moved from it, everything you saw or touched was superb. There wasn't a piece of furniture or a fixture that wasn't tastefully and exquisitely fashioned.

Bassam and a servant saw them to the guest room. Again it was a little gallery. A Pissarro over the bed, a pair of little Seurats on one wall, a Dufy on the other. The room spoke not of passion and night but of joy and sunlight. Lisa looked at Le'ith, and he just shook his head in wonder. It was not the way Saudis used their wealth. "Maybe we should have been colonized," he said facetiously.

Lisa laughed, but Bassam was confused. "What do you mean?" he said. "Is everything not all right?"

"No," Le'ith responded, "everything is fine."

"Ah." Bassam sighed in relief. "Mr. Nusseibeh will have tea with you in the garden in twenty minutes—if that will be suitable."

"Very suitable," Le'ith answered, and Bassam and the servant made their exit. Lisa started to speak, and Le'ith held his finger to his mouth in warning. Lisa sighed—and nodded.

The garden, Mr. Nusseibeh informed them, had been designed by a Japanese landscape artist he had flown in from Kyoto.

"There are many rare trees," he said. "Rare for Morocco, that is," he added with a smile. "And to achieve the waterfall and the stream and the little hillocks that create the sense of distance, we had to bring in over a thousand truckloads of dirt and rock."

"It was worth it," Lisa said. "It's beautiful."

"Well, we can try to imitate nature's beauty," he replied with a little bow to her, "but we can never equal it." It was flattery without flirtation or presumption. He might have been speaking of one of his paintings. Lisa smiled in acknowledgment. He had a coldness about him, but she hoped she was going to like him.

"You have a wonderful collection of art," Le'ith commented sociably. "If you won't be offended, it surprises me for one whose business is mining."

Nusseibeh seemed judiciously amused by the comment. Was Le'ith trying to probe?

He certainly was. Le'ith had wanted to discover something of him before he left Saudi Arabia, but he dared not make inquiries. The King had given him his name, and when Le'ith investigated the sources of potash in Morocco, he found that Nusseibeh was listed as the president of the largest producing company. Beyond that he knew nothing of him.

But Nusseibeh was obliging. "In Morocco, Mr. Safadi, if someone wants to start a business, say, shipbuilding"—he seemed to pick the illustration from the sky, but both Lisa and Le'ith realized it was no accident—"he must find a suitable Moroccan partner, and that partner will own fifty-one percent of the business. That is our national law."

He appraised the two of them for a moment, then continued. "And if one is a successful partner in shipbuilding, then one is liable to be sought out by those wanting to manufacture plastics, and television and radio sets, and lightbulbs, and paper, and industrial machines . . . or wanting to mine *potash*."

Lisa had to smile. "You are fifty-one percent of all that?"

Nusseibeh nodded. "And a few things more," he said. "Perhaps it helps explain my ability to indulge my interest in art—a weakness I acquired as a student in Paris." And he looked back at Le'ith.

Le'ith nodded, somewhat mortified. "Well, I'm here to arrange for a supply of potash and uranium for a chemical plant we are building," he said.

"I received your fax." Nusseibeh responded flatly.

Le'ith glanced around uncomfortably. How did he dare begin?

Nusseibeh studied him for a moment. "Let me help you, Mr. Safadi," he said. "I received a communication from a very revered friend of mine in Saudi Arabia saying that you would be coming to see me."

Le'ith stared at him, then glanced at Lisa. Should they come right out with it to someone they knew not at all?

Nusseibeh watched their somewhat panicked exchange of glances. "I don't know your business, but whatever it is," he said with avuncular amusement, "you must not wear your apprehensions on your sleeve. I chose to have tea here by the waterfall and to dismiss the servants because I assumed that what you wanted to talk to me about was extremely . . . 'private.' "

Le'ith hesitated for what seemed ages to Lisa. Nusseibeh just fixed his eyes on him patiently, as though he had "ages" to wait. Finally Le'ith stood and, circling the two of them and the table nervously, related the whole of his audience with the King.

When he finished, Nusseibeh stared into space, slowly fingering his mustache for a long, long time.

"What do you know of Morocco and the Jews?" he asked Le'ith at last.

"Not much," Le'ith answered. "I know Jews rose to great power in the Caliphate, living in the great cities here and in Spain."

"It was more than that," Nusseibeh said. "When the 'Christian Kings,' Isabella and Ferdinand, expelled the Jews from Spain after the fall of the Caliphate, the bulk of them came to Morocco. There were many Jews here already, but most of the refugees settled around Fez. Muhammad the Eleventh, who was sultan then, had a castle built in the center of the refugee settlements and moved into it so that no one would dare molest them.

"After Hitler's war many European Jews came here to settle too. Then, when Israel became a state, a great part of the Jewish population left Morocco to settle there. But many stayed. Many." Now *he* rose and began to pace.

For a time he didn't speak. Then he went on, "Casablanca is a very open city and therefore a very difficult place to keep a secret. But as you can imagine, the Jews who left Morocco for Israel and the Jews who stayed have not been without contact. There is a large Jewish community still in Fez. Jews come and go. If I were you, I would go to Fez—and wait."

Le'ith absorbed it and slowly nodded.

"I will set in motion a certain amount of paperwork about your potash—and your uranium." He smiled. "I am fifty-one percent of the processing too. It all begins with potash, so it's quite logical. If there are inquiries, you are simply showing your beautiful wife the sites of our historic country."

"You—you *will* contact the Mossad," Le'ith said.

"Go and wait," Nusseibeh answered tolerantly.

Le'ith shrugged away his nervousness with a self-deprecating smile. But he couldn't stop himself. "And you will tell the King?"

"I will tell no one who does not need to know," Nusseibeh answered severely. "And I suggest the same course to you. You have perhaps read of the murders in Algeria and Egypt of popular secular intellectuals. One of the most educated and profound professors of Islamic fundamentalist philosophy has justified them, saying that secularists—you 'beardless ones'—who put your brains and talent in the service of an oppressive regime must bear the consequences. Those who kill you are 'heroes.'

"If your mission goes beyond the ears of those who sympathize with you, there is no place from here to faraway Indonesia where you would be safe from one of those 'heroes.' "

He held Le'ith's gaze in a look of steel.

As the three of them walked back to the house, Le'ith tried to allay some of his doubt again. "If we should succeed, do you believe the government here would support us?"

Nusseibeh burst into laughter. It was nearly uncontrollable. "My dear Safadi," he finally croaked, "I wouldn't bet a diseased camel on the chances of your living through the next six months, but if you succeed, I can tell you there is one country where you certainly *will* be a 'hero,' welcomed with royal honors and public applause. You will probably be given the city of Fez, and—and Tangiers too if you want it."

Fez was as unlike Casablanca as it could be while still having the permissive (in Lisa's experience) approach to the outward trappings of religion.

In the first place, it was an old city. Lisa had never seen an old Arabian city, and the warren of narrow streets with their unbroken high walls and baffling twists and turns enthralled her. There was no visible demarcation between dwellings; ornate crenellations and tiny Moorish windows suggested differences in ownership, but there was no way of knowing.

More than half the people wore traditional Arab dress, but most of the women were not veiled, and the sight of a pretty girl in a short skirt and bare arms drew only the admiring gazes of men, not the sharp lashes of the muta'ween.

She and Le'ith had come almost as unenlightened and uncertain as they had to Casablanca. Nusseibeh had given them no contact, and at the recommendation of their driver they chose to register in an extraordinary hotel on a promontory in the middle of the Old Town. It had once been a palace, and it remained one. There were silken sheets and gorgeous canopied beds with fine mosquito mesh hanging over them so you could sleep with the long windows open and hear the noises of the bazaar and the life in the city below. The servants tiptoed along the hallways as though they were still in the service of the sultan. Only the lavish "American" amenities in the bathrooms gave away its modern function.

For two days they roamed the streets on foot. They found the large Jewish Quarter. It was only a continuation of the Old Town, and were it not for the synagogues and yarmulkes on some of the men, and the

Star of David on the butcher shops, you would not know you were in the Jewish Quarter. Once or twice Lisa heard bits of accented Yiddish she could not understand, but mostly they heard Arabic.

They had hired a guide from the hotel to walk with them because the maze of streets was so baffling they were warned they might never find their way out. And it was true. They had twisted and turned one day through the shadowed little passages where sunlight penetrated only a few minutes of each day and even then was filtered through rickety bamboo awnings, and they suddenly turned a corner and faced a stunning mosque. It was totally surrounded by the buildings of the Old Town, but it was so big that it opened to the sky. Sunlight glittered on its dome and illuminated its beautifully decorated walls.

They had to shield their eyes from the light, and the guide laughed at their surprise. Le'ith was awed, and so in fact was Lisa. Worshipers were going in and out, performing their ablutions in the conduits of water that flowed through its tiny courtyard. Le'ith wanted to join them.

Lisa waited as he and the guide splashed their feet and hands with water and went into the mosque. Lisa admired its lovely exterior for a time, shaking her head at the contrast between it and the surrounding labyrinth of unrelieved shades of brown. Then she became conscious of the looks she was getting from people passing by. There were quite a few women walking on their own. But she was so conspicuously Western, so blond, so out of place. For a moment she had a flash of terror and realized how hard it would be to find someone in this maze if she were ever taken. For the first time it occurred to her that she might be being followed, as she had been in Paris. She moved closer to the little railing near the entrance of the mosque, feeling its sanctity would somehow protect her.

Suddenly she smelled the stench of betel juice near her face. An elderly Arab man was right beside her, chewing betel nut and grasping for the railing.

"Don't show alarm, Lisa," he muttered in English before he spit on the ground. Lisa couldn't move, but she knew there was nothing deceptive about her expression: She was staring in frozen fear and surprise.

"Look at me," he said, spitting again, "and give me some money, as you would a beggar."

Lisa fumbled with the tiny purse she was carrying and pulled out a couple of dirhams.

"We need to know one thing," he said as he chomped on his betel. "Is it genuine or is it a scheme of the Saudi Secret Service?"

Lisa handed him the money, her hand shaking as she excoriated herself for being so terrified and inept. "It's genuine," she said. "It's absolutely genuine, but no one can know. How do you know?" She couldn't keep the alarm from her voice.

He took the money, squinted up into her face, and said, "*Shukran* [thank you]." And he shuffled away, spitting and leaning on his cane.

When they returned to the hotel they found a *Ne Pas Déranger* sign on the door to their suite. They had not placed it there. Le'ith looked at her with puzzlement, and she shrugged, but her heart was beating fast.

Le'ith turned the key warily. They entered and closed the door behind them. It was near sunset, and the whole room was russet-hued. For a moment it was hard to tell in the soft uniformity of color if anyone was there. They stood motionless until they were quite sure the room was empty. Then Le'ith walked to the bedroom and switched on the light.

"No one," he said, turning back to her.

Lisa quickly put her finger to her lips, signaling him not to speak. She turned on the light in the sitting room and started looking around. She gestured to Le'ith to pull the drapes and, even in her anxiety, had to smile as he promptly did her bidding. There was nothing in the sitting room.

As they turned in silence, the sudden amplified call of the muezzin startled them both. Lisa grabbed at her heart and sighed at him. He shook his head wryly and went back to the bedroom. "The mosque was so beautiful on the outside, what was it like on the inside?" she asked, trying to break the hushed stillness of their search with "normal" conversation.

"Mosques tend to be prettier on the outside than on the inside," he said. "There are no fancy altars like there are in your churches. Just large areas for prayer and what you would call a pulpit for the imam. Most of the decoration is—"

He stopped because Lisa had found a note under the pillows of the turned-down bed. She stared at it, then signaled him to keep talking.

"The, ah, decorations are mostly Arabic filigree. You have to be born in a desert to appreciate them."

He'd crossed to her and taken the note.

"Well, it was one of the biggest surprises of my life to see it there in the sunlight," she said, studying his face.

The note, in Arabic, had simply given an address with the words "Jewish Quarter tomorrow" and another word Lisa could not make out underneath.

Le'ith held it out to her, his finger sliding under the address indicating she memorize it. She could read the Arabic numbers easily, 16, and the street was Al Fariz. Then he took some matches from the ashtray on the bureau and burned the message.

The muezzin's call finally stopped. Le'ith looked at her, shrugged, went back into the sitting room, bowed to Mecca, and began to pray.

They struggled to make some conversation over dinner and got ready for bed quickly and silently when they returned to their suite.

Le'ith opened the drapes in the bedroom, and the windows, and they listened to the unfamiliar night sounds of the city, which had so enchanted Lisa their first two nights but now gave her a shivering sense of dread.

She put her arm over his shoulder and whispered in his ear. "What did the note say after 'Jewish Quarter tomorrow'?"

Le'ith turned and held his face close to hers, whispering his response. " 'Destroy'—that's why I burned it." She nodded her understanding, and he spoke again. "What happened outside the mosque today? You were white when we came out."

She hesitated. "I was startled by an old beggar. In all the tension it just frightened me." Le'ith groaned at her jumpiness. They lay wrapped together for a time in silence. The first two nights they had made love

with the luxury that was appropriate to their surroundings, and the close-
ness of Le'ith's body, the pressure of her breasts against his chest, made
her damp with desire even with her mind full of anxiety. She felt him
rise, and she touched him gently, rhythmically, and they shared a sort of
frenzied coupling, but it didn't stop her worrying—or his.

The next morning Le'ith bought a city map at the desk and told the
concierge that now they had been exposed to the place a little they were
going to try a day on their own.

The man smiled but warned them to be careful whom they asked
for guidance if they got lost.

When they walked out of the hotel, Le'ith suggested they take a cab
to the Jewish Quarter and then start their search on foot. He didn't want
to give an address to a cabdriver.

Lisa turned him, smiling as though they were talking about where
to have lunch. "I think we ought to walk," she said. "It's not all that
far, and why even let anyone know we're going to the quarter at all?"

Le'ith smiled. "You're right," he said. He leaned down and put his
arm around her shoulder, kissing her neck. "I love you," he whispered.
"Whatever happens, it means everything to me that you're here."

Lisa choked at his guileless intensity. But somehow she couldn't
bring herself to squeeze him back.

She tried as artfully as possible to see if they were being followed,
but she saw no one who seemed to have any interest in them. They
found the address after about twenty minutes of walking the quarter. It
was like dozens and dozens of other addresses: a tiny door in an ancient
dun building of plastered mud brick.

They climbed the narrow, uneven stairs, and a youngish Hasidic Jew
came flying down past them, looking at them askance. When they
reached the second floor, there was a man in a Moroccan djellaba squatting on the floor by one of the doors. All around them was the noise of
children playing and the drone of Arabic conversation. The man took
one look at them, shuffled a little to stand, and opened the door, ushering
them in.

When they entered the room, a tall, powerful man in Western dress
turned to face them. He had an automatic pistol raised in one hand, and

he just stood there as the man who had opened the door hand-searched Le'ith. When he moved to Lisa and started probing her dress, she reacted with a shriek. The tall man with the pistol moved his hand admonishingly, but Le'ith pivoted and smashed the man in the djellaba so hard he fell to the floor bleeding. In almost the same move Le'ith whipped around into the face of the man with the pistol. His own face was ashen. "If you feel the need to search my wife, you will arrange to have a woman do it, or I will kill you and the man who touches her." He was unarmed, but the ferocity in his eyes suggested he had a Sherman tank outside the door and the tall hood looked suddenly uncertain and defensive.

"We apologize, Mr. Safadi, and will make exactly those arrangements if it is ever necessary," a voice said.

The tall man stepped back and holstered his pistol, looking even more cowed. He put out a hand to help the man in the djellaba to his feet.

The room was tiny, with a beaded opening to another room. A stout, balding man with gentle eyes and a roseate complexion had stepped through the beads. It was he who had made the apology, and he offered his hand to Le'ith. "Please call me Uri," he said.

As he spoke, another man came from the adjoining room. It was *Adam*.

Lisa opened her mouth and almost exclaimed, but Adam darted her a look of such severity that she caught herself and looked to the floor.

"And this is your wife," Uri was saying. Lisa saw his feet moving toward her and knew he was offering his hand, but she wasn't sure she could look up without revealing her emotion.

"I want to apologize, especially to you," Uri said. "All of this was so sudden—and unusual—we had to be careful and could not be as prepared as we like to be."

Lisa looked up straight into his face. She didn't dare glance at Adam. Uri smiled very sympathetically. "I'm truly sorry," he said. "It won't happen again." Lisa simply nodded and looked back down at the floor.

The man who called himself Uri opened the door and signaled the tall hood and the man in the djellaba to wait in the hallway.

When the door closed, he ushered Le'ith and Lisa into the other room. It contained an old davenport covered with an afghan and two lounge chairs. An old rattan table perched tightly in the middle contained an ornate lamp, a samovar, and some small Arabian coffee cups.

Uri served them all and professed not to know the reason for their meeting, only that it was something of the utmost importance. Lisa did glance at Adam when he said that, but Adam's face was inscrutable.

Le'ith demanded to know if they were from the Mossad.

"Surely you don't expect us to answer that." Uri smiled. "But I can assure you that if needed, we have access to the highest echelons of the Israeli government. I understand that is what you are seeking."

Lisa was tempted to say, "Le'ith, it's all right," but of course she didn't. For a moment he remained skeptical and silent.

"I am told Mr. Nusseibeh's art collection is quite extraordinary," Uri said. Le'ith didn't answer, but it seemed to help. He waited sometime more. He only received Uri's patient smile. Eventually he began as he had with Nusseibeh and slowly related all that had brought them there.

Adam and Uri listened without expression but with total concentration. When he finished, they said nothing for a long time, and then Uri asked if they would excuse them for a few moments while they spoke in private.

Le'ith and Lisa went to the tiny outer room. Even through the noises of the building they could hear the whispering in the other room, but it was too indistinct to penetrate. Lisa took Le'ith's hand and squeezed it, trying to reassure him. *She* knew they were Mossad—or at least one of them was—but she knew Le'ith was still uncertain.

After staring out the little window for a time, Le'ith pointed out three men to Lisa. They all were in work clothes. Two were on the street about fifty feet apart, both seemingly idle, but both were watching the entrance to the building they were in. There was another on the rooftop of the building opposite. You could glimpse him only when he peered over to check the doorway, and it took a time for Lisa to catch his movement.

"The question is," Le'ith whispered, "are they Mossad or are they agents of Army Secret Service?"

"You think they followed us here?" she whispered in disbelief. She would have sworn they hadn't been followed.

"They probably didn't have to," Le'ith answered. "They knew what flight we took. I'm sure they have people in Morocco they can call on." He smirked ironically. "After all, the Mossad does."

Adam came out and asked them to come back into the inner room. When they were seated, Uri leaned forward and could not hide the excitement in his eyes.

"This is a very brilliant conception, Mr. Safadi. I want to congratulate you not only on the postulate but on the generosity of spirit that could lead you to it."

"I only think it will work," Le'ith replied emotionlessly, "if the advantages to both sides are very clear. Goodwill or 'generosity of spirit' may be products of any arrangement we make, but they are not enough to construct a settlement."

It was not cold or threatening, but Lisa could see what Rashid meant about Le'ith's capacity in business dealings.

Uri took the point, but his sense of excitement remained. "The sticking point of course will be Jerusalem," he said.

"If that issue is a sticking point, then there will be no arrangement," Le'ith said flatly.

Lisa hoped he would add some qualifying statement, but his whole attitude indicated that there would be none. She knew so many in Israel who felt the same way from the opposite point of view.

She glanced at Adam. He was studying Le'ith with such intensity that she knew they had decided someone in Israel might want this "arrangement" badly. The question was, What would it cost? The Saudis had a reputation for bargaining equal to that of any Israeli. Was Le'ith bargaining, or was the issue that cut-and-dried?

After a long silence, during which they measured each other without a sign of concession on either side, Adam finally spoke.

"Jerusalem is nonnegotiable," he said.

Le'ith turned to him very calmly. "If that is true, my wife and I will not bother you further. But we have come a long way, and I want you to consider that the Old City, which is at the crux of His Majesty's demands, already has its own Armenian Quarter, its Greek Orthodox Quarter, its Christian Quarter, its Arab Quarter, as well as its Jewish Quarter."

"Your Dome of the Rock sits on the ruins of the Jewish Temple," Uri said, his tone as calm and unargumentative as Le'ith's. "Our sacred Wailing Wall is the underpinning of your Dome."

"That is an image that could speak of cousinhood, not conflict," Le'ith replied. "And so His Majesty sees it. He would remind you that Abraham is a holy prophet to both our religions."

"Quite right," Uri answered, "and we have respected that. We have not limited access to the Dome or to the Al Asqa Mosque, nor do we intend to. You can assure His Maj—"

"That is not enough," Le'ith cut in. "His Majesty does not intend to visit the Dome or the mosque at the 'largess' of the Israeli government."

An edge had crept into his tone, and there was a flash of fire in his eyes. She knew from his past fulminations on Israel that he believed that but for the huge outpouring of American arms and money, Jerusalem would not be in Israeli hands at all. At worst it would be an international city under UN control, and it was only with American help that the Israelis had dared defy that UN resolution.

Adam stood and poured another coffee for everyone. It was the Middle Eastern elixir of the bargaining table, Lisa realized, as she watched the dark coffee flow and looked into the eyes of the men seemingly so fixed in their separate resolves.

"You're a young man, Mr. Safadi," Adam said as he poured for Le'ith. "You would not remember, but after Israel's War of Independence—after Israel was attacked by Arab countries that defied the UN resolution granting our nationhood along with Palestine's—the Jordanians seized and held the Old City. And for all the years they held it they would not allow one Jew from outside the Old City to enter to worship at the Wailing Wall."

Though he had aged and gained even more weight, Lisa was a little annoyed at Adam's talking so gravely, as though he were an old man. She didn't want him to be an old man. Le'ith only glanced at him thoughtfully and sipped his coffee.

"It is what has made us rather obdurate about who controls that sacred piece of ground," Uri added, again without an ounce of argumentation in his tone. Given his emotional control and his vocabulary, Lisa wondered who he was. He was certainly not one of those she had met or seen at the Mossad's center in Haifa, but the way Adam unconsciously deferred to him, she knew he was someone of considerable importance.

She wanted desperately to speak, but she knew this might be "bargaining," and her intervention could throw it all off. But she believed she knew the dangers in the Arab world even better than Adam. However much he had learned since he left the United States, he had been mired in Israeli politics. She had been forced to live amid *Arab* politics, and she was convinced that if this chance was lost, Israel was in more peril than it had been since that long-ago war in '48. She held her tongue, sipping her coffee in the silence as long as she could, but then she could hold it no longer.

"I am only an American," she said quietly, her head bowed, "and I don't know the history of either of your countries very well," she lied. "But I know that that war is over and if you live in the past, you will continue to fight the battles of yesterday and there will be no future. No hope for peace. What if France and Germany had taken the same stance after World War Two?"

There was another long silence. More coffee was sipped. Then Le'ith spoke. "If we come to an agreement," he said, "Saudi soldiers and Israeli soldiers are going to be jointly controlling *atomic missiles*. If they can do *that,* surely they can jointly patrol the Old City of Jerusalem. All that either side wants is control of its own holy places. It doesn't have to be a battle zone; it could be as peaceful as our having coffee at this table."

Adam glanced at Uri. Uri was contemplating the knuckles of his hands. Finally he looked up at Le'ith.

"What about East Jerusalem?" he asked, looking at Le'ith with his first show of intractableness.

Le'ith met his gaze with an equable firmness. "East Jerusalem is populated by Arabs; East Jerusalem is a functioning Arab city. If there is *no* agreement, it can be a source of a renewed and continuous intifada." He let the threat of that internal warfare hang in the air. "If Israel tries to take all Jerusalem, you will never have peace, even if you kill every Palestinian in its walls. The Arab world will never let you rest.

"In peace," he continued firmly, "East Jerusalem can be a source of trade and cultural exchange with Jewish Jerusalem, part of one of the greatest tourist and religious centers in all the world.

"But you must understand now that His Majesty is not making this offer at the sacrifice of his Arab brothers. And as potential allies you should be shrewd enough to see that nothing, *nothing,* would make His Majesty's kingdom more insecure than the charge that he had traded the slavery of his Muslim brothers in East Jerusalem for the safety of his kingdom." He paused. "East Jerusalem will be Arab. But its borders are easy to monitor, and with the Old City secured in our joint hands, there will be far more prospect of a peaceful Israeli Jerusalem than you have ever had."

Uri stared at him for a long time and then studied the white knuckles of his clasped fist again.

"Some very important people in Israel have stated that Jerusalem would never be divided and will always be Israeli," he said at last.

Le'ith smiled almost condescendingly. "Someone must suggest to those 'important people' that they look at the history of the stones on which they walk. The Romans doubtless said Jerusalem would *always* be Roman, Saladin that it would *always* be Arab, the Crusaders that it would always be Christian, the Turks that it would always be Ottoman, the British that it would always be British.

" 'Never' and 'always' are for speeches. History tends to be more realistic. One hundred years is a short time in the life of Jerusalem. Who would wager what will be even one hundred years from now? Never mind *two* or *three* hundred years."

Uri looked at him with a tight smile. "You've given this a lot of thought, Mr. Safadi." Le'ith only bowed a little in acknowledgment. Uri peered into the inflexible dark brown eyes for a moment; then he nodded in concession. A trace of his earlier excitement returned to his eyes.

"I hope you will stay in Fez for another few days," he said. "I will be one of those who will be most gratified if we can arrange to meet again."

Le'ith rose. They shook hands all around, Adam giving no indication that he knew Lisa at all.

As they went into the outer room, Le'ith turned to Adam. "Do you have people watching this building?"

Adam hesitated. "We have a few friends in the neighborhood, yes."

"On the rooftop across the way, perhaps?"

Adam frowned. "No. I don't believe we do. . . ."

Le'ith related what he'd seen.

Adam started for the window, then stopped, thinking better of it. He turned back to them. "Upstairs," he said, "there is a woman who does exquisite needlework. There's a sign on her door. Go up and purchase as much as she has ready. When you leave the building, take some of it out and talk about it as you walk away."

Le'ith nodded and took Lisa's arm.

"Do you have any idea who they might be?" Uri asked.

"They could be agents of our Army's Secret Service," Le'ith answered.

"Do they have any idea why you're here?" Adam said in alarm.

Le'ith shook his head. "No. If they did, all this would be over."

Lisa looked at Adam, thinking of the old man at the mosque who knew too much. Adam didn't react at all. "Why would they be following you then?" he asked Le'ith.

"Because I had a very long and unprecedented audience with the King."

Uri nodded his understanding slowly. "You're a valuable man, Mr. Safadi. I shall pray for your well-being."

They had breakfast in the dining room. Both of them glanced about casually, trying to look interested but unconcerned. They'd used the same technique walking home from the Jewish Quarter but had no idea how convincing they were. In any case they'd seen no one, so they weren't sure if they were being followed or not.

As one of the uniformed waiters was refilling their coffee cups, he slipped a note under Lisa's plate.

"What's the matter?" Le'ith asked as he looked up. "Have you seen something?"

"Yes," she responded distractedly. She couldn't say it was nothing when her hand was shaking and her face was colorless. "Don't look now, but didn't we see that man behind you on the left just as we were coming out of the quarter?"

Le'ith paused, concentrating.

"Now," Lisa said as the man turned to a waiter. When Le'ith glanced his way, Lisa grabbed the note and slipped it under the elastic waistband of her skirt. When she relaxed, she saw that the maître d' had been watching her. He held her eyes for moment as she looked guiltily disconcerted and then discreetly turned to other business.

"He's not anyone I noticed," Le'ith said. She couldn't hide that she was even more flustered. "I think you're a bit too nervous," he said, and began to smile. "Keep calm, and just remember, nobody can find out anything unless they torture us," he said dryly.

It made her grin despite the tension, despite the truth of it.

Upstairs in the bathroom she read the note. It was in English: "Keep faith—the bazaar. 2 o'clock." She flushed it down the toilet and agonized over how she could possibly get away from Le'ith to go off on her own.

But at a quarter to two the phone rang. It was Mr. Nusseibeh. He had a lot of details about the intended shipments of potash and uranium that he wanted to discuss with Le'ith.

Lisa sighed with relief. She signaled Le'ith, and he broke off for a moment, holding his hand over the phone.

"While you're talking business," she whispered, "I think I'll go to the bazaar." Le'ith frowned with concern. "You'd be bored anyway," she pleaded, "and it's been a long time since I've been able to shop in a place like that."

Le'ith clearly wasn't too happy but nodded and went back to his call. When Lisa left, she blew him a kiss, and he responded by shaking a finger of caution at her.

She walked the huge bazaar, almost certain she was being followed, and was beginning to think she'd somehow missed her connection or it had been called off when a girl in a chador sidled next to her at a table of silk. "Follow me," she muttered without looking. She rummaged through some silk scarves for a minute, then walked away.

Lisa followed as nonchalantly as possible. The girl started toward one of the narrow streets of the Old Town. Lisa's heart beat a bit faster. That teeming place could feel sheltered and fascinating or just plain terrifying, depending on whom you were with. Every time the girl fell out of sight around a bend, Lisa felt the urge to run to catch up, but she knew that among the others on the crowded lane there was likely to be one or more who were following them, and she didn't dare.

The girl turned up one of the many open staircases, and now Lisa felt real terror. She longed to be in a chador herself, *with* a veil preferably. In this environment her Western clothes and blue eyes were like alarms saying, "Here I am. I don't belong!"

They had climbed two flights of stairs and walked a long, rickety passageway that contained a row of doors on one side and looked down through wooden slats to a narrow courtyard below on the other. There were some men smoking in the shade and some children playing. One of the men saw her and nodded to the others. She couldn't make out what he said. Near the end of the corridor the girl took a stairway leading up to the next floor. Lisa followed, but the stairway split, and she caught just a glimpse of the girl as she disappeared at the top of the right-hand branch.

Lisa hurried, afraid to get lost in this incredible warren, and when she turned from the stairs, she was seized and a blanket put over her head! She let out a muffled cry but was lifted from her feet and bundled through a door. She heard the door close, and the blanket was taken from her head.

She was in a room full of Arabs. One of the women tossed her a chador and waved agitatedly for her to put it on. Recovered from her shock, Lisa slipped it on, and the men who had seized her squatted on the floor and began eating with the others. She had just got herself covered when they heard footsteps running up the stairs, and the woman who'd given her the chador pulled Lisa to an old sewing machine. There was a noise and some cursing in the hall. The woman gestured for Lisa to work the machine. She'd never touched one. It had a foot pedal, and she moved it up and down, her hands fumbling with the cloth when the needle started clicking. Almost immediately there was a sharp rap on the door, and it was pushed open. Frightened, Lisa started to look, but the woman nodded fiercely to the machine. The woman turned. "What do you want?" she asked sharply.

The Arabic had a different accent from what she was used to, but Lisa understood it.

Then in an accent she knew very well: "A Western woman, my master sent me to look after her." He had apparently scanned the room and looked at the blank faces because the door closed as quickly as it had opened and the footsteps ran on. They were joined by another pair, and Lisa heard the words "Try the other stairs!" And the second footsteps came running back.

Lisa started to get up, but the woman cautioned her, and they all stayed frozen, listening until they heard a rap on another door and the muted voice again. Then the woman signaled Lisa up. She looked at her work on the sewing table and muttered an imprecation.

"*Assif* [I'm sorry]," Lisa said.

The woman looked at her in amazement, then smiled, revealing four good teeth in a mouth of darkness. She took Lisa's arm and directed her toward the beaded curtain that led to another room.

Lisa entered, and as she now expected, Adam was standing there. She went into his arms, and he hugged her as though he had longed to hold her as much as she had longed to be held.

"We must be fairly quick," he said. "We've got to get you back out there where they can find you before they get too suspicious."

"We *are* being followed then," Lisa moaned.

"Yes. But don't worry, we're following them."

"Oh, God, I was not meant for this. Two of you are following us, and Le'ith and I didn't see a soul."

Adam smiled that still impish smile of his. "We're supposed to be good at it. Don't be disappointed in yourself."

"Who are they?"

"We don't know yet."

"They're Saudi, that's for sure. I think Le'ith is right. They must be agents of the Army Secret Service."

"How do you know they're Saudi?"

"I recognized the accent."

Adam looked at her—impressed.

"Don't be surprised, Adam," she said. "I've lived with that language for almost fifteen years."

Adam met her eyes; he had caught the desolation in those words and took her into his arms again. She could feel his artificial hand, and she leaned into him heavily.

"What about your 'husband'?" he asked soberly. "Is he genuine?"

"Very," she answered. And heard the same pensiveness in her voice.

"Is he in alliance with anyone else?"

"Only the King."

"You're positive of that? This could not be a trick of the military to get atomic information or to try to denude us of our own stockpile?"

Lisa smiled and shook her head. "No. I can tell you that without any doubt. This is Le'ith's idea, and his alone."

"How did he get that influential with the King?"

"That's a long story," Lisa said. "But it's not so much a matter of influence as it is that the King will hear his counsel."

"Alone? On something as momentous as this?"

"The King didn't know what it was about when they met, but when he heard Le'ith out, he agreed that it was a possible way to keep his Kingdom alive for several years to come—but it depended on total secrecy."

Adam weighed it broodingly. His hair had turned all white now, and the once playful-looking face could now look very distinguished.

"What about those people in there?" Lisa whispered.

"They don't speak English," he answered. "They've been used before. Don't worry."

"I do worry," she said brittlely, bringing his eyes and mind back to her. "If this were to get out, you know the King would deny it, would *have* to deny it. And Le'ith would almost certainly be beheaded."

Adam smiled wryly. "Don't you trust us, Lisa?"

"The old man who accosted me, how secure is he?" she asked with a censorious edge.

"He knew the *question* to ask—'Is it genuine?'—nothing more."

Lisa looked a little abashed; she might have figured that out.

"Nusseibeh confided in our section head in Casablanca," Adam explained. "He contacted us. We were thunderstruck but very tempted. It was the chief's decision to send Uri to test it out and me to see what I could find out from you."

"So you both knew everything from the start."

"No. *I* did. Uri is the man who handled the initial stages of all the negotiations for the Palestinian Peace Accord both in Norway and Egypt. We thought we should let him hear it firsthand and come to a judgment without our input."

"And what judgment did he come to?"

Adam shook his head. "He didn't confide that to me. He's flown to Israel. We'll see when he comes back—if he comes back."

"I hope to God it's positive."

Adam studied her. "Have you fallen in love with this 'arranged' husband of yours?"

Lisa shook her head. "But I think he's too decent to betray without a lot of pain," she answered. "And the thought that all these years could accomplish something so good for them and so good for Israel has made me more content with myself than I have been since that day you first took me to Haifa."

Adam grazed her chin affectionately with his fist. Then he turned and sat on the huge, sagging bed that took up most of the room. With his remaining hand he pinched his eyes in fatigue and concern.

"What is your worry?" Lisa asked.

"Can't you imagine? We'd be risking our best and most secret weapons to a 'joint' enterprise in Saudi Arabia, where every unit will be isolated hundreds of miles from Israel."

"The Saudis don't fear Israel," Lisa said, hunching down on her heels before him. "They fear Iran and Iraq and the fundamentalists . . . just as the Israelis do."

"If Iran or Iraq attacked Saudi Arabia, the United States would act in a minute. They're importing more Saudi oil now than they did in the days before the price rise."

"Perhaps. But what if there is an *internal* revolution, *instigated* by Iran or Iraq? You yourself said that was a danger."

He touched her cheek playfully, as if she were still nineteen.

"I *would* worry about that, but whoever takes over Saudi Arabia will still want to *sell* its oil—be they sheikhs or imams."

"Yes," Lisa answered confidently. "They will sell to Japan and Europe. *Maybe* to the United States, but they will certainly use the proceeds to buy arms and lavish money on Hamas and the Islamic Jihad and Fatah because the extreme fundamentalists want to eliminate Israel; it's their primary goal.

"I know them better than you do now, and they look at Israelis the way Israelis sometimes look at Palestinians," she went on fervently, "as though they were the Nazis, *and* the Spanish Inquisitors, *and* the Crusaders, and all the enemies of Jews throughout history rolled into one. Well, that's the way they see *Israelis,* as the arrogant people who through the years of their denigration under the British and French— and the most hated of all, *us,* the Americans—humiliated them time and again. I have spent most of my adult life in that atmosphere, and believe me, if the fanatic imams seize power in Saudi Arabia, Israel will suffer more than anyone quibbling about a few feet of Jericho can ever imagine."

Adam had been peering at her with a growing sense of astonishment. She knew what he was thinking. She leaned forward, letting her knees rest on the floor and folded her arms across his lap. "You may not have believed everything Mother wrote you at the time," she said quietly, "but I wasn't a dummy when I first came to Israel. And I'm not a dummy now."

Adam reached down and slowly stroked her hair.

Chapter 29

The wait for the man called Uri seemed endless. The Israelis were holding an election, and the Arab extremists who wanted no peace with Satan's daughter blew up a bus in the middle of Tel Aviv, and there were cries for revenge. The leader of the Likud party, a man who had decried the peace initiative from the beginning, became Prime Minister of Israel. Le'ith was in despair; so was Lisa.

But the man called Uri did come back. A week after the election Nusseibeh called Le'ith and said he should take his lovely wife to see Marrakesh. Lisa and Le'ith were uncertain. Maybe it was designed to keep up the cover story that they were "seeing" Morocco; maybe it was a way to tell them to go home.

They stayed at La Mamounia, famous for a dozen historic meetings and for being Winston Churchill's favorite resort. Outside its walls was the chaos of a city that was somewhere between ancient Fez and modern Casablanca. But inside it was a grand thirties European spa with Moorish overtones, its rooms looking out over its acres of garden and the Atlas Mountains in the distance in a way that made you believe that you were in the middle of an empty landscape.

Lisa had had the shock of her life when she went for an early-morning swim and came face-to-face with a large naked bosom. She was doing the breaststroke, and so was the owner of the generous breasts. The two women bubbled to the top. "Sorry," Lisa gulped.

The woman shook her head good-naturedly and sputtered in a thick French accent, "The whole pool and we bump into each other! *Mon*

Dieu!" And she paddled off. It seemed in such great contrast with the dark thoughts in Lisa's mind, the dark events at the other end of the Mediterranean. By afternoon Lisa realized that however discreetly women dressed in the street, the vacationing French chose to sunbathe at the hotel as bare-chested as they did in Cap d'Antibes. Despite his own problems, it clearly distracted Le'ith. He tried not to look but bore the expression Lisa had seen several times in California when some "American" behavior totally flummoxed him.

For a day they waited and worried. They wandered the immense souk, watched a snake charmer and a busload of uniformed English schoolgirls who had whistled and cheered a handsome flame swallower in a way that somehow made Lisa very homesick, then walked back to the hotel so Le'ith could enjoy his poolside embarrassment, all the time wondering if they were being followed, and by whom, or whether any-one cared anymore.

The next morning they were having breakfast—by the pool—when a bellhop came with a message that their car was waiting. He said their chauffeur recommended they might want to take sweaters as it might be cool.

Le'ith was elated, but on the way out he whispered, "It would be nice to know if we're driving to see the Mossad or the Army Secret Service." Lisa had the same icy feeling, and the memory of hearing that Youssef had been trained by American Special Forces came unwillingly to her mind.

The chauffeur began by saying, "No speak English." When Le'ith addressed him in Arabic, he looked frightened and just shook his head. They couldn't get him to talk.

He recklessly careered through the streets, then suddenly made a U-turn and left the city and started toward the mountains. After a time he turned onto a road that became quite narrow and started to climb. He finally swung onto a well-kept dirt road and approached a large ranch house and the fences of a huge estate.

It was Adam who greeted them. He was with another man Lisa recognized from Haifa. Adam made first-name introductions, using a false one for himself.

Inside, Adam took them to a grand room with a huge stone fireplace and magnificent views out over the ranch and the mountains. Uri was waiting for them with a handsome man wearing jodhpurs and leather boots. He introduced himself as their host, Nadi Abu Libdeh.

He offered them fattoosh, hummus, and coffee and excused himself, leaving with Adam. There was an awkward pause. Then a round-faced distinguished-looking man who vaguely resembled Abba Eban came down the stairs. Uri introduced him as Aaron.

After they'd shaken hands, Aaron gestured them to a table by the long windows overlooking the ranch. It was Uri who began. "You will understand our delay, but I can report that our government has considerable interest in your proposal, Mr. Safadi."

He was going to say more, but Le'ith cut him off immediately. " 'Interest' is not quite sufficient," he said firmly. "For my part, I cannot risk going ahead on 'interest.' "

It was calm and authoritative, but its bluntness clearly discomforted the man called Aaron. Lisa was impressed by Le'ith's unwillingness to be cowed by Aaron's obvious stature, but she hoped he wouldn't push too audaciously. She knew they both had been hoping desperately for some sign of any interest at all.

"Well, perhaps a 'decision' can be given," Uri said after a hesitation. "But there are still some issues that need clarification."

Le'ith simply nodded. His strength, Lisa realized, was that he seemed utterly without concern as to whether their decision was going to be positive or negative.

"One problem area for us," Uri continued, "is the question of bringing Syria and Egypt into this agreement. Is that something His Majesty is fixed on?"

"Yes," Le'ith answered without hesitation. "We have a small population and thousands of miles of border. If it were assumed that this agreement benefited only Israel and Saudi Arabia, the reaction in Syria and Egypt would be catastrophic. Their hostility would be a constant threat to the Kingdom and to peace. That is why His Majesty's proposal for an economic development plan includes them and Jordan."

"And that plan would be *totally* separate from the military agreement between your country and ours?" Uri persisted.

"Separate—but linked," Le'ith answered flatly. "Both agreements must be announced at the same time." His tone left no room for discussion.

The distinguished-looking Aaron spoke for the first time. "It is our belief," he stated, "that nothing can keep Egypt from exploding." He was as calm and firm as Le'ith. "The Islamic fundamentalists grow more powerful every day; they kill policemen, ministers of government, artists, tourists, and for every one the government imprisons or executes, ten more spring up in their place."

Le'ith faced him, examining him a moment for depth, it seemed. Then he leaned forward with a personal intensity.

"I have been frightened myself by the images of hysterical fundamentalism in Egypt," he said with a voice filled with emotion, and Lisa remembered the night they had watched the film of the assassination of Sadat. "It is a problem that has kept me awake many nights. But I realized that I *know* many fundamentalists," he went on, "and I know that some of the best brains in Islam, some of the most humane people in the *world,* are fundamentalists. So why do these educated college professors and idealistic young students allow what is happening in Egypt to go on?

"I'll tell you why. Because besides ideology, fundamentalist groups provide schools and health clinics and food and even jobs. They give hope and the promise of dignity to people who live in filth and poverty, while all around them 'secular' functionaries profit from corruption and care about the future not at all."

The emotion, after his almost bloodless bargaining, created a moment of silence. Le'ith's eyes remained fixed on Aaron, but then he leaned back in his chair.

"But how do you propose to end corruption in a system that breeds it?" Uri asked.

"Do what the fundamentalists want to do," Le'ith answered. "Take the instruments of power from the corrupt."

Aaron grinned spontaneously. It wasn't condescending; it was as though Le'ith had told a great joke. Unpredictably Le'ith smiled back.

"I know there are corrupt Israelis," he said, "and corrupt Saudis. But in general our societies function with some justice. If we create an economic development plan—with Saudi money primarily—it will be *jointly* controlled. Israeli bankers and economists, Saudi bankers and economists, along with, in Egypt, Egyptian bankers and economists. But all *three* would control and monitor the disbursal of money and the choice of projects. And all three would have to *agree*."

He paused and looked at the two of them. "Point one," he said, "you have many more educated technocrats in banking, engineering, and economics than we have, or the Egyptians have, so how fast the Egyptian economy and social structure repaired itself would depend very much on you. Point two, once it does, I guarantee the ground support for the extreme fundamentalists will all but vanish."

"Really?" Uri said skeptically.

"Yes," Le'ith responded confidently. "Because most people do not normally approve of murder." His eyes began to sparkle with a smile again. "And because we all know that, very few of us have the appetite for ardent fundamentalism—in any religion. If our stomachs and pockets are full, we think of better things to devote our energy to."

Aaron slowly shook his head, not in disapproval but in acknowledgment of the potency of the argument. "Was all this the King's idea?" he asked.

Le'ith grinned. "The idea of an economic development plan was the King's. The nature of its operation was mine."

Aaron smiled again. Lisa sensed he was beginning to like Le'ith. "Saudi finances are not as liquid as they once were," Aaron pointed out. "How does His Majesty expect to find the capital for that size enterprise?"

"Japan, the Common Market, the United States all desperately need our oil—*and* a stable Middle East. Our oil reserves can act as guarantees for any immediate loans that might be necessary."

There was a long pause. Then Aaron slowly got up and stood at the window, staring out. It was some time before he spoke. "There is no way of contacting the King directly, were it even the Prime Minister who sought it?"

"No," Le'ith answered. "There is no way of doing that without exposing everything. There is no avenue of approaching the King unknown to his royal brothers. In the long run they must agree," he continued, "but to open it to them now would finish it before it ever got started."

"So that means you are our sole contact?"

"Yes. But I remind you that it was the King who led me to Mr. Nusseibeh. And if I am misleading you, at worst you will have lost some time and some few expenses. If I am not, there is perhaps a once-and-for-all opportunity to create a secure Middle East, one where your country might at last be an accepted part."

"What assurance do we have that the two royal princes *will* agree?" Uri persisted.

"None," Le'ith replied, "other than the fact that the King saw the value of it, and he believes that if we can bring it off, his royal brothers will see its value too."

Aaron sighed. He turned back to the window, and they waited silently for a long time.

"Do you have a safe contact in Egypt?" he asked ultimately.

"I have friends, close friends, but not for this sort of thing," Le'ith answered.

Aaron continued to stare at the horizon. "Perhaps we can help you with that," he said.

Chapter 30

It all broke apart in Egypt.

Without knowing, they both were to blame. Le'ith faxed Rashid, saying that instead of flying directly back from Casablanca, he was stopping in Cairo for a few days to show Lisa the Pyramids, while Lisa acted from the day they arrived on the assumption that since the man called Aaron had given them an Egyptian contact who had access to President Mubarak, Israel was committed.

For a time neither had a clue that anything was wrong. Le'ith didn't want to stay at the homes of any of his friends because though he trusted them, he thought it would be too difficult to come and go as they might have to. The tourist trade was so badly hit they had their choice of hotels and took a suite on the top floor of the new Sheraton that gave them views of the Pyramids and the traffic on the Nile.

From the moment they landed Lisa was struck by an almost tangible sense of danger, not from what they were attempting but from the city itself. She only vaguely remembered it from a long-ago tour, so full of history and beauty, a beauty that came both from its setting and from the accumulation of civilizations that had inhabited it. It should have been a city to walk at leisure or ride through indolently in one of the horse carriages that waited by every bridge and taxi stand.

But there was an indescribable tension in the air that made Aaron's words "nothing can keep Egypt from exploding" seem uncannily prophetic. Hostility snapped at them everywhere like sparks from a faulty wire; people on the street glared icily or looked through them altogether.

They had walked for a time the first night and were harassed and cursed by beggars who stole up slyly to make their appeals and then slipped away muttering curses whether you gave them something or not.

Even in this international zone of wealth, the words "Islam is the solution!" were scrawled in figures of rage on walls and etched defiantly in the concrete sidewalks. When they got back to the hotel, they saw that someone had spit a huge ugly blob of red betel juice onto the back of Le'ith's pants. He closed his eyes in anger and a kind of rueful disillusionment.

They heard sirens throughout the night—it was like New York City—and in the morning when they went out to their balcony for breakfast, they saw a crowd gathered on one of the tree-lined side streets. A wailing police car rounded the corner, and the crowd split and exposed three white-suited policemen standing over the body of a man, a huge puddle of blood circling his head.

Unlike the bobbies, who had once trained them, the police all carried menacing semiautomatic rifles, but even they looked edgily insecure. Most of the crowd was dressed in Western clothes, and several just glanced at the scene and walked on as though the sight were too habitual to be worth their tarrying; the others fell back as the police waved their rifles at them in quick-tempered admonition.

"Maybe it's going to be harder than I thought," Le'ith said dispiritedly.

"No," Lisa replied. "If you give people hope, you can change even this."

He shrugged ambiguously.

That night they had dinner on the paddle steamer *Queen of the Nile*. Before they left the hotel, they had stayed on their balcony to watch the river change through a dozen hues of gold to dark purple. The breathtaking view was accompanied by half a dozen amplified calls from muezzins at mosques dotted around them. After their summons ended, Le'ith went to the sitting room and prayed longer than was his wont. In the car he held her hand as he used to do when they went to the movies in Los Angeles long ago.

They were to rendezvous with Uri, who was already seated when they arrived. The maître d' led them past his table, and Lisa was thankful they were moving because sitting across from him was "Aunt Connie."

Lisa had recovered enough from the shock when they reached their table not to alert Le'ith, but she quickly buried herself in the menu to avoid saying anything until she was sure she had control of herself.

Le'ith had, as agreed, made a reservation for a table near the band. Lisa found the noise deafening, but eventually people began to dance, and as an unorganized group pushed around their table to reach the tiny dance floor, the boy clearing their first course slipped an envelope to Le'ith. It had disappeared by the time the boy lifted his tray.

When they returned to the hotel, Le'ith opened the note. A car was to pick him up at ten; the note recommended "Mrs. Safadi" remain in their suite.

"How do they know what hotel we're in?" Lisa groaned.

"Well, we registered under my name—"

"But we could be in one of twenty different hotels, or we could have stayed with one of your friends." She shook her head. "I would swear we were not followed yesterday. *We* chose the cab at the airport, and I kept watching behind us."

"In that traffic it wouldn't have been too hard to keep track of us." He grinned. "Look, we're not spies. Just let them arrange things; then we'll try to do what *we* are good at."

"*You* are good at," Lisa corrected.

Le'ith was flattered. "I'm glad I'm not here alone, I'll tell you that."

And Lisa was flattered. She was really feeling that they were doing this together and, despite the miasmic aura of danger, felt a contentment deeper than any she could remember.

Lisa was about to open the door after the buzzer had sounded when she had a second thought. She peered through the peephole. Facing her was Linn, Dr. Nordheimer, the Swedish psychologist–cum–Mossad agent from whom she had last received a lecture in Riyadh.

She opened the door, and Linn came in quickly, checking the hallway behind her. Once inside she relaxed, slipped off the little hijab she wore over her graying blond hair, and gave Lisa a smile and a hug.

"Well, time hasn't done much to you," she said. "You look marvelous."

"I'm doing something I believe in." Lisa grinned.

"We're all supposed to be doing that, though I admit some things are easier than others." She looked at Lisa almost sympathetically. "You wouldn't have a drink, would you?"

Lisa went to the minibar, which was buried in a beautiful mahogany cabinet.

Linn took straight whiskey on ice, four of the little bottles in one glass, a quantity that reinforced all Lisa had heard about the Swedish capacity for alcohol.

"Lovely view," Linn said. "We know who was following you."

The way she said it Lisa knew she was not about to hear good news. Linn took another drink of whiskey, and it was a drink, not a sip.

"It was not agents of Army Secret Service," she continued. "They were agents of the King's."

Lisa was baffled. In the first place she hadn't known the King had a separate corps of agents, and second she couldn't imagine why he had sent them to follow Le'ith.

"Why?" she asked. "Do you know why?"

Linn nodded. "He wanted to protect you in case you were double-crossed by the Moroccans. His Majesty's tribal background has apparently given him a heightened sense of conspiracy."

"With all the brothers and half brothers he has, all wanting to be king, it's probably what's kept him alive."

"That may be," Linn replied cynically. She sprawled on one of the couches. "Why don't you toss me some peanuts or something? I probably shouldn't do this on an empty stomach."

Lisa went to the minibar and gave her a choice. "Are they still following us?" she asked.

"No. One is dead. The other is being held incommunicado by one of our teams in Fez."

Lisa froze. Linn looked up at her and shrugged miserably. "The word on your husband's plan was very high, and they wanted to know who was following you, and why."

"What does that mean?" Lisa asked sharply.

"It means the King's agents didn't want to say why they were following you, and one of our people went a little too far in demanding an answer."

Lisa was dumbstruck. "You mean you killed him?"

"That was not the intention."

"They tortured him to death?"

"Until the end they didn't know he was an agent of the King's! But in any case there was never an intention to kill him."

Lisa sank onto a footstool, holding her head in her hands. "How can Le'ith ever explain it? You don't know. This is enough to kill the whole plan."

"I *do* know," Linn corrected. "And there's no reason for the King ever to discover the Mossad was involved."

"Oh, God! I always thought you people knew what you were doing!"

"There is one considerable benefit from the information," Linn said calmly. "Not everyone was convinced your husband was actually empowered to speak for the King. Now they are certain."

Lisa shook her head silently. "Was Adam involved in this?" she asked numbly.

"No. Quite a different sort of person handles work like that."

"Where is Adam?"

"Not here," was the only answer Linn was prepared to give. "Sandra, your 'Aunt Connie,' has replaced him because she's known to you and she knows this city far better than he." She looked at Lisa again and finished her drink. "And I know it best of all."

"What are you doing here?" Lisa pried listlessly.

"Interviewing Muslim women on their sex lives," Linn replied archly. "That's my cover, but you'd be surprised, I've published more from research I've done on these 'travels' than I ever did at the university.

I'm making quite a reputation for myself." She said it joylessly, and Lisa was sufficiently recovered from her own shock to realize that Linn was as distressed by what had happened to the King's agent as she was.

"We learned that the King was to be kept informed by a rotating agent, someone in his personal household," Linn continued. "Has Le'ith met with anyone like that?"

Lisa shook her head. "Was he to contact Le'ith or just the agents?"

"Neither of them seemed to know. But whoever it is may contact Le'ith and will want to know about the disappearance of the two who were following you. We don't want you to tell Le'ith anything, so he will be as surprised by the news as you were, and you should act the same.

"But," she continued, "Le'ith is bound to tell them that he alerted the Mossad to the fact that you were being watched. That's when we want you to remind Le'ith that he was followed home from his meeting with the King by agents of the Army Secret Service, and for all you know they were *still* following you and *are* still following you."

"In other words, you want to blame the Saudi Army for what the Mossad did."

"We simply want to open the possibility." Her expression changed to something quite harsh. It made her look much older. "Are you concerned about seeing your husband's plan succeed or pursuing 'justice' in the case of this unfortunate soldier in a war we all are reluctantly fighting?"

It carried the same tone of reproval she had used with Lisa back in Riyadh. It angered Lisa, but she knew Linn was right. Nevertheless she got some of her own back. "I assure you, by putting it on the Army, you'll create a breach between the King and Prince Sultan that can cause a lot of damage—even to the acceptance of Le'ith's plan."

Linn looked at her. "It's the price of the mistake, I'm afraid, but my, you've become quite the little Saudi, haven't you?"

Lisa looked flustered, and Linn laughed and looked at her with something like compassion. "I would have another drink," she said, "but I mustn't stay too long." She sighed and walked to the door.

"There is one more thing," she added. "You have heard of the Islamic Group the Gaama al Islamiya?"

"No," Lisa replied.

"They're the action arm of the fundamentalists here. They're the ones who've bombed banks, killed tourists—and Egyptians they consider traitors to Islam. They are everywhere, they're extremely powerful, and they're ruthless beyond your wildest nightmares.

"Sandra recommends, and I heartily agree, that you wear a chador while you are here. You went walking last night, and you looked like a tourist and, worst of all, an American tourist."

"How do you know we went walking last night?" Lisa said irritably.

Linn grimaced. "I'm sure there were others who knew it too, and we can't protect you here as we could in Morocco." She smiled. "It's not your fault, but even after all these years you still walk like an American college girl, Lisa. I'm envious. But this is not the place to display it.

"We can't order you," she said. "But we would if we could. This has become a very dangerous city, and we want you to get out of it in one piece."

Over the next few days Le'ith went to two more meetings without Lisa. During the second one Aunt Connie/Sandra made a brief visit to the hotel. Like Linn, she embraced Lisa like an old friend or perhaps an errant daughter. Through the faked funeral, her dad's real death, and that horrendous weekend in Geneva, they had become close despite Lisa's awareness that Sandra still questioned her competence.

In fact after the hugs Sandra held up a bag and revealed that the purpose of her visit was to bring Lisa a chador. She herself was wearing one—as an example, Lisa thought. When she saw her at the *Queen of the Nile* with Uri, she'd been dressed in a very becoming suit.

After Linn's appeal Lisa had purchased a couple of long dresses and done her hair up in a knot every time she went out, but it was apparently not enough.

"You don't know the dangers of this city, Lisa." Sandra scolded her. "Ninety-nine tourists out of a hundred will be all right, but you are a double target. The system is so corrupt and so penetrated by those who are fundamentalists or are so dissatisfied they think fundamentalism is the only answer that it's almost impossible for the government to keep anything secret. It's like the United States during the Vietnam War; there are leaks everywhere, even at the very highest level. You're much too identifiable in everything you wear. Yesterday you wore a long dress, but the bodice was so tight and the fabric so sheer that—"

"I was wearing a long slip!" Lisa protested.

Sandra looked at her sharply. "You're a beautiful girl, you always have been and have doubtless grown to like it, but you are being a fool! You may see thin blouses and short skirts here, but they are worn by Egyptians, and even *they* are in danger these days. They're liable to end up having their hair shorn. *You* are liable to end up dead.

"You've worn a chador for years in Saudi Arabia. Indulge me, put your vanity aside, and wear one for a few more days here in Cairo!"

Even Lisa's Bubbie, who had sometimes chastised her for thinking too much of herself, had never spoken to her with such severity, and Lisa's face was flushed with anger—and a touch of shame.

"You are becoming very valuable to us." Sandra continued more gently. "Please, please, use your discretion."

Lisa bent from her gaze, but she was still angry. "I've given up much of my life to be here. I don't think it's necessary that I be spoken to like a teenage delinquent."

"I know how much you've sacrificed," Sandra said appeasingly. "I would hate to see it jeopardized by something as trivial as vanity."

Lisa grimaced. She felt she couldn't win.

"Tell Le'ith you're frightened and want to wear a chador. And use that beauty of yours to induce him to wear a djellaba. Pick him out a white silken one and tell him how handsome he looks in it."

It was a ten-minute visit that seemed like ten hours, but in the end she did exactly as Sandra recommended.

Le'ith was even relieved to be wearing a djellaba and, being a true

Saudi male at heart, was more comfortable with his wife sheltered from the hungry male eyes that stalked the Cairo streets.

There were to be still more meetings, and again Lisa was instructed not to go. At twilight on the second day they strolled like an Egyptian couple up and down the al-A'ma channel quay. Le'ith told her that his central idea had been embraced immediately; what was dragging everything out was Egyptian reluctance to have development money destined for them be in the virtual control of the Saudis and the Israelis—an "impossible affront to their sovereignty."

"What it is, is an 'impossible' assault on their draining the well for their own fields and letting their neighbors eat sand," he said.

"How can they be so blind?"

Le'ith shook his head. "I think they all think they can steal their own fortunes and flee to Switzerland before the ax falls. . . . They don't think of the family and the future the same way we do," he reflected soberly.

Lisa wanted to put her arm in his, but it was not something properly done in a chador and djellaba, so she bumped him with her shoulder. When he turned questioningly, she said, "There are times your second wife admires you a great deal."

"She'd better wait until I've succeeded," he replied.

The next morning, when she was in the hotel on her own, the phone startled Lisa. It hadn't rung once since they'd come to Cairo. Her hand was shaking when she picked it up.

"Hey, Golden One," came the familiar voice. "I'm at the airport, and I want you to come get me. We have some talking to do before that brother of mine knows I'm here. Is he with you now?"

"No," Lisa answered. She wanted to cry and laugh with joy.

"Good," Reena snapped. "I was going to suggest you tell him that it was the concierge asking if you wanted tickets to the belly dancing, but we'll save that one."

Lisa laughed. "How in God's name did you know where we were?"

"Le'ith sent a fax from the hotel. We all know where you are."

Lisa took a cab. She knew she would be followed, and this time she actually thought she saw the bearded driver of a motorbike keeping track of the cab. But if the only person Reena wanted to keep in the dark about her arrival in Cairo was Le'ith, then let them follow, Lisa thought.

At the airport she found Reena dressed stunningly. It was designer wear for travel, comfortable, alluring, even risqué, a great outfit to meet men in.

Reena laughed on seeing Lisa in her chador. "I should have left on my black," she scoffed. "I changed the minute I got on the plane because I thought I'd have to compete with you." They hugged and walked toward the exit, Lisa justifying her "native garb" by saying Le'ith felt more comfortable with her being dressed like that.

"Well, Le'ith's right," Reena declared. "The men in this town are awful. They'll pinch your bottom on a street corner. I've seen them put their hands right on a girl's breast. Western girl, of course, dressed in a sweater." She shook her head. "I don't know, Arab men can be very nice in Paris or London, but all the worst in them comes out in this place."

Reena wanted to stay in a different hotel, so they drove straight to the Hilton. It was near enough, but she could ignore them if she chose. Lisa glimpsed the bearded man on the motorbike again. Her assumption was it was the Mossad, and at least she wouldn't get another lecture from Sandra. But that thought reminded her chillingly that Reena knew Sandra as "Aunt Connie," from both the funeral and Geneva, and if she should ever bump into her here in Cairo, it could produce a disaster that could ruin everything. Her euphoria at having Reena there dissipated into another terrible fear.

When they settled into Reena's room, things did not become better. Reena paid off the bellhop and immediately went to the minibar and broke open a split of champagne. She poured a glass for herself, a glass for Lisa. She lifted her glass and touched Lisa's. "I think you're in trouble, little sister-in-law, but I hope not." She peered into Lisa's eyes and drank. Lisa knew her reaction looked anything but innocent, and Reena's capacity to read her made her all the more disconcerted.

Reena curled up on the couch. "Le'ith had an audience with the King," she stated.

Lisa nodded, looking as composed as she could.

"The Army Secret Service had him followed for a time, trying to determine what it was all about." Lisa waited. Reena took another sip of champagne. "Then they decided it only had to do with some chemical plant and lost interest." She looked at Lisa. "Is all this news to you?"

Lisa didn't dare lie to her. She simply shook her head.

"Um-hmm. So all was well until Le'ith sent that fax to Rashid that he was taking you here to see the Pyramids—'because you'd never seen them before.'" She was watching Lisa very closely now. "True or not, everyone knows this is not the time to take a blond American to see the Pyramids, especially if you love her and are very protective of her. On top of that our mutual friend Youssef announced that you had told him you'd already seen the Pyramids—on a high school tour."

"None of this sounds very drastic." Lisa shrugged dismissively.

But Reena had kept her eyes fixed on her. "Unfortunately for me, but perhaps fortunately for you, Youssef has taken an occasional renewed interest in Ulti's body. And he told her that he had you now. You were a member of the Mossad and you had lured Le'ith to Cairo either to destroy him or to get him to convince the King to do a deal with Israel."

Lisa wanted to laugh, but the words were too close to the mark for that. She just shook her head as though responding to another of Youssef's fantasies. "Le'ith and I are here to—"

"No, no," Reena interjected quickly. "I don't want to know. What I want you to do is look me in the eye and tell me you are not betraying Le'ith."

In relief Lisa looked directly at her and said with total sincerity, "I am not betraying Le'ith."

Reena held her eyes for a long moment, then grinned and said, "Let's open another split of champagne."

As she went to get the bottle, she half turned to Lisa. "Well, I'm on your side, but your troubles aren't over. Youssef is either here in Cairo now, or coming very soon. And he has convinced someone in Army Secret Service to send a unit of agents over here to find out what Le'ith is up to, and they have apparently accepted his theory that you are working for the Mossad."

Fortunately she was bending over the minibar and couldn't see the panic on Lisa's face.

When Lisa returned to her hotel, she knew she had to contact Sandra as soon as she could, but she had no idea how. For a time she paced the hotel suite, fearing Le'ith might come back before she could think of anything. Then it struck her. Five minutes later she walked out of the lobby into the street in high heels, a skirt that stopped just above her knees, and a sheer blouse that revealed the lace bra beneath it and a fair quantity of what that bra held.

She tried not to walk like an American college girl. For her own safety she hoped she only looked "European," a Dane or a Norwegian perhaps, with shapely legs and a nice bust.

She stayed within four blocks of the hotel and jumped at every sound. But the worst she suffered were some groans and a single pinch on her bottom.

When she got back to the hotel suite, she was certain Sandra or Linn would be at the door or on the phone within an hour.

Twenty minutes later the phone rang, and Lisa grabbed it excitedly. "Yes" was all she said.

A faint voice called to her. "Lisa . . . Lisa."

Lisa didn't recognize the voice. "Yes, this is Lisa," she answered cautiously.

"Lisa, it's Reena," the weak, high voice said. "Please . . . help me."

It sounded like Reena, and it didn't sound like Reena. Was it Youssef trying to lure her out of the hotel? "What's wrong?" she said. "Is it you, Reena?"

"Please—help me. . . ." And the voice began to sob.

Lisa was torn. Was it someone imitating Reena? The voice sounded so strained. But as she listened, the sobbing became more anguished. If it *was* Reena, she had to do something. "Reena, I'm coming," she said. "I'll be there right away."

She hung up, grabbed her chador, and flung it over her as she trotted to the elevator. She wished she'd changed her high heels, but she didn't want to go back.

At the Hilton she got an assistant manager and said her sister-in-law was in some trouble, and she wanted him to accompany her to the room. The man looked at her calculatingly. She was in a chador; she had blue eyes and an American accent. Lisa could read his thoughts as his eyes passed over her. She held out her hand with her engagement and wedding rings. They were probably worth more than he made in a decade. It was the right status symbol: married and rich. He got a key and took her to Reena's floor.

They rang the bell and could hear sound in the room, but there was no response. The assistant manager shrugged; he was beginning to suspect this was a wasted trip. He put the key in the door and knocked as he opened it. "This is the management, is anyone—"

A deep moan cut him off. Lisa pushed around him down the little corridor past the bathroom and the closet and saw Reena lying on the bed. Her waist and legs were drenched in blood.

"No, no!" Reena screamed. "Get him out! Get him out!"

Lisa turned and pushed the assistant manager toward the door. He was now desperately curious. "Get the house doctor," Lisa whispered. "And hurry!" She gave him another shove and closed the door behind him.

She ran back and took another look at Reena, who was curled up on her side, rocking slightly, her anguished face staring at Lisa. There was a terrible stench of intestines.

Lisa kicked off her shoes and hurried into the bathroom. She soaked one towel as quickly as she could, grabbed the rest of the pile and rushed back into the bedroom.

Reena reached a hand out to her. It was covered with blood. Lisa knelt by her and kissed her hand, then put her arm around Reena's head and held her, kissing her forehead as Reena sobbed in gasps of torment. "I'm in such pain," she murmured. "Oh, Allah be merciful, I'm in such pain."

Lisa tried to soothe her. With one hand she took the wet towel and wiped at the blood around her waist. She could see an open wound on one side a little below her waist angling down toward her groin. Reena shrieked in pain as Lisa moved the towel over it.

"Don't touch it! Please, don't touch it."

"I've got to stop the bleeding," Lisa said compassionately. "I'll just pack the towels around it gently."

She stood and started to place a clean towel on the wound, and then she saw that there was another cut on the other side and still another right up the middle almost to her navel. Lisa tried to remove a bit of the torn dress to see the damage, but again Reena screamed in pain, so she simply covered it all. She went into the bathroom again and brought out the bath towels and washclothes to add to the pile, hoping they would cut the flow and allow the blood to clot. She had an anguished thought about how far the doctor might have to come to reach the hotel.

When she knelt at Reena's side again and took her hand, Reena shook her head and tears poured from her eyes. Lisa cradled her head again.

"Can you tell me?" Lisa said. "Who was it?"

"Youssef . . . it was Youssef."

Lisa held her tighter, beginning to cry herself. "I can't believe it," she said. "Youssef couldn't do this to you."

Reena choked a sob and tried to smile. "You've . . . caused me a lot . . . of trouble, Golden One."

"But why?" Lisa croaked. "Why?"

"They—they followed us. Some of the Army agents. He—he knew I'd warned you."

"But, God," Lisa sobbed, "why do *this* to you?"

Reena closed her eyes in pain and rocked back and forth. She tried to smile again through her contorted face. "He—he wanted . . . to know how I knew."

Her breath was getting shorter, but she tried to go on. "He had . . . only told Ulti. . . ." She groaned in agony as she said the name, an agony as much mental as physical. Lisa held her tightly, saying, "Reena, Reena," over and over again.

"And he—he figured it out," she sobbed, "why—why Ulti . . . would tell me." She broke down again, her pain engulfing her in grief.

Lisa couldn't see for her own tears now. She kept stroking Reena's hair and kissing her, trying to share her torment.

"He—he had them . . . rape me . . . and then they held . . . me down . . . and—and he cut me. There's—there's nothing left of me down there."

Lisa clutched her, and the two of them cried as one.

The doctor came about five minutes later. Reena wailed that she didn't want anyone to see her, but Lisa held her tenderly as the doctor gave her a shot and she finally lost consciousness.

By the time the ambulance came the doctor said she'd lost so much blood he was not sure she could survive an operation. Lisa herself was covered with that blood, and she went through the lobby with the stretcher and into the ambulance without looking right or left.

At the hospital there was a question of obtaining matching blood for a transfusion, and it took Lisa a little time to realize they were asking for a bribe. She gave them her gold watch.

Once the doctors took Reena away, Lisa realized that she would have to tell Le'ith something. He would have to know where she was at least and, if he was at the hotel when she returned, how she got the blood on her clothes. What she knew she could not tell him—not at this moment—was what had actually happened.

She called the hotel, and fortunately he was still not there. She left a message saying she was having a late lunch at Shepheard's, just for a change of scene. She might spend some time in the hotel shops, but she'd be back in time for dinner.

She had washed some of the blood from her face and hands and poured enough cold water on her chador and blouse to make them look smudged rather than dark red when one of the interns called her to Reena's room.

When she got to her ward, a very sympathetic nurse asked her to wait, the emergency surgeon wanted to speak to her.

The emergency surgeon was Indian. He looked earnest and too young.

"You would be Miss Safadi's—"

"Sister-in-law," Lisa answered. Besides the unkempt state of her clothes, she knew her face bore the strain of the last harrowing hour. "I love her very much," she said as the tears rolled down her cheek.

"Yes, yes, of course," he said sympathetically. "I must unfortunately tell you that the prognosis is not good. She is very weak, of course, and perhaps you can help, but she does not want us to operate. That is very important right now. Of course we need her permission. I would ask you to—to please keep that in mind when you speak to her." He smiled somberly. "Perhaps together we can make her pull through. Let's hope so."

Deferentially and unexpectedly he held out his hand, and Lisa shook it numbly. The nurse took her to Reena's room.

When Lisa went in, Reena's eyes were closed, and her breathing was so restricted she was wheezing. The usually lively face was sallow and drawn, and Lisa remembered the little girl who had been left in the desert to make it or not make it.

She went to her side and took her hand. Reena stirred and partially opened her eyes. "They've doped me up," she said. "I only feel the pain in my head."

"You've got to fight to stay alive," Lisa said softly. "I need you. There's no one else I can smoke pot with."

Reena forced a wan smile, but she shook her head, "I made up my mind hours ago," she said with weighted finality. "We shouldn't waste their time."

Lisa started to speak, but Reena shook her head again. Her voice was very weak, and Lisa had to bend to hear her. "You have some things to do for me . . . tell Huda I loved her . . . and Le'ith . . . and you." Tears were running from Lisa's eyes, but not Reena's. She had "submitted." "Do what you can . . . to protect Ulti. . . . It was my sin. . . . Don't let him do to her . . . what he did to me."

Lisa shook her head. She would do everything, even tell Le'ith, to prevent that.

Reena's thumb moved along Lisa's hand. "I can feel it going," she said, "all loose and relaxed. It's a lesson. I was just beginning to think life was worth it."

Lisa was sobbing silently. "Please don't go, Reena." She wept. "Please."

Reena closed her eyes; then she frowned and opened them a crack. "Lisa, watch out for Youssef. . . ." The frown evaporated, and she grimaced in what might have been a smile. Her eyes had closed again. Lisa felt a tiny squeeze on her hand.

Ten minutes later the kind Indian doctor said she had "passed away."

Lisa held Reena's head in her arms, hugging her, squeezing her, crying until she thought she would never stop.

Chapter 31

Before Lisa left the hospital, she was asked to accompany the nurse to the administration office. She had blotched her face with cold water, but it still looked swollen from crying. When she arrived there was a police inspector waiting for her, with the chief medical officer.

The police had been notified by the hotel, and now they had been informed that the lady registered as Reena Safadi had died. From the evidence it would be a case of murder.

Lisa tried to think before she opened her mouth, but she was too shattered and too filled with hatred for Youssef to work it out.

She stolidly gave her own name, their hotel, their address in Riyadh; she agreed to a detective's coming with her to take the details of her passport. When asked if she knew who had attacked her sister-in-law, she hesitated, then answered, "Yes." She hesitated again, then said in a broken voice, "It was Reena's half brother Youssef Ibrahim Safadi." When they asked why, she hesitated once more, cried, and said she did not know. Did she know where Youssef Safadi was at this time? She shook her head no.

After the detective had left the hotel suite, Lisa went out on the balcony and stared at the fabled river and the city it had spawned and thought of how fleeting her life and grief were when set against all the horrendous and brutal things that had happened on this very stretch of shoreline. But that could not keep her from sobbing again for Reena.

When she was finally able to stop, she went back in and saw the clock by the telephone and could hardly believe that it was only four. She felt she'd lived through a week.

She went into the bedroom and flopped out on the bed, knowing she should first change clothes. But the phone rang before she'd had even a moment's rest. She knew before she picked it up that it had to be Sandra or Linn. It was almost the same; it was the concierge saying the car she'd ordered was waiting. That was their way, Lisa thought. It seemed years since she'd put on her skirt and sexy blouse and sauntered out into the street. Now she had to pull herself together and warn them of Youssef and the band of agents who were buzzing around the city someplace.

She changed, calling down to one of the shops in the hotel to have a new chador sent to the room. While she waited, she put her blood-soaked blouse and skirt and her smudged and bedraggled chador into a laundry bag and buried it behind the extra pillows in the closet. Just seeing the blood made her cry again.

It wasn't until she was in the car with another strange driver who refused to speak that she had the icy thought that perhaps it was Youssef who'd sent this car. Her heart started to race. She tried—heatedly—to make the driver respond to her questions, but he wouldn't.

They finally pulled up to a town house in one of those rows that looked like a piece of London. She told the driver in Arabic that she wouldn't leave the car until he told her who had sent him. He would only say the "agency" no matter what she screamed at him. She sat back in silence and affected an unyielding adamancy. Traffic went by, some time passed, but he seemed not to care. Finally she cursed him with all the foul words she knew and slammed out of the car. Her anger sustained her to the door, and then she began to shake. She decided that whatever happened, she was not going to go in until she was sure. She rang the bell, took a step back, and prepared to run screaming down the street. A strange man opened the door.

"Come in, Lisa," he said.

"I'm not coming in until I see Sandra or Linn," Lisa answered, and took a further step back. Another man appeared behind the first.

"Will I do?" he asked. In the shadows she couldn't make him out, but she instantly recognized the voice. It was Adam.

Four of them sat around the little parlor with its stuffed furniture and white linen antimacassars. Linn, Adam, the man, Yair, who had opened the door and was a local agent, and Lisa.

Lisa kept hold of her emotions enough to tell them coherently about Reena and Youssef and those he'd brought with him to Cairo. She was stunned by their lack of response. Adam nodded slightly, looking sickened at Reena's fate, but otherwise nothing.

"I bring some news too," he said solemnly. "After many hours of debate, many days really, the Cabinet has decided *not* to accept the King's offer."

Lisa was devastated. "I can't believe it," she gasped. It was as if somebody had hit her in the stomach. "It's—it's not possible. Can't they see what this *means*?"

Adam shook his head glumly. "A lot of people feel the same way, but that's their decision."

"Do you know why?" she pleaded.

Adam shrugged. "I guess you might call it our kind of fundamentalist thinking: You can't trust the Arabs. Saudis supported the PLO when it was at its most extreme; they support Hamas now. They will use our skills to build up their own capacity until they can turn on Israel and destroy us."

It was a compelling litany, but Lisa didn't accept any of it. "All of that is past tense," she argued. "Hell, none of them wanted Israel at first. God, the French accepted the *Germans* as partners—even after World War One *and* World War Two. And—and what about the United States and Japan? And the *Chinese* and Japan? People don't have to stay enemies forever."

"Many of the people making that decision have suffered a great deal," Linn replied in extenuation. "It's not an easy call. Ten years from now they might prove to be right." It was not argumentative, just a statement that obviously covered her own disappointment.

Lisa shook her head and sank back in her chair despondently. It was something she had feared since the election, but she had put it out of her mind—especially after Uri had returned and Aaron had given them the contact in Egypt.

She could hardly keep herself from crying again. Not only did she believe in Le'ith's plan, but now Reena's death was a joke; it was for nothing, nothing at all. That's why they didn't care about Youssef. It was *all* a joke, all of it. At last she looked across desolately at Adam. He was starting to say something when there was the sound of the lock turning in the front door. A small light Lisa had not seen went on in the corner. "It's all right," Yair said, and got up and went to the door. Lisa could hear him free the latch, and he returned with Sandra. The light went out.

Sandra simply nodded to Lisa, then sat in an armchair and sighed. She was wearing another business suit, and she looked very tired.

"Tea?" Yair suggested. Sandra nodded.

"I'll fix it," Linn offered, and she rose and went off down the hallway.

Sandra lifted her eyes to Adam and numbly shook her head no.

Adam sat back and suddenly looked very tired himself. He didn't speak for a moment. Then he turned to Lisa. "There's something else, Lisa," he said ominously. "It's not good news either, but it's Sandra's area, and I think she'd better explain."

Lisa looked across at her, but Sandra didn't seem to want to talk about anything. The sun was setting, and Yair got up and pulled the drapes. Then he turned on a couple of table lamps. Lisa's eyes went from one to the other, and she knew they were going to face her with something overwhelming.

"Your husband is going to a secret meeting tomorrow," Sandra said. "He's being introduced to a man he's been told is capable of persuading the Egyptians to accept the guidelines on expenditures we've finally hammered out."

Lisa glanced at Adam. He looked down, avoiding her eyes.

"We have reason to know that this is a trap of the Gaama, the Islamic Group. They have had wind of our meetings, but they don't know what they're about. They intend to find out from your husband."

"Le'ith would never tell any—" Lisa stated in dissent, but then she understood. "They're going to torture him," she blurted.

Adam didn't answer, but Linn did. She had returned with a tea tray. "And in this case if they kill him, it won't be accidental," she said in obvious requital to Lisa's outburst against the Mossad.

Yair helped Linn pass around teacups. "In fact, when they find out, they will almost certainly kill him to put an end to it," he said.

Lisa looked at them all incredulously. "Well, tell him not to go," she protested, frightened by their avoidance of the obvious. "Or let me tell him," she entreated.

"We hope you will try," Sandra continued. "But in case you fail, and he expects you to accompany him, which we believe is part of the plan because he would of course be more likely to speak if there were a threat of rape or torture to you"—Lisa's mouth opened, and she could hardly breathe—"then you must go with him, not allowing any hint of suspicion. When you are well into the slums, in the area controlled by the Gaama, a truck will be unloading in the very narrow street, and the car will have to stop. It will be just past an intersection with another small street. There will be some gunfire to justify your running, and you must immediately open your door and run back to that intersecting street and turn right. Don't look back, and don't stop running until you see a car door open for you."

Lisa stammered, looking desperately at Adam.

"Listen to me, Lisa," Sandra persisted. "You run back and turn *right*—and run until a car door opens for you."

Lisa stared at her. "You mean I'm supposed to save myself and let them kill Le'ith?" She couldn't *believe* them.

"Lisa, we are taking enormous risks to save *you!*" Adam interjected. When she looked back at him, he spoke more gently. "We never leave our own," he said, "even though in that area we will be putting several people at risk."

His tone, their attitude were like hands clutching at her throat. She had lived with the idea that she would humiliate Le'ith and betray him, but she suddenly grasped that if he were to die and it was through her doing, she would rather die with him than live with what she'd done.

"Why—why can't we save him?" she stammered.

"Because," Adam explained somberly, "there is someone like you—a mole—in the Gaama. At great risk he has told us what is happening, and if we ever revealed it, his death would undoubtedly be slower and much more painful than your husband's is liable to be."

Lisa immediately grasped the dilemma. She buried her face in her hands, then peered up desperately at Adam. "Can't we save them *both*?" she pleaded.

"Infiltrating the Gaama is the most difficult and dangerous job we have ever performed," Sandra said uncompromisingly. "This person has spent more years than you have, not living in luxury but in prisons, in slums, in danger from the police and everyone around him year after year. If there *is* a fundamentalist revolution in Egypt, he will be invaluable to us. We cannot 'save' him and sacrifice all he has done, and can do, for one Saudi sheikh, however well-meaning he might be."

"But why not tell Le'ith it's hopeless, that it's doomed anyway because the Israeli Cabinet has turned it down?" she implored.

"We've *tried*," Sandra said dejectedly. "Tried desperately. Uri spent over an hour with him after the meeting today, telling him it was hopeless. But your husband is a very determined man." She shook her head. "It's the first time we realized how very much he wanted this for Saudi Arabia. He'd more or less convinced us we could take it or leave it as far as he was concerned."

"He does want it, and so do I," Lisa responded.

Sandra stiffened. "Your husband told Uri that he's convinced that if he can get a final acceptable agreement from the Egyptians, we will change our minds, that we will *have* to change our minds. He's determined to go to that meeting."

A dozen images of Le'ith went through Lisa's mind: the days they had spent in the valley while he thought this all through, the night they had made love after his meeting with the King, his joy at having her with him in Fez. . . . And she remembered the fanatic mania, the hatred in the eyes of the fundamentalists they'd seen in the prisons after Sadat's assassination. She choked on her tears, and Adam sat on the arm of her chair and cradled her shoulders in his arm.

After she had regained some control, Sandra studied her and took a long sip of tea. She wiped her mouth and faced Lisa with that look of doubt of her competence that Lisa had seen so often. "There is one possibility that remains," she said sternly, "and that is that *you* talk him out of it tonight.

"I'm not sure how you can do that without giving yourself away." Sandra continued with the same severity. "But give *yourself* away before you ever reveal the slightest *hint* of what is going to happen tomorrow. Not the slightest! Debriefing Uri every night, I have learned one thing about your husband, and that is that he is very, very intelligent. And very perceptive. To be honest, Lisa, neither your life nor his is worth what you would destroy if you abuse the information we have given you." Her look at Lisa expressed no doubt on that subject.

"Worth more than *our* lives too," Adam added in gentler tones. "You've handled Le'ith superbly, and I don't want to try to give you advice, but perhaps you could get him talking about what Uri told him and then suggest that maybe he should give up for now, that maybe another change in government or the situation might create an opportunity later."

Lisa still couldn't give up. "If you save me, won't you be giving away the mole anyway?" she pleaded.

Adam shook his head. "If we knew something, we would have saved you both. But for us to grab a Mossad agent being taken into Gaama territory by an Arab sheikh will not seem unreasonable *or* suspicious."

"Tell him you're frightened," Linn suggested, "that you want to go back to your valley."

Lisa didn't know. Le'ith *was* so perceptive. But after feeling hopeless, she at least had something to cling to, and she was going to try, try with all her brain and all her heart.

"If you do succeed," Sandra continued, "we must know so that we avoid the risks of sending people into a Gaama quarter to save you. It's not something we can do in five minutes. So tomorrow morning you must induce him to have breakfast at the Terrace Restaurant. Linn will meet you in the ladies' room. *Don't* look for her. Just go at some point, and she will be there."

Lisa nodded.

Sandra's attitude remained coldly skeptical and admonishing, but then she half smiled at the despondent Lisa. "I sincerely wish you luck—for his sake . . . and yours." It was as genuine as anything else she had said, and its unexpectedness caught Lisa unaware and touched her.

She guessed they knew what she was discovering: that she had a feeling for Le'ith far deeper than she had ever faced.

Chapter 32

Le'ith wanted time to think, and he wanted to talk it out with Lisa. Uri's waylaying him after the meeting and confronting him with a reverse he'd thought had long ago been avoided not only desolated him but forced a reappraisal of his whole strategy. When he left their secret rendezvous, the driver of his car was the one who had clandestinely told him that he could lead him to the one man in all Egypt who could truly influence President Mubarak. The driver, Kamal, had been Uri's driver during the Palestinian negotiations in Cairo, so Le'ith knew he was trustworthy, and he knew too that drivers often hear more than even the "best informed." Beyond that, Kamal had a rugged peasant strength and taciturnity that Le'ith found reassuring.

When they went by the Sinan Pasha Mosque, Le'ith asked him to turn back. He decided what he also needed just then was some time in reflective prayer, and it was almost sunset. Kamal thought it was his duty to wait or go in with Le'ith, but Le'ith told him that he preferred to be alone, and he preferred to *walk* back to the hotel. Kamal seemed a little concerned, as well he might in that very marginal neighborhood, but he only bowed. "Nine-thirty," he said.

Le'ith nodded. "Don't worry, you be at the entrance, I'll be there." Kamal bowed again, but Le'ith saw the flicker of misgiving in his eyes. "And I will bring my wife," he added. "I accept what you say, and believe me, in my wife's case, you will see that it's an advantage I'm not liable to forget."

Kamal had told him that this conservative, idiosyncratic man of remarkable influence and power had a weakness for the appeal in an intelligent woman's eyes, and as Le'ith finished his ablutions with the washing of his feet, he almost smiled at the thought of Lisa in a veil and the impact the wisdom and blue of her eyes would make.

After prayers he went back over a longer route than he need have, but he wanted to walk along the river. The elegant Corniche was safe, and the shimmering reflections of the streetlights and the tall apartment buildings on the muddy water gave him a reassuring sense of peace. He had bargained in negative atmospheres before, and he felt certain that if he could carry the Egyptians in a way that would convince the Israelis that the country could be pulled back from the abyss, he would win in the end. When he looked back, he had almost expected it to be harder than it had turned out to be. The biggest hurdle, he believed, had been the first, the King. With that behind him, he had to prevail. He also believed fate, this time in the form of Kamal, was on his side.

Just after he had crossed the Qasr an-Nil Bridge and was approaching the hotel, a green Mercedes screeched to a stop a few feet ahead of him. The back door flew open, and *Youssef* stepped out. He smiled at Le'ith's surprise and, with a little bow and gesture of his hand, invited him into the car.

Le'ith was taken totally off-guard. Youssef had been far from his thoughts, and the jolt of seeing him there in Cairo face-to-face was more than he could immediately adjust to. His inclination was just to say no and walk on. His feelings for Youssef were so mixed, but the animosity between them had grown beyond civility, and he believed he would really feel affection for him again only when he was standing over his grave.

"Come on, Le'ith," Youssef appealed. "Just a short ride, then right back to your hotel and the arms of your beautiful wife."

Mentioning Lisa was not the subtlest thing for him to do, of course, but who expected subtlety from Youssef? Le'ith grunted; the brazen stupidity somehow made him feel more comfortable, and he got into the car.

There were two men in the front seat, neither of them known to Le'ith, but he guessed they were Army Secret Service because they both sat with squared shoulders as if they were on parade. The car left the curb about as fast as it had stopped. Twice they did U turns, with one of the men facing back, watching through the rear window all the time. Finally they headed out toward the Pyramids.

The Mercedes pulled to a stop near a little plaza where a few half-empty busloads of tourists were unloading for an evening visit to the floodlit spectacles. No one had spoken since Le'ith got in the car. Youssef turned to him now. "Let's walk among the wonders of our ancestors," he said with a smirk. The two men didn't move as he and Le'ith got out.

They avoided the crowds and the guides and walked off into the desert beyond the field of lights. It was from here that the three tombs were most impressive, most beautiful.

Youssef finally turned to him. "What are you doing in Cairo, Le'ith?" he asked with a sly grin.

Le'ith looked at him coldly, trying to figure what he was after. "It's not family business," he answered.

"Oh!" Youssef exclaimed. "I thought you were showing Lisa the Pyramids." Le'ith just stared at him without answering. "Well," Youssef went on, "you never believed me when I told you your blond wife was with the Mossad, did you?"

"Did you bring me here to repeat that fantasy?"

"Yes"—Youssef smiled—"that's exactly why I brought you here. Remember her dear 'Aunt Connie,' the one I told you had set up that 'accident' in Geneva? The one who so conveniently had to leave the city before you arrived? Well, by some odd coincidence, she's here in Cairo, *now*."

Le'ith frowned despite himself. Youssef grinned and went on. "Lisa met with her today at a safe house for the Mossad. We followed her there, and we saw 'Aunt Connie' enter the house *after* she arrived and dear Lisa leaving about half an hour later on her own. For your comfort she went back to the hotel, where she is probably lying on the bed waiting for your return."

Le'ith grabbed him by his shirt and pulled him to him, but Youssef was as strong as Le'ith and, once over the surprise of Le'ith's move, grabbed Le'ith's shirt and held him off as fiercely as he was being held. "Your envy is going to be the end of you, Youssef," Le'ith avowed. But a seed of doubt had been planted, and he was driven to deal with it. "If you have no proof but your mouth, I'm telling you now I'm cutting you off from the household permanently. You may take your wives and go. And do it before I return." And he shoved Youssef off.

Youssef laughed. "You didn't hear me. I saw the woman myself. The one who came to me in the hospital, who dined with me, who called Lisa her *niece*."

"Why should I believe you?"

"Because it will save your life."

"Really? Lisa is going to kill me, is she?" Le'ith mocked.

"Maybe. But if not Lisa, somebody."

"And how do *you* know this?" His scorn was about equal to his anger.

"Oh, I can't tell you everything, but I do know they've decided you're expendable."

"Horseshit!" Le'ith exploded, but Youssef's relentless calm was uncharacteristic when he was lying or pushing, and it was eroding Le'ith's confidence.

"I'm telling you, Le'ith. My 'associates' don't know what you're up to, but they know you're up to something. They also know you've been written off. The Mossad has written you off."

"And how do your 'associates' know all this?" Le'ith sneered.

"I don't know, Le'ith," Youssef responded with mocking self-assurance. "Spying on Israel is not my field. *How* they know *what* they know is not something I care about—or something they want to reveal to someone whose brother is married to an agent of the Mossad!" He moved to inches from Le'ith's face, and Le'ith pushed him off again but with less force. Youssef's conviction had sapped his own certainty.

Youssef shook his head with a kind of insolent benevolence. "I'm trying to save your life, Le'ith, though why I'm not sure."

Le'ith looked at him icily. "Because if I died, the family would put Rashid at its head, and you couldn't stand that."

At last Le'ith had hit a nerve. Youssef glared and seemed ready to leap across the sand at him, but he only raised his middle finger defiantly in Le'ith's face. "Fuck you, Le'ith! Fuck you with the dong of a camel! I pray to Allah they kill you and cover your body with dogshit!"

He turned and strode off toward the lights and the three stolid monuments.

Le'ith roamed the desert floor for a long time.

Chapter 33

Lisa went from nervousness to exhaustion as she waited for what seemed an eternity for Le'ith to return to the hotel. She had spent the entire ride back thinking of some plausible excuse for having been gone so long. So at first she was relieved that he hadn't arrived. But she knew he'd left Uri, and then Uri had reported to Sandra, and then Sandra had come to the safe house. She couldn't imagine where he'd gone.

Initially she pushed her concern aside and practiced ways of convincing him it was best to drop his plan for now and go back to Saudi Arabia. She covered every inducement she could think of, from little Ibrahim to his duties to the tribe, and still, there was no sign of him. She began to wonder if he'd had an accident or if the police had reached him and taken him to see Reena at the morgue.

When he finally arrived, it was almost ten o'clock and she was so exhausted she wanted only to sleep. She accepted her exhaustion as a gift; at least she was less likely to seem nervous. But Le'ith was not inclined to talk. He said he'd gone to see a friend and was too tired to recount what happened at the meeting. She'd lived with him too long for her not to recognize almost instantly that something was wrong between them. And despite his "visiting a friend" at dinnertime, he was excessively hungry and ordered a meal while they prepared for bed.

He moved about the suite, watching her in her silk peignoir but avoiding her touch in the way he had done when Youssef had first accused her long ago, and it finally broke through her deadened mind that perhaps Youssef had gotten to him again. Was Youssef "the friend" he'd spent the hours with? The thought was enough to snap her out of her lethargy.

Le'ith was eating, staring broodingly out over the lights along the river. She knelt beside him and took a handful of rice and dipped it in the lamb and smiled at him as she put it in her mouth. He usually loved her to do that and would lean to her and kiss her full mouth. But he only looked at her with a wry smile and lifted his eyes back out to the river.

"Did anything at all special happen at the meeting to make you so thoughtful?" she said as lightheartedly as she could.

He shook his head. "No. Nothing really. Just another day of frustration."

She put her hand in the rice again, and this time he waited until she'd withdrawn it before he took another bite himself, and that convinced her Youssef *had* gotten to him. He had not provided proof, she was sure of that. Le'ith wouldn't be sitting there if he'd known. It was doubt that was in Le'ith's mind—monstrous doubt—not conviction.

Her mind raced. If he had to discover the truth about her, this was probably the best time of all. So she was with the Mossad, well, he and the Mossad were united in trying to achieve this agreement. But whatever Youssef had told him, she was sure he had not told him about tomorrow, and even at the risk of confirming Youssef's accusations she somehow had to prevent tomorrow from happening.

The other thing she was sure of was that Le'ith could not have heard about Reena. He was far too emotional a man to hide that, and if he knew, she was convinced Youssef might well be dead by now.

Her voice cracked when she spoke the words, but she fought to control her emotion.

"I have something I must tell you, Le'ith," she said, sitting back on her haunches, tossing back her hair. It was a posture he was especially vulnerable to, but that had not entered her mind until he glanced at her, then turned away quickly with his jaw clenched.

She knew exactly how she would tell him. She wouldn't mention Ulti—or the Mossad. But Le'ith gave her no chance.

"I'd rather not talk tonight, Lisa. I would rather you went to bed."

It was a Saudi man speaking to his chattel, polite in this case but just as firm, and Lisa knew if she defied it, it would only produce an explosion, and he would hear nothing. Given the anguish that had leaked into her words, she was amazed at his cold disinterest, but she dared not confront it. "All right, Le'ith," she answered, and rose very slowly and went into the bedroom.

It was several minutes before he came in, and then he spent an interminable time in the bathroom before he turned out the lights and came to bed. She reached out to put her arm around him, but he turned away from her, and she simply touched his shoulder and withdrew. She knew from experience this was not the time to push herself on him.

"What is it you wanted to talk about?" he asked coldly.

"It's about Youssef," she answered, her voice croaking again, despite her effort to remain calm. "Youssef and—"

He cut her off peremptorily. "I'm sure anything about Youssef can wait till tomorrow. Right now I'm very tired, and I want to be rested for the morning."

She held her breath. Tears had come to her eyes. Dare she just spill it out, just say, "Youssef killed Reena," or should she wait until morning when both of them might be less fraught but when time would be so precious? She lay silently, crying, thinking of Reena.

"I have a special meeting tomorrow morning," Le'ith mumbled surlily, ignoring the tears she knew he must be aware of. "We leave at ninethirty. I'd like you to come with me."

Lisa's heart beat faster. "Reena is dead, Le'ith," she blurted out, and despite herself, she started to sob. "She came to Cairo to see us, and Youssef killed her. He killed her so savagely." She was crying uncontrollably. Le'ith had switched on the bedside light and was staring at her rigidly, his face white in shock and disbelief.

"He killed her because she told me that he was here with a team of Secret Service agents from the Army trying to find out why you were here and what you were doing."

There was no doubt that he believed her. It was as though she had told him some truth he already knew. His eyes suddenly looked wounded and vulnerable. "When did this happen?" he asked feebly.

"Today," she said, "this morning." She put her hand on his and pulled herself closer. "Le'ith, I'm afraid. I want to go back to the valley and stay there forever."

"Where is Reena?" he asked.

"In the city morgue. . . ."

He stared into nothingness for a time. She slipped up into his arms and felt a wash of relief as he put his arms around her and held her. "Can't we just take a plane back to Riyadh tomorrow? Surely everything's too dangerous now."

Le'ith's arms held her a little tighter. He answered slowly and solemnly, "I must go to this meeting tomorrow, now more than ever. . . . Then I will deal with Youssef."

Lisa was terrified. She had somehow made it worse. Sandra's words rang in her head; she mustn't give anything away, but somehow she had to stop him. The thoughts of Reena and her last minutes with her at the hospital had kept her on the verge of tears, and she gave in to them, sobbing from deep within her. "Please, Le'ith, can't we just go home?"

Le'ith lay motionless for a moment, then took her by the shoulders and turned her so that she was looking directly at him. Through the tears she could see the layers of pain lying in the wells of his dark eyes. "I need to know one thing, Lisa. One thing truthfully." His voice was almost a whisper as he seemed to peer into her soul. "Do you really want to go back to the valley forever?"

"Yes," she answered desperately and truthfully. "Yes, more than anything."

Le'ith studied her eyes for a moment, then pulled her to him. His voice cracked when he said, "Then it's all right. We'll go to the meeting, and I will see to Youssef later."

She started to protest, but he hushed her. "We need to sleep," he said. "Tomorrow is going to be a very long day." She wanted desperately to argue, but she had run out of reasons and answers. She would have to wait till morning and hope the light of day would make him less adamant or her own mind more fertile.

He squeezed her tightly and kissed the top of her head, and though her mind was full of dread, her exhausted body, nestled so securely in his arms, eventually dragged her down into sleep.

Chapter 34

When Lisa woke in the morning, the other side of the bed was empty. She sat up with a start. The bathroom door was open, and she couldn't hear any sound from there. She got up quickly, threw on her peignoir, and went into the living room. "Le'ith," she called. But there was no answer. She looked out on the balcony. No sign of him, and the city was already moving on its noisy daily round. She looked at the clock. It was eight thirty-five. She cursed her exhaustion and ran to the phone. She called the Terrace Restaurant.

"Yes, madame, *Said* Safadi is having breakfast now," the maître d' answered.

"Please tell him his wife is on the way down and ask him to wait," she pleaded. She hung up before he could answer. She ran to the bedroom, knowing she would skip makeup and only uncertain about whether she should wear a chador or not. Wearing it might make her seem more submissive, and he might listen to her. Or it might make him feel more the Saudi man, and he *wouldn't* listen to her. She decided the strongest hold she had on him was "the ally" he'd found in California. She threw the chador over her arm and handed it to the maître d' when she entered the restaurant.

The dress she wore was white with a pattern of blue flowers and a flattering cleavage. Le'ith rose when she came to the table, and his eyes took her in, this time with a warmth that made her feel she'd made the right choice.

She wanted to talk to him immediately because he had finished his breakfast, but the waiter hovered and a busboy filled her water glass, while another asked if she wanted coffee.

She quickly ordered fruit and a croissant and waited until they were alone.

"You were very quiet this morning." She smiled.

"You were sleeping so soundly," he said, and then he grinned. "You were snoring."

"Well, I'll admit," she retorted, "I slept sound enough not to hear *your* snoring." They had teased each other on this subject many times and always in good humor. "Le'ith," she continued gently, "I want to go home. I'm afraid of this city."

"We'll go soon," he said, and touched her hand affectionately.

"I don't want to wait for another meeting, Le'ith. Who knows what Youssef is up to?"

He started to speak, but the waiter came with her fruit, and another offered her orange juice. When they'd gone, he had obviously decided not to discuss it. "I didn't want to disturb you this morning," he said affectionately, "so I haven't shaved. We need to hurry, so I must get back to the room. Please excuse me."

Lisa started to rise. "I'll go with you. I'm not hungry anyway."

Le'ith turned to her with a flash of irritation. She was being persistent in a way that offended his Saudi manhood.

"We are going to the meeting," he said sharply. Then more gently: "I must see this through for a number of reasons, Lisa, but one of them now is Reena. That, I know, you, of all people, will understand." He held her in a gaze that made her pale with its haunting, loving evocation of Reena. Then he touched her arm, rose, and went off, leaving her stunned in fear and defeat.

She was utterly overwhelmed for several minutes, wiping at tears that kept falling across her cheeks, staring at her food, knowing there was no way left now. She had played every card and somehow played them wrong.

It was almost nine-thirty when she remembered that she had to notify Linn. She couldn't mess that up too.

She walked as calmly as she could to the ladies' room, but she almost lost her equilibrium more than once. Her head was pounding, and she felt dizzy and nauseous. She couldn't push those crazed faces screaming hate at the camera from her mind. They would take their venom out on Le'ith.

When she reached the ladies' room, there was only one other woman there, a pretty girl wearing sultry makeup and a chador. A distinctly Egyptian combination, she remembered thinking. The girl left. Lisa looked around, then called out softly, "Linn!" There was no answer. Then something thumped behind her, and she turned. A foot was sticking awkwardly out of one of the stalls.

Lisa moved to the stall in what seemed like slow motion. She knew before she opened the door. When she did, Linn tumbled all the way to the bloodied floor. Her throat had been slit from ear to ear.

When Lisa staggered out of the ladies' room, Le'ith was impatiently waiting for her, holding her chador. For a moment she was paralyzed. He started to walk toward her, and she realized it was her final chance. She turned from him and spoke loudly to the maître d'. "There's a woman in there; she's been murdered!"

The maître d' looked embarrassed and then panicked by the reactions of his customers. Several people just got up quickly and started leaving the terrace. He signaled a couple of waiters and busboys, and they hurried toward the hall leading to the rest rooms.

Le'ith grabbed Lisa's arm. "Come on," he said quietly. "We've got to get out of here."

"But there's a woman in there. Her throat's slit!" She resisted his tug at her, hoping someone would demand they all stay put, but Le'ith gripped her more firmly.

"Lisa, people get their throats slit in this town often. Now, come on, I'm not missing this meeting." He half pulled her out of the terrace and across the lobby as the chaos on the terrace grew and people started running to it from the lobby.

When they pushed through the revolving door, Le'ith looked

around quickly and led her to an old black English Oxford. "I know it's upset you," he told her, "but it's not something that involves us. We can't help anyone in there, and it's not our responsibility."

Lisa thought, I wanted to help *you,* and it *is* our responsibility! But Le'ith opened the back door of the car and let her in. Then he ran around to the other side. "Let's go, Kamal," he said. "There's been some trouble back there. I don't want to get caught up in it."

The driver, a stout, thick-necked man with huge eyes, started the car and moved out of the line of cars deftly but without undue speed. He's experienced, Lisa thought; he's not going to do anything that will call attention to us. . . . And her hopes sank.

Once they were safely away from the hotel, Le'ith handed her her chador. "You'd better slip this on," he said. "And do you have a veil? I'm told Mr. Kabir is a very conservative man."

Lisa nodded. She carried a veil in her purse the way she used to carry lipstick. As she put it on, she was aware of the driver watching her, and she wondered if he was anticipating the pleasure of ripping off her black clothing and raping her while his comrades held her and Le'ith was forced to watch. She wanted to scream out, "Le'ith, we can't! We've got to stop!" But she thought of the mole, someone who had lived through God knows what hell in the boiling summers and the damp, cold winters, who had been beaten in prisons, who had lived afraid always of what he might cry out in his sleep, while spending his fugitive days preaching hate against the country he loved. She knew, whatever she wanted to spare Le'ith, she could not betray that unknown soldier.

The car had entered a part of Cairo she had never seen. At first the cluttered streets, teeming with people and run-down cars, were a kaleidoscope of color: clothing, in reds and yellows and blues, hanging on outdoor racks; creaky wooden stands of fruit and vegetables; color-splashed signs for shirts, umbrellas, herbal medicines, Coca-Cola, and at a large intersection three huge cinemas with immense, garish drawings of luscious, big-breasted women and handsome men wielding swords or Uzis. Gradually her eye caught the scrawls, high on building walls, or running down the wooden telephone poles, always in black characters set against white: "Islam Is the Solution!" It was like a death's-head in an eighteenth-century drawing, sudden, striking reminders of what life was really about.

They passed from the bustle of the busy streets into another section of the city. It was like taking a step closer to hell. Lisa's heart had started racing the moment they entered it. These were not streets in any American sense; they were not straight; there were no sidewalks, no lawns, just buildings thrust awkwardly against one another with only tiny dirt pathways separating them. Every foot into the area made her feel more claustrophobic. The redbrick and crumbling concrete buildings were swarming with life, but that was inside, like bugs on the underside of a rotten log; they heard only an occasional shout, and color had all but vanished. Faded clothing hung from lines tied to bits of rusted metal, here and there a young man walked in jeans and a drab shirt, but what women you saw wore black chadors and veils, the men djellabas. The streets were covered with refuse, and chickens and goats roamed them as if they were open fields.

Every street had its dismantled van or car rusting among the other rubble, but what traffic there had been just disappeared. They saw a battered van loaded with plastic bottles moving far ahead of them, and some scooter-trucks bouncing along some of the side streets. But now the signs, "Islam Is the Solution!," were everywhere. Their car, so old and ordinary on the city's main thoroughfares, was an object of envy here. Children screamed out excitedly at it, and the men eyed it with suspicion and enmity.

Le'ith sensed her fear and moved closer to her. He moved his arm gently back and forth against her, as much of a gesture as one dared make in a fundamentalist area, where Lisa knew women had been dragged from cars and beaten for exposing a small portion of their hair.

She was beginning to choke and swallowed repeatedly. She knew the moment was coming soon, and the touch of his arm made everything worse. She couldn't see how they'd ever get her out of an area like this, and if they could, the thought of what was going to happen to Le'ith made her stomach churn. If she only had the courage, she would die with him.

Then, ahead of them, she saw the battered van angle in toward a building; a pile of rubble across from it blocked the street to anything bigger than a goat. Their own car passed an intersecting street. Lisa desperately glanced up and down it. It was half a market street, with a few women on their haunches, their wares spread out before them. There were a couple of old cars and a van. And she suddenly glimpsed an old truck following them.

Their driver started honking his horn but kept moving toward the battered van. Despite herself, Lisa clutched at Le'ith's leg. She was breathing so hard there was no masking her panic. He turned to her just as their car stopped before the van, the driver sitting on his horn. Suddenly—long before she was ready!—machine-gun fire sounded almost in their ears! It struck the car, and there were shouts and more gunfire. She turned to Le'ith, tears running down her face, then swung around, pushing off him, and opened the door and raced down the street, holding her chador above her knees. Gunfire traced after her, and there was more shooting—much more—and wild shouts and cries of pain! She ran past the old truck. Two men were standing in the back, shooting Uzis. She glanced at them in terror and didn't dare look back.

She rounded the corner, and people were running, screaming, into buildings, the market women trying to scoop up their needlework and pots, and as Lisa ran toward the cars, not knowing which she should run to, there were shots on this street and more cries of pain. And the gunfire kept coming from the street they had been on as though it were a battlefield.

A woman running to a building entrance bumped her, and she fell, losing one of her shoes. She pulled herself up as quickly as she could but fell again on her own chador. She kicked off her other shoe and pulled up the chador so she could stand and ran on. Now the shouting seemed all around her, and there were several running feet coming after her.

As she neared the first car, the door opened, and Lisa could see a woman in a chador holding it open. She sprinted to it, tears blurring her vision. As she got near, she heard Sandra's voice: "Hurry, Lisa! Hurry!" When she got to the door, she recognized Sandra's eyes. Sandra swung back to the driver's seat, and Lisa had started to throw herself in when machine-gun fire burst right at her back. She saw it rip through Sandra, spattering blood over the razed and punctured windshield. A huge hand grabbed her and swung her away from the car and slammed her against the building wall. She could feel blood run down her forehead, and the hand turned her and grabbed her neck, holding her fiercely against the wall.

It was *Le'ith*!

His eyes burned with rage and pain. "Youssef was right!" He slapped her viciously across the face. Her head rang with the sting. "All the time!" he screamed. "All the time!" And he slapped her fiercely again, and when she turned her head back, he hit her with all his might with the back of his hand. She heard the bone snap and felt the blood run from her nose, and her head pounded as if everything had been broken. "May Allah damn you for eternity!" Lisa was blind from the blood running from her forehead, but even in her own agony she heard the tears in his rage.

"Le'ith! Le'ith!" a voice yelled out. Lisa became aware of the continued sounds of gunfire and shouting and the distant but piercing wail of sirens.

Le'ith pulled her by her neck from the wall and dragged her to a car and threw her into the backseat. He hit her to force her feet in, then slammed the door, and the car drove off hurriedly without him, its horn blaring while bullets ricocheted off it.

Lisa tried to pull herself up. She wiped the blood from her eyes and could see as they careered around a bend that the street led up a little incline to a narrow road. The car bounced onto the road, turned, and sped away. They could hear several sirens now, but no gunfire. As the car raced on, the man beside the driver turned back and grabbed the hood of Lisa's chador, pulling it down and ripping away the veil. She pulled back, but he wanted nothing more. He just looked at her, his face filled with hate, and he spit a huge blob of phlegm into her face. By the time they reached their destination she was covered with blood and the spit of them both.

Chapter 35

Youssef had made a bad choice. When he had gone through passport control, he had listed the Semiramis Hotel as his prospective residence in Cairo. He had not moved out when the police came looking for him. The doorman warned him they were waiting in the lobby and received the staggering tip he expected from a Saudi in trouble. Youssef walked briskly to the cab rank and instructed a reluctant driver to take him where he knew no policeman would follow.

Nowhere in the Arab world is there a place like the "City of the Dead." A vast, dusty expanse at the eastern end of Cairo where endless cemeteries are interspersed here and there with sometimes grandiose mosque-shrines. Decades ago the poor fellahin, who came to the city from their serfdom on the estates along the Nile, made it their illegal home. Shacks, tents, sheet-metal hovels rose over the numberless unmarked graves. There was no city water, no sewers, no garbage disposal—and no police. As the years went on, the population multiplied uncontrollably, goats and chickens proliferated, disease flourished, drugs and arms and sometimes children were bought and sold. But when the police took an interest, it was too late. The Gaama controlled the City of the Dead. The sale of drugs stopped, and a few police were killed to discourage their taking further interest.

It was a place where Youssef should have been safe. But he had sent a team of the special agents he had brought with him to follow Le'ith. They'd seen the bitch Linn, whom he'd identified from a picture taken outside the Mossad safe house, and, as he had instructed them, made sure she would never betray an Arab again. But they had lost Le'ith when they tried to follow him through the old city, and they had returned to his hotel to wait for his return.

Bored with sitting in their car, two of them got out and walked up and down the entranceway, looking for the old black Oxford. Le'ith drove past them in a gray Rolls-Royce. His friend Hazem was at the wheel, and three of Hazem's steelworkers were in the backseat.

As he passed by, Le'ith instantly recognized the green Mercedes, the squared shoulders, and the impassive faces. He had come to change his clothes—and to call the morgue. While he was in the hotel doing that, Youssef's team of Army Secret Service agents found themselves facing the guns of three very formidable-looking men. They were Hazem's steelworkers.

Le'ith rented a gleaming new van at the hotel. He left the parking lot and followed the gray Rolls-Royce out of the hotel entrance. Around the corner he picked up Youssef's Army Secret Service agents—three men, one woman—and two of the steelworkers, who had already blackened one eye and bloodied one pair of lips. The third steelworker followed them in the green Mercedes the Army agents had been traveling in.

Two hours later Le'ith and the three steelworkers entered the City of the Dead in the green Mercedes. They all were dressed in striped gray djellabas and were armed with rapid firing automatic pistols equipped with silencers—all except Le'ith. Le'ith carried only a knife.

The girl had been the first to break under the brutal attention of the steelworkers, and they had quickly learned the location of Youssef's hideaway. They found him there with the remaining two agents. There was a short, extremely bloody firefight, which only Youssef survived.

Foreigners do not drive in Saudi Arabia. They are permitted to, but if you are allowed entry into the country, it is not wise to do so. Should you be involved in an automobile accident when you are driving and someone dies, whoever is at fault, the family of the person killed will want the life of someone in your family in fair and equal recompense. This is accepted by everyone, even the drivers you hire, though they are usually Egyptian or Lebanese who hope the difficulty of pursuit of one of their family will postpone the inevitable for a long, long time. *Inshallah*.

So when the body of Youssef was ultimately found, it was not surprising that there were signs of a massive struggle and Youssef's face was frozen in a ghastly grimace that mirrored the jagged gore at the center of his totally castrated torso.

Le'ith was going to bury him there among the dead, but he decided he had been wrong. He wouldn't feel affection for Youssef, even standing over his grave.

Chapter 36

Lisa had begun to recognize parts of the city even before the car crossed the big bridge to az-Zamalik Island. They pulled through the electronically controlled gates of an imposing estate. The two men drove directly to the large garage. They pulled Lisa from the car and spit on her again as they hauled her roughly up an outside stairs to an apartment above the garage. She caught a glimpse of the tower of the Sheraton beyond the trees of the Sports Club and thought ironically how this fatal and disastrous day had begun less than half a mile away. Upstairs they shoved her into a little room that contained some old furniture, boxes of magazines, and broken toys. They smashed the lightbulb and locked her in.

She was kept in the room the rest of the day and all through the night. She could tell roughly what the time was by the sounds of the city. Twice she had to go to the toilet and pounded on the door, begging someone to let her go. She heard voices, but they ignored her, and she emptied a box and sat it in the corner and felt more humiliated than she had when she was being covered with spittle.

All night her head ached, her legs hurt, and she cried a dozen times. She didn't know what Le'ith would do to her. One part of her rejoiced that he was still alive, but he obviously knew that she had run from him because he was supposed to die. His face had been so full of fury and pain when he hit her she knew his pride might well lead him to have her pay with her own life under a hail of stones.

She had cried herself out and only ached from her bruises and hunger when, sometime in the morning, an elderly woman in a chador was let into the room by a man. She carried a pan of water and a torn, dirty towel. She wouldn't speak to Lisa but simply held the bowl out to her with the towel draped over her arm. Lisa sipped from the bowl; she was as desperately thirsty as she was hungry. Then she washed at the blood on her face, but without a mirror she couldn't tell how much she'd cleaned. She daubed at the cut on her forehead, but she could feel that the blood had dried, and she didn't want to reopen the wound. Her nose was swollen and tender, and she assumed her eyes were black. She wanted to wash her legs where they had been scraped when she fell, but the man was in the door, and she didn't dare raise her frayed chador. After she'd done the best she could, she put the damp towel back over the woman's arm, and the woman turned and went out of the room. The door closed, and Lisa was in the dark again.

It seemed hours later when the two men who had brought her opened the door and faced her again. Although the midday light half blinded her, she could see they had shaved and washed and changed clothes. Still, they treated her just as roughly as before when they hauled her back down the stairs. A gray Rolls-Royce was pulling out of one of the garage doors. When it turned and came to a stop, one of the men opened the back door. He shoved Lisa in and followed. The other man went around and sat on her other side. The car moved forward a bit, then stopped, and the chauffeur got out.

Le'ith and another man about his age came from a side door of the manorlike house. Le'ith's face was knotted in some kind of personal hell. He had two cuts on his cheek and another along his neck, but they were nothing compared with the wounds in his eyes. Lisa had never seen him so tormented, and it made her believe he was going to do something to her that he did not want to do.

At the front of the car the other man shook his head at him in disgust and walked back into the house. Le'ith got into the driver's seat without looking at Lisa and, after the chauffeur had closed the door behind him, spun the wheels on the gravel drive, hurtling the car around the half circle toward the gates. They opened without his having to slow, and he skidded onto the road, pounding the horn as his only concession to the possibility of other traffic.

They drove out over the bridge again into the older part of the city. Lisa kept her eyes on the rear-vision mirror, hoping he might glance back at her, but he avoided it as assiduously as she watched it.

When the traffic finally forced him to slow, she spoke to him in English, hoping the two men would not understand, so he need feel no humiliation.

"Le'ith, I want—" she began.

"Don't try to save yourself!" His voice was hoarse from arguing or shouting, and it almost cracked from the effort of screaming at her. He looked in the mirror, and she could see the fierce anger and torment in his eyes.

"I don't care about saving myself," she responded instinctively, meaning it more than she could ever have believed. "I just want you to know I was doing what I thought was my duty, not what I wanted to—"

"Shut up! Shut up!!" His voice cracked again, and he was looking at her with rage. She sat back, just looking into his eyes. When he saw that she had stopped, the rage subsided into a cold, wounded hate. "I wish I had it in me to kill you myself," his raspy voice growled.

They drove on toward the outskirts of town. They passed a neglected park, and Le'ith suddenly turned down a road beside it and stopped. In the distance Lisa could see a couple of women in chadors with baby carriages and a young girl pushing a small child on a swing. The man on Le'ith's side opened the door, and the other man pushed Lisa as the first man grabbed her arm and hauled her out.

Lisa turned to Le'ith. He was not two feet from her. "Le'ith—"

He glared at her. "If you say you love me," he croaked harshly, "I'll kill you right now." He reached his hand back, and the man in the car handed him a gun. He pointed it right at her, and she could see that he *wanted* her to speak. It was all he would need.

The man beside her let go of her arm and got back into the car, slamming the door. Le'ith kept the gun pointed at her, and her knees were shaking because she could sense his maniacal need to pull the trigger. He finally tossed it blindly into the backseat, then reached into his suit pocket and threw something on the ground. She jumped back from it, and the car sped off.

She bent down; it was a manila envelope. Inside she found several hundred Egyptian pounds and her passport. She looked up. The Rolls was turning a corner in the distance.

"I love you, Le'ith . . ." she uttered to nobody at all.

Chapter 37

Lisa slept in the kibbutz, in the "ghetto." It was the only place she felt any shred of peace. Everyone got up long before dawn and left her alone till it was time to return. She lay on her cot listening to the chatter, and it refreshed her even though she never took part. She was one of the "older" ones now, and the young volunteers didn't think of her as one of them. A couple of days she went out in the fields and worked, feeling it might lift her spirits to do something physical. She simply found it mindless drudgery.

She usually had dinner with Adam and Deborah, but she often just broke into tears looking at Deborah. Yassi, who was only two when Lisa first came to adore him, had been, like every Israeli boy and girl, called up in the reserves. He had served in Gaza, and Lisa had seen the pictures of him in uniform, looking like a kid in junior high school dressed up like a soldier, his face all sunburned and wearing that same bursting-with-the-joy-of-life smile he had as a two-year-old.

But one Friday night there'd been a riot. Palestinian youths had ambushed a patrol of their hated "jailors," bombarding them with stones. Yassi and the others had given chase. Scores of youths suddenly appeared, stones flew from every direction, and the frightened Israeli troops opened fire. Two Palestinians were killed, and seven badly injured. The only Israeli loss was Corporal Yassi Braun. In the swirling dark chaos he had been killed by "friendly fire."

Deborah had turned totally gray. The lines on her face, which had always been living patterns of love and warmth and motherhood, had become deep imprints of tragedy. She, who had worked all her life in hospitals, bringing children into the world, comforting those leaving it, could not deal with this second loss in her own life. Only once, when she'd shown Lisa Yassi's last picture, had she said, "Your children should never die before you do." Otherwise she never spoke of it, but it was always present in her face. They had scraped together the money to send David back to America, to Antioch College in Ohio, where Adam and Deborah had first met as undergraduates.

Adam had the double burden of dealing with Yassi's loss himself and with Deborah's depression. He wanted them to adopt a child, but for the moment Deborah wouldn't hear of it. To think of Yassi's being dead after the tragedy of Sophie's and Ben's loss hurt Lisa so much she couldn't offer much help to either of them. She cried at the mention of his name and the thought of what he meant to them.

Adam was one of those who had debriefed her when she'd first come back. There wasn't much she knew that they didn't already know. For her part, she learned that they had infiltrated four Mossad agents simply to provide cover for her escape. When they started firing, they got return fire not only from Gaama marksmen, as they had expected, but from a truckload of gunmen who went for them *and* the Gaama. Besides Sandra, they lost two of the Mossad agents, and the other two were so badly wounded they would be out of action for months. For a time of course they also believed they had lost Lisa.

Lisa explained her belief that Youssef had gotten to Le'ith and warned him. She'd thought Le'ith had accepted that Youssef's accusations were false, but he'd obviously taken precautions to protect himself in case he was mistaken.

"Do you know who the gunmen were?" she'd asked.

A young man with red hair and a freckled face had answered. "Your husband has a friend, Hazem Jaabari, whose family owns a large iron and steel works. The Gaama have taken to attacking it, as they have anything that keeps the present regime functioning: industrial sabotage, threats to his family, their workers. Like several other Egyptian industrialists, they reacted by creating their own little personal army. It's about as ruthless as the opposition. It was his army of steelworkers who took on the Gaama and our agents."

It had all been so devastating Lisa's interest was only mild curiosity. She was deeply hurt by the loss of Sandra and Linn, but she was too benumbed to react with anything except despair that it had all been for nothing. That hurt her most, that and the loss of Reena.

They were leaving the room when one thought occurred to her. "Did Le'ith know he was going to be killed?" she asked.

Someone immediately closed the door. Everyone looked around. Then the fat, bald-headed man who'd first interviewed her had answered. "Yes, we believe he did know. All this created a great deal of internal investigation of what went wrong. It seems the agent who was running our safe house in Cairo, a Druze we had recruited because of his knowledge of Cairo, was securing his retirement by having healthy deposits of U.S. dollars made in his name in a bank in Liechtenstein."

"Yair?" Lisa had whispered incredulously.

The fat, bald-headed man nodded gravely. "We have reason to believe that everyone going in or out of that house has been photographed and therefore compromised in a way that prohibits their further use in the field. Yair alleged that he passed only 'insignificant' information that didn't endanger Israel, so it is very likely he would have considered the information on your husband in that category."

The accumulation of mischance had finally penetrated Lisa's personal desolation. "It's been a terrible disaster, hasn't it?" she'd commented to no one in particular.

"Yes, it has," the fat, bald-headed man answered. "But we are in a business where there are disasters and sometimes incredible victories; one is often the price of the other."

She had spent the rest of the day with Adam. They'd journeyed down to Tel Aviv, where Lisa was going to get a "nose job" at the expense of the Mossad. In a very unexpected way she was joining hundreds of her ethnic sisters. She'd joked with Adam about it, but mostly they'd just looked out the window and thought their own thoughts.

At her request they had gone early so they could make a detour to

Yad Vashem. She'd asked Adam to wait, and she'd walked slowly on her own to the Children's Memorial, that place of incredible beauty with its curved walls and columns of glass reflecting the thousands and thousands of candles. It was something like heaven, Lisa had thought when she first saw it. She wanted to see it again before she left Israel forever. It was so perfectly crafted that it seemed not like a building at all. There was no sense of ceilings or floors; it was as if you were suspended in space in the midst of a celestial dance of soft, shimmering light, and the only sound was the hushed, rhythmic voices of the cantors speaking the names of all the children who had perished in the chambers of death, intoning one name after another, ritually, without emotion, endlessly, day and night, the thousands and thousands and thousands.

The beauty took you beyond the images of gaunt, frightened children being herded into ovens and carried you into "heaven," where each tiny victim had become a point of light in a world of peace and beauty.

She'd stayed there a long time, absorbing the sense that her life had not been wasted. One of those candles was worth all that she had sacrificed—and more. Next to even one, her personal grief was only that, a piece of life, a life she had been granted by God or chance instead of a flickering candle in this wondrous hall.

They'd gone on down to Tel Aviv, and she'd met the young surgeon who was going to realign the bone of her nose. He was handsome and witty and very considerate. She'd stayed three days.

From the time she'd left Cairo she'd felt as if someone had tied a knot in her head. It was like thirst; there was no release from it except to drink. Only her thirst was Le'ith. She wanted him to hold her, to forgive her. She knew that if he put his arms around her, she would be able to breathe again, that the knot would just dissolve. But she also knew that she would never see him again and that if she did, he might well kill her or have her killed.

In her despair she grasped at anything, even the thought that the arms of the handsome Dr. Tzadom might quench that longing a little. He tried from the moment she arrived in his office. The next morning she'd let him kiss her in her room in the hospital. It was something, it was physical, but it was not relief. He came back an hour later, and they had—sex. She couldn't call it anything else. It was the closest thing to masturbation she had ever experienced without its actually being masturbation. She felt no relief, only self-disgust and a bizarre sense of betrayal.

He'd operated that afternoon. That night he came to her room again. He held her hand and asked her to stay in Tel Aviv for a week or two; his wife was on a visit to her parents in France. She shoved him away in fury, but even as the blood rose in her bandaged face she saw the paradox: Here she was longing for a man she was married to, along with another woman who had borne him two sons while she was next door waiting as it were, and that was somehow all right, while this good doctor was morally repugnant in a way that made her scream insults at him so loudly it drew the night nurse and a warder.

She had gone back to the kibbutz and hibernated. After a week she decided finally that she had to return to America. She would change her environment, and maybe all this world, Le'ith included, would seem nothing more than some strange interlude.

She didn't wire or phone her mother, but she said a tearful good-bye to Deborah and Adam, promising to return soon, making them promise to come visit America, they'd been away too long.

She didn't want Adam to drive her to the airport; she couldn't stand the idea of them waiting around for her departure. There was a bus that went directly to the Tel Aviv airport. Once there she booked her flight to Florida, but she couldn't get out that day, a Saturday. The thought of Tel Aviv did not appeal to her, so she took another bus up to Jerusalem. She loved that city and wandered its streets, filled with Arabs and Jews, for several melancholy hours, then had a late dinner and went to bed—in a room she had taken at the old American Colony Hotel in the Arab Quarter. Her last good-bye.

The next morning she grabbed her bags from the jitney bus she had taken from Jerusalem and raced for the airport entrance. They had been delayed in traffic and she was afraid she was going to miss her flight. When she got to the top of the stairs, Adam was standing there. She stopped for a second in surprise but circled him.

"What are you doing here?" She smiled. "We've said good–bye, and I'm late."

Somebody took hold of her bag without forcing her to release it, and that did stop her.

"We've been looking all over for you," Adam said. There was now another man standing on the other side of her.

"What's the matter?" she asked.

Adam had a very funny look on his face. "The Cabinet has changed its mind, Lisa," he said in a cross between gravity and optimism. "They want you to go back to Saudi Arabia."

Chapter 38

She took off from London on British Airways. The flight was nonstop to Riyadh and then on to Singapore. She traveled business class, and everyone in her section was English, but there were Saudis in first class and some in the main cabin.

When they lifted off, she was shaking, and her mouth had gone dry. No matter how she rationalized it, she knew that by putting herself on Le'ith's home soil, she was inviting the retribution she had only narrowly avoided in Cairo. And when she landed in Saudi Arabia, she would be a traitor, a spy from a country the Kingdom was at war with. So if Le'ith didn't have her stoned, the government might well have her beheaded, that punishment it still practiced with alarming frequency.

She had discussed all these things with Adam and even with Deborah, who had repeatedly begged her not to go. There were three arguments for risking it. Le'ith hadn't killed her in Cairo—or had her killed. She was going with an offer for something she knew he truly wanted. Lastly, the very fact that she would return to such danger was an evidence of the sincerity of the Israeli government's change of heart. She was in a way the ultimate hostage for its commitment.

But Lisa knew the weight Reena's death would hold in the family. She knew that her betrayal of Le'ith through a lifetime was, in Saudi terms, a sin for which stoning would be a generous sentence. And she, above all, knew that everything in Le'ith's life, all that he had worked for, had been destroyed by the fact that he had married and loved and been deceived by an agent of the Mossad. Should his enemies, or the enemies of his plan, come to know of her presence, they both might end up being beheaded.

Despite all that, she had accepted the arguments, "rationalizations" Deborah called them, for going because in her heart she wanted more than anything in life to see Le'ith. The moment they talked to her about returning, the knot of depression that had haunted her days and kept her staring blindly at the ceiling in the night had lifted as if somebody had turned on a light in a darkened room. It had just gone, and from that moment on she knew all the agonizing about her going back—both among the Mossad and with Adam and Deborah—meant nothing. She was going back.

Maybe she was being naive in a way more appropriate to her late teens than her late thirties, but she didn't care. In the safety of Haifa and the kibbutz there was only one possible course for her. She longed for him beyond reason, beyond any fear of life or future. She at last realized that she loved him beyond reason, beyond self.

But now that she was racing toward Riyadh, the memories of the square before the Great Mosque, the frenzied crowd, the grim figure of the executioner all came back with a force she had suppressed in Haifa. Even the smell of the aircraft, with its offering of Saudi dishes, brought back the sense of isolation she'd always felt under the endless sky in that vast land that had for hundreds of years kept itself aloof from the rest of the world. It had its own life, its own views of justice and retribution, and they were as harsh as its landscape. And now she was afraid, afraid as she'd never been in the three days of discussion about the dangers she was racing to at more than six hundred miles an hour.

In those days they had of course appealed to her feeling toward Israel. The rejection of Le'ith's concept had never been total, they told her. Ironically those who had opposed it were the younger members of the Cabinet. But even after they had sent their message to Egypt, the arguments had gone on. The senior members had argued a truth they knew: that Israel survived in today's world only because of the United States. But they could see too that the American era was dying. America was too compromised economically and politically to sustain any serious overseas venture that required a genuine commitment of money and American lives for the benefit of some other country.

The younger members, who had lived only with Israel's military power and its dominance of its neighbors, argued that American money and arms were only a part of its strength and that in any case the United States would come back; it was too dynamic a society to flounder long.

But history was against it. Like empires before it, Britain had its day of challenge, World War I, and that power seemed verified by its victory, but by World War II it was already a secondary power, and the United States was the giant.

So too America was the victor in the Cold War, but it was Japan and the other Asian nations that were the powers in the new world. It was Toyota, Honda, Sony that were found in every corner of the world. And across the whole spectrum of economic life, from banks to computer-driven elevators in Singapore-financed skyscrapers in Johannesburg to Los Angeles, the same was true.

And the leader of the new parade, Japan, had no oil. Furthermore, it had already proved with Iran that it would double-cross the West to secure the massive quantities of petroleum products it needed to propel its industrial machine.

Most important, Japan had no blood ties with Israel. There was no historic link, no "Jewish" lobby in the Japanese Diet. The children of Israel's next generation would have no red, white, and blue colossus to lean on; they would be facing an Asian leviathan more interested in oil than in preserving the state of Israel. And should there be a fundamentalist sweep of the whole Middle East, the United States could never summon the political will to combat it, especially when the cost would be the cutoff of all Middle Eastern oil.

And if it came to war, where could the United States mount a defense of Israel, even if a future Congress and a future president could agree that it was worth both the cost in American lives and the loss of oil? With all of Saudi Arabia at their disposal it had taken weeks to prepare to invade Kuwait. Where could they deploy their forces in a fight for Israel? Islamic Turkey? Hardly. The whole of the Arabian Peninsula and all of North Africa would not only be closed to them, but a source of possible attack. Would oil-hungry NATO be willing to become a base for a war against Islam in defense of Israel? Given France's and Germany's relations with the Arab world, no one was willing to argue it. And, in any case, Europe is hundreds of miles from Israel.

It was the power of these arguments that finally prevailed.

Then, as if to seal it all, came the bombing of the American Air Force housing unit in Dhahran: nineteen airmen killed, more than fifty injured, a crater eighty-five feet across and thirty-five feet deep, the whole facade of a concrete and steel building totally destroyed. The power of the explosion and the skill of its delivery were evidence that the terrorist group behind it was both organized and well equipped. Those who had scorned the idea that the Saudi monarchy was in any danger suddenly had second thoughts. War or no war, there was not one member of the Cabinet who did not dread the idea of an extremist Islamic group's ruling Saudi Arabia. And now it was recognized that this was a real possibility—if not today, tomorrow.

So Le'ith's plan began to make sense. There was less fear of a trap, more realization that the alliance he proposed could be beneficial to the Saudis as well. But now they had no idea of what its chances were. Had Le'ith already destroyed any possibility of it with the King? Would Le'ith—or the King—ever again accept the honesty of their desire to bring it to fruition?

Lisa was the one avenue to discover how the matter stood and possibly help them begin again.

But in Haifa, it seemed, it was only Lisa who could not sense the terrible nature of her personal risk.

Now, as the plane began its descent to Riyadh, she did. If Le'ith *had* revealed everything to the King, she would be beheaded. That, she knew, was certain. And in all probability she would be tortured first for information, maybe even turned over to the Army Secret Service.

The iota of hope that Le'ith would not act like a Saudi man was what put her on board the plane, and it was all that made her rise from her seat and walk in her long dress with its high collar to the exit instead of clinging firmly to her seat and flying on to Singapore.

She was met by a driver from London's Westminster Bank. It is not easy to get into Saudi Arabia, especially for a woman. But the Mossad of course had contacts. She was going in as "married personnel," the wife of an investment banker working in Riyadh. She had been provided with a false passport and a marriage certificate to prove that she was not Jewish.

Her "husband" actually existed. His rank was sufficient that no one made an issue of the fact that he was illegally bringing in his "first cousin" from America to see a country he had told a million stories of but was off limits to any but real wives. He put her up in the flat of one of their executives who was off to Dubai. Lisa found the bank's compound exactly like the American compound she had visited eons ago with—who was it?—yes, Anne Kregg, the lonely woman whose husband was an American banker. This compound had the same air-conditioned luxury, the green grass, the swimming pool; only the homemade beer and the accents were different.

As she rode to it, the streets of Riyadh made her feel strangely at home—and stiff with fear. The scarcity of women, and those you did see dressed in strict purdah, walking in pairs or a step behind their men, never looking right or left. The traffic, all male. Rich Saudis in their Mercedes or Rolls, oblivious to all the foreign workmen about them, being chauffeured like princes in a land of slaves. Poor Saudis, driving their taxis like Arab horsemen on the charge. It all reminded her of how strict the society was, how fierce and fundamentalist at the core. She had stepped out of it and had, without conscious awareness, stopped thinking as she had thought when she was a part of it. As it all returned to her, she knew her life hung on a very unrealistic thread.

The first night at the bank's compound she didn't sleep at all. What had seemed so easy in Haifa now seemed almost impossible. How was she even going to contact Le'ith? She knew she had to confront him in person if she was to have any chance at all, but how? It was dawn and a couple of English jocks were swimming in the pool before she finally thought of a way that might work.

Lisa slept all that next day. She wanted to look her very best. At night she took a sleeping pill and slept some more.

During the third day she swam, spent some time in the sun, and relaxed in the comfort of the flat, listening to Brahms and Mozart.

She had ordered her driver to pick her up at five-thirty. At ten to six she told him to wait down the street and walked up to the front door of Grandfather's house, for so she still thought of it.

Bushra opened the door. For a moment she just stared at Lisa in amazement. Then she bent, almost bursting into tears, and kissed her foot. Lisa was too frightened and too astonished even to withdraw.

Moustafa appeared in the hallway. He had lost none of his head of household hauteur, but for a moment he too was stunned into silence. Lisa helped Bushra up to her feet and gestured for her to close the door. She wanted to establish her authority from the beginning.

"Madame," Moustafa finally said with a bow, "the sheikh is not here. If you would like to—"

"He *is* in Riyadh," Lisa declared as though she knew, but fearing tremulously that she might have made a terrible mistake.

"Yes, of course," Moustafa replied with a firmness meant to quell her assertiveness. "But at the moment he is not in, and if you would like to—"

"Moustafa," Lisa said coolly, "I know exactly what I would like to do. But before I do it, I want you to call together the servants, and I want you all to go to your dining room and to remain there until my husband or I instruct you to do otherwise."

Moustafa stared at her flabbergasted; then his eyes narrowed in fury. He opened his mouth to speak, but Lisa didn't give him the chance.

"*Now,* Moustafa," she commanded harshly. "I don't have a lot of time, and I don't want to have to deal with disciplining you first. I have other things to speak to the sheikh about."

If Moustafa had had the power to kill, Lisa would not have had to wait for the executioner. He glared fire at her but gestured to Bushra and went off to the kitchen. Lisa went into Grandfather's study. She heard some scurrying about by the younger servants, and then the house was quiet.

She stepped back into the hall. No one was in sight. She went to the front door and cracked it open. Then she went back into the study and waited.

It seemed an eternity, but she eventually heard the car pull up. Heard the chauffeur's footsteps and his opening the car door, then Le'ith's walk to the house. She couldn't swallow, and her heart was beating so hard she could see its movement in her breast. She heard the door push open and Le'ith step across the threshold. She hurriedly undid the neck of her dress, unbuttoning it so that just a bit of cleavage showed.

"Moustafa?" Le'ith inquired irritably.

Lisa reached for a book on the table and dropped it.

She heard his feet moving across the polished floor. She felt the blood rise to her face. The study door pushed open, and Le'ith came in inquiringly—and stopped.

They had been apart only for weeks, but it seemed a lifetime. His face looked worn, and she was more aware of the gray at his temples. He looked at her blankly, as though she were a vision. Not anger, not surprise, just a deeper strain of sadness.

Lisa smiled wanly. She wanted so badly to hold him. "I'm here on business, Le'ith," she said quietly.

"You've always been here on business," he replied mordantly.

"It's not true!" she exclaimed. "It began as business. It didn't stay business."

"Is that why you planned to have me killed?"

"It was never 'planned'; *they* didn't want you to be killed . . . and it was the last thing I wanted."

He grinned bitterly. "Really? You knew the Gaama was going to kill me; *they* knew the Gaama was going to kill me. I suppose you were all 'too busy' to let me know."

"I begged you not to go—please remember that." Even now she knew she couldn't tell him about the mole, but he should remember that she tried to stop him.

He stood there thoughtfully for a moment, then lifted his eyes to her. "Perhaps you'd just better tell me what your business is now."

She started to relate all she'd learned in Haifa. She had only stumbled through a part of it when he gave her a look that made her stop.

He was staring at her, but she could see that the engines of his mind were dealing with something outside her. Finally he focused on her again. "There was a mole," he said flatly.

Lisa just looked at him, not answering verbally or by any signal in her face.

"An Israeli mole in the Gaama . . . and you chose him over me."

She tried to remain expressionless, but she swallowed reflexively and couldn't stop the motion in her neck. His eyes burned into her; then he shrugged cynically, but Lisa knew him, and she could see the hurt in that shrug. "Please go on," he said.

When she finished, he went to his favorite chair and sat looking into space as he kneaded his hands. She waited a long time as he weighed it all, but her desire to know was so great she finally interrupted. "Have you spoken to the King?"

He grimaced. "No . . . but the King is not a fool. He knows it has gone wrong, or I wouldn't be here without something to show him. He's not given me an audience yet, and I haven't pushed for one. It's not easy for him to precipitate a quarrel with his brothers; they function as a government because nothing is hidden. That is why this was so singular a chance."

"Whatever has happened between us," she pleaded, "the stakes are the same for your country and Israel. The same dangers exist, the same opportunities."

He looked up at her. "Are you Israeli?" he asked coldly.

"No, Le'ith. I am an American from Philadelphia. But I *am* Jewish. . . . Like you, a follower of Moses and Abraham—but a daughter of David."

"Do you know the danger you're in?"

Lisa sat down on the floor before him, as she so often had, and looked at him with the love she knew she felt. "Yes, I know the danger I am in."

For a moment she thought he was going to reach out to her, but he turned away.

"You may not. We're *both* in some danger."

"Why you? Have you told anyone what happened?"

Now he looked back at her, but there was a sudden tempest in his eyes. "Have I told anyone how Reena died? No. Have I told anyone how Youssef died? No."

"Is Youssef dead?" she whispered, afraid to let the words carry in the house.

Le'ith nodded slowly. "Yes, he died in a car accident with Reena."

Lisa stared at him. She guessed what that meant, and his expression confirmed it. "Who would believe Reena and Youssef would travel in the same car?" she said fearfully.

"They were coming to see us: you and me and your *aunt Connie*." His eyes were ice. "That's where you are now. You've gone back to America to live with your aunt Connie. We quarreled, and I spoke the words 'I divorce you' three times before my friend Hazem Jaabari."

Lisa absorbed it. That explained Bushra's astonishment and Moustafa's bristling hostility. But now it was her turn to surprise him. " 'Aunt Connie' was the driver of the car that was to rescue me," she said.

"The one in the chador?" he murmured in shock.

"Yes. The one you killed."

Le'ith shook his head sardonically. "I thought it was probably a man dressed as a woman." He looked deep into her eyes. "You were the one I wanted to kill."

There was no sense that his lethal bitterness was not still there; it was only that the fire of his wrath had tempered.

"Are you in danger from the Army about Youssef's death?" she asked.

"Yes. For Youssef's death and several others. No one knows what happened, but not one of those who accompanied Youssef returned."

"*No* one knows?" she asked penetratingly.

He smiled almost as he used to smile at her. "No one in the *Army Secret Service* knows." Then more soberly: "But Colonel Ansari has me followed everywhere, and they are waiting."

"Le'ith, why not put it together again? We can try. It was so close."

"And what guarantee would I have that the Israeli Cabinet and its minions"—he stared at her bitterly—"would not perform as they have in the past?"

"Well, I am *one* hostage," she said. He laughed mockingly at that. It hurt her. She had thought she was making some progress. But she continued. "And they are prepared to send Aaron and Uri to Riyadh on false passports. They will come to you and of course would instantly be vulnerable to arrest and would face the same death I am facing. But you could, if you preferred, hold them hostage for your safety and as a guarantee of Israeli commitment."

Le'ith considered that more seriously. She tried to give it more weight. "You should know that Uri was a primary negotiator of the Palestinian accord and Aaron is the attorney and personal adviser of the Prime Minister. You know too that Israelis do not give up on one unranked soldier, so you can be certain they are not going to sacrifice men of this importance without reason. They want you to be convinced they will be with you until the negotiations succeed or someone outside their control brings them to an end."

Le'ith pondered it calculatingly. "Iran is still there, Le'ith," she pursued, "and the Iraqis. And you saw the power of the fundamentalists in Egypt. Nothing outside of *us* has changed."

Le'ith stood, avoiding her, and walked to the window. He thought for a time. "I would want the hostages," he said, "but I'm not sure where I could keep them without the Army's somehow discovering it."

She wanted to rush to him. But she stayed where she was and tried to keep the excitement from her voice. "They could be kept in the valley. Send Abdel back to the compound for some reason and put Rashid in charge of the farm."

Le'ith turned to her. "Rashid is Reena's *brother*."

"Yes," she responded calmly. "All you need do is tell him what happened. Rashid will keep the secret, but you know if anything goes wrong, he will kill your hostages without hesitation. All three of us."

Le'ith nodded slowly; she could see he thought he could trust that.

Then he looked at her with a twisted smile. "The one called Ephraim means something to you."

It was the name Adam had given himself in Morocco. She nodded. "He would have to come too," Le'ith demanded. "I need some guarantee *you* won't betray me again."

Lisa wanted to cry. "I'm sure he will come," she said. "There is a message you are to phone to London if you want to go ahead. To bring Ephraim all you need to add are the words 'Deal will not go through unless the uncle of Mrs. Safadi is included in the party to Riyadh.' "

It caught Le'ith off-balance. "Your *uncle*?"

"Yes, and I love him very much."

Le'ith lifted his eyebrows, "Like you 'loved' me?" he mocked.

"Yes, Le'ith. Very much like I loved you. Like I love you now."

Chapter 39

The car picked her up at the English compound. It was almost midnight, and she didn't recognize the driver or the car. For a moment when she saw it she groaned. To go through another journey not knowing if Le'ith or the Army Secret Service was going to be at the end . . . But she got in, and the car drove directly to the airport. It went to the private sector, but not the place where Le'ith leased his space. It stopped by a small service area, closed for the night. Le'ith came from behind the shed and opened the door for her. The driver drove off without a word. Le'ith touched her for the first time, pulling her back into the shadows, where they waited for several minutes, with him watching any car that moved anywhere in the sector.

When he was at last sure that they had eluded any surveillance, he led her to an aircraft Lisa had never seen. When Le'ith called the tower for clearance, he gave Najib's name and Najib's family compound as his destination.

They flew in silence for an hour. Lisa took the copilot's seat even though Le'ith had pointedly put his charts and computer on it. She held them in her lap until he asked for them. He avoided looking at her and flew with his face in a rigid knot of isolation.

The dimmed panel lights were all that illuminated him, and the land he stared at so grimly was sable black before and behind them; only the sky was alight with thousands of glittering stars. Were it not for the whine of the engines it would have been like floating in space.

"Can you tell me why you did it?" he said finally, breaking the frigid silence.

Lisa tried. She told him about the kibbutz, about her uncle Noah, and Adam and Deborah, and the shelling that had killed little Sophie and Ben. She tried to describe to a man who had come from generations who called the same stretch of land home what it was like never to have a country of your own.

Le'ith never responded, never commented. Before they landed at the compound, he asked her to move to the back and, when they landed, to lie down and put a blanket over her. He didn't want Abdel to know she was there. She saw the kerosene pots and a few lights of the valley, and she felt a deep well of homesickness. She had, after all, lived on that plot of land most of her adult life.

Le'ith locked the plane, and it seemed a long time before he came back in the Land Rover to get her. He let her sleep in "their" bedroom, though of course he slept elsewhere, but she thought it was a sign that perhaps the ice was cracking.

Abdel had gone and Rashid was flying in from Riyadh by the time Le'ith had one of the women waken Lisa. She showered and found clothes in the closet that made her look as appealing as possible without looking American or "improper." She put on a red and white scarf.

When she asked for him, she was told he'd gone riding. She went to the stables. Saladin was not in his stall. She asked the men if they knew where Le'ith had gone.

"One of the riding boys saw him on the ridge," the groom answered.

She went back to the house and got the Land Rover. She drove along the trail on the east ridge. The valley spread out like some kind of Shangri-la on her right. On her left were miles and miles of utter barrenness.

She saw a horseman far ahead, riding toward her. In seconds she could tell it was Saladin, and then, as they neared a bit more, she saw the grim countenance of Le'ith.

She stopped the Land Rover and got out. She waited for him, not smiling, but she took off her scarf. He pulled up before her; both he and Saladin were covered with sweat. He had been working something out of his system. For a moment he just looked at her coldly, and she wondered if he was going to go on without speaking to her.

"I admire your horse a great deal, *Said*," she ventured archly.

He shook his head scoffingly. She stepped forward and stroked Saladin's lifting, arching nostril. He nuzzled her. She hugged his great head and blew gently in his ear, then stepped back and looked up again at Le'ith. His eyes were fixed on Saladin's neck. For a moment he held them there, then swung around and dismounted. He tied Saladin's reins to the spare wheel of the Land Rover and walked to the edge of the ridge, looking down at the valley.

Lisa walked slowly to his side, but she kept a distance. Below them were wheat fields cut by the wandering orange trees, in pink and white flower now. The palm orchards' emerald greens contrasted with the light green of the new wheat. In the far distance, where the fences of the "ranch" were just visible, the pastures were still another hue. It was so beautiful, and Lisa felt attached to every piece of it.

When Le'ith finally spoke, his voice was dry and cracked like the soil at their feet. "And through all this . . . from the first night in the tent, even the first night at Lake Tahoe, it was all a performance."

Lisa shook her head, but her answer was as calm as she could make it. "No. It was never *all* performance. From the very beginning, despite myself, part of it was always you. At first I hated it that I couldn't make it just a duty, a job to perform. But then I decided that the fact that I liked you, the fact that you thrilled me, was part of the game. It made it easier. I would be your mistress. Part yours, but never all yours. But as the years went on, you became my life, Le'ith. At the end I realized that you were my fate from that first day, that you *are* my life."

He grimaced bitterly. "Until you were asked to sacrifice it . . ."

"Yes, in more pain and despair than you can imagine I chose all the generations, all the suffering through the centuries that had called me to do it in the first place, but for me I knew it would mean tragedy. I knew as we drove through those narrow streets that I was betraying more than the man I love. I was betraying the life God had given me, betraying my life for my people's life . . . and it hurt like the thrust of a knife."

He didn't move. His eyes dwelled on the distance before them.

"All that I have come to be would have died with you, Le'ith. All that I am as a person, all of that, is yours. Ours. I love you more than a lifetime can show. . . . What I did, I did for all those others, all those ghosts that we are raised with . . . and for others to come, so that they may not be ghosts as well."

Her own voice was cracked now, and her vision was clouded with emotion, but she could see there was no reaction from him, only the dark, luminous eyes searching the valley floor below as though seeking the truth in some hidden fault in the land.

But at last she went to him and touched him, and he did not move. She stepped in front of him, crossing her arms, taking his arms and folding them around her. They were limp and unresponsive.

She looked out over the valley that had meant so much to them both.

"I love you, Le'ith," she said, squeezing his arms gently. "I have come back to you because I love you."

For a moment only the desert silence, the pawing of Saladin. Then she felt the pressure of his chin on her head, and, gradually, his limp arms began to tighten around her. She leaned back into him and bit her quivering lip as she felt the warm tears fall on her hair. . . .

"Maybe we could have that child now," she said, clutching him more tightly . . . "I would love it so. . . ."